RANDOM
HOUSE

LARGE
PRINT

THE PARIS VENDETTA

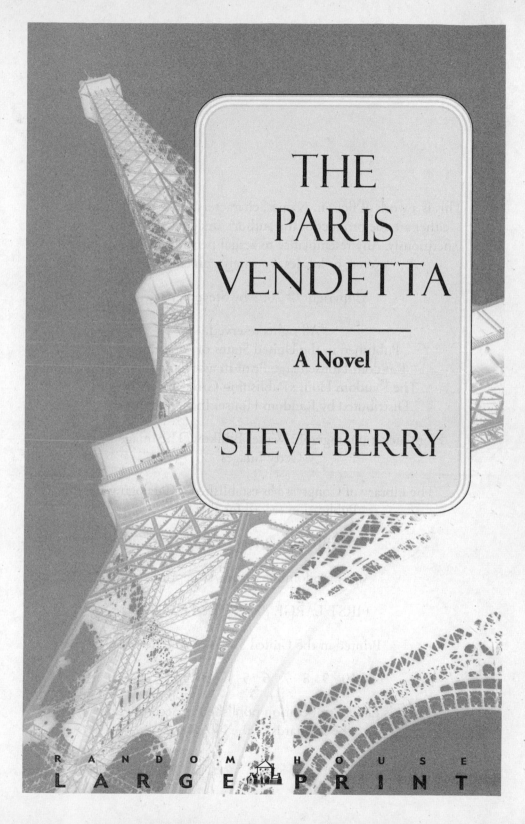

THE PARIS VENDETTA

A Novel

STEVE BERRY

RANDOM HOUSE
LARGE PRINT

Copyright © 2009 by Steve Berry

All rights reserved.
Published in the United States of America by
Random House Large Print in association with
The Random House Publishing Group, New York.
Distributed by Random House, Inc., New York.

Front jacket photograph: Walter Bibikow/The Image Bank/
Getty Images

The Library of Congress has established a Cataloging-in-
Publication record for this title.

ISBN: 978-0-7393-2868-2

www.randomhouse.com/largeprint

FIRST LARGE PRINT EDITION

Printed in the United States of America

10 9 8 7 6 5 4 3 2 1

This Large Print edition published in accord with
the standards of the N.A.V.H.

For Gina Centrello, Libby McGuire,
Kim Hovey, Cindy Murray,
Christine Cabello, Carole Lowenstein,
and Rachel Kind

With Thanks and Deep Appreciation

ACKNOWLEDGMENTS

To my agent, Pam Ahearn—I offer another bow of deep gratitude. We've come a long way, haven't we? To Mark Tavani, Beck Stvan, and the wonderful folks at Random House Promotions and Sales, thanks again for a terrific job. You're all, without question, the best.

A special thanks to a fine novelist and friend, James Rollins, who saved me from drowning in a Fijian pool; to Laurence Festal, who offered invaluable assistance with the French language; and to my wife, Elizabeth, and Barry Ahearn, who found the title.

Finally, this book is dedicated to Gina Centrello, Libby McGuire, Kim Hovey, Cindy Murray, Christine Cabello, Carole Lowenstein, and Rachel Kind.

Seven marvelous ladies.

Professionals, one and all.

Collectively, they've brought implacable wisdom, consistent leadership, and a vibrant creativity to all of my novels.

No writer could ask for anything more.

It's an honor to be a part of your team.

This one's yours.

Money has no motherland;
financiers are without patriotism and
without decency: their sole object is gain.
—Napoleon Bonaparte

History records that the money changers
have used every form of abuse, intrigue,
deceit, and violent means possible to
maintain their control over governments.
—James Madison

Let me issue and control a nation's
money and I care not who writes the
laws.
—Mayer Amschel Rothschild

THE PARIS VENDETTA

PROLOGUE

GÉNÉRAL NAPOLEON BONAPARTE DISMOUNTED from his horse and stared up at the pyramid. Two more lay in succession nearby, but this was the grandest of the three.

What a mighty prize his conquest had yielded.

The ride south yesterday from Cairo, through fields bordering muddy irrigation canals, and the quick trek across windblown sand, had been uneventful. Two hundred armed men had accompanied him, as it was foolhardy to venture this far out into Egypt alone. He'd left his contingent a mile away, camped for the night. The day had been another arid scorcher, and he'd intentionally waited until sunset before visiting.

He'd arrived ashore, near Alexandria, fifteen months ago with 34,000 men, 1,000 guns, 700 horses, and 100,000 rounds of ammunition. He'd quickly advanced south and taken the capital, Cairo, his aim being to disorganize any resistance through rapidity and surprise. Then he'd fought the Mamelukes not far from here, in a glorious conflict he'd dubbed the Battle of the Pyramids. Those former Turkish slaves had ruled Egypt for five hundred years, and what a sight—there had been thousands of warriors, dressed in colorful garb, mounted atop magnificent stallions. He could still smell the cordite, feel the roar of cannon, hear the snap of muskets, the screams of dying men. His troops, many veterans of the Italian campaign, had fought bravely. And while suffering only two hundred French dead, he'd captured virtually the entire enemy army, gaining total control of lower Egypt. One reporter had written that **a handful of French subdued a quarter of the globe.**

Not exactly true, but it sounded wonderful.

The Egyptians had dubbed him Sultan El Kebir—a title of respect, they'd said. During the past fourteen months, ruling this nation as commander in chief, he'd discovered that, as other men loved the sea, so he loved the desert. He also loved the Egyptian way of life, where possessions counted little and character much.

They also trusted providence.

As did he.

"Welcome, Général. Such a glorious evening for a visit," Gaspard Monge called out in his usual cheerful tone.

Napoleon enjoyed the pugnacious geometer, an older Frenchman, son of a peddler, blessed with a wide face, deep-set eyes, and a fleshy nose. Though a learned man, Monge always toted a rifle and a flask and seemed to crave both revolution and battle. He was one of 160 scholars, scientists, and artists—**savants,** the press had labeled them—who had made the journey from France with him, since he'd come not only to conquer but to learn. His spiritual role model, Alexander the Great, had done the same when invading Persia. Monge had traveled with Napoleon before, in Italy, ultimately supervising the looting of that country, so he trusted him.

To a point.

"You know, Gaspard, as a child I wanted to study science. During the revolution, in Paris, I attended several lectures on chemistry. But alas, circumstances made me an army officer."

One of the Egyptian workers led his horse away, but not before he grabbed a leather satchel. He and Monge now stood alone, luminous dust dancing in the shadow of the great pyramid.

"A few days ago," he said, "I performed a calculation and determined that these three pyramids contain enough stone to build a wall a meter wide and three meters high around the whole of Paris."

Monge seem to ponder his assertion. "That could well be true, Général."

He smiled at the equivocation. "Spoken like a doubting mathematician."

"Not at all. I just find it interesting how you view these edifices. Not in relation to the pharaohs, or the tombs they contain, or even the amazing engineering used to construct them. No. You view these only in terms related to France."

"That is hard for me not to do. I think of little else."

Since his departure, France had fallen into impossible disarray. Its once great fleet had been destroyed by the British, isolating him here in Egypt. The ruling Directory seemed intent on warring with every royalist nation, making enemies of Spain, Prussia, Austria, and Holland. Conflict, to them, seemed a way to prolong their power and replenish a dwindling national treasury.

Ridiculous.

The Republic was an utter failure.

One of the few European newspapers that had made its way across the Mediterranean predicted it was only a matter of time before another Louis sat on the French throne.

He had to return home.

Everything he cherished seemed to be crumbling.

"France needs you," Monge said.

"Now you speak like a true revolutionary."

His friend laughed. "Which you know I am."

Seven years ago Napoleon had watched as other revolutionaries stormed the Tuileries Palace and dethroned Louis XVI. He'd then faithfully served the new Republic and fought at Toulon, afterward promoted to brigadier general, then to Général of the Eastern Army, and finally commander in Italy. From there he'd marched north and taken Austria, returning to Paris a national hero. Now, barely thirty, as Général of the Army of the Orient, he'd conquered Egypt.

But his destiny was to rule France.

"What a superfluity of wonderful things," he said, admiring again the great pyramids.

During the ride from his camp he'd spied workers busy clearing sand from a half-buried sphinx. He'd personally ordered the excavation of the austere guardian, and was pleased with the progress.

"This pyramid is closest to Cairo, so we call it the First," Monge said. He pointed at another. "The Second. The farthest is the Third. If we could but read the hieroglyphs, we could perhaps know their true labels."

He agreed. No one could understand the strange signs that appeared on nearly every one of the ancient monuments. He'd ordered them copied, so many drawings that his artists had expended all of the pencils brought from France. It had been Monge who devised an ingenious way to melt lead bullets into Nile reeds and fashion more.

"There may be hope there," he said.

And he caught Monge's knowing nod.

They both knew that an ugly black stone found at Rosetta, inscribed with three different scripts— hieroglyphs, the language of ancient Egypt, demotic, the language of current Egypt, and Greek—might prove the answer. Last month he'd attended a session of his Institut Egypt, created by him to encourage his **savants,** where the discovery had been announced.

But much more study was needed.

"We are making the first systematic surveys of these sites," Monge said. "All who came before us simply looted. We shall memorialize what we find."

Another revolutionary idea, Napoleon thought. Fitting for Monge.

"Take me inside," he ordered.

His friend led him up a ladder on the north face, to a platform twenty meters high. He'd come this far once before, months ago, with some of his commanders, when they'd first inspected the pyramids. But he'd refused to enter the edifice since it would have required him to crawl on all fours before his subordinates. Now he bent down and wiggled into a corridor no more than a meter high and equally as wide, which descended at a mild gradient through the pyramid's core. The leather satchel swung from his neck. They came to another corridor hewn upward, which Monge entered. The gradient now climbed, heading toward a lighted square at the far end.

They emerged and were able to stand, the wondrous site filling him with reverence. In the flickering glow of oil lamps he spied a ceiling that rose nearly ten meters. The floor steeply planed upward through more granite masonry. Walls projected outward in a series of cantilevers that built on each other to form a narrow vault.

"It is magnificent," he whispered.

"We've started calling it the Grand Gallery."

"An appropriate label."

At the foot of each sidewall a flat-topped ramp, half a meter wide, extended the length of the gallery. A passage measuring another meter ran between the ramps. No steps, just a steep incline.

"Is he up there?" he asked Monge.

"**Oui,** Général. He arrived an hour ago and I led him to the King's Chamber."

He still clung to the satchel. "Wait outside, below."

Monge turned to leave, then stopped. "Are you sure you wish to do this alone?"

He kept his eyes locked ahead on the Grand Gallery. He'd listened to the Egyptian tales. Supposedly, through the mystic passageways of this pyramid had passed the illuminati of antiquity, individuals who'd entered as men and emerged as gods. This was a place of "second birth," a "womb of mysteries," it was said. Wisdom dwelled here, as God dwelled in the hearts of men. His **savants** wondered what fundamental urge had inspired this Herculean engineering labor, but for him there could be but one explanation—and he understood the obsession—the desire to exchange the narrowness of human mortality for the breadth of enlightenment. His scientists liked to postulate how this may be the most perfect building in the world, the original Noah's Ark, maybe the origin of languages, alphabets, weights, and measures.

Not to him.

This was a gateway to the eternal.

"It is only I who can do this," he finally muttered.

Monge left.

He swiped grit from his uniform and strode ahead, climbing the steep grade. He estimated its length at about 120 meters and he was winded when he reached the top. A high step led into a low-ceilinged gallery that flowed into an antechamber, three walls of which were cut granite.

The King's Chamber opened beyond, more walls of polished red stone, the mammoth blocks fitted so close only a hairbreadth remained between them. The chamber was a rectangle, about half as wide as long, hollowed from the pyramid's heart. Monge had told him that there may well be a relationship between the measurements of this chamber and some time-honored mathematical constants.

He did not doubt the observation.

Flat slabs of granite formed a ceiling ten meters above. Light seeped in from two shafts that pierced the pyramid from the north and the south. The room was empty save for a man and a rough, unfinished granite sarcophagus without a lid. Monge had mentioned how the tubular drill and saw marks from the ancient workmen could still be seen on it.

And he was right. He'd also reported that its width was less than a centimeter greater than the width of the ascending corridor, which meant it had been placed here **before** the rest of the pyramid was built.

The man, facing the far wall, turned.

His shapeless body was draped in a loose surtout, his head wrapped in a wool turban, a length of calico across one shoulder. His Egyptian ancestry was evident, but remnants of other cultures remained in a flat forehead, high cheekbones, and broad nose.

Napoleon stared at the deeply lined face.

"Did you bring the oracle?" the man asked him.

He motioned to the leather satchel. "I have it."

Napoleon emerged from the pyramid. He'd been inside for nearly an hour and darkness had now swallowed the Giza plain. He'd told the Egyptian to wait inside before leaving.

He swiped more dust from his uniform and straightened the leather satchel across his shoulder. He found the ladder and fought to control his emotions, but the past hour had been horrific.

Monge waited on the ground, alone, holding the reins of Napoleon's horse.

"Was your visit satisfactory, **mon** Général?"

He faced his **savant.** "Hear me, Gaspard. Never speak of this night again. Do you understand me? No one is to know I came here."

His friend seemed taken aback by his tone.

"I meant no offense—"

He held up a hand. "Never speak of it again. Do you understand me?"

The mathematician nodded, but he caught Monge's gaze as he glanced past him, upward, to the top of the ladder, at the Egyptian, waiting for Napoleon to leave.

"Shoot him," he whispered to Monge.

He caught the shock on his friend's face, so he pressed his mouth close to the academician's ear. "You love to tote that gun. You want to be a soldier. Then it is time. Soldiers obey their commander. I don't want him leaving this place. If you don't have the guts, then have it done. But know this. If that man is alive tomorrow, our glorious mission on behalf of the exalted Republic will suffer the tragic loss of a mathematician."

He saw the fear in Monge's eyes.

"You and I have done much together," Napoleon made clear. "We are indeed friends. Brothers of the so-called Republic. But you do not want to disobey me. Not ever."

He released his grip and mounted the horse.

"I am going home, Gaspard. To France. To my destiny. May you find yours, as well, here, in this godforsaken place."

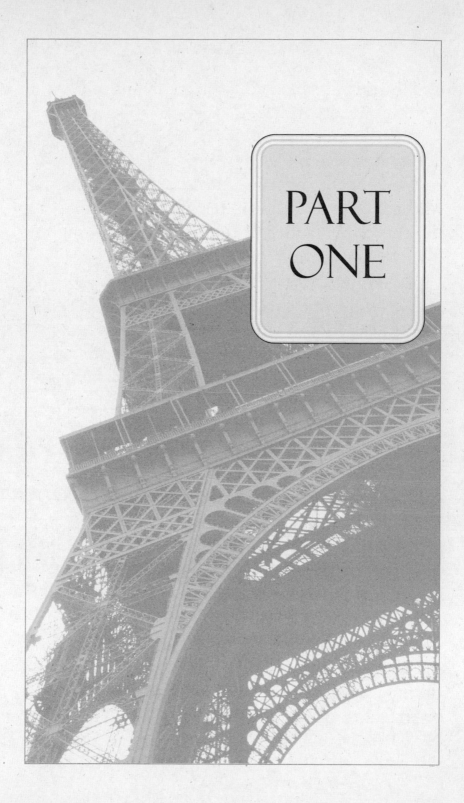

PART ONE

ONE

THE BULLET TORE INTO COTTON MALONE'S left shoulder.

He fought to ignore the pain and focused on the plaza. People rushed in all directions. Horns blared. Tires squealed. Marines guarding the nearby American embassy reacted to the chaos, but were too far away to help. Bodies were strewn about. How many? Eight? Ten? No. More. A young man and woman lay at contorted angles on a nearby patch of oily asphalt, the man's eyes frozen open, alight with shock—the woman, facedown, gushing blood. Malone had spotted two gunmen and immediately shot them both, but never saw the third, who'd clipped him with a single round and was now trying to flee, using panicked bystanders for cover.

Dammit, the wound hurt. Fear struck his face like a wave of fire. His legs went limp as he fought to raise his right arm. The Beretta seemed to weigh tons, not ounces.

Pain jarred his senses. He sucked deep breaths of sulfur-laced air and finally forced his finger to work the trigger, which only squeaked, and did not fire.

Strange.

More squeaks could be heard as he tried to fire again.

Then the world dissolved to black.

Malone awoke, cleared the dream from his mind—one that had recurred many times over the past two years—and studied the bedside clock.

12:43 AM.

He was lying atop the bed in his apartment, the nightstand's lamp still on from when he'd plopped down two hours ago.

Something had roused him. A sound. Part of the dream from Mexico City, yet not.

He heard it again.

Three squeaks in quick succession.

His building was 17th century, completely remodeled a few months ago. From the second to the third floor the new wooden risers now announced themselves in a precise order, like keys on a piano.

Which meant someone was there.

He reached beneath the bed and found the rucksack he always kept at the ready from his Magellan Billet days. Inside, his right hand gripped the Beretta, the same one from Mexico City, a round already chambered.

Another habit he was glad he hadn't shucked.

He crept from the bedroom.

His fourth-floor apartment was less than a thousand square feet. Besides the bedroom, there was a den, kitchen, bath, and several closets. Lights burned in the den, where a doorway opened to the stairway. His bookshop consumed the ground floor, and the second and third floors were used exclusively for storage and work space.

He found the doorway and hugged the inner jamb.

No sound had revealed his advance, as he'd kept his steps light and his shoes to the carpet runners. He still wore his clothes from yesterday. He'd worked late last night after a busy Saturday before Christmas. It was good to be a bookseller again. That was supposedly his profession now. So why was he holding a gun in the middle of the night, every one of his senses telling him danger was nearby?

He risked a glance through the doorway. Stairs led to a landing, then angled downward. He'd switched off the lights earlier before climbing up for the night, and there were no three-way switches. He cursed himself for not including some during the remodeling. One thing that had been added was a metal banister lining the stair's outer edge.

He fled the apartment and slid down the slick brass rail to the next landing. No sense announcing his presence with more creaks from other wooden risers.

Carefully, he glanced down into the void.

Dark and quiet.

He slid to the next landing and worked his way around to where he could spy the third floor. Amber lights from Højbro Plads leaked in through the building's front windows and lit the space beyond the doorway with an orange halo. He kept his inventory there—books bought from people who, every day, lugged them in by the boxload. "Buy for cents, sell for euros." That was the used-book business. Do it enough and you made money. Even better, every once in a while a real treasure arrived inside one of the boxes. Those he kept on the second floor, in a locked room. So unless someone had forced that door, whoever was here had fled into the open third floor.

He slid down the last railing and assumed a position outside the third-floor doorway. The room beyond, maybe forty by twenty feet, was littered with boxes stacked several feet high.

"What do you want?" he asked, his back pressed to the outer wall.

He wondered if it had only been the dream that had sparked his alert. Twelve years as a Justice Department agent had certainly stamped paranoia on his personality, and the last two weeks had taken a toll—one he hadn't bargained for but had accepted as the price of truth.

"Tell you what," he said. "I'm going back upstairs. Whoever you are, if you want something, come on up. If not, get the hell out of my shop."

More silence.

He started for the stairs.

"I came to see you," a male said from inside the storage room.

He stopped and noted the voice's nuances. Young. Late twenties, early thirties. American, with a trace of an accent. And calm. Just matter-of-fact.

"So you break into my shop?"

"I had to."

The voice was close now, just on the other side of the doorway. He retreated from the wall and aimed the gun, waiting for the speaker to show himself.

A shadowy form appeared in the doorway.

Medium height, thin, wearing a waist-length coat. Short hair. Hands at his sides, both empty. The face blocked by the night.

He kept the gun aimed and said, "I need a name."

"Sam Collins."

"What do you want?"

"Henrik Thorvaldsen is in trouble."

"What else is new?"

"People are coming to kill him."

"What people?"

"We have to get to Thorvaldsen."

He kept the gun aimed, finger on the trigger. If Sam Collins so much as shuddered he'd cut him down. But he had a feeling, the sort agents acquired through hard-fought experience, one that told him this young man was not lying.

"What people?" he asked again.

"We need to go to him."

He heard glass break from below.

"Another thing," Sam Collins said. "Those people. They're coming after me, too."

TWO

GRAHAM ASHBY STOOD ATOP THE PLACE DU DUJON
and admired the tranquil harbor. Around him,
crumbly pastel houses were stacked like crates
among churches, the olden structures overshad-
owed by the plain stone tower that had become his
perch. His yacht, **Archimedes,** lay at anchor half a
kilometer away in the Vieux Port. He admired its
sleek, illuminated silhouette against the silvery
water. Winter's second night had spawned a cool
dry wind from the north that swept across Bastia. A
holiday stillness hung heavy, Christmas was only
two days away, but he could not care less.

The Terra Nova, once Bastia's center of military
and administrative activity, had now become a
quarter of affluence with lofty apartments and
trendy shops lining a maze of cobbled streets. A few
years ago, he'd almost invested in the boom, but

decided against it. Real estate, especially along the Mediterranean shoreline, no longer brought the return it once had.

He gazed northeast at the Jetée du Dragon, an artificial quay that had not existed just a few decades ago. To build it, engineers had destroyed a giant lion-shaped rock dubbed the Leone, which once blocked the harbor and had figured prominently in many pre-twentieth-century engravings. When **Archimedes** had cruised into the protected waters two hours ago, he'd quickly spotted the unlit castle keep upon which he now stood—built by the island's 14th century Genoese governors—and wondered if tonight would be the night.

He hoped so.

Corsica was not one of his favorite places. Nothing but a mountain springing from the sea, 115 miles long, 52 miles wide, 5,500 square miles, 600 miles of coast. Its geography varied from alpine peaks to deep gorges, pine forests, glacial lakes, pastures, fertile valleys, and even some desert. At one time or another Greeks, Carthaginians, Romans, Aragonese, Italians, Brits, and the French had conquered, but none had ever subjugated the island's rebellious spirit.

Another reason why he'd passed on investing. Far too many variables in this unruly French **département.**

The industrious Genoese founded Bastia in 1380 and built fortresses to protect it, his tower perch one of the last remaining. The town had served as the capital of the island until 1791, when Napoleon decided that his birthplace, Ajaccio, in the south, would be better. He knew the locals had still not forgiven the little emperor for that transgression.

He buttoned his Armani overcoat and stood close to a medieval parapet. His tailored shirt, trousers, and sweater clung to his fifty-eight-year-old frame with a reassuring feel. He bought all his ensembles at Kingston & Knight, as had his father and grandfather. Yesterday a London barber had spent half an hour trimming his gray mane, eliminating those pale waves that seemed to make him look older. He was proud at how he retained the appearance and vigor of a more youthful man and, as he continued to gaze out past a dark Bastia, at the Tyrrhenian Sea, he savored the satisfaction of a man who'd truly arrived.

He glanced at his watch.

He'd come to solve a mystery, one that had tantalized treasure hunters for more than sixty years, and he detested tardiness.

He heard footsteps from the nearby staircase that angled its way twenty meters upward. During the day, tourists climbed to gawk at the scenery and snap pictures. At this hour no one visited.

A man appeared in the weak light.

He was small, with a headful of bushy hair. Two deep lines cut the flesh from above the nostrils to his mouth. His skin was as brown as a walnut shell, the dark pigments heightened by a white mustache.

And he was dressed like a cleric.

The skirts of a black soutane swished as he walked closer.

"Lord Ashby, I apologize for my lateness, but it could not be helped."

"A priest?" he asked, pointing to the robe.

"I thought a disguise best for tonight. Few ask questions of them." The man grabbed a few breaths, winded from the climb.

Ashby had selected this hour with great care and timed his arrival with English precision. But everything was now out of kilter by nearly half an hour.

"I detest unpleasantness," he said, "but sometimes a frank, face-to-face discussion is necessary." He pointed a finger. "You, sir, are a liar."

"That I am. I freely admit."

"You cost me time and money, neither of which I like to expend."

"Unfortunately, Lord Ashby, I find myself in short supply of both." The man paused. "And I knew you needed my help."

Last time he'd allowed this man to learn too much.

A mistake.

Something had happened in Corsica on September 15, 1943. Six crates were brought west from Italy by boat. Some said they were dumped into the sea, near Bastia, others believed they were hauled ashore. All accounts agreed that five Germans participated. Four of them were court-martialed for leaving the treasure in a place that would soon be in Allied hands, and they were shot. The fifth was exonerated. Unfortunately he was not privy to the final hiding place, so he searched in vain for the rest of his life.

As had many others.

"Lies are all the weapons I possess," the Corsican made clear. "It's what keeps powerful men like you at bay."

"Old man—"

"I dare say, I'm not much older than you. Though my status is not as infamous. Quite a reputation you have, Lord Ashby."

He acknowledged the observation with a nod. He understood what an image could do to, and for, a person. His family had, for three centuries, possessed a controlling interest in one of England's oldest lending institutions. He was now the sole holder of that interest. The British press once described his luminous gray eyes, Roman nose, and flick of a smile as the **visage of an aristocrat.** A reporter a few years ago labeled him **imposing,** while another described him as **swarthy and saturnine.** He didn't necessarily mind the reference to his dark complexion—something his half-Turkish mother had bestowed upon him—but it bothered him that he might be regarded as sullen and morose.

"I assure you, good sir," he said. "I am not a man you should fear."

The Corsican laughed. "I should hope not. Violence would accomplish nothing. After all, you seek Rommel's gold. Quite a treasure. And I might know where it waits."

This man was as obtrusive as he was observant. But he was also an admitted liar. "You led me on a tangent."

The dark form laughed. "You were pushing hard. I can't afford any public attention. Others could know. This is a small island and, if we find this treasure, I want to be able to keep my portion."

This man worked for the Assemblée de Corse, out of Ajaccio. A minor official in the Corsican regional government, who possessed convenient access to a great deal of information.

"And who would take what we find from us?" he asked.

"People here, in Bastia, who continue to search. More who live in France and Italy. Men have died for this treasure."

This fool apparently preferred conversations to move slowly, offering mere hints and suggestions, leading by tiny degrees to his point.

But Ashby did not have the time.

He signaled and another man exited the stairway. He wore a charcoal overcoat that blended well with his stiff gray hair. His eyes were piercing, his thin face tapered to a pointed chin. He walked straight to the Corsican and stopped.

"This is Mr. Guildhall," Ashby said. "Perhaps you recall him from our last visit?"

The Corsican extended his hand, but Guildhall kept his hands in his coat pockets.

"I do," the Corsican said. "Does he ever smile?"

Ashby shook his head. "Terrible thing. A few years ago Mr. Guildhall was involved in a nasty altercation, during which his face and neck were slashed. He healed, as you can see, but the lasting effect was nerve damage that prevents the muscles in his face from fully functioning. Hence, no smile."

"And the person who slashed him?"

"Ah, an excellent inquiry. Quite dead. Broken neck."

He saw that his point had been made, so he turned to Guildhall and asked, "What did you find?"

His employee removed a small volume from his pocket and handed it over. In the weak light he noted the faded title, in French. **Napoleon, From the Tuileries to St. Helena.** One of countless memoirs that had appeared in print after Napoleon died in 1821.

"How . . . did you get that?" the Corsican asked.

He smiled. "While you made me wait here atop the tower, Mr. Guildhall searched your house. I'm not a total fool."

The Corsican shrugged. "Just a dull memoir. I read a lot on Napoleon."

"That's what your co-conspirator said, too."

He saw that he now commanded his listener's total attention. "He and I, and Mr. Guildhall, had a great talk."

"How did you know of Gustave?"

He shrugged. "It wasn't hard to determine. You

and he have searched for Rommel's gold a long time. You are each, perhaps, the two most knowledgeable people on the subject."

"Have you harmed him?"

He caught the alarm in the question. "Heavens no, my good man. Do you take me for a villain? I am of an aristocratic family. A lord of the realm. A respectable financier. Not a hoodlum. Of course, your Gustave lied to me as well."

A flick of his wrist and Guildhall grabbed the man by a shoulder and one trouser leg projecting from the soutane. The tiny Corsican was vaulted upward between the parapets, Guildhall sliding him out and adjusting his grip to both ankles, the body now upside down outside the wall, twenty meters above stone pavement.

The soutane flapped in the night breeze.

Ashby poked his head out another parapet. "Unfortunately, Mr. Guildhall does not have the same reservations toward violence as I harbor. Please know that if you utter a sound of alarm, he'll drop you. Do you understand?"

He saw a head bob up and down.

"Now, it's time you and I have a serious conversation."

THREE

MALONE STARED AT THE FEATURELESS FORM OF SAM Collins as more glass shattered below.

"I think they want to kill me," Collins said.

"In case you haven't noticed, I have a gun pointed at you, too."

"Mr. Malone, Henrik sent me here."

He had to choose. The danger in front of him, or the one two floors down.

He lowered the gun. "You led those people downstairs here?"

"I needed your help. Henrik said to come."

He heard three pops. Sound-suppressed shots. Then the front door banged open. Footsteps thumped across the plank floor.

He motioned with the gun. "In there."

They retreated into the third-floor storage room, seeking refuge behind a stack of boxes. He realized the intruders would immediately head toward the top floor, drawn by lights. Then, once they realized no one was there, they would start searching. Trouble was, he didn't know how many had come to visit.

He risked a peek and saw a man transition from the third-floor landing to the fourth floor. He motioned for quiet and to follow. He darted for the doorway and used the brass railing to slide down to the next landing. Collins mimicked his action. They repeated the process down to the final flight of stairs that led to ground level and the bookshop.

Collins moved toward the last railing, but Malone grabbed his arm and shook his head. The fact that this young man would do something that stupid showed either ignorance or a deceptive brilliance. He wasn't sure which, but they couldn't linger here for long, considering there was an armed man above them.

He motioned for Collins to remove his coat.

The dark face seemed to hesitate, unsure about the request, then relented and slipped it off without a sound. Malone grabbed the thick wool bundle, sat on the rail, and slowly wiggled halfway down. With the gun firmly gripped in his right hand, he tossed the coat outward.

Pops erupted as the garment was peppered with bullets.

He slid the remainder of the way down, left the railing, and vaulted behind the front counter as more rounds thudded into wood around him.

He pinpointed a location.

The shooter was to his right, near the front windows, where the shop's History and Music categories were shelved.

He came to his knees and sent a round in that direction.

"Now," he yelled at Collins, who seemed to sense what was expected, fleeing the stairway and leaping behind the counter.

Malone knew they'd have more company shortly, so he crept to the left. Luckily, they weren't hemmed in. During the recent remodel he'd insisted that the counter be open at both ends. His shot had not been sound-suppressed, so he wondered if anyone outside had heard the loud retort. Unfortunately, Højbro Plads stayed fairly deserted from midnight to dawn.

He scooted to the end, Collins beside him. His gaze stayed locked on the stairway as he waited for the inevitable. He spotted a dark form, growing in size as the attacker from upstairs slowly aimed his gun around the corner.

Malone fired and caught the man in the forearm.

He heard a grunt and the gun disappeared.

The first gunman laid down enough fire to allow the man on the stairway to flee toward him.

Malone sensed a stalemate. He was armed. So were they. But they probably carried more ammunition than he, since he'd failed to bring a spare magazine for the Beretta. Luckily, they didn't know that.

"We need to aggravate them," Collins whispered.

"And how many is **them**?"

"Looks like two."

"We don't know that." His mind drifted back to the dream, when he'd once before made the mistake of failing to count to three.

"We can't just sit here."

"I could give you to them and go back to sleep."

"You could. But you won't."

"Don't be so sure."

He still remembered what Collins had said. **Henrik Thorvaldsen is in trouble.**

Collins eased past and reached for the fire extinguisher behind the counter. Malone watched as Collins yanked the safety pin and, before he could object, fled the counter and spewed a chemical fog into the bookshop, using a rack of shelves for cover, propelling retardant toward the gunmen.

Not a bad move except—

Four pops came in reply.

Bullets sprang from the fog, sinking into wood, pinging off stone walls.

Malone sent another round their way.

He heard glass crash in a tingling crescendo, then running footsteps.

Moving away.

Cold air rushed over him. He realized they'd escaped through the front window.

Collins lowered the extinguisher. "They're gone."

He needed to be sure, so he kept low, eased away from the counter and, using more shelves for cover, rushed through the dissipating fog. He found the end row and risked a quick look. Smoky air retreated out into the frigid night through a shattered plate-glass window.

He shook his head. Another mess.

Collins came up behind him. "They were pros."

"How would you know?"

"I know who sent them." Collins laid the fire extinguisher upright on the floor.

"Who?"

Collins shook his head. "Henrik said he'd tell you."

He stepped to the counter and found the phone, dialing Christiangade, Thorvaldsen's ancestral estate nine miles north of Copenhagen. It rang several times. Usually Jesper, Thorvaldsen's chamberlain, answered, no matter the hour.

The phone continued to ring.

Not good.

He hung up and decided to be prepared.

"Go upstairs," he said to Collins. "There's a rucksack on my bed. Grab it."

Collins ran up the wooden risers.

He used the moment to dial Christiangade one more time and listened as the phone continued to ring.

Collins thumped his way down the stairs.

Malone's car was parked a few blocks over, just outside old town, near the Christianburg Slot. He grabbed his cell phone from beneath the counter.

"Let's go."

FOUR

ELIZA LAROCQUE SENSED THAT SHE WAS CLOSE TO success, though her flying companion was making the task difficult. She sincerely hoped that this hastily arranged overseas trip would not be a waste of time.

"It's called the Paris Club," she said in French.

She'd chosen 15,000 meters over the north Atlantic, inside the sumptuous cabin of her new Gulfstream G650, to make one last pitch. She was proud of her latest state-of-the-art toy, one of the first off the assembly line. Its spacious cabin accommodated eighteen passengers in plush leather seats. There was a galley, a roomy lavatory, mahogany furnishings, and mega-speed Internet video modules connected by satellite to the world. The jet flew high, fast, long, and reliably. Thirty-seven million, and worth every euro.

"I'm familiar with that organization," Robert Mastroianni said, keeping to her native language. "An informal group of financial officials from the world's richest countries. Debt restructuring, debt relief, debt cancellation. They float credit and help struggling nations pay back their obligations. When I was with the International Monetary Fund, we worked with them many times."

A fact she knew.

"That club," she said, "grew out of crisis talks held in Paris in 1956 between a bankrupt Argentina and its creditors. It continues to meet every six weeks at the French Ministry of the Economy, Finance, and Industry, chaired by a senior official of the French treasury. But I'm not speaking of that organization."

"Another of your mysteries?" he asked, criticism in his tone.

"Why must you be so difficult?"

"Perhaps because I know it irritates you."

Yesterday she'd connected with Mastroianni in New York. He hadn't been pleased to see her, but they'd dined out last night. When she'd offered him a ride back across the Atlantic, he'd accepted.

Which surprised her.

This would be either their last conversation—or the first of many more.

"Go ahead, Eliza. I'm listening. Of course, there's nothing else I can do but listen to you. Which, I suspect, was your plan."

"If you felt that way, then why fly home with me?"

"If I'd refused, you would have simply found me

again. This way we can resolve our business, one way or the other, and I receive a comfortable flight home as the price for my time. So please, go ahead. Make your speech."

She quelled her anger and declared, "There's a truism born of history. 'If a government can't face the challenge of war, it ends.' The sanctity of law, citizen prosperity, solvency—all those principles are readily sacrificed by any state when its survival is challenged."

Her listener sipped from a champagne flute.

"Here's another reality," she said. "Wars have always been financed by debt. The greater the threat, the greater the debt."

He waved her off. "And I know the next part, Eliza. For any nation to involve itself in war, it must have a credible enemy."

"Of course. And if they already exist, **magnifico.**"

He smiled at her use of his native tongue, the first break in his granite demeanor.

"If enemies exist," she said, "but lack military might, money can be provided to build that might. If they don't exist—" She grinned. "—they can always be created."

Mastroianni laughed. "You have such a diabolical way."

"And you don't?"

He glared at her. "No, Eliza. I don't."

He was maybe five years older, equally as rich,

and though aggravating, could be quite charming. They'd just dined on succulent beef tenderloin, Yukon Gold potatoes, and crisp green beans. She'd learned he was a simple eater. No spices, garlic, or hot pepper. A unique palate for an Italian, yet a lot about this billionaire was unique. But who was she to judge? She harbored a number of her own idiosyncracies.

"There is another Paris Club," she said. "One much older. Dating to the time of Napoleon."

"You've never mentioned this fact before."

"You never showed any interest, until now."

"May I be frank?"

"By all means."

"I don't like you. Or more accurately, I don't like your business concerns or your associates. They are ruthless in their dealings, and their word means nothing. Some of your investment policies are questionable at best, criminal at worst. You've pursued me for nearly a year with tales of untold profits, offering little information to support your claims. Perhaps it's your Corsican half, and you simply can't control it."

Her mother had been Corsican, her father a Frenchman. They'd married young and stayed together for more than fifty years. Both were now dead, she their only heir. Prejudice regarding her ancestry was nothing new—she'd encountered it many times—but that didn't mean she accepted it gladly.

She stood from her seat and removed their dinner plates.

Mastroianni grabbed her arm. "You don't need to serve me."

She resented both his tone and grasp, but did not resist. Instead she smiled, switched to Italian, and said, "You're my guest. It's the proper thing."

He released his grip.

She'd staffed the jet only with two pilots, both forward behind a closed cockpit door, which was why she'd attended to the meal. In the galley, she stored the dirty plates and found their dessert in a small refrigerator. Two luscious chocolate tarts. Mastroianni's favorite, she'd been told, bought from the Manhattan restaurant they'd visited last evening.

His countenance changed when she laid the treat before him.

She sat across from him.

"Whether you like me or my companies, Robert, is irrelevant to our discussion. This is a business proposition. One that I thought you would be interested in entertaining. I have taken great care in making my selections. Five people have already been chosen. I'm the sixth. You would be the seventh."

He pointed to the tart. "I wondered what you and the garçon were discussing before we left last night."

He was ignoring her, playing a game of his own.

"I saw how much you enjoyed the dessert."

He grabbed a sterling-silver fork. Apparently his

personal dislike of her did not extend to her food, or her jet, or the possibility of the money to be made.

"Might I tell you a story?" she asked. "About Egypt. When then-Général Napoleon Bonaparte invaded in 1798."

He nodded as he savored the rich chocolate. "I doubt you would accept a no. So, by all means."

Napoleon personally led the column of French soldiers on the second day of their march south. They were near El Beydah, only a few hours away from the next village. The day was hot and sunny, just like all of the others before it. Yesterday Arabs had viciously attacked his advance guard. Général Desaix had nearly been captured, but a captain was killed and another adjutant général taken prisoner. A ransom was demanded, but the Arabs disputed the booty and eventually shot the captive in the head. Egypt was proving a treacherous land—easy to conquer, difficult to hold—and resistance seemed to be growing.

Ahead, on the side of the dusty road, he spotted a woman with a bloody face. In one arm she cradled a baby, but her other arm was extended, as if in self-defense, testing the air before her. What was she doing here, in the scorching desert?

He approached and, through an interpreter,

learned that her husband had pierced both her eyes. He was mortified. Why? She dared not complain and simply pleaded for someone to care for her child, who seemed near death. Napoleon ordered that both her and the baby be given water and bread.

That done, a man suddenly appeared from beyond a nearby dune, enraged and full of hate.

Soldiers came alert.

The man ran forward and snatched the bread and water from the woman.

"Forbear," he screamed. "She has forfeited her honor and tarnished mine. That infant is my disgrace. It is an offspring of her guilt."

Napoleon dismounted and said, "You are mad, monsieur. Insane."

"I am her husband and have the right to do as I please."

Before Napoleon could respond, a dagger appeared from beneath the man's cloak and he inflicted a mortal wound to his wife.

Confusion ensued as the man seized the baby, held it in the air, then dashed it to the ground.

A shot cracked and the man's chest exploded, his body thudding to the dry earth. Captain Le Mireur, riding behind Napoleon, had ended the spectacle.

Every soldier seemed shocked by what they'd seen.

Napoleon himself was having trouble concealing his dismay. After a few tense moments he ordered the column ahead but before remounting his horse, he noticed that something had fallen from beneath the dead man's cloak.

A roll of papyri held tight by a string.

He retrieved it from the sand.

Napoleon commandeered quarters for the night in the pleasure house of one of his most resolute opponents, an Egyptian who'd fled into the desert with his Mameluke army months ago, leaving all of his possessions to be enjoyed by the French. Stretched out on downy carpets strewn with velvet cushions, the général was still troubled by the appalling show of inhumanity he'd witnessed earlier on the desert road.

He'd been told later that the man had done wrong stabbing his wife, but if God had wanted her vouchsafed for infidelity, she should have already been received into someone's house and kept on charity. Since that had not occurred, Arab law would not have punished the husband for his two murders.

"Then it is a good thing we did," Napoleon declared.

The night was quiet and dull, so he decided to examine the papyri he'd found near the body. His savants had told him how the locals routinely pillaged sacred sites, stealing what they could to either sell or reuse. What a waste. He'd come to discover this country's past, not destroy it.

He popped the string and unrolled the bundle discovering four sheets, written in what appeared to be Greek. He was fluent in Corsican, and could finally speak and read passable French, but beyond that foreign languages were a mystery.

So he ordered one of his translators to appear.

"It's Coptic," the man told him.

"Can you read it?"

"Of course, Général."

"What a horrible thing," Mastroianni said. "Killing that infant."

She nodded. "That was the reality of the Egyptian campaign. A bloody, hard-fought conquest. But I assure you, what happened there is why you and I are having this conversation."

FIVE

SAM COLLINS SAT IN THE PASSENGER SEAT AND watched as Malone sped out of Copenhagen, heading north on the Danish coast highway.

Cotton Malone was exactly what he'd expected. Tough, gutsy, decisive, accepting the situation thrown at him, doing what needed to be done. He even fit the physical description Sam had been given. Tall, burnished blond hair, a smile that betrayed little emotion. He knew about Malone's twelve years of Justice Department experience, his Georgetown legal education, eidetic memory, and love of books. But now he'd seen firsthand the man's courage under fire.

"Who are you?" Malone asked.

He realized he couldn't be coy. He'd sensed Malone's suspicions, and didn't blame him. A stranger breaks into his shop in the middle of the night and armed men follow? "U.S. Secret Service. Or at least I was until a few days ago. I think I'm fired."

"Why's that?"

"Because nobody there would listen to me. I tried to tell them. But no one wanted to hear."

"Why did Henrik?"

"How'd you—" He caught himself.

"Some folks take in stray animals. Henrik rescues people. Why'd you need his help?"

"Who said I did?"

"Don't sweat it, okay? I was once one of those strays."

"Actually, I'd say it was Henrik who needed help. He contacted me."

Malone shifted the Mazda into fifth gear and sped down the blackened highway, a hundred yards or so away from a dark Øresund sea.

Sam needed to make something clear. "I didn't work White House detail at Secret Service. I was in currency and financial fraud."

He always laughed at the Hollywood stereotype of agents wearing dark suits, sunglasses, and skin-toned earpieces surrounding the president. Most of the Secret Service, like him, worked in obscurity, safeguarding the American financial system. That was actually its primary mission, since it grew out of the Civil War, created to prevent Confederate counterfeiting. Only after the assassination of William McKinley, thirty-five years later, had it assumed presidential protection responsibility.

"Why'd you come to my bookshop?" Malone asked.

"I was staying in town. Henrik sent me to a

hotel yesterday. I could tell something was wrong. He wanted me away from the estate."

"How long have you been in Denmark?"

"A week. You've been gone. Just got back a few days ago."

"You know a lot about me."

"Not really. I know you're Cotton Malone. Former naval officer. Worked with the Magellan Billet. Now retired."

Malone tossed him a glance that signaled rapidly depleting patience with his evasion of the original question.

"I run a website on the side," Sam said. "We're not supposed to do stuff like that, but I did. World Financial Collapse—A Capitalist Conspiracy. That's what I called it. It's at Moneywash.net."

"I can see why you're superiors might have a problem with your hobby."

"I can't. I live in America. I have a right to speak my mind."

"But you don't have a right to carry a federal badge at the same time."

"That's what they said, too." He could not hide the defeat in his voice.

"What did you say on this site of yours?" Malone asked him.

"I told the truth. About financiers, like Mayer Amschel Rothschild."

"Expressing those First Amendment rights of yours?"

"What does it matter? That man wasn't even American. Just a master with money. His five sons were even better. They learned how to convert debt into fortune. They were lenders to the crowns of Europe. You name it and they were there, one hand to give money out, the other to take even more back."

"Isn't that the American way?"

"They weren't bankers. Banks operate with funds either deposited by customers or created by the government. They worked with personal fortunes, lending them out at obscene interest rates."

"Again, what's wrong with that?"

He shifted in his seat. "That's the attitude that allowed them to get away with what they did. People say, 'So what? It's their right to make money.' No, it's not." The fire in his belly surged. "The Rothschilds made a fortune financing war. Did you know that?"

Malone did not reply.

"Both sides, most times. And they didn't give a damn about the money they loaned. In return, they wanted privileges that could be converted into profit. Things like mining concessions, monopolies, importation exceptions. Sometimes they were even given the right to certain taxes as a guarantee."

"That was hundreds of years ago. So the hell what?"

"It's happening again."

Malone slowed for a sharp curve. "How do you know that?"

"Not everyone who strikes it rich is as benevolent as Bill Gates."

"You have names? Proof?"

He went silent.

Malone seemed to sense his dilemma. "No, you don't. Just a bunch of conspiracy crap you posted on the Internet that got you fired."

"It's not far-fetched," he was quick to say. "Those men came to kill me."

"You sound almost glad they did."

"It proves I was right."

"That's a big leap. Tell me what happened."

"I was cooped up in a hotel room, so I went out for a walk. Two guys started following me. I hauled ass and they kept coming. That's when I found your place. Henrik told me to wait at the hotel until I heard from him, then make contact with you. But when I spotted those two I called Christiangade. Jesper said to find you pronto, so I headed for your shop."

"How'd you get inside?"

"Pried open the back door. It's real easy. You need an alarm."

"I figure if somebody wants to steal old books, they can have 'em."

"What about guys who want to kill you?"

"Actually, they wanted to kill you. And by the way, that was foolish breaking in. I could have shot you."

"I knew you wouldn't."

"Glad you knew that, 'cause I didn't."

They rode in silence for a few miles, coming ever closer to Christiangade. Sam had made this journey quite a few times over the past year.

"Thorvaldsen's gone to a lot of trouble," he finally said. "But the man he's after acted first."

"Henrik's no fool."

"Maybe not. But every man meets his match."

"How old are you?"

He wondered about the sudden shift in topic. "Thirty-two."

"You've been with the service how long?"

"Four years."

He caught Malone's drift. Why had Henrik needed to connect with a young, inexperienced Secret Service agent who ran an off-the-wall website? "It's a long story."

"I've got time," Malone said.

"Actually, you don't. Thorvaldsen has been aggravating a situation that can't stand much more irritation. He needs help."

"That the conspiratorialist talking, or the agent?"

Malone gunned the Mazda and sped down a straightaway. More black ocean stretched to their right, the lights of a distant Sweden on the horizon.

"It's his friend talking."

"Obviously," Malone said, "you have no idea about Henrik. He's afraid of nothing."

"Everybody's afraid of something."

"What's your fear?"

He pondered the question, one he'd asked himself several times over the past few months, then answered honestly. "The man Thorvaldsen's really after."

"You going to tell me a name?"

"Lord Graham Ashby."

SIX

CORSICA

Ashby returned to **Archimedes** and hopped from the tender onto the aft platform. He'd brought the Corsican back with him, after acquiring the man's undivided attention atop the tower. They'd shed the ridiculous soutane and the man had given them no trouble on the journey.

"Escort him to the main salon," Ashby said, and Guildhall led their guest forward. "Make him comfortable."

He climbed three teak risers to the lighted pool. He still held the book that had been retrieved from the Corsican's house.

The ship's captain appeared.

"Head north, along the coast, at top speed," Ashby ordered.

The captain nodded, then disappeared.

Archimedes' sleek black hull stretched seventy meters. Twin diesels powered her at twenty-five knots, and she could cruise transatlantic at a respectable twenty-two knots. Her six decks accommodated three suites, an owner's apartment, office, gourmet kitchen, sauna, gym, and all the other amenities expected on a luxury vessel.

Below, engines revved.

He thought again about that night in September 1943.

All accounts described calm seas with clear skies. Bastia's fishing fleet had been lying safe at anchor within the harbor. Only a solitary motor launch sliced through the waters offshore. Some said the boat was headed for Cape Sud and the River Golo, situated at the southern base of Cap Corse, Corsica's northernmost promontory—a finger-like projection of mountains aimed due north to Italy. Others placed the boat in conflicting positions along the northeastern coast. Four German soldiers had been aboard the launch when two American P-39s strafed the deck with cannon fire. A dropped bomb missed and, thankfully, the planes ended their attack without finishing off the vessel. Ultimately, six wooden crates were hidden somewhere either on or near Corsica, a fifth German, on shore, aiding the other four's escape.

Archimedes eased ahead.

They should be there in under thirty minutes.

He climbed one more deck to the grand salon where white leather, stainless-steel appointments, and cream Berber carpet made guests feel comfortable. His 16th-century English estate was replete with antiquity. Here he preferred modernity.

The Corsican sat on one of the sofas nursing a drink.

"Some of my rum?" Ashby asked.

The older man nodded, still obviously shaken.

"It's my favorite. Made from first-press juice."

The boat surged forward, acquiring speed, the bow quickly scything through the water.

He tossed the Napoleon book on the sofa beside his guest.

"Since we last talked, I have been busy. I'm not going to bore you with details. But I know four men brought Rommel's gold from Italy. A fifth waited here. The four hid the treasure, and did not reveal its location before the Gestapo shot them for dereliction of duty. Unfortunately, the fifth was not privy to where they secreted the cache. Ever since, Corsicans like you have searched and distributed false information as to what happened. There are a dozen or more versions of events that have caused nothing but confusion. Which is why, last time, you lied to me." He paused. "And why Gustave did the same."

He poured himself a shot of rum and sat on the sofa opposite the Corsican. A wood-and-glass table rested between them. He retrieved the book and laid it on the table, "If you please, I need you to solve the puzzle."

"If I could, I would have long ago."

He grinned. "I recently read that when Napoleon became emperor, he excluded all Corsicans from the administration of their island. Too untrustworthy, he claimed."

"Napoleon was Corsican, too."

"Quite true, but you, sir, **are** a liar. You know how to solve the puzzle, so please do it."

The Corsican downed the rest of his rum. "I should have never dealt with you."

He shrugged. "You like my money. I, on the other hand, should never have dealt with you."

"You tried to kill me on the tower."

He laughed. "I simply wanted to acquire your undivided attention."

The Corsican did not seem impressed. "You came to me because you knew I could provide answers."

"And the time has come for you to do that."

He'd spent the past two years examining every clue, interviewing what few secondary witnesses remained alive—all of the main participants were long dead—and he'd learned that no one really knew if Rommel's gold existed. None of the stories about its origin, and journey from Africa to Germany, rang consistent. The most reliable account stated that the hoard originated from Gabès, in Tunisia, about 160 kilometers from the Libyan border. After the German Afrika Korps commandeered the town for its headquarters, its three thousand Jews were told that for "sixty hundredweight of gold" their lives would be spared. They were given forty-eight hours to produce the ransom, after which it was packed into six wooden crates, taken to the coast, and shipped north to Italy. There the Gestapo assumed control, eventually entrusting four soldiers with transporting the crates west to Corsica. What the containers contained remained unknown, but the Jews of Gabès were wealthy, as were the surrounding Jewish communities, the local synagogue a famous place of pilgrimage—the recipient, through the centuries, of many jeweled artifacts.

But was the treasure gold?

Hard to say.

Yet it had acquired the name **Rommel's gold**—thought to be one of the last great caches from World War II.

The Corsican held out his empty glass and Ashby rose to refill it. He might as well indulge the man, so he returned with a tumbler three-quarters full of rum.

The Corsican enjoyed a long swallow.

"I know about the cipher," Ashby said. "It's actually quite ingenious. A clever way to hide a message. The Moor's Knot, I believe it's called."

Pasquale Paoli, a Corsican freedom fighter from the 18th century, now a national hero, had coined the name. Paoli needed a way to effectively communicate with his allies, one that assured total privacy, so he adapted a method learned from the Moors who, for centuries, had raided the coastline as free-booting pirates.

"You acquire two identical books," Ashby explained. "Keep one. Give the other to the person to whom you want to send the message. Inside the book you find the right words for the message, then communicate the page, line, and word number to the recipient through a series of numbers. The numbers, by themselves, are useless, unless you have the right book."

He tabled his rum, found a folded sheet of paper in his pocket, and smoothed the page out on the glass-topped table. "These are what I provided you the last time we spoke."

His captive examined the sheet.

XCV	CCXXXVI	CXXVIII	CXCIV	XXXII
IV	XXXI	XXVI	XVIII	IX
VII	VI	X	II	XI

"They mean nothing to me," the Corsican said.

He shook his head in disbelief. "You're going to have to stop this. You know it's the location of Rommel's gold."

"Lord Ashby. Tonight, you've treated me with total disrespect. Hanging me from that tower. Calling me a liar. Saying that Gustave lied to you. Yes, I had this book. But these numbers mean nothing with reference to it. Now we are sailing to someplace that you have not even had the courtesy to identify. Your rum is delicious, the boat magnificent, but I must insist that you explain yourself."

All his adult life Ashby had searched for treasure. Though his family were financiers of long standing, he cherished the quest for things lost over the challenge of simply making money. Sometimes the answers he sought were discovered from hard work. Sometimes informants brought, for a price, what he needed to know. And sometimes, like here, he simply stumbled upon the solution.

"I would be more than happy to explain."

SEVEN

DENMARK, 1:50 AM

HENRIK THORVALDSEN CHECKED THE CLIP AND made sure the weapon was ready. Satisfied, he gently laid the assault rifle on the banquet table. He sat in the manor's great hall, beneath an oak beam ceiling, surrounded by armor and paintings that conveyed the look and feel of a noble seat. His ancestors had each sat at the same table, dating back nearly four hundred years.

Christmas was in less than three days.

What was it, nearly thirty years ago that Cai had climbed atop the table?

"You must get down," his wife demanded. "Immediately, Cai."

The boy scampered across the long expanse, his open palms threading the tops of high-backed chairs on either side. Thorvaldsen watched as his son avoided a gilded centerpiece and raced ahead, leaping into his outstretched arms.

"You're both impossible," his wife said. "Totally impossible."

"Lisette, it's Christmas. Let the boy play." He held him close in his lap. "He's only seven. And the table has been here a long time."

"Papa, will Nisse come this year?"

Cai loved the mischievous elf who, legend said, wore gray woolen clothes, a bonnet, red stockings, and white clogs. He dwelled in the lofts of old farmhouses and enjoyed playing jokes.

"To be safe," the boy said, "we'll need some porridge."

Thorvaldsen smiled. His own mother had told him the same tale of how a bowl of porridge, left out on Christmas Eve, kept Nisse's jokes within limits. Of course, that was before the Nazis slaughtered nearly every Thorvaldsen, including his father.

"We shall have porridge," Lisette said. "Along with roasted goose, red cabbage, browned potatoes, and cinnamon rice pudding."

"With the magic almond?" Cai asked, wonder in his voice.

His wife stroked the boy's thin brown hair. "Yes, my precious. With the magic almond. And if you find it, there will be a prize."

Both he and Lisette always made sure Cai found the magic almond. Though he was a Jew, Thorvaldsen's father and wife had been Christian, so the holiday had found a place in his life. Every year he and Lisette had decorated an aromatic fir with homemade wood and straw baubles and, per tradition, never allowed Cai to see their creation until after Christmas Eve dinner, when they all gathered and sang carols.

My, how he'd enjoyed Christmas.

Until Lisette died.

Then, two years ago, when Cai was murdered, the holiday lost all meaning. The past three, including this one, had been torture. He found himself every year sitting here, at the end of the table, wondering why life had been so cruel.

This year, though, was different.

He reached out and caressed the gun's black metal. Assault rifles were illegal in Denmark, but laws did not interest him.

Justice.

That's what he wanted.

He sat in silence. Not a light burned anywhere in Christiangade's forty-one rooms. He actually relished the thought of a world devoid of illumination. There his deformed spine would go unnoticed. His leathery face would never be seen. His bushy silver hair and bristly eyebrows would never require trimming. In the dark, only a person's senses mattered.

And his were finely tuned.

His eyes searched the dark hall as his mind kept remembering.

He could see Cai everywhere. Lisette, too. He

was a man of immeasurable wealth, power, and influence. Few heads of state, or imperial crowns, refused his requests. His porcelain, and reputation, remained among the finest in the world. He'd never seriously practiced Judaism, but he was a devoted friend of Israel. Last year he'd risked everything to stop a fanatic from destroying that blessed state. Privately, he supported charitable causes around the world with millions of the family's euros.

But he was the last Thorvaldsen.

Only the most distant of relatives remained, and damn few of them. This family, which had endured for centuries, was about to end.

But not before justice was administered.

He heard a door open, then footsteps echoed across the black hall.

A clock somewhere announced two AM.

The footsteps stopped a few meters away and a voice said, "The sensors just tripped."

Jesper had been with him a long time, witnessing all of the joy and pain—which, Thorvaldsen knew, his friend had felt as well.

"Where?" he asked.

"Southeast quadrant, near the shore. Two trespassers, headed this way."

"You don't need to do this," he said to Jesper.

"We need to prepare."

He smiled, glad his old friend could not see him. For the past two years he'd battled near-constant waves of conflicting emotion, involving himself with quests and causes that, only temporarily, allowed him to forget that pain, anguish, and sorrow had become his companions.

"What of Sam?" he asked.

"No further word since his earlier call. But Malone called twice. I allowed the phone to ring, as you instructed."

Which meant Malone had done what he'd needed him to do.

He'd baited this trap with great care. Now he intended to spring it with equal precision.

He reached for the rifle.

"Time to welcome our guests."

EIGHT

Eliza sat forward in her seat. She needed to command Robert Mastroianni's complete attention.

"Between 1689 and 1815, England was at war for sixty-three years. That's one out of every two in combat—the off years spent preparing for more combat. Can you imagine what that cost? And that was not atypical. It was actually common during that time for European nations to stay at war."

"Which, you say, many people actually profited from?" Mastroianni asked.

"Absolutely. And winning those wars didn't matter, since every time a war was fought governments incurred more debt and financiers amassed more privileges. It's like what drug companies do today. Treating the symptoms of a disease, never curing it, always being paid."

Mastroianni finished the last of his chocolate tart. "I own stock in three of those pharmaceutical concerns."

"Then you know what I just said is true."

She stared him down with hard eyes. He returned the glare but seemed to decide not to engage her.

"That tart was marvelous," he finally said. "I confess to a sweet tooth."

"I brought you another."

"Now you're bribing me."

"I want you to be a part of what is about to happen."

"Why?"

"Men like you are rare commodities. You have great wealth, power, influence. You're intelligent. Innovative. As with the rest of us, you are certainly tired of sharing great portions of your results with greedy, incompetent governments."

"So what is about to happen, Eliza? Explain the mystery."

She could not go that far. Not yet. "Let me answer by explaining more about Napoleon. Do you know much about him?"

"Short fellow. Wore a funny hat. Always had a hand stuck inside his coat."

"Did you know more books have been written about him than any other historical figure, save perhaps Jesus Christ."

"I never realized you were such the historian."

"I never realized you were so obstinate."

She'd known Mastroianni a number of years, not as a friend, more as a casual business associate.

He owned, outright, the world's largest aluminum plant. He was also heavy into auto manufacturing, aircraft repair, and, as he'd noted, health care.

"I'm tired of being stalked," he said. "Especially by a woman who wants something, yet can't tell me what or why."

She decided to do some ignoring of her own. "I like what Flaubert once wrote. **History is prophecy, looking backwards.**"

He chuckled. "Which perfectly illustrates your peculiar French view. I've always found it irritating how the French resolve all their conflicts on the battlefields of yesterday. It's as if some glorious past will provide the precise solution."

"That irritates the Corsican half of me sometimes as well. But occasionally, one of those former battlefields can be instructive."

"Then, Eliza, do tell me of Napoleon."

Only for the fact that this brash Italian was the perfect addition to her club did she continue. She could not, and would not, allow pride to interfere with careful planning.

"He created an empire not seen since the days of Rome. Seventy million people were under his personal rule. He was a man at ease with both the reek of gunpowder and the smell of parchment. He actually proclaimed **himself** emperor. Can you imagine? A mere thirty-five years old, he snubs the pope and places the imperial crown upon his own head." She allowed her words to take root, then said, "Yet for all that ego, Napoleon built, specifically for himself, only two memorials, both small theaters that no longer exist."

"What of all the buildings and monuments he erected?"

"Not one was created in his honor, or bears his name. Most were not even completed till long after his death. He even specifically vetoed the renaming of the Place de la Concorde to Place Napoleon."

She saw that Mastroianni was learning something. Good. It was about time.

"In Rome he ordered the Forum and Palatine cleared of rubble and the Pantheon restored, never adding any plaque to say that he'd done such. In countless other cities across Europe he ordered improvement after improvement, yet nothing was ever memorialized to him. Isn't that strange?"

She watched as Mastroianni cleared his palate of chocolate with a swish of bottled water.

"Here's something else," she said. "Napoleon refused to go into debt. He despised financiers, and blamed them for many of the French Republic's shortfalls. Now he didn't mind confiscating money, or extorting it, or even depositing money in banks, but he refused to borrow. In that, he was totally different from all who came before him, or after."

"Not a bad policy," he muttered. "Leeches, every one of the bankers."

"Would you like to be rid of them?"

She saw that prospect seemed pleasing, but her guest kept silent.

"Napoleon agreed with you," she said. "He flatly rejected the American offer to buy New Orleans and sold them, instead, the entire Louisiana Territory, using the millions from that sale to build his army. Any other monarch would have kept the land and borrowed money, from the leeches, for war."

"Napoleon has been dead a long time," Mastroianni said. "And the world has changed. Credit **is** today's economy."

"That's not true. You see, Robert, what Napoleon learned from those papyri I told you about is still relevant today."

She saw that she'd clearly tickled his interest as she drew close to her point.

"But of course," he said, "I cannot learn of that until I agree to your proposal?"

She sensed control of the situation shifting her way. "I can share one other item. It may even help you decide."

"For a woman I do not like, who offered me such a comfortable flight home, fed me the finest beef, served the best champagne, and, of course, the chocolate tart, how can I refuse?"

"Again, Robert, if you don't like me, why are you here?"

His eyes focused tight on hers. "Because I'm intrigued. You know that I am. Yes, I'd like to be rid of bankers and governments."

She stood from her seat, stepped aft to a leather sofa, and opened her Louis Vuitton day satchel. Inside rested a small leather-bound volume, first published in 1822. **The Book of Fate, Formerly in the Possession of and Used by Napoleon.**

"This was given to me by my Corsican grandmother, who received it from her grandmother." She laid the thin tome on the table. "Do you believe in oracles?"

"Hardly."

"This one is quite unique. It was supposedly found in a royal tomb in the Valley of the Kings, near Luxor, by one of Napoleon's **savants.** Written in hieroglyphs, it was given to Napoleon. He consulted a Coptic priest, who translated it orally to Napoleon's secretary, who then converted it into German for secrecy, who then gave it to Napoleon." She paused. "All lies, of course."

Mastroianni chuckled. "Why is that not surprising?"

"The original manuscript was indeed found in Egypt. But unlike the papyri I mentioned earlier—"

"Which you failed to tell me about," he said.

"That comes with a commitment."

He smiled. "A lot of mystery to your Paris Club."

"I have to be careful." She pointed to the oracle on the table. "The original text was written in Greek, probably part of the lost library at Alexandria. Hundreds of thousands of similar scrolls were stored in that library, all gone by the 5th century after Christ. Napoleon did indeed have this transcribed, but not into German. He couldn't read that language. He was actually quite poor with foreign languages. Instead, he had it converted to Corsican. He did keep this oraculum with him, at all times, in a wooden cabinet. That cabinet had to be discarded after the disastrous Battle of Leipzig in 1815, when his empire first began to crumble. It is said that he risked his life trying to retrieve it. A Prussian officer eventually found and sold it to a captured French general, who recognized it as a possession of the emperor. The general planned to return it, but died before he could. The cabinet eventually made it to Napoleon's second wife, Empress Marie Louise, who did not join her husband in his forced exile on St. Helena. After Napoleon's death, in 1821, a man named Kirchenhoffer claimed that the empress gave the manuscript to him for publication."

She parted the book and carefully thumbed though the opening pages.

"Notice the dedication. HER IMPERIAL HIGHNESS, THE EX-EMPRESS OF FRANCE."

Mastroianni seemed not to care.

"Would you like to try it?" she asked.

"What will it do?"

"Predict your future."

NINE

MALONE'S INITIAL ESTIMATE REGARDING SAM Collins had been correct. Early thirties, with an anxious face that projected a mix of innocence and determination. Thin, reddish blond hair was cut short and matted to his head like feathers. He spoke with the same trace of an accent Malone had first detected—Australian, or maybe New Zealand—but his diction and syntax were all American. He was antsy and cocky, like a lot of thirty-somethings, Malone himself once included, who wanted to be treated like they were fifty.

One problem.

All of them, himself once again included, failed to possess those extra twenty years of mistakes.

Sam Collins had apparently tossed away his Secret Service career, and Malone knew that if you failed with one security branch, rarely did another extend a hand.

He wheeled the Mazda around another tight curve as the coastal highway veered inland into a darkened, forested expanse. All of the land for the next few miles, between the road and sea, was owned by Henrik Thorvaldsen. Four of those acres belonged to Malone, presented unexpectantly by his Danish friend a few months ago.

"You're not going to tell me why you're here, in Denmark, are you?" he asked Collins.

"Can we deal with Thorvaldsen? I'm sure he'll answer all of your questions."

"More of Henrik's instructions?"

A hesitation, then, "That's what he said to tell you—if you asked."

He resented being manipulated, but knew that was Thorvaldsen's way. To learn anything meant he'd have to play along.

He slowed the car at an open gate and navigated between two white cottages that served as the entrance to Christiangade. The estate was four centuries old, built by a 17th-century Thorvaldsen ancestor who smartly converted tons of worthless peat into fuel to produce fine porcelain. By the 19th century Adelgate Glasvaerker had been declared the Danish royal glass provider. It still held that title, its glassware reigning supreme throughout Europe.

He followed a grassy drive lined by trees bare to winter. The manor house was a perfect specimen of Danish baroque—three stories of brick-encased sandstone, topped with a curving copper roof. One wing turned inland, the other faced the sea. Not a light burned in any window. Normal for the middle of the night.

But the front door hung half open.

That was unusual.

He parked, stepped from the car, and walked toward the entrance, gun in hand.

Collins followed.

Inside, the warm air reeked with a scent of boiled tomatoes and a lingering cigar. Familiar smells for a house that he'd visited often during the past two years.

"Henrik," Collins called out.

He glared at the younger man and whispered, "Are you a complete idiot?"

"They need to know we're here."

"Who's **they**?"

"The door was open."

"Precisely my point. Shut up and stay behind me."

He eased across polished flagstones to the hardwood of a nearby corridor and followed a wide hall, past the conservatory and billiard parlor, to a ground-floor study, the only light courtesy of a three-quarter winter moon stealing past the windows.

He needed to check something.

He threaded his way through the furniture to an elaborate gun cabinet, fashioned of the same rich maple that encased the rest of the salon. He knew that at least a dozen hunting rifles, along with several handguns, a crossbow, and three assault rifles were always displayed.

The beveled glass door hung open.

One of the automatic weapons was gone, as were two hunting rifles. He reached for one of the pistols. A Welby target revolver—blued finish, six-inch barrel. He knew how Thorvaldsen admired the weapon. None had been made since 1945. A bitter scent of oil filled his nostrils. He checked the cylinder. Six shots. Fully loaded. Thorvaldsen never displayed an empty gun.

He handed it to Collins and mouthed, **You can use it?**

The younger man nodded.

They left the room through the nearest doorway.

Familiar with the house's geography, he followed another corridor until he came to an intersection. Doors framed with elaborate molding lined both sides of the hall, spaced sufficiently apart to indicate that the rooms beyond were spacious.

At the far end loomed a pedimented entrance. The master bedchamber.

Thorvaldsen hated climbing stairs, so he'd long ago occupied the ground floor.

Malone stepped to the door, slowly turned the knob, and pushed the slab of carved wood open without a sound.

He peered inside and inventoried the silhouettes of tall, heavy furniture, the drapes open to the silvery night. A rug filled the center, its edge a good five paces from the doorway. He spied the duvets on the bed and noticed a mound, signaling where someone may be sleeping.

But something was wrong.

Movement to the right caught his attention.

A form appeared in a doorway.

Light flooded the room.

He raised a hand to shield his eyes from the burning rays and caught sight of Thorvaldsen, a rifle muzzle pointed straight at him.

Jesper appeared from the walk-in closet, gun leveled.

Then he saw the bodies.

Two men, lying on the floor at the far side of the bed.

"They thought me stupid," Thorvaldsen said.

He did not particularly enjoy being caught in a trap. The mouse never did have much fun. "Is there a reason I'm here?"

Thorvaldsen lowered his weapon. "You've been away."

"Personal business."

"I spoke to Stephanie. She told me. I'm sorry, Cotton. That had to be hell."

He appreciated his friend's concern. "It's over and done with."

The Dane settled onto the bed and yanked back the covers, revealing only pillows beneath. "Unfortunately, that kind of thing is never done with."

Malone motioned at the corpses. "Those the same two who attacked the bookshop?"

Thorvaldsen shook his head, and he spotted pain in Thorvaldsen's tired eyes.

"It's taken me two years, Cotton. But I finally found my son's murderers."

TEN

"NAPOLEON STRONGLY BELIEVED IN ORACLES AND prophecy," Eliza told her flying companion. "That was the Corsican in him. His father once told him that fate and destiny were **written in the sky.** He was right."

Mastroianni did not seem impressed.

But she was not to be deterred.

"Josephine, Napoleon's first wife, was a Creole from Martinique, a place where voodoo and the magical arts flourished. Before leaving that island and sailing for France, she had her fortune told. She was assured that she would marry young, be unhappy, widowed, and would later become more than the queen of France." She paused. "She married at 15, was extremely unhappy, became widowed, and later rose to be not queen, but empress of France."

He shrugged. "More of the French way of looking backward to find answers."

"Perhaps. But my mother lived her life by this

oracle. I was like you once, a nonbeliever. But I now have a different opinion."

She opened the thin book.

"There are thirty-two questions to choose from. Some are basic. **Shall I live to old age? Shall the patient recover from illness? Have I any or many enemies? Shall I inherit property?** But others are more specific. You spend a few moments formulating the question, and are even allowed to substitute a word or two in the query." She slid the volume before him. "Choose one. Something that perhaps you may already know. Test its power."

A shrug and a wink conveyed his amusement.

"What else do you have to do?" she asked.

He surrendered and examined the list of questions, finally pointing to one. "Here. **Shall I have a son or daughter?**"

She knew he'd remarried last year. Wife number three. Maybe twenty years younger. Moroccan, if she remembered correctly.

"I had no idea. Is she pregnant?"

"Let's see what the oracle says."

She caught the warning of suspicion in a quick twitch of his eyebrow.

She handed him a notepad. "Take the pencil and mark a row of vertical lines across the page of at least twelve. After twelve, stop where you please."

He threw her a strange look.

"It's how it works," she said.

He did as she instructed.

|||||||||||||||||||||||||

"Now, mark four more rows of vertical lines, one line each, under the first. Don't think about it, just do it."

"At least twelve?"

She shook her head. "No. Any number you like."

She watched as he marked the page.

||||||||||||||||||

|||||||||

|||||||||||

|||||||||||||||||||||||||||||||||

"Now count all five rows. If the number is even, place two dots to the side. If it's odd, one dot."

He took a moment and made the calculation, ending up with a column of five rows of dots.

She examined the results. "Two odds, three evens. Random enough for you?"

He nodded his head.

She opened the book to a chart.

"You chose question 32." She pointed to the bottom and a row marked 32. "Here, at the top of the page are the dot possibilities. In the column for your chosen combination, two odd, three even, for question 32, the answer is R."

She thumbed through and stopped at a page with a capital R at the top.

"On the answer page are the same dot combinations. The oracle's reply to the two odd, three even combination is the third one down."

He accepted the book and read. A look of astonishment came to his face. "That's quite remarkable."

She'd allowed herself a smile.

" 'A son will be born who, if he receives not timely correction, may prove a source of trouble to thee.' I am, indeed, having a son. In fact, we only learned that a few days ago. Some prenatal testing has revealed a developing problem that the doctors want to correct while the baby is in the womb. It's risky to both mother and baby. We've told no one the situation, and are still debating the treatment." His original dismay faded. "How is that possible?"

"Fate and destiny."

"Might I try again?" he asked.

She shook her head. "The oracle warns that an inquirer may not ask two questions on the same day, or ask on the same subject within the same lunar month. Also, questions asked under the light of the moon are more likely to be accurate. It's what, nearly midnight, as we head east toward the sun?"

"So there's another day soon coming."

She smiled.

"I must say, Eliza, that is impressive. There are thirty-two possible answers to my question. Yet I randomly chose the precise one that satisifed my inquiry."

She slid the pad close and flipped to a clean page. "I haven't consulted the oracle today. Let me try."

She pointed to question 28.

Shall I be successful in my current undertaking?

"Does that refer to me?" His tone had clearly softened.

She nodded. "I came to New York specifically to see you." She leveled her gaze. "You will make an excellent addition to our team. I choose carefully, and I chose you."

"You are a ruthless woman. More than that, you're a ruthless woman with a plan."

She shrugged. "The world is a complicated place. Oil prices go up and down with no reason or predictability. Either inflation or recession runs rampant across the globe. Governments are helpless. They either print more money, which causes more inflation, or regulate the situation into another recession. Stability seems a thing of the past. I have a way to deal with all those problems."

"Will it work?"

"I believe so."

His swarthy face seemed as strong as an iron, his eager eyes finally conveying decisiveness. This entrepreneur, affected by the same dilemmas that she and the others faced, understood. The world was indeed changing. Something had to be done. And she might have the solution.

"There is a price of admission," she said. "Twenty million euros."

He shrugged. "Not a problem. But surely you have other revenue sources?"

She nodded. "Billions. Untraced and untouched."

He pointed to the oracle. "Go ahead, make your marks and let's learn the answer to your question."

She gripped the pencil and slashed five rows of vertical lines, then counted each row. All even numbers. She consulted the chart and saw that the answer was Q. She turned to the appropriate page and found the message that corresponded.

She resisted the urge to smile, seeing that his passions were now thoroughly aroused. "Would you like me to read it to you?"

He nodded.

" 'Examine strictly the disposition of thy intended partner and, if it is in accord with thine own, fear not but happiness will attend you both.' "

"Seems the oracle knows what I'm to do," he said.

She sat silent and allowed the drone of jet engines to sweep through the cabin. This skeptical Italian had just learned what she'd known for all of her adult life—what her Corsican mother and grandmother had taught her—that the direct transmission of provenance was the most empowering form of knowledge.

Mastroianni extended his hand.

They shook, his grip light and sweaty.

"You may count me a part of whatever you have in mind."

But she wanted to know, "Still don't like me?"

"Let's reserve judgment on that one."

ELEVEN

MALONE DECIDED A STROLL IN THE PLAZA would clear his head. Court had started early and not recessed till well after the noon hour. He wasn't hungry, but he was thirsty, and he spotted a café on the far side of the expanse. This was an easy assignment. Something different. Observe and make sure the conviction of a drug-smuggler-turned-murderer happened without a hitch. The victim, a DEA supervisor out of Arizona, had been shot execution-style in northern Mexico. The agent had been a personal friend of Danny Daniels, president of the United States, so Washington was watching carefully. The trial was in its fourth day and probably would end tomorrow. So far, the prosecution had done a good job. The evidence was overwhelming. Privately, he'd been briefed about a turf war between the defendant and several of his Mexican competitors—the trial apparently an excellent way for some of the reef sharks to eliminate a deep-water predator.

From some nearby belfry came the fiendish clamor of bells, barely discernible over Mexico City's daily drone. Around the grassy plaza, people sat in the shade of bushy trees, whose vibrant color tempered the severity of the nearby sooty buildings. A blue marble fountain shot slender columns of foamy water high into the warm air.

He heard a pop. Then another.

A black-skirted nun fifty yards away dropped to the ground.

Two more pops.

Another person, a woman, fell flat.

Screams pierced the air.

People fled in every direction, as if an air-raid warning had been issued.

He noticed little girls in sober, gray uniforms. More nuns. Women in bright-colored skirts. Men in somber business suits.

All fleeing.

His gaze raked the mayhem as bodies kept dropping. Finally, he spotted two men fifty yards away with guns—one kneeling, the other standing, both firing.

Three more people tumbled to the ground.

He reached beneath his suit jacket for his Beretta. The Mexicans had allowed him to keep it while in the country. He leveled the gun and ticked off two rounds, taking down both shooters.

He spotted more bodies. Nobody was helping anyone.

Everybody simply ran.

He lowered the gun.

Another crack rang loud and he felt something pierce his left shoulder. At first there was no sensation, then an electric charge surged through him and exploded into his brain with a painful agony he'd felt before.

He'd been shot.

From a row of hedges a man emerged. Malone noticed little about him save for black hair that curled from under the rakish slant of a battered hat.

The pain intensified. Blood poured from his shoulder, soaking his shirt. This was supposed to be a low-risk courtroom assignment. Anger rushed through him, which steeled his resolve. His attacker's eyes grew impudent, the mouth chiseled into a sardonic smile, seemingly deciding whether to stay and finish what he started or flee.

The gunman turned to leave.

Malone's balance was failing, but he summoned all his strength and fired.

He still did not recall actually pulling the trigger. He was told later that he fired three times, and two of the rounds found the target, killing the third assailant.

The final tally? Seven dead, nine injured.

Cai Thorvaldsen, a young diplomat assigned to the Danish mission, and a Mexican prosecutor, Elena Ramirez Rico, were two of the dead. They'd been enjoying their lunch beneath one of the trees.

Ten weeks later a man with a crooked spine came to see him in Atlanta. They'd sat in Malone's den, and he hadn't bothered to ask how Henrik Thorvaldsen had found him.

"I came to meet the man who shot my son's killer," Thorvaldsen said.

"Why?"

"To thank you."

"You could have called."

"I understand you were nearly killed."

He shrugged.

"And you are quitting your government job. Resigning your commission. Retiring from the military."

"You know an awful lot."

"Knowledge is the greatest of luxuries."

He wasn't impressed. "Thanks for the pat on the back. I have a hole in my shoulder that's throbbing. So since you've said your peace, could you leave?"

Thorvaldsen never moved from the sofa, he simply stared around at the den and the surrounding rooms visible through an archway. Every wall was sheathed in books. The house seemed nothing but a backdrop for the shelves.

"I love them, too," his guest said. "I've collected books all my life."

"What do you want?"

"Have you considered your future?"

He motioned around the room. "Thought I'd open an old-book shop. Got plenty to sell."

"Excellent idea. I have one for sale, if you'd like it."

He decided to play along. But there was something about the tight points of light in the older man's eyes that told him his visitor was not joking. Hard hands searched a suit coat pocket and Thorvaldsen laid a business card on the sofa.

"My private number. If you're interested, call me."

That was two years ago. Now he was staring at Henrik Thorvaldsen, their roles reversed. His friend was the one in trouble.

Thorvaldsen remained perched on the edge of the bed, an assault rifle lying across his lap, his face cast with a look of utter defeat.

"I was dreaming about Mexico City earlier,"

Malone said. "It's always the same each time. I never can shoot the third guy."

"But you did."

"For some reason, I can't in the dream."

"Are you okay?" Thorvaldsen asked Sam Collins.

"I went straight to Mr. Malone—"

"Don't start that," he said. "It's Cotton."

"Okay. Cotton took care of them."

"And my shop's destroyed. Again."

"It's insured," Thorvaldsen made clear.

Malone stared at his friend. "Why did those men come after Sam?"

"I was hoping they wouldn't. The idea was for them to come after me. That's why I sent him into town. They apparently were a step ahead of me."

"What are you doing, Henrik?"

"I've spent the past two years searching. I knew there was more to what happened that day in Mexico City. That massacre wasn't terrorism. It was an assassination."

He waited for more.

Thorvaldsen pointed at Sam. "This young man is quite bright. His superiors don't realize just how smart he is."

Malone spotted tears glistening on the rims of his friend's eyes. Something he'd never seen before.

"I miss him, Cotton," Thorvaldsen whispered, still staring at Sam.

He laid a hand on the older man's shoulders.

"Why did he have to die?" Thorvaldsen whispered.

"You tell me," Malone said. "Why did Cai die?"

"PAPA, HOW ARE YOU TODAY?"

Thorvaldsen so looked forward to Cai's weekly telephone calls and he liked that his son, though thirty-five years old, a part of Denmark's elite diplomatic corp, still called him Papa.

"It's lonely in this big house, but Jesper keeps things interesting. He's trimming the garden, and he and I disagree on how much cutting he should do. He's a stubborn one."

"But Jesper is always right. We learned that long ago."

He chuckled. "I shall never tell him. How are things across the ocean?"

Cai had asked for and received assignment to the Danish consulate in Mexico City. From an early age his son had been fascinated with Aztecs and was enjoying his time near that long-ago culture.

"Mexico is an amazing place. Hectic, cluttered, and chaotic, while at the same time fascinating, challenging, and romantic. I'm glad I came."

"And what of the young lady you met?"

"Elena is quite wonderful."

Elena Ramirez Rico worked for the federal prosecutor's office in Mexico City, assigned to a special investigative unit. Cai had told him some about it, but much more about her. Apparently, his son was quite taken.

"You should bring her for a visit."

"We talked about that. Maybe at Christmas."

"That would be wonderful. She would like the way Danes celebrate, though she might find our weather uncomfortable."

"She's taken me to many archaeological sites. She's so knowledgeable about this country's history"

"You seem to like her."

"I do, Papa. She reminds me of Mother. Her warmth. Her smile."

"Then she has to be lovely."

"Elena Ramirez Rico," Thorvaldsen said, "prosecuted cultural crimes. Mainly art and artifact thefts. That's big business in Mexico. She was about to indict two men. One a Spaniard, the other a Brit. Both major players in the stolen artifact business. She was murdered before that could happen."

"Why would her death matter?" Malone asked him. "Another prosecutor would have been assigned."

"And one was, who declined to pursue the case. All charges were dropped."

Thorvaldsen studied Malone. He saw that his friend fully understood.

"Who were the two men she was prosecuting?" Malone asked.

"The Spaniard is Amando Cabral. The Brit is Lord Graham Ashby."

TWELVE

CORSICA

Ashby sat on the sofa, sipping his rum, watching the Corsican as **Archimedes** continued its cruise up the coast, following Cap Corse's rocky east shore.

"Those four Germans left something with the fifth," Ashby finally said. "That has long been rumor. But I discovered it to be fact."

"Thanks to information I provided, months ago."

He nodded. "That's right. You controlled the missing pieces. That's why I came and generously offered what I knew, along with a percentage of the find. And you agreed to share. "

"That I did. But we've found nothing. So why have this conversation? Why am I a captive?"

"Captive? Hardly. We're simply taking a short cruise aboard my boat. Two friends. Visiting."

"Friends don't assault each other."

"And neither do they lie to each other."

He'd approached this man over a year ago, after learning of his connection with that fifth German who'd been there in September 1943. Legend held that one of the four soldiers Hitler executed encoded the treasure's location and tried to use the information as a bargaining chip. Unfortunately for him Nazis didn't bargain, or at least never in good faith. The Corsican sitting across from him, surely trying to determine just how far this charade could be taken, had stumbled upon what that ill-fated German had left behind—a book, an innocuous volume on Napoleon—which the soldier had read while imprisoned in Italy.

"That man," Ashby said, "learned of the Moor's Knot." He pointed to the table. "So he created those letters. They were eventually discovered by that fifth participant, after the war, in confiscated German archives. Unfortunately, he never learned the book's title. Amazingly, you managed to accomplish that feat. I rediscovered these letters and, the last time we met, provided them to you, which showed my good faith. But you didn't mention anything about knowing the actual book title."

"Who says I know it?"

"Gustave."

He saw the shock on the man's face.

"Have you harmed him?" the Corsican asked again.

"I paid him for the information. Gustave is a

talkative individual, with an infectious optimism. He's also now quite rich."

He watched as his guest digested the betrayal.

Mr. Guildhall entered the salon and nodded. He knew what that meant. They were near. Engines dulled as the boat slowed. He motioned and his acolyte left.

"And if I decipher the Moor's Knot?" the Corsican asked, after apparently connecting the dots.

"Then you, too, shall be rich."

"How rich?"

"One million euros."

The Corsican laughed. "The treasure is worth a hundred times that."

Ashby stood from the sofa. "Provided there's one to find. Even you admit that it may all be a tale."

He stepped across the salon and retrieved a black satchel. He returned and poured out its contents on the sofa.

Bundles of euros.

The bureaucrat's eyes widened.

"One million. Yours. No more hunting for you. "

The Corsican immediately leaned forward and slid the book close. "You are most persuasive, Lord Ashby."

"Everyone has a price."

"These Roman numerals are clear. The top row are page numbers. The middle set, line numbers. The last show the position of the word. Angling ties the three rows together."

XCV CCXXXVI CXXVIII CXCIV XXXII
IV XXXI XXVI XVIII IX
VII VI X II XI

He watched as the Corsican thumbed though the old book, locating the first page, 95, line 4, word 7. "Santa. Which makes no sense. But if you add the two words after, it does. Santa Maria Tower."

The steps were repeated four more times.

Santa Maria Tower, convent, cemetery, marker, Ménéval.

Ashby watched, then said, "A well-chosen book. Its text describes Napoleon's exile on St. Helena, along with his early years on Corsica. The correct words would all be there. That German was smart."

The Corsican sat back. "His secret has stayed hidden for sixty years. Now here it is."

He allowed a friendly smile to sweeten the atmosphere.

The Corsican examined the euros. "I'm curious, Lord Ashby. You're a man of obvious wealth. You certainly don't need this treasure."

"Why would you say that?"

"You search simply for the joy of it, don't you?"

He thought of his careful plans, his calculated risks. "Things lost interest me."

The ship slowed to a stop.

"I search," the Corsican said, holding up a wad of euros, "for the money. I don't own such a big boat."

Ashby's worries from earlier, on the cruise south from France, had finally receded. His goal was now in sight. He wondered if the prize would be worth all this trouble. That was the problem with things lost—sometimes the end did not justify the means.

Here was a good example.

Nobody knew if six wooden crates were waiting to be found and, if so, what was actually inside them. It could be nothing more than silver place settings and some gold jewelry. The Nazis were not particular about what they extorted.

But he wasn't interested in junk. Because the Corsican was wrong. He needed this treasure.

"Where are we?" he was finally asked.

"Off the coast, north of Macinaggio. At the Site Naturel de la Capandula."

Cap Corse, above Bastia, was dotted with ancient watchtowers, empty convents, and Romanesque churches. The extreme northern tip comprised a national wilderness zone with few roads and even fewer people. Only gulls and cormorants claimed it as home. Ashby had studied its geography. The Tour de Santa Maria was a ruined three-story tower that rose from the sea, a mere few meters from shore, built by the Genoese in the 16th century as a lookout post. A short walk inland from the tower stood the Chapelle Santa Maria, from the 11th century, a former convent, now a tourist attraction.

Santa Maria Tower, convent, cemetery, marker, Ménéval.

He checked his watch.

Not yet.

A little longer.

He motioned at the Corsican's glass. "Enjoy your drink. When you're done, there's a tender ready to take us ashore. Time for us to find Rommel's gold."

THIRTEEN

DENMARK

SAM WATCHED THORVALDSEN WITH CONCERN, recalling what one of his Secret Service instructors had taught him. **Stir a person up and they think. Add anger and they usually screw up.**

Thorvaldsen was angry.

"You killed two men tonight," Malone made clear.

"We've known this night would come," Thorvaldsen said.

"Who's **we**?"

"Jesper and me."

Sam watched as Jesper stood obedient, clearly in agreement.

"We've been waiting," Thorvaldsen said. "I tried to contact you last week, but you were away. I'm glad you came back. I needed you to look after Sam."

"How'd you find out about Cabral and Ashby?" Malone asked.

"Private detectives working for the past two years."

"You've never mentioned this before."

"It wasn't relevant to you and me."

"You're my friend. I'd say that made it relevant."

"Perhaps you're right, but I chose to keep what I was doing to myself. I learned a few months ago that Ashby tried to bribe Elena Rico. When that failed, Cabral hired men to shoot her, Cai, and a lot of others to mask the crime."

"A bit grandiose."

"It sent a message to Rico's successor. Which worked. He was much more agreeable."

Sam listened, amazed at how his life had changed. Two weeks ago he was an obscure Secret Service agent chasing questionable financial transactions through a maze of dull electronic records. Background work—secondary to the field agents. He'd genuinely wanted to work the field, but had never been offered the chance. He believed himself up to the challenge—he'd reacted well back at Malone's bookshop—but staring at the corpses across the room, he wondered. Thorvaldsen and Jesper had killed those men. What did it take to do that? Could he?

He watched as Jesper stretched two body bags on the floor. He'd never actually seen someone who'd been shot dead. Smelled the rusty scent of blood. Stared into glassy eyes. Jesper handled the corpses with a cool detachment, stuffing them into the bags, not seeming to care.

Could he do that, too?

"What's the deal with Graham Ashby?" Malone asked. "Sam here made a point to mention him to me. I assume that was at your insistence."

Sam could tell Malone was both irritated and concerned.

"I can answer that," Sam said. "He's a rich Brit. Old, old money, but his actual worth is unknown. Lots of hidden assets. He got caught up in something a few years ago. Retter der Verlorenen Antiquitäten. Retrievers of Lost Antiquities. A group of people who stole art that was already stolen and traded it among themselves."

"I remember that," Malone said. "That's when they found the Amber Room."

Sam nodded. "Along with a ton of other lost treasures when they raided the participants' homes. Ashby was implicated, but nothing was ever proven. Amando Cabral worked for one of the members. Acquisitors, they called them. The ones who did the actual collecting. " He paused. "Or stealing, depending on how you look at it."

Malone seemed to comprehend. "So Ashby got himself into trouble in Mexico City with collecting?"

Thorvaldsen nodded. "The case was building, and Elena Ramirez Rico was on the right path. She'd eventually tie Cabral and Ashby together, so Ashby decided she had to be eliminated."

"There's more," Sam said.

Malone faced him.

"Ashby is also involved with another covert group that's working a more widespread conspiracy."

"Is that the agent talking, or the webmaster?" Malone asked.

He shook off the skepticism. "It's real. They intend to wreak havoc with the world's financial systems."

"That seems to be happening without their efforts."

"I realize that you think I'm nuts, but economics can be a powerful weapon. It could be argued that it is the ultimate weapon of mass destruction."

"How do you know about this secret group?"

"There are some of us who've been watching. I have an acquaintance in Paris who found this one. They're just getting started. They've tinkered here and there with currency markets. Small stuff. Things few would even notice, unless paying close attention."

"Which you and your friends have apparently been doing. You probably told your superiors, and they didn't believe you. I assume the problem is a lack of proof."

He nodded. "They're out there. I know it, and Ashby is a part of them."

"Cotton," Thorvaldsen said, "I met Sam about a year ago. I came across his website and his unconventional theories, especially his opinions relative to Ashby. There's a lot he says that makes sense." The older man smiled at Sam. "He's bright and ambitious. Perhaps you might recognize those qualities?"

Malone grinned. "Okay. I was young once, too. But apparently Ashby knows you're after him. And he knows about Sam."

Thorvaldsen shook his head. "I don't know about that. The men tonight came from Cabral. I specifically provoked him. I wasn't sure if Sam would be a target. I was hoping Cabral's anger would focus on me, but I told Sam to find you if he needed help."

Jesper dragged one of the bagged bodies from the room.

"They came by boat," Thorvaldsen said. "It'll be found tomorrow adrift in the Øresund, a long way from here."

"And what are you going to do now?" Malone asked.

Thorvaldsen sucked a succession of quick breaths. Sam wondered if his friend was okay.

"Ashby likes to acquire art and treasure that is either unknown, unclaimed, or stolen," Thorvaldsen finally said. "No lawyers, legal battles, or press to worry about. I've studied the Retrievers of Lost Antiquities. They were around for a long time. Pretty clever, actually. To steal what's already stolen. Ashby's Acquisitor was a man named Guildhall, who still works for him. Cabral was hired by Ashby, after the Retrievers were exposed, for some specialized tasks. Cabral went after some of the items that weren't recovered when the Retrievers were caught, things Ashby knew existed. The list of what was recovered when the Retrievers were finally discovered is staggering. But Ashby may have moved on to other things, trading treasure hunting for something on a grander scale." Thorvaldsen faced Sam. "Your information makes sense. All of your analysis on Ashby, so far, has proven accurate."

"But you don't see any new financial conspiracy," Malone said.

The Dane shrugged. "Ashby has lots of friends, but that's to be expected. After all, he heads one of England's largest banks. To be honest, I've confined my investigation only to his association with Cabral—"

"Why not just kill him and be done with it? Why all these games?" Malone asked.

The answer to both questions struck Sam immediately. "Because you **do** believe me. You think there is a conspiracy."

Thorvaldsen's countenance beamed with a mild delight, the first sign of joviality Sam had seen on his friend's face in a while.

"I never said I didn't."

"What do you know, Henrik?" Malone asked. "You never move in the dark. Tell me what you're holding back."

"Sam, when Jesper returns, could you help him with that final bag. It's a long way to the boat. Though he'd never say it, my old friend is getting up in age. Not as spry as he once was."

Sam didn't like being dismissed, but saw that Thorvaldsen wanted to talk to Malone alone. He realized his place—he was an outsider, not in any position to argue. Not a whole lot different from when he was a kid, or from the Secret Service, where he was the low man on the pole as well. He'd done what Thorvaldsen wanted and made contact with Malone. But he'd also helped thwart attackers in Malone's bookshop. He'd proven he was capable. He thought about protesting, but decided to keep quiet. Over the past year he'd said plenty to his supervisors in Washington, surely enough to get him fired. He desperately wanted to be a part of whatever Thorvaldsen was planning.

Enough to swallow his pride and do as he was told.

So when Jesper returned, he bent down and said, "Let me help you."

As he grabbed feet sheathed in thick plastic, carrying a corpse for the first time in his life, Malone looked at him. "This financial group you keep talking about. You know a lot about them?"

"My friend in France knows more."

"You at least know its name?"

He nodded. "The Paris Club."

FOURTEEN

CORSICA

ASHBY STEPPED ONTO THE DESOLATE CAP CORSE
shore, its dirty sand grass-strewn, its rocks invested
with prickly maquis. On the eastern horizon, far
across the water, he spied the lights of Elba. The
crumbling Tour de Santa Maria sprang from the surf
twenty meters away, the shadowy ruin torn and con-
vulsed with the look of something utterly besieged.
The winter night was a balmy 18° Celsius, typical
for the Mediterranean, and the main reason why so
many tourists flocked to the island this time of year.

"We are going to the convent?" the Corsican
asked him.

He motioned and the tender motored away. He
carried a radio and would contact the ship later.
Archimedes rested at anchor, in a calm expanse,
just offshore.

"Indeed we are. I checked a map. It's not far."

He and his cohort carefully eased their way

across the granite, following a defined footpath among the maquis. He caught the distinctive scent of the aromatic scrub, a blend of rosemary, lavender, cistus, sage, juniper, mastic, and myrtle. Not as strong this time of year as it was in spring and summer when Corsica erupted in a blaze of pink and yellow blossoms, but nonetheless pleasant. He recalled that Napoleon, while first exiled on nearby Elba, had remarked that on certain days, with a westerly wind, he could smell his homeland. He imagined himself one of the many Moorish pirates who'd raided this coastline for centuries, using the maquis to mask their trail and shield a retreat. To defend against those raids, the Genoese had erected watchtowers. The Tour de Santa Maria was one of many—each round, nearly twenty meters high, with walls over a meter thick, a cistern in the lower part, living section in the middle, an observatory and fighting platform on top.

Quite an engineering achievement.

Something about history stirred him.

He liked following in its footsteps.

On a dark night in 1943 five men had managed something extraordinary, something that he had only in the past three weeks been able to comprehend. Unfortunately, the fool of small stature, with a devil-may-care personality, walking ahead of him, had interfered with success. This venture needed to end. Here. Tonight. Ventures far more critical lay ahead.

They abandoned the rocky shoreline and crossed a ridge into a forest of oak, chestnut, and olive trees. Silence had settled about them. Ahead rose the Chapelle Santa Maria. The convent had stood since the 11th century, a tall, gunpowder-gray rectangle of vitrified stone, with a plank roof and a belfry.

The Corsican stopped. "Where do we go? I've never been here."

"Never visited this national preserve? Seems a must for any resident of this island."

"I live in the south. We have our own natural wonders."

He motioned left, through the trees. "I am told there's a cemetery behind the convent."

He now led the way, a nearly full moon illuminating the path. Not a light shone anywhere. The nearest village was miles away.

They rounded the ancient building and found an iron archway that opened into a graveyard. His research had revealed that the medieval lords of Cap Corse had been afforded a certain latitude by their Genoese masters. Positioned so far north, on a mountainous, inhospitable strip of land that cleaved the sea, those Corsican lords had profited from both the French and the Italians. Two local families once shared territorial control. The da Gentiles and da Mares. Some of the da Mares were buried here, behind the convent, in graves centuries old.

Three beams of light suddenly appeared from the blackness. Electric torches, switched on at their approach.

"Who's there?" the Corsican called out.

One of the beams revealed a stiff face. Guildhall.

The Corsican faced Ashby. "What is this?"

Ashby motioned ahead. "I'll show you."

They walked toward the lights, threading a path through crumbling stone markers, maybe fifty or so overgrown with more fragrant maquis. As they came closer the lights revealed a rectangle dug into the earth, maybe a meter and a half deep. Two younger men stood with Guildhall, holding shovels. Ashby produced his own flashlight and shone its beam on a gravestone, which revealed the name MÉNÉVAL.

"He was a da Mare, from the 17th century. Those four German soldiers used his grave as their hiding place. They buried six crates here, just as the Moor's Knot revealed from the book. **Santa Maria Tower, convent, cemetery, marker, Ménéval.**"

He adjusted the angle of the light and revealed the inside of the freshly excavated grave.

Empty.

"No crates. No Ménéval. Nothing. Can you explain that?"

The Corsican did not offer a reply.

Ashby had not expected one. With his light, he revealed the faces of the other two men, then said, "These gentlemen have worked for me a long time.

As has their father. Once, so did their uncles. They are absolutely loyal. Sumner," he called out.

From the darkness more forms appeared, and a new torch beam revealed two more men.

"Gustave," the Corsican said, recognizing one of the faces as his co-conspirator. "What are you doing here?"

"This man, Sumner, brought me."

"You sold me out, Gustave."

The other man shrugged. "You would have done the same."

The Corsican laughed. "That I would. But we have both been made rich."

Ashby noticed they spoke Corsican, so he added, in their language, "I apologize for this inconvenience. But we needed privacy to conclude our business. And I needed to know if there was, indeed, anything to find."

The Corsican motioned to the empty hole. "As you can see, Lord Ashby, there are no crates. No treasure. As you feared."

"Which is entirely understandable, given you both recently found the crates and carted them away."

"That's preposterous," the Corsican said. "Completely, utterly false."

Time for all pretense to end. "I have spent three years searching for Rommel's gold. It has cost me much time and money. Six months ago I finally located that fifth German's family. He lived a long life and died in Bavaria a decade ago. His widow, for a fee of course, allowed me inside her home. Among his belongings, I found the Roman numerals."

"Lord Ashby," the Corsican said. "We have not betrayed you."

"Sumner, if you please, inform these gentlemen what you found."

The shadowy form motioned at Gustave with his light. "Buried in this bugger's backyard. Six crates." The voice paused. "Full of gold bars bearing the swastika."

Ashby savored the revelation. He hadn't known, to this moment, what they'd discovered. While he'd hosted the Corsican, Sumner Murray and his sons had located Gustave, outside Bastia, and determined whether his suspicions proved correct. And while they'd sailed north, the Murrays had driven up the coast highway. Then Mr. Guildhall had come ashore and excavated the grave.

"I dealt with you in good faith," Ashby told the two liars. "I offered you a percentage of the find, and I would have honored that agreement. You chose to deceive me, so I owe you nothing. I withdraw the one million euros I extended you both."

He'd read of the famed Corsican **vendettas**— blood feuds that erupted between families and generated body counts normally associated with national civil wars. Usually begun over trivial matters of honor, the murderous fights could smolder for decades. The da Gentiles and da Mares had, for centuries, fought each other, some of the victims of those feuds decaying in the ground around him. Officially, **vendettas** no longer existed, but Corsican politics continued to be riddled with remnants. Assassination and violence were common. The political tactic even had a name. **Règlement de comte.** Settling of scores.

Time to settle this score.

"Normally I would have my solicitor deal with you."

"A lawyer? You plan to sue us?" the Corsican asked.

"Heavens, no."

The Corsican laughed. "I was beginning to wonder. Can't we make some sort of arrangement? We did, after all, supply part of the answer. Can we keep the money you have already given us in return?"

"To do that, I would have to forgive your deceit."

"It's my nature," the Corsican said. "I can't help it. How about half the money for our trouble?"

He watched as Guildhall slowly backed away from the two men. Sumner and the two younger Murrays had already retreated, sensing what was about to happen.

"Half seems a bit much to me," he said. "How about—"

Two pops disturbed the night.

Both Corsicans lurched as bullets from Guildhall's gun pierced their skulls. Their bodies went limp, then flesh and bones collapsed forward, tumbling into the open grave.

Problem solved.

"Cover this up and make sure it's unnoticed." He knew the Murrays would handle things.

Mr. Guildhall came close, and Ashby asked, "How long will it take to retrieve the gold?"

"We have it already. It's in the truck."

"Excellent. Load it on **Archimedes.** We need to leave. Tomorrow, I have business elsewhere."

FIFTEEN

DENMARK

MALONE AND THORVALDSEN LEFT THE BEDROOM and walked toward Christiangade's main foyer. There Thorvaldsen climbed a staircase to the next floor, where he followed a wide corridor adorned with Danish art and antiques to a closed door. Malone knew where they were headed.

Cai's room.

Inside was an intimate chamber, with high ceilings, soft-colored plaster walls, and a four-poster English bed.

"He always called this his **thinking space,**" Thorvaldsen said, switching on three lamps. "This room was redecorated many times. It went from a nursery, to a little boy's room, to a young man's haven, to a grown man's retreat. Lisette loved changing it."

He knew the subject of Thorvaldsen's late wife was taboo. In the two years they'd been together they'd discussed her but once, and then only fleetingly. Her portrait remained downstairs, more photographs of her scattered throughout the house. It seemed only visual reminders were permitted of this sacred memory.

He'd never before been allowed in Cai's room, and he noticed more visual reminders here, too—shelves littered with knickknacks.

"I come here often," Thorvaldsen said.

He had to ask, "Is that healthy?"

"Probably not. But I have to hold on to something, and this room is all I have left."

He wanted to know what was happening so he kept his mouth shut and his ears open and indulged his friend. Thorvaldsen stooped against a dresser adorned with family photographs. An abyss of unfathomable grief seemed to engulf him.

"He was murdered, Cotton. Gunned down in the prime of his life for nothing more than the proving of a point."

"What evidence do you have?"

"Cabral hired four shooters. Three went to that plaza—"

"And I killed them." His vehemence at that reality alarmed him.

Thorvaldsen faced him. "Rightly so. I found the fourth. He told me what happened. He saw what you did. How you shot the two. He was to cover the third man, the one who shot you, but fled the plaza when you started firing. He was terrified of Cabral, so he disappeared."

"So why not have Cabral prosecuted?"

"Not necessary. He's dead."

Then he knew. "He's in one of those body bags?"

Thorvaldsen nodded. "He came to finish me himself."

He caught what was not said. "Tell me the rest."

"I didn't want to speak in front of Sam. He's so eager. Perhaps too eager. He believes himself right and wants vindication or, more correctly, validation. I hate that he was almost harmed."

Thorvaldsen's gaze returned to the dresser. Malone watched as emotions writhed within the older Dane.

"What did you discover?" Malone quietly asked.

"Something I never expected."

SAM CLIMBED ABOARD THE BOAT AS JESPER TIED the other craft to the stern. Cold Scandinavian winter air burned his face. They'd laid both bodies, outside the bags, in the other boat and were now towing the craft into the open sound. Jesper had already told him how strong currents would sweep the boat toward Sweden, where it would be found after the sun rose.

What an exhausting night.

So much was happening.

Three days ago Thorvaldsen had predicted that the situation would escalate, and it certainly had.

"You do a lot for Henrik," he said to Jesper over the outboard's roar.

"Herre Thorvaldsen has done a lot for me."

"Killing people is a little above and beyond, wouldn't you say?"

"Not if they deserve it."

The waters were choppy from a stiff northerly breeze. Luckily, Jesper had provided him with a thick wool coat, insulated gloves, and scarf.

"Is he going to kill Cabral and Ashby?" he asked.

"Senor Cabral is dead."

He didn't understand. "When did that happen?"

Jesper motioned to the boat they were towing. "He underestimated Herre Thorvaldsen."

He stared back at the dark hull containing two corpses. He hadn't liked being dismissed, and now wondered even more what Thorvaldsen and Malone were discussing. Jesper still had not answered his question about killing Ashby, and Sam realized he wasn't going to. This man was absolutely loyal, and replying would mean breaching that commitment to Thorvaldsen.

But his silence said it all.

"ASHBY IS ON A TREASURE HUNT," THORVALDSEN said. "A treasure that has eluded people for a long time."

"So what?"

"It matters. I'm not sure how, just yet. But it matters."

Malone waited.

"Young Sam is right about a conspiracy. I haven't told him, but my investigators confirmed numerous recent meetings of five people, who gather in Paris."

"His Paris Club?"

Thorvaldsen shrugged.

"People have a right to meet."

He noticed a light sweat on Thorvaldsen's forehead, even though the room was not warm.

"Not these people. I determined they've been experimenting. In Russia last year, they affected the national banking system. In Argentina, they artificially devalued stocks, bought low, then reversed everything and sold for huge profits. More of the same in Colombia and Indonesia. Small manipulations. It's as if they're testing the waters, seeing what can be done."

"How much harm could they do? Most nations have more than adequate protections on their financial systems."

"Not really, Cotton. That's a boast most governments cannot support. Especially if those attacking the system know what they're doing. And notice the countries they picked. Places with oppressive regimes, limited or no democracy, nations that flourish with centralized rule and few civil rights."

"You think that matters?"

"I do. These financiers are well schooled. I've checked them out. And they're well led."

He caught a note of mockery.

"Elena Rico was targeting Ashby and Cabral. I've learned a lot about Graham Ashby. He would have handled Rico's death more discreetly. But his ally was tasked with the kill, and did it his way. I imagine Ashby wasn't pleased with that slaughter in the plaza, but he had no room to complain about it, either. It did the job."

Malone did not like the hollow feeling in his stomach, which seemed to worsen by the minute. "You going to kill him? Like Cabral?"

Thorvaldsen simply stared at the photographs.

"Ashby is unaware of Cabral's attacks on me tonight. The last thing Cabral would have wanted is for Ashby to know he's been exposed. That's why he came himself."

Thorvaldsen spoke mechanically, as if all had been decided. But there was still something else. Malone could sense it. "What's really happening here, Henrik?"

"It's a complicated tale, Cotton. One that started the day Napoleon Bonaparte died."

SIXTEEN

Ashby was thrilled. Rommel's gold was now safely stored aboard **Archimedes.** A quick estimate, applying the current price, told him the stash was worth at least sixty to seventy million euros, maybe as much as a hundred million. The lying Corsican's prediction had proven correct. He'd off-load the bullion in Ireland, where it could be kept in one of his banks, safe from British inspectors. No need to convert hard metal into cash. Not yet, anyway. The worldwide price was still rising, the forecasts promising more increases, and besides, gold was always a good investment. He now possessed more than enough collateral to secure any immediate financing he may need.

All in all, an excellent evening.

He entered **Archimedes'** grand salon. The Corsican's rum still lay on the table between the sofas. He lifted the tumbler, stepped out onto the deck, and tossed the glass into the sea. The thought of drinking from the same tumbler as that lying cheat disgusted him. The Corsican had every intention of confiscating the gold **and** being paid a million euros. Even in the face of irrefutable exposure, the lying bureaucrat had continued the charade.

"Sir."

He turned. Guildhall stood just inside the salon.

"She's on the phone."

He'd been expecting the call, so he walked into an adjacent lounge, a warm room adorned with polished woods, soft fabrics, and split-straw marquetry papering the walls. He sat in a club chair and lifted the phone.

"**Bonsoir,** Graham," Eliza Larocque said.

"Are you still in the air?" he asked in French.

"We are. But the flight has been a good one. Signor Mastroianni has agreed to sign the pact. He will deposit his earnest money immediately, so expect a transfer."

"Your instincts proved correct."

"He'll make a fine addition. He and I have had a wonderful conversation."

If nothing else, Eliza Larocque was persuasive. She'd appeared at his English estate and spent three days tantalizing him with the possibilities. He'd investigated and learned that she was descended from a long line of wealth, her Corsican ancestors first rebels then aristocracy who wisely fled the French Revolution—then smartly returned when the time was right. Economics was her passion. She held degrees from three European universities. She headed her family concerns with hands-on management, dominant in wireless communication, petrochemicals, and real estate. **Forbes** had estimated her wealth at nearly twenty billion. He'd always thought that figure high, but noticed that Larocque never corrected its quotation. She lived both in Paris and to the south, on a family estate in the Loire Valley, and had never married, which he'd thought odd, too. Her voiced passions were classical art and contemporary music. Strange, those contradictions.

And her flaw?

Too quick to violence.

She saw it as the means to almost every end.

Personally, he wasn't opposed to its use—tonight had demonstrated the inherent need—but he tempered its application.

"How has your weekend been so far?" Larocque asked him.

"I've enjoyed a peaceful cruise on the Mediterranean. I love my boat. It's a pleasure I so rarely savor."

"Far too slow for me, Graham."

They each loved their toys. Larocque cherished planes—he'd heard about her new Gulfstream.

"You'll be at the meeting Monday?" she asked.

"We are cruising toward Marseille now. I'll fly out from there."

"And so I shall see you then."

He hung up the phone.

He and Larocque had become quite the team.

He'd joined her group four years ago, anteing up his twenty-million-euro initiation fee. Unfortunately, ever since, his financial portfolio had taken a massive beating, which had forced him to tap deep into his family reserves. His grandfather would have chastised him for taking such foolish risks. His father would have said, **So what, take more.** That dichotomy accounted, in many ways, for his present financial precariousness. Both men were long dead, yet he continued to try to please each.

When the Retrievers of Lost Antiquities had been exposed, it had taken all he could muster to keep Europol at bay. Luckily, proof had been scarce and his political connections strong. His private art cache had not been discovered, and he still maintained it. Unfortunately, that precious hoard could never figure into his bottom line.

Thankfully, he now controlled a stash of gold.

Problem solved.

At least for the foreseeable future.

He noticed the Corsican's book—**Napoleon, From the Tuileries to St. Helena**—lying on the chair beside him. One of the stewards had brought it from the salon, along with the briefcase once again full of euros.

He lifted the book.

How did an unremarkable child, born to modest Corsican parents, rise to such greatness? At its height the French Empire comprised 130 **départements,** deployed over 600,000 troops, ruled

70,000,000 subjects, and maintained a formidable military presence in Germany, Italy, Spain, Prussia, and Austria. From those conquests Napoleon amassed the largest treasure hoard in human history. He gathered loot at unprecedented levels, from every nation he conquered. Precious metals, paintings, sculptures, jewels, regalia, tapestries, coins—anything and everything of value seized for the glory of France.

Much of it had been returned after Waterloo.

But not all.

And what remained had metamorphosed into legend.

He opened the book to a section he'd read a few days ago. Gustave had willingly surrendered his copy, upon a down payment on the promised one million euros. The book's author, Louis Etienne Saint-Denis, had served as Napoleon's valet from 1806 to 1821. He voluntarily went into exile with Napoleon, first on Elba, then St. Helena. He maintained Napoleon's library and, since the emperor's penmanship was atrocious, prepared clean copies of all dictation. Nearly every written account from St. Helena had been penned in his hand. Ashby had been drawn to Saint-Denis' memoir. One chapter in particular had caught his attention. He again found the page.

His Majesty hated St. Helena, a British dot on the world map, west of Africa, hammered by wind and rain, ringed by steep cliffs. Napoleon's thoughts upon seeing his island prison in 1815 remained his thoughts throughout. "Disgraceful. Not an attractive place. I would have done better to remain in Egypt."

But in spite of the trials which Napoleon had to suffer, the memory of his power was always an agreeable dream. "I placed all of my glory," he said, "in making the French the first people of the universe. All of my desire, all of my ambition, was that they should surpass the Persians, the Greeks, and the Romans, as much in arms as in the sciences and arts. France was already the most beautiful, the most fertile country. In a word, it was already worthy to command the world as was ancient Rome. I should have accomplished my end if marplots, conspirators, men of money, immoral men, had not raised up obstacle after obstacle and stopped me in my march. It was no small accomplishment to have succeeded in governing the principal part of Europe and to have subjected it to a unity of laws. Nations directed by a just, wise, enlightened government would, in time, have drawn in other nations, and all would have made one family. When once everything had been settled I should have established a government in which the people would have nothing to dread from arbitrary authority. Every man would have been a man and simply subject to the common law. There would be nothing privileged, only merit. But there are those who would not have liked that to be. Debt barons who thrive upon the greed and idiocy of others. My goal was always to rid France of debt. Their desire was to drive France deeper into the abyss. Never were loans meant to be employed to meet current expenditures, whether they be civil or military. One has only to consider what loans can lead to in order to realize their danger. I strove against them. Finance would never have possessed the power to embarrass the government since, if that had been the case, the bankers and not the leaders of government would have controlled. The hand that gives is above the hand that takes. Money has no motherland. Financiers are without patriotism and without decency. Their sole object is gain."

He'd never realized Napoleon's passionate convictions regarding money lending. Previous and later French monarchs easily succumbed to the lure of debt, which had only hastened their downfall. Napoleon resisted. Which, ironically, may have hastened his end as well.

One other item in the book had drawn his eye.

He thumbed through the brittle yellow pages and found the critical reference in the introduction, written in 1922, by a professor at the Sorbonne.

Saint-Denis died in 1856. He left to the city of Sens some of the articles which he had preserved in memory of his Emperor: two volumes of Fleury de Chaboulon with notes in Napoleon's handwriting; two atlases in which Napoleon had made some notations in pencil; the folio volume of the campaigns of Italy; a copy of **The Merovingian Kingdoms 450–751 A.D.;** personal relics; a coat with epaulettes; a cockade from a hat; a piece of the St. Helena coffin; and a bit of one of the willows which grew over the Emperor's tomb. His final words were specific, "My daughters should always remember that the Emperor was my benefactor and, consequently, theirs. The greater part of what I possess I owe to his kindness."

Ashby had known of some of the items Saint-Denis left the city of Sens. The two volumes of Fleury de Chaboulon. The atlases. The folio volume of the campaigns of Italy. But a copy of **The Merovingian Kingdoms 450–751 A.D.?**
That was new.
Perhaps the answer he sought lay with it?

SEVENTEEN

DENMARK

THORVALDSEN HAD COME TO CAI'S ROOM FOR strength. The time for resolution had arrived. He'd plotted this path carefully, planned every detail, anticipated the possible moves. He believed himself ready. All that remained was to enlist Cotton Malone's help. He'd almost called his friend Cassiopeia Vitt, but decided against it. She'd try to stop him, tell him there was another way, while Malone would understand, particularly given what had happened over the past couple of weeks.

"Napoleon died peacefully on May 5, 1821, just after six o'clock in the evening," he explained to Malone. "One observer noted, **he went out as the light of a lamp goes out.** He was buried on St. Helena, but exhumed in 1840 and returned to Paris, where he now lays in the Hôtel des Invalides. Some say he was murdered, slowly poisoned. Others say natural causes. Nobody knows. Nor does it matter."

He caught sight of a knotted tail stretched across one of the shelves. He and Cai had flown the kite one summer afternoon, long ago. A flash of joy passed through him—a rare feeling, both won-drous and uncomfortable.

He forced his mind to concentrate and said, "Napoleon stole so much that it's beyond compre-hension. On his way to Egypt, he conquered Malta and acquired coin, art, silver plate, jewels, and five million francs' worth of gold from the Knights of Malta. History says it was lost at sea, during the Battle of Abukir Bay. Isn't it interesting how we title battles, as if they were some great dramatic epic? When the British destroyed the French fleet in August 1798, seventeen hundred sailors died. Yet we give it a title, like some novel."

He paused.

"The Malta treasure was supposedly on one of the ships that went down, but no one knows if that is actually the case. There are many more sto-ries like that. Homes, castles, entire national trea-suries looted. Even the Vatican. Napoleon remains the only person to have successfully plundered the church's wealth. Some of that booty made it back to France in an official capacity, some didn't. There was never any adequate inventory. To this day, the Vatican maintains there are items unac-counted for."

As he spoke, he fought with the ghosts this sa-cred room hosted, their presence like a chain of missed opportunities. He'd so much wanted for Cai to inherit his Thorvaldsen birthright, but his son had wanted first to commit himself to public service. He'd indulged the desire since he, too, when young, had satisfied his curiosity with a trip around the world. The planet had seemed so different then. People didn't get shot while simply enjoying their lunch.

"When Napoleon died, he left a detailed will. It's long, with numerous monetary bequests. Something like three million francs. Most were never honored, as there were no funds from which to pay them. Napoleon was a man in exile. He'd been dethroned. He had little, besides what he'd brought to St. Helena. But to read his will, you would think him wealthy. Remember, it was never intended that he would leave St. Helena alive."

"I never understood why the Brits didn't just kill him," Malone said. "He was an obvious danger. Hell, he escaped from his first exile, in Elba, and wreaked havoc in Europe."

"That's true, and when he finally surrendered himself to the British, that surprised a lot of people. He wanted to go to America, and they almost let him, then decided better. You're right—he was a real danger. And nobody wanted any more wars. But killing him would have posed other problems. Martyrdom, for one. Napoleon was revered, even in defeat, by many French and British. Of course, there is also another explanation."

He caught sight of his face in the mirror above the dresser, his eyes, for once, alight with energy.

"It was said he harbored a secret, one the British wanted to learn. Untold wealth, all that unaccounted-for loot, and the English wanted it. The Napoleonic Wars had been costly. That's why they kept him alive."

"To bargain with him?"

He shrugged. "More likely waiting for Napoleon to make a mistake and they'd learn the treasure's location."

"I've read about his time on St. Helena," Malone said. "It was a constant struggle of wills between him and Hudson Lowe, the British commander. Down to even how he should be addressed. Lowe referred to him as **Général.** Everyone else called him **Your Majesty.** Even after he died, Lowe wouldn't allow the French to place **Napoleon** on the tombstone. He wanted the politically neutral **Napoleon Bonaparte.** So they buried him in an unmarked grave."

"Napoleon was clearly a polarizing figure," Thorvaldsen said. "But his will is most instructive, written three weeks before he died. There's a provision, to his valet, Saint-Denis, where he left a hundred thousand francs and then directed him to take his copy of **The Merovingian Kingdoms 450–751 A.D.** and another four hundred of his favorite volumes from his personal library, and to care for the books until Napoleon's son reached sixteen. He was then to deliver the books to the son. Napoleon's son lived to age twenty-one, but died a virtual prisoner in Austria. He never saw those books."

Anger crept into his voice. For all his faults, every account ever written acknowledged how much Napoleon loved his son. He'd divorced his beloved Josephine and married Marie Louise of Austria simply because he needed a legitimate male heir, one that Josephine could not supply. The boy was but four when Napoleon had been exiled to St. Helena.

"It is said that within those books was the key to finding Napoleon's cache—what the emperor skimmed for himself. He supposedly secreted that wealth away, in a place only he knew. The amount was enormous."

He paused again.

"Napoleon possessed a plan, Cotton. Something he was counting on. You're right, he played a game of wills with Lowe on St. Helena, but nothing was ever resolved. Saint-Denis was his most loyal servant, and I'm betting Napoleon trusted him with the most important bequest of all."

"What does this have to do with Graham Ashby?"

"He's after that lost cache."

"How do you know that?"

"Suffice it to say that I do. In fact, Ashby desperately needs it. Or, more accurately, this Paris

Club needs it. Its founder is a woman named Eliza Larocque, and she holds information that may lead to its discovery."

He glanced away from the dresser, toward the bed where Cai had slept all his life.

"Is all this necessary?" Malone asked. "Can't you let it go?"

"Was finding your father necessary?"

"I didn't do it to kill anyone."

"But you had to find him."

"It's been a long time, Henrik. Things have to end." The words carried a somber tone.

"Since the day I buried Cai, I swore that I would discover the truth about what happened that day."

"I'm going to Mexico," Cai said to him. "I'm to be chief deputy of our consulate there."

He saw the excitement in the young man's eyes, but had to ask, "And when does all this end? I need you to take over the family concerns."

"As if you'd actually let me decide anything."

He admired his son, whose wide shoulders stretched straight as a soldier's, his body lithe as an athlete's. The eyes were identical to his from long ago, brittle blue, boyish at first glance, disconcertingly mature on further acquaintance. In so many ways he was like

Lisette. Many times he felt as if he were actually talking to her again.

"I would allow you to make decisions," he made clear. "I'm ready to retire."

Cai shook his head. "Papa, you will never retire."

He'd taught his son what his father had taught him. People can be read by gauging what they wanted in life. And his son knew him well.

"How about only another year with public service," he said. "Then home. Is that acceptable?"

A feeling of remorse filled him.

Another year.

He faced Malone.

"Cotton, Amando Cabral killed my only child. He's now dead. Graham Ashby likewise will be held accountable."

"So kill him and be done with it."

"Not good enough. First I want to take from him all that is precious. I want him humiliated and disgraced. I want him to feel the pain I feel every day." He paused. "But I need your help."

"You've got it."

He reached out and clasped his friend's shoulder.

"What about Sam and his Paris Club?" Malone asked.

"We're going to deal with that, too. It can't be ig-nored. We have to see what's there. Sam derived much of his information from a friend in Paris. I'd like for you two to pay that man a visit. Learn what you can."

"And when we do, are you going to kill all of them, too?"

"No. I'm going to join them."

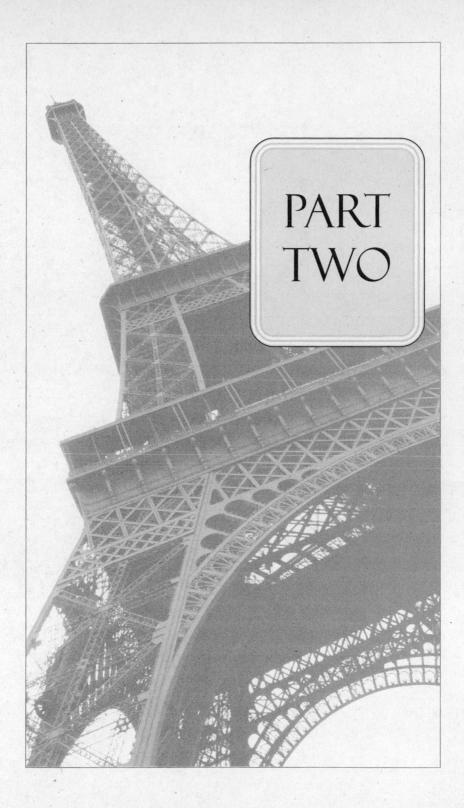

PART
TWO

EIGHTEEN

MALONE LOVED PARIS. HE REGARDED IT AS A delightful conjunction of old and new, every corner volatile and alive. He'd visited the city many times when he worked with the Magellan Billet, and knew his way around its medieval hovels. He wasn't happy, though, with this assignment.

"How did you get to know this guy?" he asked Sam.

They'd flown from Copenhagen on a midmorning flight directly to Charles de Gaulle Airport and taken a taxi downtown into the boisterous Latin Quarter, named long ago for the only language then permitted within the university precinct. Like almost everything else, Napoleon abolished the use of Latin, but the name stuck. Officially known as the fifth **arrondissement,** the quarter remained a haven for artists and intellectuals. Students from the nearby Sorbonne dominated its cobblestones, though tourists were drawn to both the ambience and the staggering array of shops, cafés, galleries, bookstalls, and nightclubs.

"We met online," Sam said.

He listened as Sam told him about Jimmy Foddrell, an American expatriate who'd come to Paris to study economics and decided to stay. Foddrell had started a website three years ago—GreedWatch.net—that became popular among the New Age/world conspiratorialist crowd. The Paris Club was one of its more recent obsessions.

You never know, Thorvaldsen had said earlier. **Foddrell is getting his information somewhere, and there might be something we can use.**

Since Malone couldn't argue with that logic, he'd agreed to come.

"Foddrell has a master's in global economics from the Sorbonne," Sam told him.

"And what has he done with it?"

They stood before a squatty-looking church labeled ST.-JULIEN-LE-PAUVRE, supposedly the oldest in Paris. Down Rue Galande, off to their right, Malone recognized the line of old houses and steeples as one of the most painted scenes of the Left Bank. To their left, just across a busy boulevard and the tranquil Seine, stood Notre Dame, busy with Christmastime visitors.

"Nothing I know of," Sam said. "He seems to work on his website—big into worldwide economic conspiracies."

"Which makes it tough to get a real job."

They left the church and walked toward the Seine, following a well-kept lane checkered by winter sunlight. A chilly breeze stirred leaves along the dry pavement. Sam had emailed Foddrell and requested a meeting, which led to another email exchange, which finally instructed them to go to 37 Rue de la Bûcherie, which Malone now saw was, of all things, a bookshop.

Shakespeare & Company.

He knew the place. Every Parisian guidebook noted this secondhand shop as a cultural landmark. More than fifty years old, started by an American who modeled it after and named it for Sylvia Beach's famous Parisian store from the early 20th century. Beach's kindness and free lending policies made her den mother to many a noted writer—Hemingway, Pound, Fitzgerald, Stein, and Joyce included. This reincarnation was little of that, yet it had managed to carve for itself a popular bohemian niche.

"Your friend a book guy?" Malone asked.

"He mentioned this place once. He actually lived here for a while, when he first came to Paris. The owner allows it. There are cots among the shelves inside. In return, you have to work around the store and read a book each day. Sounded a little goofy to me."

He grinned.

He'd read about those boarders, who called themselves tumbleweeds, some staying for months at a time. And he'd visited the shop in years past, but he actually preferred another secondhand vendor, The Abbey Bookstore, a couple of blocks over, which had provided him with some excellent first editions.

He stared at the eclectic wooden façade, alive with color, which seemed unsteady on its stone foundations. Empty wooden benches lined the storefront beneath rickety casement windows. Christmas being only forty-eight hours away explained why the sidewalk was busy, and why a steady flow of people paraded in and out of the shop's main doors.

"He told us to go upstairs," Sam said, "to the mirror of love. Whatever that is."

They entered.

Inside reeked of age, with twisted oak beams overhead and cracked tiles underfoot. Books were stacked haphazardly on sagging shelves that stretched across every wall. More books were piled on the floor. Light came from bare bulbs screwed into tacky brass chandeliers. People bundled in coats, gloves, and scarves browsed the shelves.

He and Sam climbed a red staircase to the next floor. At the top, amid children's books, he caught sight of a long wall mirror plastered with handwritten notes and photos. Most were thank-yous from people who'd resided in the shop over the years. Each loving and sincere, reflecting an admiration for their apparent once-in-a-lifetime experience.

One card, a bright pink, taped near the center, caught his eye.

Sam, remember our talk last year.
Who I said was right.
Check out his book in the Business section.

"You've got to be kidding," Malone muttered. "Is this guy on medication?"

"I know. He's paranoid as hell. Always has been. He dealt with me only after he confirmed that I worked with the Secret Service. Always with a password, though, which changed all the time."

Malone was seriously wondering if this was worth the trouble. But he wanted to confirm a hunch, so he stepped across the upper floor, ducked through a low doorway that bore the curious admonition BE NOT INHOSPITABLE TO STRANGERS LEST THEY BE ANGELS IN DISGUISE, to a casement window.

When they'd left the churchyard and strolled toward the shop, he'd first noticed the man. Tall, rail-thin, dressed in baggy khaki pants, a waist-length navy coat, and black shoes. He'd stayed a hundred feet behind them and, as they'd loitered out front, their tail had stopped, too, near one of the cafés.

Now Skinny was entering the shop below.

Malone needed to be sure, so he turned from the window and asked, "Does Foddrell know what you look like?"

Sam nodded. "I sent him a picture."

"I assume he did not reciprocate?"

"I never asked."

He thought again of the mirror of love. "So tell me, who is it Foddrell said was right?"

NINETEEN

ASHBY STROLLED INTO WESTMINSTER ABBEY AMID a crowd that had just emerged from several tour buses.

His spine always tingled when he entered this shrine.

Here was a place that could recount English history back more than a millennium. A former Benedictine monastery, now the seat of government and heart of the Anglican Church. Every English monarch, save two, since the time of William the Conqueror had been crowned here. Only its French influences bothered him, though understandable given that the design had been inspired by the great French cathedrals at Reims, Amiens, and Sainte-Chapelle. But he'd always agreed with how one British observer described Westminister.

A great French thought expressed in excellent English.

He stopped at the gate and paid his admission, then followed a throng into Poets' Corner, where visitors congregated near wall monuments and statuary depicting images of Shakespeare, Wordsworth, Milton, and Longfellow. Many more of the greats lay around him, among them Tennyson, Dickens, Kipling, Hardy, Browning. His gaze surveyed the chaotic scene and finally settled on a man standing before Chaucer's tomb, sporting a glen-plaid suit with a cashmere tie. A pair of caramel-colored gloves sheathed empty hands and a handsome style of Gucci loafers protected his broad feet.

Ashby approached and, as he admired the tomb's five-hundred-year-old stonework, asked, "Do you know the painter Godfrey Kneller?"

The man scrutinized him with a pair of rheumy eyes whose amber color was both distinctive and disturbing. "I believe I do. A great court artist of the 18th century. He's buried at Twickenham, I believe."

The reference to Twickenham signaled the correct response, the strained Irish accent an interesting touch. So he said, "I'm told Kneller harbored a great aversion toward this place, though there is a memorial dedicated to him near the east cloister door."

The man nodded. "His exact words, I believe, were, **By God I will not be buried in Westminster. They do bury fools there.**"

The quotation confirmed that this was the man

he'd talked with on the telephone. The voice then was different, more throaty, less nasal, no accent.

"Top of the morning to you, Lord Ashby," the man said, adding a smile.

"And what should I call you?"

"How about Godfrey? In honor of the great painter. He was quite correct in his assessment of the souls laid to rest within these walls. There are a great many fools buried here."

He took in the man's coarse features, scrutinizing a cob nose, satchel mouth, and scrubby salt-and-pepper beard. But it was the reptilian amber eyes, framed by bushy eyebrows, that arrested his attention.

"I assure you, Lord Ashby, this is not my real appearance. So don't waste your time memorizing it."

He wondered why someone who went to so much trouble to be in disguise allowed his most noticeable feature—the eyes—to remain so startling. But all he said was, "I like to know about the men I do business with."

"And I prefer to know nothing as to my clients. But you, Lord Ashby, are an exception. You, I have learned a great deal about."

He wasn't particularly interested in this demon's mind games.

"You're the sole shareholder of a great British banking institution, a wealthy man who enjoys life. Even the queen herself counts you as an adviser."

"And surely, you possess an equally exciting existence."

The man smiled, revealing a gap between his front teeth. "I have no interests, other than pleasing you, my lord."

He did not appreciate the sarcasm, but let it pass. "Are you prepared to carry through on what we discussed?"

The man ambled toward a row of monuments, gazing at the memorials like the other visitors surrounding them. "That depends if you're prepared to deliver, as I requested."

He reached into his pocket and removed a set of keys. "These open the hangar. The plane is there, waiting with a full tank of petrol. Its registration is Belgian, its owner fictitious."

Godfrey accepted the keys. "And?"

The gaze from the amber eyes brought a new wave of uncomfortableness. He handed over a slip of paper. "The number and pass code for the Swiss account, as you requested. Half payment is there. The other half will come after."

"The timetable you wanted is two days from now. Christmas Day. Is that still correct?"

Ashby nodded.

Godfrey pocketed the keys and the paper. "Things certainly will change then."

"That's the whole idea."

The man gave a slight chuckle and they strolled farther into the cathedral, stopping before a plaque that indicated a date of death in 1669. Godfrey motioned to the wall and said, "Sir Robert Stapylton. Do you know him?"

He nodded. "A dramatic poet, knighted by Charles II."

"As I recall, he was a French Benedictine monk who turned Protestant and became a servant of the Crown. Gentleman Usher of the Privy Chamber to Charles, I believe."

"You know your English history."

"He was an opportunist. A man of ambition. Someone who did not let principle interfere with objective. A lot like you, Lord Ashby."

"And you."

Another chuckle. "Hardly. As I've made clear, I am but hired help."

"Expensive help."

"Good help always is. Two days' time. I'll be there. You be sure to not forget your final obligation."

He watched as the man called Godfrey disappeared into the south ambulatory. He'd dealt with many people in his life, but the amoral despot who'd just left genuinely made him uneasy. How long he'd been in Britain was unknown. The first call came a week ago, and the details of their relationship had subsequently been finalized through more unexpected calls. Ashby had easily arranged his end of the bargain, and he'd been patiently waiting for confirmation that Godfrey had done the same.

Now he knew.

Two days.

TWENTY

THORVALDSEN HAD BEEN DRIVEN SOUTH, FROM
Paris, to a quiet French hollow sheltered by vine-
clad hills. The château sat moored like a ship in the
middle of the meandering Cher, about fifteen kilometers from where the muddy river entered the
more majestic Loire. Bridging the waterway, its
charming frontage of brick, stone, turrets, spires,
and a conical slate roof bordered on the fantastical.
Not gray, or severely constructed for defense, or decaying from neglect, instead it cast a whimsical air
of medieval majesty.

He sat in the château's main salon beneath
chestnut rafters, magnificent in their centuries-old
workmanship. Two wrought-iron electric cande-
labra provided harsh light. The paneled walls were
dotted with superb canvases by Le Sueur, a work by
Van Dyck, and some first-rate oil portraits of what

he assumed were cherished ancestors. The château's owner sat across from him in an exquisite Henri II leather armchair. She possessed a charming voice, quiet manners, and memorable features. From everything he knew about Eliza Larocque, she was clear-sighted and decisive, but also stubborn and obsessive.

He could only hope that the latter trait proved correct.

"I'm somewhat surprised by your visit," she said to him.

Though her smile seemed sincere, it flashed too automatically.

"I've known of your family for many years," he told her.

"And I know your porcelain. We have quite a collection in the dining room. Two circles, with a line beneath—that symbol represents the ultimate in quality."

He bowed his head, acknowledging her compliment. "My family has worked for centuries to establish that reputation."

Her dark eyes displayed a peculiar mixture of curiosity and caution. She was clearly uneasy, and trying hard to conceal it. His detectives had informed him of her jet's arrival. They'd then tracked her from Orly Airport until sure of her destination. So while Malone and Sam trawled for information in Paris, he'd headed south to do some fishing of his own.

"I have to say, Herre Thorvaldsen," she said,

keeping to English, "I agreed to see you out of curiosity. I flew from New York last night, so I'm a bit fatigued and not up to visitors."

He watched her face, a pleasant composition of graceful curves, noticing the corners of her mouth as they angled into another smile of an accomplished manipulator.

"Is this your family's country estate?" he asked, trying to keep her off guard, and he caught a momentary flush of annoyance.

She nodded. "Built in the 16th century. Modeled after Chenonceau, which stands not far from here. Another idyllic wonder."

He admired a dark oak mantelpiece across the room. Unlike other French homes he'd visited, which were bare and suggestive of tombs, this house was clearly no sepulcher.

"You realize, Madame Larocque, that my financial resources are substantially greater than yours. Perhaps by as much as ten billion euros."

He studied her high cheekbones, serious eyes, and firm mouth. He thought the stark contrast between her creamy patina and her ebony hair intentional. Given her age, he doubted if the hair color was natural. She was, without question, an attractive woman. Confident and smart, too. Accustomed to having her way—unaccustomed to bluntness.

"And how would the fact of your obvious wealth interest me?"

He allowed a measured pause to break the natural flow between them, then said, "You've insulted me."

Puzzlement crept into her eyes. "How is that possible? We just met."

"I control one of the largest and most successful corporations in Europe. My ancillary businesses, which include oil and gas, telecommunications, and manufacturing, stretch globally. I employ more than eighty thousand people. My annual revenues far exceed those of all your entities combined. Yet you insult me."

"Herre Thorvaldsen, you must explain yourself."

She was off guard. But that was the beauty of blind attacks. The advantage always lay with the attacker. True in Mexico City two years ago—equally true here today.

"I want to be a part of what you're planning," he declared.

"And what is that?"

"Though I wasn't on your jet last evening, I can only surmise Robert Mastroianni—a friend of mine, by the way—has been extended an invitation. Yet I am to be shunned."

She kept her face as stone cold as a grave marker. "An invitation to what?"

"The Paris Club."

He decided to not allow her the luxury of a response. "You have a fascinating ancestry. Directly descended from Carlo Andrea Pozzo di Borgo, who was born near Ajaccio, Corsica, on March 8, 1764. He became the implacable foe of Napoleon Bonaparte. With marvelous skill, he manipulated international politics to the eventual undoing of his lifelong enemy. A classic Corsican **vendetta.** His weapons not guns or bombs, but the intrigues of diplomacy. Its coup de grâce, the destiny of nations."

He paused while her mind chewed on his facts.

"Don't be alarmed," he said. "I'm not an enemy. Quite the contrary. I admire what you are doing, and want to be a part."

"Assuming for a moment that what you say is even partly true, why would I entertain such a request?"

Her voice was warm and lazy, signaling not the slightest hint of alarm. So he allowed his face to take on an equal look of shrewdness. "The answer to that is quite simple."

She was listening.

"You have a security leak."

TWENTY-ONE

MALONE FOLLOWED SAM BACK DOWNSTAIRS, where they located a row of cluttered shelves marked BUSINESS.

"Foddrell and I email each other a lot," Sam said. "He's big against the Federal Reserve system. Calls it a giant conspiracy that will be the downfall of America. Some of what he says makes sense, but most of his views are really out there."

He smiled. "Good to see you have limits."

"Contrary to what you think, I'm not a fanatic. I just think that there are people out there who can manipulate our financial systems. Not to take over the planet or destroy the world. Just for greed. An easy way to get, or stay, rich. What they do can affect national economies in a lot of ways, none of which are good."

He didn't disagree, but there was still the matter of proof. Before they'd left Christiangade he'd perused both Sam's and Jimmy Foddrell's web-sites. Not all that dissimilar, except, as Sam noted, Foddrell's predicted global gloom and doom in a more radical tone.

He grabbed Sam by the shoulder. "What exactly are we looking for?"

"That note upstairs is talking about a book, written by a certified financial planner, who's also into the same kind of things Foddrell and I talk about. A few months ago, I found a copy and read it."

He released his grip and watched as Sam scanned the crowded shelves.

Malone's trained eye also assessed the books. He saw that they were a hodgepodge of titles, most of which he would have never bought from people who lugged them into his shop by the crateful. He assumed that since they were for sale in Paris, on the Left Bank, a few hundred yards from the Seine and Notre Dame, their value elevated.

"Here it is."

Sam removed an oversized gold-colored paper-back, titled **The Creature from Jekyll Island: A Second Look at the Federal Reserve.**

"Foddrell had to leave this here," Sam said. "There's no way there just happened to be a copy. It's pretty obscure."

People continued to browse. More wandered in from the cold. Malone casually searched for Skinny, but didn't see him. He was reasonably sure what was happening, but decided patience was the call of this day.

He relieved Sam of the book and thumbed through the pages until he spotted a slip of paper pressed inside.

Back to the mirror.

He shook his head.

They returned to the upper floor and saw written on the same pink note that had led them downstairs:

**Café d'Argent, 34 Rue Dante
Thirty minutes**

Malone stepped back across the upper floor to the casement window. The plane trees below stood lifeless, limbs bare as brooms, their spindly shadows already lengthening in the midafternoon sun. Three years ago he and Gary had visited the International Spy Museum in Washington, DC. Gary had wanted to learn about what his father did for a living, and the museum turned out to be fascinating. They'd enjoyed the exhibits and he'd bought Gary a book, **Handbook of Practical Spying,** a lighthearted look at spy craft. One of the chapters, titled "Keeping Caution from the Wind," explained how contacts could be safely approached.

So he waited, knowing what was coming.

Sam stepped close.

He heard the door below open, then close, and he spotted Skinny leaving the shop holding what appeared, in color and shape, to be the Jekyll Island book from downstairs.

"It's an old ploy that nobody ever uses," he said. "A way to check out who wants to meet you. Your friend has been watching too many spy movies."

"He was here?"

He nodded. "He seemed interested in us when we were out front, then came inside and, I assume, hid behind the shelves downstairs while we found the book. Since you sent him your picture, he knew who to look for. Once satisfied that I looked okay, he came back up here before we did, and went back down a minute ago."

"You think that's Foddrell?" Sam asked, pointing.

"Who else could it be?"

ELIZA CAME ALERT. NOT ONLY DID HENRIK THORvaldsen know her business, he apparently knew something she didn't. "A security leak?"

"One of the individuals, part of your Paris Club, is not what he appears to be."

"I haven't said that any club exists."

"Then you and I have nothing more to talk about."

Thorvaldsen rose.

"I've enjoyed my visit to your estate. If you ever come to Denmark, I would be pleased to host you at my home, Christiangade. I'll leave you now so you may rest from your trip."

She gave a cautious laugh. "Are you always so grandiose?"

He shrugged. "Today, two days before Christmas, I took the time to travel here and speak with you. If you insist that there is nothing for us to discuss, then I shall leave. The presence of your security problem will eventually become obvious. Hopefully, the damage will be minimal."

She'd acted so carefully, choosing her members with deliberate care, limiting the total to seven, herself included. Each recruit had signaled acceptance by anteing a twenty-million-euro initiation. Each had also taken an oath of secrecy. Early efforts in South America and Africa had generated unprecedented profits, and secured everyone's continued allegiance, since nothing fortified a conspiracy better than success. Yet this Dane of immense wealth and influence, an outsider, seemed to know everything.

"Tell me, Herre Thorvaldsen, are you seriously interested in joining?"

His eyes twinkled for a moment. She'd struck a chord.

He was a squat man, made even shorter by a crooked spine and bent knees. He wore a baggy sweater, oversized corduroy trousers, and dark sneakers, perhaps as a way to mask the deformity. His thick silver hair hung long, unkempt. His tufted eyebrows flared bushy, like wire brushes. Wrinkles in his face had evolved into deep clefts.

He could have easily been mistaken for a homeless person, but maybe that was the whole idea.

"Can we stop the pretense?" he asked. "I came for a specific reason. One, I hoped, was to our mutual benefit."

"Then, by all means, let us talk."

His impatience seemed to recede as he sensed her concession.

He sat. "I learned of your Paris Club through careful investigation."

"And what piqued your interest?"

"I became aware of some skillful manipulation occurring in certain foreign currency exchanges. Clearly, not natural occurrences. Of course, there are sites on the Internet that profess to know a lot more about you, and your activities, than I do."

"I've read some of those. You surely know that such postings are nonsense."

"I would agree." He paused. "But one in particular caught my eye. I believe it's called Greed-Watch. That site has surely been striking a bit too close to home. I like the quotation at the top of its home page, from Sherlock Holmes. **There is nothing more deceptive than an obvious fact.**"

She knew the site and its webmaster, and Thorvaldsen was correct. It had struck close. Which was why, three weeks ago, she'd ordered remedial measures. She wondered, did this man know about those, too? Why else mention that specific website?

Thorvaldsen reached into his trouser pocket,

withdrew a folded sheet of paper, and handed it to her. "I printed that off GreedWatch yesterday."

She unfolded and read.

Has an Antichrist Come?

If you analyze the current systematic conquering of the independent countries of the world you can easily find that, behind all of these aggressions, a pattern of unique power emerges that includes economy, military, media, and politicians. I will try to present that this power belongs to the world's financiers. I think an Antichrist is at the head of these tyrants. Her name is Eliza Larocque. She wants to rule the world, totally invisibly, by the secretly possessed economic power her family has built through centuries.

There is no safer and more profitable business than lending money to countries. Like financiers joining together, refusing to compete with one another, and manipulating markets and currency to their collective advantage pose a grave threat. Larocque and her associates possess a hierarchically organized structure that buys or acquires shares in everything valuable in the global market. They may, for instance, possess Coca-Cola and PepsiCo and, from the top of their Olympus, watch these companies fight each other on the market. But thanks to the capitalist system and its secret business regulation policy, nobody except them is able to know. By controlling the governments in the Western countries, they control the whole Western world. If you follow global political policy you can easily see that democratically elected leaders of countries change, but policy follows the interests of the rich and therefore stays more or less the same. Numerous elements point out the fact that there is an invisible organization that rules the world. The facts I have collected about Eliza Larocque tells me that she leads that organization. I am talking here about a conspiracy that captures almost the whole world.

She smiled. "Antichrist?"

"Granted, the wording is unorthodox, the conclusions bold, but it is on the right track."

"I assure you, Herre Thorvaldsen, the last thing I want is to rule the world. Far too much trouble."

"I agree. You simply want to manipulate it to the mutual advantage of you and your colleagues. If that manipulation has some . . . political fallout . . . so what? It's profit that matters." Thorvaldsen paused. "That's why I'm here. I'd like to share in those profits."

"You couldn't possibly need money."

"Nor could you. But that's not the point, is it?"

She asked, "And what would you have to offer, in return for that sharing?"

"One of your members is in financial trouble. His portfolio has been stretched to the breaking point. He's heavily in debt. His lifestyle demands massive amounts of capital, money he simply does not have. A series of bad investments, overextensions, and carelessness have brought him to the verge of collapse."

"Why does this man interest you?"

"He doesn't. But in order to command your attention, I knew that I would have to provide something that you don't already know. This seemed ideal for that purpose."

"And why should I care about this man's troubles?"

"Because he's your security leak."

Her spine shivered. Everything she'd envisioned could be in jeopardy if one of the chosen had sold out the others.

She needed to know, "Who is this man?"

"Lord Graham Ashby."

TWENTY-TWO

ENGLAND

A LATE LUNCH WAS WAITING FOR ASHBY WHEN HE
returned to Salen Hall. His paternal family's ancestral seat was a classical battlemented manor,
perched amid twenty-four forested hectares to
which Ashbys had held the title since 1660.

He entered the main dining room and took his
customary seat at the north end of the table where a
portrait of his great-grandfather, the sixth duke of
Ashby, a close confidant of Queen Victoria I,
watched his back. Outside, frigid December air
swirled with white flakes—a prelude, he believed, to
a coming snow and Christmas, just two days away.

"I heard you'd returned," a female voice said.

He glanced up from the table at Caroline. She
was wearing a full-length silk charmeuse gown,
bare legs slipping in and out of a high-cut slit. A ki-
mono-style robe covered her thin shoulders, open
in front, the gown's golden coloring matching her
long, curly hair.

"I see you've dressed as a good mistress should."

She smiled. "Isn't that my job? To please the master?"

He liked their give-and-take. His wife's prudish ways had long ago become tiresome. She lived in London, her apartment filled with pyramids under which she lay for hours each day, hoping their magical power would cleanse her soul. He hoped the apartment would burn, with her inside it, but no such luck had come his way. He'd been lucky, though, in that they were childless, estranged for years, which explained his many mistresses, Caroline the latest and longest lasting.

Three things, though, distinguished Caroline from all of the others.

First, she was extraordinarily beautiful—a collection of the best physical attributes he'd ever seen gathered around one spine. Second, she was brilliant. Her degrees, one from the University of Edinburgh, the other from University College of London, were in medieval literature and applied ancient history. Her master's thesis had been devoted to the Napoleonic Age and its effects on modern political thought, especially as it impacted European unification. Finally, he genuinely liked this woman. Her sensuous ways stimulated him in ways he'd never thought possible.

"I missed you last night," she said as she sat at the table.

"I was on the boat."

"Business or pleasure?"

She knew her place, he'd give her that. No jealousies. No demands. Strangely, though, he'd never cheated on her. And he often wondered if she was equally as loyal. But he realized the path of privacy flowed two ways. They were each free to do as they pleased.

"Business," he said, then added, "as always."

A footman appeared and laid a plate on the table before him. He was delighted to see a celery heart wrapped in ham, smothered in the tart cheese sauce he loved.

He lapped his napkin and lifted a fork.

"No, thank you," Caroline said to him. "I'm not hungry. None for me."

He caught the sarcasm but kept eating. "You're a big girl. I assume you'd have something brought if you wanted it."

She had the run of the estate, the staff at her complete disposal. His wife never visited the house anymore. Thank goodness. Unlike her, Caroline treated the employees with kindness. She actually did a good job looking after things, which he appreciated.

"I ate a couple of hours ago," she said.

He finished his celery and was pleased by the entrée the footman presented. Roasted partridge with sweet dressing. He acknowledged his pleasure with a nod and signaled for another pat of butter for his roll.

"Did you find the damn gold?" she finally asked.

He'd intentionally kept silent about his success in Corsica, waiting for her to inquire. More of their give-and-take.

Which he knew she liked, too.

He gripped another fork. "Right where you said it would be."

She'd been the one who'd discovered the connection between Gustave's and the Corsican's books and the Roman numerals. She'd also discovered, from some research conducted in Barcelona a few weeks ago, the Moor's Knot. He was glad to have her on his side, and knew what was now expected of him.

"I'll have a few bars set aside for you."

She nodded her appreciation. "And I'll see to it that you have a lovely evening tonight."

"I could use some relaxation."

The charmeuse in her gown shimmered as she edged closer to the table. "That solves your money problems."

"For the foreseeable future. I estimated as much as a hundred million euros in gold."

"And my few bars?"

"A million. Maybe more, depending on how lovely my evening is tonight."

She laughed. "How about dress-up? The schoolgirl sent to the headmaster's office? That's always fun."

He was feeling good. After a disastrous couple of years, things were finally starting to go right. The bad times had begun when Amando Cabral had grown careless in Mexico and nearly brought them both down. Thankfully, Cabral solved that problem. Then a combination of poor investments, failing markets, and inattention cost him millions. With near-perfect timing, Eliza Larocque had appeared at his estate and offered salvation. It had taken all he could do to amass the twenty million euros needed to buy his admittance, but he'd managed.

Now he'd finally generated room to breathe.

He finished his entrée.

"I have a surprise for you," Caroline said.

This woman was a rare combination. Part tramp, part academician, and quite good at both.

"I'm waiting," he said.

"I think I may have discovered a new link."

He caught her amused expression and asked, "Think?"

"Actually, I know I have."

TWENTY-THREE

PARIS

SAM FOLLOWED MALONE AS THEY FLED THE BOOK-
store into the brisk afternoon. Foddrell had turned
away from the Seine and plunged deeper into the
Latin Quarter's chaotic streets, each one crowded
with excited holiday revelers.

"There's no way to know if anyone's on your tail
in this crowd," Malone said. "But he knows our
faces, so let's stay back."

"He doesn't seem to care if anyone's following.
He hasn't looked back once."

"He thinks he's smarter than everyone else."

"He's going to the Café d'Argent?"

"Where else?"

They kept a normal pace, submerged within the
sweeping tide of commerce. Cheese, vegetables,
fruit, chocolate, and other delicacies, displayed in
wooden bins, spilled into the street. Sam noticed
fish lying on gleaming beds of ice, and meat, boned

and rolled, chilling in refrigerated cases. Farther on, an ice-cream shop offered Italian gelato in a variety of tempting flavors.

Foddrell stayed a hundred feet ahead.

"What do you really know about this guy?" Malone asked.

"Not a whole lot. He latched on to me maybe a year ago."

"Which, by the way, is another reason the Secret Service doesn't want you doing what you're doing. Too many crazies, too many risks."

"Then why are we here?" he asked.

"Henrik wanted us to make contact. You tell me, why is that?"

"Are you always so suspicious?"

"It's a healthy affliction. One that'll prolong your life."

They passed more cafés, art galleries, boutiques, and souvenir shops. Sam was pumped. Finally, he was in the field, doing what agents did.

"Let's split up," Malone said. "Less chance of him recognizing us. That is if he bothers to look back."

Sam drifted to one side of the street. He'd been an accounting major at college and almost a CPA. But a government recruiter, who'd visited the campus during his senior year, steered him toward the Secret Service. After graduation, he'd applied and passed the Treasury test, a polygraph exam, complete physical, eye test, and drug screen.

But he was rejected.

Five years later he made it the second time around, after working as an accountant at several national firms, one of which became heavily implicated in a corporate reporting scandal. At the Secret Service's training center he'd been schooled in firearms, use of force, emergency medical techniques, evidence protection, crime detection, even open-water survival. Then he'd been assigned to the Philadelphia field office, working credit card abuse, counterfeiting, identity theft, and bank fraud.

He knew the score.

Special agents spent their first six to eight years in a field office. After that, depending on performance, they were transferred to a protective detail, where they stayed for another three to five years. Following that, most returned to the field, or transferred to headquarters, or a training office, or some other DC-based assignment. He could have possibly worked overseas in one of the international offices, since he was reasonably fluent in French and Spanish.

Boredom was the reason he'd turned to the Internet. His website had allowed him to explore avenues that he wanted to work as an agent. Investigating electronic fraud had little to do with safeguarding the world's financial systems. His website provided a forum in which he could express himself. But his extracurricular activities had generated the one thing an agent could never afford. Attention to himself. Twice he was reprimanded. Twice he ignored his superiors. The third time he'd been officially questioned, just two weeks ago, which caused him to flee, flying to Copenhagen and Thorvaldsen. Now here he was, in the liveliest, most picturesque section of Paris, on a cold December day, following a suspect.

Ahead, Foddrell approached one of the quarter's countless bistros, the quaint sign out front announcing Café d'Argent. Sam slowed and searched the crowd for Malone, finding him fifty feet away. Foddrell disappeared through the front door, then reappeared at an inside table that abutted a plate-glass window.

Malone walked over. "All that paranoia and he ends up framed out for the world to see."

Sam still wore the coat, gloves, and scarf Jesper had provided last night. He could also still see the two corpses. Jesper had cast them away with no ceremony, as if killing was routine. And maybe it was for Henrik Thorvaldsen. He actually knew little about the Dane, other than that he seemed interested in what Sam thought.

Which is a lot more than he could say for anyone else.

"Come on," Malone said.

They entered the bistro's brightly lit interior, decorated in a 1950s motif using chrome, vinyl, and neon. The climate was noisy and smoky. Sam caught Foddrell staring at them, clearly recognizing their faces, reveling in his anonymity.

Malone walked straight to where Foddrell sat and slid out one of the vinyl chairs. "You had enough fun?"

"How do you know who I am?" Foddrell asked.

Malone pointed at the book in Foddrell's lap. "You really should have covered that up. Can we dispense with the drama and get on with this?"

THORVALDSEN LISTENED AS THE MANTELPIECE clock struck half past three, the hour confirmed by more clocks chiming throughout the château. He was making progress, maneuvering Eliza Larocque into a corner where she'd have no choice but to cooperate with him.

"Lord Ashby is broke," he made clear.

"You have facts to back this up?"

"I never speak without them."

"Tell me about my security leak."

"How do you think I learned what I know?"

She threw him a keen, dissecting glance. "Ashby?"

He shook his head. "Not directly. He and I have never met nor spoken. But there are others he's spoken to, people he approached for financial assistance. They wanted assurances that their loans would be repaid, so he gave them a unique guarantee, one that involved explaining what he was part of. He was quite vocal about the profits to be made."

"And you don't plan to tell me any names?"

He assumed a rigid pose. "Why would I do such a thing? What value would I be then?" He knew she had no choice but to accept his offerings.

"You're quite a problem, Herre Thorvaldsen."

He chuckled. "That I am."

"But I'm beginning to like you."

"I was hoping we might find common ground." He pointed at her. "As I mentioned earlier, I've studied you in detail. Especially your ancestor, Pozzo di Borgo. I found it fascinating how both the British and the Russians made use of his **vendetta** with Napoleon. I love what he said in 1811, on learning of the birth of the emperor's heir. **Napoleon is a giant who bends down the mighty oaks of the primeval forest. But some day the woodland spirits will break from their disgraceful bondage, then the oaks will suddenly rebound and dash the giant to the earth.** Quite prophetic, as that's precisely what happened."

He knew this woman sought strength from her heritage. She spoke of it often, and with pride. In that respect they were similar.

"Unlike Napoleon," she said, "di Borgo remained a true Corsican patriot. He loved his homeland and always placed its interests first. When Napoleon finally occupied Corsica for France, di Borgo's name was specifically excluded from the list of those granted political amnesty. So he fled. Napoleon hunted him all over Europe. Di Borgo, though, managed to elude capture."

"And, at the same time, maneuvered the emperor's downfall. Quite a feat."

Thorvaldsen had been schooled on how Pozzo di Borgo exerted pressure on the French court and cabinet, inflaming the jealousies of Napoleon's many brothers and sisters, eventually becoming a conduit for any and all French opposition. He served with the British at their embassy in Vienna, becoming **persona grata** in Austrian political circles. Then his real opportunity came when he entered the Russian diplomatic service, as commissioner to the Prussian army. Eventually, he became the tsar's right hand in all affairs connected with France and convinced Alexander not to make peace with Napoleon. For twelve years he skillfully kept France embroiled in controversy, knowing Napoleon could fight, and win, on only so many fronts. In the end his efforts worked, but his life was one of unrecognized success. History hardly mentioned him. He died in 1842, mentally deranged but incredibly wealthy. His assets were bequeathed to nephews, one of whom was Eliza Larocque's ancestor, whose descendants multiplied that wealth a hundred times over, establishing one of the great European fortunes.

"Di Borgo carried the **vendetta** to its end," he said, "but I wonder, madame, did your Corsican ancestor, in his hatred of Napoleon, have an ulterior purpose?"

Her cold eyes communicated a look of begrudging respect. "Why don't you tell me what you already know."

"You're looking for Napoleon's lost cache. That's why Lord Ashby is part of your group. He is—shall we politely say—a **collector.**"

She smiled at the word. "I see I made a serious error not approaching you long ago."

Thorvaldsen shrugged. "Thankfully, I do not hold a grudge."

TWENTY-FOUR

PARIS

MALONE'S PATIENCE WITH JIMMY FODDRELL WAS wearing thin. "All this cloak-and-dagger crap isn't necessary. Who the hell's after you?"

"You have no idea how many people I've riled up."

Malone waved off the younger man's fear. "News flash. Nobody gives a damn. I've read your site. It's a bunch of garbage. And by the way, there's medication you can take that'll ease your paranoia."

Foddrell faced Sam. "You said you had someone who wanted to learn. Who had an open mind. It's not this guy, is it?"

"Teach me," Malone said.

Foddrell's thin lips parted to show the top of a gold tooth. "Right now, I'm hungry."

Foddrell motioned for a waiter. Malone listened as the younger man ordered pan-fried veal kidneys in a mustard sauce. Just the thought of that turned his stomach. Hopefully, they'd be done talking before the food arrived. He declined ordering anything for himself.

"I'll take the **côte de boeuf,**" Sam said.

"For what?" Malone asked.

"I'm hungry, too."

He shook his head.

The waiter left and he again asked Foddrell, "Why are you so afraid?"

"There are some powerful people in this town who know all about me."

Malone told himself to let the fool talk. Somewhere, somehow, they might stumble onto a nugget or two.

"They make us follow them," Foddrell said. "Even though we don't know it. They create policy, and we don't know it. They create our needs and possess the means to satisfy them, and we don't know it. We work for them, and, we don't know it. We buy their products, and—"

"Who is **they**?" he asked.

"People like the U.S. Federal Reserve. One of the most powerful groups in the world."

He knew he shouldn't ask, but, "Why do you say that?"

"I thought you said this guy was cool," Foddrell said to Sam. "He doesn't know spit."

"Look," Malone answered, "I've been into the whole alien autopsy, Area 51 thing, for the past few years. This monetary stuff is new to me."

Foddrell pointed a nervous finger. "Okay, you're a funny man. You think this is all a big joke."

"Why don't you just explain yourself?"

"The Federal Reserve makes money from thin air. Then it loans it back to America and gets repaid by the taxpayers with interest. America owes the Federal Reserve trillions upon trillions. Just the annual interest on that debt, which by the way is mostly controlled by private investors, is approximately eight times bigger than the wealth of the richest man on the planet. It'll never be paid off. A lot of people are getting filthy rich off that debt. And it's all a cheat. If you or I printed money, then loaned it out, we'd go to jail."

Malone recalled something he'd read earlier on Foddrell's website. Supposedly, John Kennedy had wanted to end the Federal Reserve and signed Executive Order 11110, which instructed the U.S. government to retake control of the nation's money supply from the Reserve. Three weeks later, Kennedy was dead. When Lyndon Johnson took office, he immediately rescinded that order. Malone had never heard such an accusation before, so he'd checked further and read Executive Order 11110, an innocuous directive whose effect, had it been carried through, would have actually strengthened, rather than weakened, the Federal Reserve system. Any relation to the signing of that order and Kennedy's assassination was purely coincidental. And Johnson never rescinded the order.

Instead, it was purged decades later along with a host of other outdated regulations.

More conspiratorial bullshit.

He decided to get to the point. "What do you know about the Paris Club?"

"Enough to know that we need to be afraid."

ELIZA STARED AT THORVALDSEN AND SAID, "HAVE you ever wondered what money can really do?"

Her guest shrugged. "My family has amassed so much, over such a long time, I never think about it. But it certainly can provide power, influence, and a comfortable life."

She assumed a calm air. "It can also do much more. Yugoslavia is an excellent example."

She saw he was curious.

"Supposedly, in the 1980s, the Yugoslavs were an imperial, fascist regime that committed crimes against humanity. After free elections in 1990, the people of Serbia chose the socialist party, while the people from other Yugoslav republics chose to implement more pro-Western governments. Eventually, the U.S. started a war with Serbia. Prior to that, though, I watched as world policy gradually weakened Yugoslavia, which, at that time, had one of the best economies in Eastern Europe. The U.S.–Serbian war, and subsequent dismantling of

Yugoslavia, destroyed any idea that a socialist economy might be a good thing."

"Serbia was clearly oppressive and dangerous," Thorvaldsen said.

"Who says? The media? Were they any more oppressive than say, North Korea, China, Iran? Yet no one advocates war with them. **Take a match and make a forest fire.** That's what one diplomat told me at the time. The aggressions on Serbia were heavily supported by the mainstream media, along with influential leaders all over the world. That aggression lasted for more than ten years. All of which, by the way, made it quite easy, and far less expensive, to buy the entire former Yugoslav economy."

"Is that what happened?"

"I know of many investors who took full advantage of that catastrophe."

"You're saying all that happened in Serbia was contrived?"

"In a manner of speaking. Not actively, but certainly tacitly. That situation proved that it's entirely feasible to take advantage of destructive situations. There is profit in political and national discord. Provided, of course, that the discord ends at some point. It's only then that a return can be made on any investment."

She was enjoying discussing theory. Rarely was she afforded an opportunity. She wasn't saying anything incriminating, only repeating observations that many economists and historians had long noted.

"The Rothschilds in the 18th and 19th centuries," she said, "were masters of this technique. They managed to play all sides, generating enormous profit at a time when Europeans fought among themselves like children on a playground. The Rothschilds were wealthy, international, and independent. Three dangerous qualities. Royal governments could not control them. Popular movements hated them, because they were not answerable to the people. Constitutionalists resented them because they worked in secret."

"As you are attempting to do?"

"Secrecy is essential for the success of any cabal. I'm sure, Herre Thorvaldsen, you understand how events can be quietly shaped by the simple granting or withholding of funds, or affecting the selection of key personnel, or just maintaining a daily intercourse with decision makers. Being behind the scenes avoids the brunt of public anger, which is directed, as it should be, to open political figures."

"Who are largely controlled."

"As if you don't own a few." She needed to steer the conversation back on point. "I assume you can produce evidence on Lord Ashby's treachery?"

"At the appropriate time."

"Until then, I am to take your word about Lord Ashby's statements to these unknown financiers?"

"How about this. Allow me to join your group

and we shall together discover if I am truthful or a liar. If I am a liar, you can keep my twenty-million-euro admittance fee."

"But our secrecy would have been compromised."

"It already is."

Thorvaldsen's sudden appearance was unnerving, yet it could also be a godsend. She'd meant what she'd said to Mastroianni—she believed in fate.

Perhaps Henrik Thorvaldsen was meant to be a part of her destiny?

"Might I show you something?" she asked.

MALONE WATCHED AS THE WAITER RETURNED WITH bottled water, wine, and a breadbasket. He'd never been impressed with French bistros. Every one he'd ever visited was either overpriced, overrated, or both.

"Do you really like pan-fried kidneys?" he asked Foddrell.

"What's wrong with them?"

He wasn't about to explain the many reasons why ingesting an organ that rid the body of urine was bad. Instead, he said, "Tell me about the Paris Club."

"You know where the idea came from?"

He saw that Foddrell was enjoying his superior status. "You were a little vague with that on your website."

"Napoleon. After he conquered Europe, what he really wanted was to settle back and enjoy. So he assembled a group of people and formed the Paris Club, which was designed to make it easier for him to rule. Unfortunately, he never was able to use the idea—too busy fighting war after war."

"Thought you said he wanted to stop fighting?"

"He did, but others had different ideas. Keeping Napoleon fighting was the best way to keep him off guard. There were people who made sure he always had a crop of enemies at his doorstep. He tried to make peace with Russia, but the tsar told him to stuff it. So he invaded Russia in 1812, an act that nearly cost him his whole army. After that, it was all downhill. Three years later, bye-bye. Deposed."

"Which tells me nothing."

Foddrell's gaze fixed out the window, as if something suddenly caught his attention.

"There a problem?" Malone asked.

"Just checking."

"Why sit by the window for all to see?"

"You don't get it, do you?"

The question declared a growing annoyance at being dismissed so easily, but Malone could not care less. "I'm trying to understand."

"Since you've read the website, you know that Eliza Larocque has started a new Paris Club. Same idea. Different time, different people. They meet in a building on the Rue l'Araignée. I know that for a fact. I've seen them there. I know a guy who works for one of the members. He contacted me through the website and told me about it. These people are plotting. They're going to do what the Rothschilds did two hundred years ago. What Napoleon wanted to do. It's all a grand conspiracy. The New World Order, coming of age. Economics their weapon."

Sam had sat silent during the exchange. Malone realized that he must see that Jimmy Foddrell existed light-years past any semblance of reality. But he couldn't resist, "For somebody who's paranoid, you never even asked my name."

"Cotton Malone. Sam told me in his email."

"You don't know anything about me. What if I'm here to kill you? Like you say, they're everywhere, watching. They know what you view on the Internet, what books you check out from the library, your blood type, your medical history, your friends."

Foddrell began to study the bistro, the tables busy with patrons, as though it were a cage. "I gotta go."

"What about your pan-fried kidneys?"

"You eat them."

Foddrell sprang from the table and darted for the door.

"He deserved that," Sam said.

Malone watched as the goofy fellow fled the eatery, studied the crowded sidewalk, then rushed ahead. He was ready to leave, too. Especially before the food arrived.

Then something caught his attention.

Across the busy pedestrian-only street, at one of the art stalls.

Two men in dark wool coats.

Their attention had instantly alerted when Foddrell appeared. Then they followed their gaze, walking swiftly, hands in their pockets, straight after Jimmy Foddrell.

"They're not tourists," Sam said.

"You got that right."

TWENTY-FIVE

SALEN HALL

ASHBY LED CAROLINE THROUGH THE LABYRINTH of ground-floor corridors to the mansion's north-ernmost wing. There they entered one of the many parlors, this one converted into Caroline's study. Inside, books and manuscripts lay scattered across several oak tables. Most of the volumes were more than two hundred years old, bought at consider-able expense, located in private collections from as far away as Australia. Some, though, had been stolen by Mr. Guildhall. All were on the same sub-ject.

Napoleon.

"I found the reference yesterday," Caroline said as she searched the stacks. "In one of the books we bought in Orleans."

Unlike himself, Caroline was fluent in both modern and old French.

"It's a late 19th-century treatise, written by a

British soldier who served on St. Helena. I'm amused how these people so admired Napoleon. It's beyond hero worship, as if he could do no wrong. And this one's by a Brit, no less."

She handed him the book. Strips of paper protruding from its frayed edges marked pages. "There are so many of these accounts it's hard to take any of them seriously. But this one is actually interesting."

He wanted her to know that he may have found something, too. "In the book from Corsica that led to the gold, there's a mention of Sens."

Her face lit up. "Really?"

"Contrary to what you might think, I can also discover things."

She grinned. "And how do you know what I think?"

"It's not hard to comprehend."

He told her about the book's introduction and what Saint-Denis had bequeathed to the city of Sens, especially the specific mention of one volume, **The Merovingian Kingdoms 450–751 A.D.**

He saw that something about that title seemed significant. Immediately, she stepped to another of the tables and rummaged through more stacks. The sight of her, so deep in thought, but dressed so provocatively, excited him.

"Here it is," she said. "I knew that book was important. In Napoleon's will. Item VI. **Four hundred volumes, selected from those in my library of which I have been accustomed to use most,**

including my copy of The Merovingian Kingdoms 450–751 A.D., **I direct Saint-Denis to take
care of them and to convey them to my son
when he shall attain the age of sixteen years.**"

They were slowly piecing together a puzzle that
had not been meant to be deciphered in such a
backward manner.

"Saint-Denis was loyal," she said. "We know he
faithfully kept those four hundred books. Of
course, there was no way to ever deliver them. He
lived in France after Napoleon's death, and the son
stayed a prisoner of the Austrians until he died in
1832."

"Saint-Denis died in 1856," he said, recalling
what he'd read. "Thirty-five years he stored those
books. Then he bequeathed them to the city of
Sens."

She threw him a sly smile. "This stuff charges
you, doesn't it?"

"You charge me."

She pointed at the book he held. "Before I gladly
perform my mistress responsibilities, read what's at
the first marker. I think it might enhance your en-
joyment."

He parted the book. Flakes of dried leather from
the brittle binding fluttered to the floor.

Abbé Buonavita, the elder of the two priests
on St. Helena, had been for some months crip-
pled to the point where he was really not able

to leave his room. One day Napoleon sent for him and explained that it would be better and more prudent for him to return to Europe than to remain at St. Helena, whose climate must be injurious to his health, while that of Italy would probably prolong his days. The Emperor had a letter written to the imperial family requesting payment to the priest of a pension of three thousand francs. When the abbé thanked the Emperor for his goodness he expressed his regret at not ending his days with him to whom he had meant to devote his life. Before he left the island, Buonavita made a last visit to the Emperor, who gave him various instructions and letters to be transmitted to the Emperor's family and the pope.

"Napoleon was already sick when Buonavita left St. Helena," Caroline said. "And he died a few months later. I've seen the letters Napoleon wanted delivered to his family. They're in a museum on Corsica. The Brits read everything that came to and from St. Helena. Those letters were deemed harmless, so they allowed the abbé to take them."

"What's so special about them now?"

"Would you like to see?"

"You have them?"

"Photos. No sense going all the way to Corsica and not taking pictures. I snapped a few shots when I was there last year researching."

He studied her piquant nose and chin. Her raised eyebrows. The swell of her breasts. He wanted her.

But first things first.

"You brought me gold bars," she said. "Now I have something for you." She lifted a photo of a one-page letter, written in French, and asked, "Notice anything?"

He studied the jagged script.

"Remember," she said. "Napoleon's handwriting was atrocious. Saint-Denis rewrote everything. That was known to everyone on St. Helena. But this letter is far from neat. I compared the writing with some we know Saint-Denis penned."

He caught the mischievous glow in her eyes.

"This one was written by Napoleon himself."

"Is that significant?"

"Without question. He wrote these words without Saint-Denis' intervention. That makes them even more important, though I didn't realize how important until earlier."

He continued to gaze at the photo. "What does it say? My French is not nearly as good as yours."

"Just a personal note. Speaks of his love and devotion and how much he misses his son. Not a thing to arouse the suspicion of any nosy Brit."

He allowed himself a grin, then a chuckle. "Why don't you explain yourself, so we can move on to other business."

She relieved him of the photo and laid it on the

table. She grabbed a ruler and positioned the straightedge beneath one line of the text.

dESIR PROFOd dE SAVOIR QUE VOUS

"You see?" she asked. "It's clearer with the ruler underneath."

And he saw. A few of the letters were raised from the others. Subtle, but there.

"It's a code Napoleon used," she said. "The Brits on St. Helena never noticed. But when I found that account of how Napoleon sent the letters through the abbé, ones he wrote himself, I started looking at these more closely. Only this one has the raised lettering."

"What do the letters spell?"

"Psaume trente et un."

That he could translate. "Psalm thirty-one." Though he did not understand the significance.

"It's a specific reference," she said. "I have it here." She lifted an open Bible from the table. **"Turn your ear to me, come quickly to my rescue; be my rock of refuge, a strong fortress to save me. Since you are my rock and my fortress, for the sake of your name lead and guide me. Free me from the trap that is set for me."** She glanced up from the book. "That fits Napoleon's exile perfectly. Listen to this part. **My life is consumed by anguish and my years by groaning; my strength fails because of** my affliction, and my bones grow weak. Because of all my enemies, I am in utter contempt of my neighbors; I am a dread to my friends—those who see me on the street flee from me. I am forgotten by them as though I were dead."

"The lament of a man defeated," he said.

"By the time he wrote the letter he knew the end was near."

His gaze immediately locked on the copy of Napoleon's will, lying on the table. "So he left the books to Saint-Denis and told him to hold them until the son was sixteen. Then he mentioned the one book specifically and sent out a coded letter feeling sorry for himself."

"That book about the Merovingians," she said, "could be the key."

He agreed. "We must find it."

She stepped close, wrapped her arms around his neck, and kissed him. "Time for you to take care of your mistress."

He started to speak, but she silenced him with a finger to his lips.

"After, I'll tell you where the book is located."

TWENTY-SIX

PARIS

SAM COULDN'T BELIEVE THAT TWO MEN WERE actually following Jimmy Foddrell. Malone had been right in the bistro to attack the pedantic moron. He wondered if his superiors at the Secret Service viewed him in the same bewildered way. He'd never been that extreme, or that paranoid, though he had defied authority and advocated similar beliefs. Something about him and rules just didn't mix.

He and Malone kept pace through the warren of tight streets filled with heads burrowed into heavy coats and sweaters. Restaurateurs braved the cold, hawking their menus, trying to attract diners. He savored the noises, smells, and movements, fighting their hypnotic effect.

"Who do you think those two guys are?" he finally asked.

"That's the problem with fieldwork, Sam. You never know. It's all about improvising."

"Could there be more of them around?"

"Unfortunately, there's no way to know in all this chaos."

He recalled movies and TV shows where the hero always seemed to sense danger, no matter how crowded or how far away. But in the hubbub assaulting them from every angle, he realized there'd be no way to perceive anything as a threat until it was upon them.

Foddrell kept walking.

Ahead the pedestrian-only way ended at a busy thoroughfare identified as Boulevard St. Germain—a turmoil of taxis, cars, and buses. Foddrell stopped until a nearby signal thickened traffic to a standstill, then he rushed across the four lanes, thick with a clot of people.

The two men followed.

"Come on," Malone said.

They raced forward, reaching the curb as traffic signals to their right cycled back to green. Not stopping, he and Malone darted across the boulevard, finding the other side just as motors accelerated past them in high, eager tones.

"You cut it close," Sam said.

"We can't lose them."

The sidewalk's inner edge was now lined by a waist-high stone wall that supported a wrought-iron fence. People hustled in both directions, their faces bright with energy.

Having no immediate family had always made the holiday season lonely for Sam. The past five

Christmases he'd spent on a Florida beach, alone. He never knew his parents. He was raised at a place called the Cook Institute—just a fancy name for an orphanage. He'd come as an infant, his last day a week after his eighteenth birthday.

"I have a choice?" he asked.

"You do," Norstrum said.

"Since when? There's nothing here but rules."

"Those are for children. You're now a man, free to live your life as you please."

"That's it? I'm can go? Bye-bye. See you later."

"You owe us nothing, Sam."

He was glad to hear that. He had nothing to give.

"Your choice," Norstrum said, "is simple. You can stay and become a larger part of this place. Or you can leave."

That was no choice. "I want to go."

"I thought that would be the case."

"It's not that I'm not grateful. It's just that I want to go. I've had enough of—"

"Rules."

"That's right. Enough of rules."

He knew that many of the instructors and caretakers had been raised here, too, as orphans. But another rule forbid them from talking about that. Since he was leaving, he decided to ask, "Did you have a choice?"

"I chose differently."

The information shocked him. He'd never known the older man had been an orphan, too.

"Would you do me one favor?" Norstrum asked.

They stood on the campus green, among buildings two centuries old. He knew every square inch of each one, down to their last detail, since everyone was required to help maintain things.

Another of those rules he'd come to hate.

"Be careful, Sam. Think before you act. The world is not as accommodating as we are."

"Is that what you call it here? Accommodating?"

"We genuinely cared for you." Norstrum paused. "I genuinely cared for you."

Not once in eighteen years had he heard such sentiment from this man.

"You are a free spirit, Sam. That's not necessarily a bad thing. Just be careful."

He saw that Norstrum, whom he'd known all his life, was being sincere.

"Perhaps you'll find rules on the outside easier to follow. God knows, it was a challenge for you here."

"Maybe it's in my genes."

He was trying to make light, but the

comment only reminded him that he had no parents, no heritage. All he'd ever known lay around him. The only man who'd ever given a damn stood beside him. So out of respect, he extended his hand, which Norstrum politely shook.

"I had hoped you'd stay," the older man quietly said.

Eyes filled with sadness stared back at him.

"Be well, Sam. Try to always do good."

And he had.

Graduating college with honors, finally making it to the Secret Service. He sometimes wondered if Norstrum was still alive. It had been fourteen years since they'd last spoken. He'd never made contact simply because he did not want to disappoint the man any further.

I had hoped you'd stay.

But he couldn't.

He and Malone turned a corner onto a side street, off the main boulevard. Ahead, the sidewalk rose toward the next intersection, and another wall with an iron fence stretched to their right. They followed the slow shuffle of feet to the corner and turned. A taller wall, topped with battlements, replaced the fence. Attached to its rough stone hung a colorful banner that announced MUSÉE NATIONAL DU MOYEN AGE, THERMES DE CLUNY.

Cluny Museum of Medieval History.

The building that rose beyond the wall was a

crenellated Gothic structure topped with a sloping slate roof, dotted with dormers. Foddrell disappeared through an entrance, and the two men followed.

Malone kept pace.

"What are we doing?" Sam asked.

"Improvising."

MALONE KNEW WHERE THEY WERE HEADED. THE Cluny Museum stood on the site of a Roman palace, the ruins of its ancient baths still inside. The present mansion was erected in the 15th century by a Benedictine abbot. Not until the 19th century had the grounds become state-owned, displaying an impressive collection of medieval artifacts. It remained one of the must-sees on any Parisian itinerary. He'd visited a couple of times and recalled the inside. Two stories, one exhibit room opening into the next, one way in and out. Tight confines. Not a good place to go unnoticed.

He led the way as they entered a cloistered courtyard and caught sight of the two tails stepping through the main door. Maybe thirty camera-clad visitors milled in the courtyard.

He hesitated, then headed for the same entrance.

Sam followed.

The chamber beyond was a stone-walled ante-
room converted into a reception center, with a
cloakroom and stairway that led down to
toilets. The two men were buying tickets from a
cashier, then they turned and climbed stone risers
into the museum. As they disappeared through a
narrow doorway, he and Sam purchased their own
tickets. They climbed the same risers and entered a
crowded gift shop. No sign of Foddrell, but the two
minders were already passing through another low
doorway to their left. Malone caught sight of com-
plimentary English brochures that explained the
museum and grabbed one, quickly scanning the
layout.

Sam noticed. "Henrik says you have a photo-
graphic memory. Is that true?"

"Eidetic memory," he corrected. "Just a good
mind for detail."

"Are you always so precise?"

He stuffed the brochure into his back pocket.
"Hardly ever."

They entered an exhibit room illuminated by
both sunlight from a mullioned window and some
strategically placed incandescent floods that ac-
cented medieval porcelain, glass, and alabaster.

Neither Foddrell nor his tails were there.

They hustled into the next space, containing
more ceramics, and caught sight of the two men
just as they were exiting at the far side. Both rooms,
so far, had been active with talkative visitors and

clicking cameras. Malone knew from the brochure that ahead lay the Roman baths.

At the exit he spotted the two as they passed through a tight corridor, painted blue and lined with alabaster plaques, that opened into a lofty stone hallway. Down a flight of stone steps was the **frigidarium.** But a placard announced that it was closed for renovations and a plastic chain blocked access. To their right, through an elaborate Gothic arch, a brightly lit hall housed remnants of statues. Folding metal chairs were arranged before a platform and podium. Some sort of presentation space that was clearly once an exterior courtyard.

Left led deeper into the museum.

The two men turned that way.

He and Sam approached and cautiously peered inside the next room, which rose two stories, naturally lit from an opaque ceiling. Rough-hewn stone walls towered forty feet. Probably once another courtyard, between buildings, now enclosed and displaying ivories, capital fragments, and more statuary.

Foddrell was nowhere to be seen, but Tweedledum and Tweedledee were headed toward the next exhibit space, which opened at the top of more stone risers.

"Those two are after me," someone yelled, disturbing the library-like silence.

Malone's head craned upward.

Standing at a balustrade, on what would be the

upper floor of the next building, pointing downward at the two men they were following, was a woman. Perhaps early thirties, with short-cut brownish hair. She wore one of the blue smocks that Malone had already noticed on other museum employees.

"They're after me," the woman screamed. "Trying to kill me."

TWENTY-SEVEN

LOIRE VALLEY

THORVALDSEN FOLLOWED LAROCQUE FROM THE drawing room as they strolled farther into the château, out over the Cher, which flowed beneath the building's foundations. Before coming, he'd learned the estate's history and knew that its architecture had been conceived in the early 16th century, part of François I's gallant, civilized court. A woman initially formulated the design, and that feminine influence remained evident. No power was asserted by buttressed walls or overwhelming size. Instead, inimitable grace evoked only a pleasant affluence.

"My family has owned this property for three centuries," she said. "One owner built the central château on the north shore, where we were just seated, and a bridge to connect to the river's south bank. Another erected a gallery atop the bridge."

She motioned ahead.

He stared at a long rectangular hall, maybe sixty meters or more in length, the floor a black-and-white checkerboard, the ceiling supported by heavy oak beams. Streams of sunshine slanted inward through symmetrically placed windows that stretched, on both sides, from end to end.

"During the war, the Germans occupied the estate," she said. "The south door at the far end was actually in the free zone. The door on this end the occupied zone. You can imagine what trouble that created."

"I hate Germans," he made clear.

She appraised him with a calculating gaze.

"They destroyed my family and country, and tried to destroy my religion. I can never forgive them."

He allowed the fact that he was Jewish to register. His research on her had revealed a long-held prejudice against Jews. No specific reason that he could identify, just an inbred distaste, not uncommon. His vetting had also exposed another of her many obsessions. He'd been hoping she'd escort him through the château—and ahead, beside the pedimented entrance to another of the many rooms, illuminated by two tiny halogens, hung the portrait.

Right where he'd been told.

He stared at the image. Long ugly nose. A pair of oblique eyes, deeply set, casting a sidelong cunning glance. Powerful jaw. Jutting chin. A conical hat sheathing a nearly bare skull that made the figure look like a pope or a cardinal. But he'd been much more than that.

"Louis XI," he said, pointing.

Larocque stopped. "You are an admirer?"

"What was said of him? **Loved by the commons, hated by the great, feared by his enemies, and respected by the whole of Europe. He was a king.**"

"No one knows if it's an authentic image. But it has a strange quality, wouldn't you say?"

He recalled what he'd been told about the stink of theater that hung around Louis XI's memory. He ruled from 1461 to 1483 and managed to forge for himself a wondrous legend of greatness. In actuality, he was unscrupulous, openly rebelled against his father, treated his wife villainously, trusted few, and showed no mercy on anyone. His passion was the regeneration of France after the disastrous Hundred Years' War. Tirelessly, he planned, plotted, and bribed, all with the aim of gathering under one crown lost lands.

And he succeeded.

Which cemented him a sainted place in French history.

"He was one of the first to understand the power of money," he said. "He liked to buy men, as opposed to fighting them."

"You are a student," she said, clearly impressed. "He grasped the importance of commerce as a political tool, and laid the foundations for the modern nation-state. One where an economy would be more important than an army."

She motioned and they entered another of the rooms, this one with walls sheathed in warm leather and windows screened by draperies the color of port wine. An impressive Renaissance hearth sheltered no fire. Little furniture existed, other than a few upholstered chairs and wooden tables. In the center stood a stainless-steel glass case, out of place with the room's antiquity.

"Napoleon's 1798 invasion of Egypt was a military and political fiasco," she told him. "The French Republic sent its greatest general to conquer, and he did. But ruling Egypt was another matter. In that, Napoleon did not succeed. Still, there is no denying that his Egyptian occupation changed the world. For the first time the splendor of that mysterious and forgotten civilization was revealed. Egyptology was born. Napoleon's **savants** literally discovered, beneath the millennial sands, pharaonic Egypt. Typical Napoleon—an utter failure masked by partial success."

"Spoken like a true descendant of Pozzo di Borgo."

She shrugged. "While he lies in glory at the Invalides, my ancestor, who quite possibly saved Europe, is forgotten."

He knew this was a sore point so, for the moment, he left the subject alone.

"While in Egypt, though, Napoleon did manage

to discover a few things of immense value." She motioned at the display case. "These four papyri. Encountered by accident one day, after Napoleon's troops shot a murderer on the side of the road. If not for Pozzo di Borgo, Napoleon may have used these to consolidate power and effectively rule most of Europe. Thankfully, he was never allowed the chance."

His investigators had not mentioned this anomaly. On Ashby, he'd spared no expense, learning everything. But on Eliza Larocque he'd targeted his inquiries. Perhaps he'd made a mistake?

"What do these papyri say?" he casually asked.

"They are the reason for the Paris Club. They explain our purpose and will guide our path."

"Who wrote them?"

She shrugged. "No one knows. Napoleon believed them from Alexandria, lost when the library there disappeared."

He had some experience with that artifact, which wasn't as lost as most people thought. "Lots of faith you place in an unknown document, written by an unknown scribe."

"Similar to the Bible, I believe. We know virtually nothing of its origin, yet billions model their lives on its words."

"Excellent point."

Her eyes beamed with the confidence of a guileless heart. "I've shown you something dear to me. Now I want to see your proof on Ashby."

TWENTY-EIGHT

PARIS

MALONE WATCHED AS TWO MEN, GARBED IN rumpled blue blazers and ties, museum ID badges draped around their necks, rushed into the exhibit space. One of the men who'd followed Foddrell, a burly fellow with shocks of unkempt hair, reacted to the assault and punched the lead Blazer in the face. The other minder, with gnomic, flat features, kicked the second Blazer to the floor.

Guns appeared in the hands of Flat Face and Burly.

The woman above, who'd started the melee, fled the balustrade.

Patrons noticed the weapons and voices rose. Visitors rushed past where Malone and Sam stood, back toward the main entrance.

Two more Blazers appeared on the opposite side.

Shots were fired.

Stone walls, a tile floor, and a glass ceiling did

little to deaden the sound and the bangs pounded into Malone's ears with the force of an explosion.

One of the Blazers collapsed.

More people raced past him.

The other Blazer disappeared from sight.

Flat Face and Burly vanished.

The museum's geography flashed through Malone's brain. "I'm going to double back around. There's only one other way out of the building. I'll cut them off there. You stay here."

"And do what?"

"Try not to get shot."

He assumed that museum security would close the exits and the police would arrive shortly. All he had to do was occupy the two gunmen long enough for all that to happen.

He raced back toward the main entrance.

SAM HAD LITTLE TIME TO THINK. THINGS WERE happening fast. He immediately decided that he wasn't going to sit still—no matter what Malone ordered—so he bolted through the towering, sunlit exhibit room, where the shooting had occurred, to the man in a blue blazer, lying facedown, bleeding, his body limp as a rag.

He knelt down.

Eyes glassed over in a distant stare barely blinked.

He'd never before seen someone actually shot. Dead? Yes. Last night. But this man was still alive.

His gaze raked the scene around him as he inventoried more capitals, statues, and sculptures. Plus two exits—one a door, locked with an iron hasp, the other an open archway that led into a windowless space. He spotted a tapestry hanging from that room's far wall and saw a stairway that led up.

All visitors had fled, the museum unnervingly quiet. He wondered about security personnel, employees, or police. Surely the authorities had been called.

Where was everyone?

He heard footsteps. Running. His way. Back from where he and Malone had entered—where Malone had gone.

He did not want to be detained. He wanted to be a part of what was happening.

"Help's on the way," he said to the downed man.

Then he ran into the next room, leaping up the steps to the upper floor.

MALONE RETURNED TO THE GIFT SHOP AND elbowed his way through the crowds that were clamoring to exit through the museum's entrance.

Excited voices boomed in several languages.

He kept shouldering his way through the throng and fled the gift shop, entering an adjacent chamber that the museum brochure had identified as the location for luggage lockers and a stairway that visitors used to descend from the upper floor. At the top, he should be able to backtrack and intercept Burly and Flat Face as they advanced through the museum.

He bounded up the wooden staircase two steps at a time and entered an empty hall that displayed armor, knives, and swords. A tapestry depicting a hunting scene adorned one of the walls. Locks sealed all of the glass cases. He needed a weapon, so he hoped the museum would understand.

He grabbed hold of a chair that abutted another wall and slammed its metal leg into the case.

Glass shards clattered to the floor.

He tossed the chair aside, reached in, and removed one of the short swords. Its edges had been sharpened, most likely to enhance its display. A card inside the case informed visitors that it was a 16th century weapon. He also removed a hand shield identified as from the 1500s.

Both sword and shield were in excellent condition.

He gripped them, looking like a gladiator ready for the arena.

Better than nothing, he reasoned.

SAM RACED UP THE STAIRS, ONE HAND SLIDING across a slick brass banister. He listened at the landing, then climbed the final flight to the museum's top floor.

No sound. Not even from below.

He kept his steps light and his right hand firm on the railing. He wondered what he was going to do. He was unarmed and scared to death, but Malone might need help, just like in the bookstore last night.

And field agents helped one another.

He came to the top.

A wide archway opened to his left into a tall room with bloodred walls. Directly ahead of him was an entrance to an exhibit labeled LA DAME À LA LICORNE.

The Lady and the Unicorn.

He stopped and carefully peered around the archway into the red room.

Three shots cracked.

Bullets pinged off stone, inches from his face, stirring up dust, and he reeled back.

Bad idea.

Another shot came his way. Windows to his right, adjacent to the stairway landing, shattered from an impact.

"Hey," a voice said, nearly in a whisper.

His eyes shot right and he spotted the same woman from before, the one who'd started the mayhem with her scream, standing inside the recessed entrance for the Lady and the Unicorn exhibit. Her short hair was now pushed back from her face, her eyes bright and alert. Her two open palms displayed a gun.

She tossed him the weapon, which he caught.

His left hand clamped the grip, finger on the trigger. He hadn't fired a weapon since his last visit to the Secret Service shooting range. What, four months ago? But he was glad to have the thing.

He met her intense gaze and she motioned that he should fire.

He sucked a deep breath, swung the gun around the archway's edge, and pulled the trigger.

Glass broke somewhere in the red room.

He fired again.

"You could at least try and hit one of them," she said from her hiding place.

"If you're so damn good, you do it."

"Toss it back and I will."

TWENTY-NINE

ELIZA SAT IN THE DRAWING ROOM, CONCERNED BY the unexpected complications that had arisen during the past few hours. Thorvaldsen had left for Paris. Tomorrow they'd talk more.

Right now she needed guidance.

She'd ordered a fire and the hearth now burned with a lively blaze, illuminating the motto carved into its mantel by one of her ancestors.

S'IL VIENT À POINT, ME SOUVIENDRA.

If this castle is finished, I will be remembered.

She sat in one of the upholstered armchairs. The display case, which held the four papyri, stood to her right. Only the crackling embers disturbed the silence. She'd been told that it might snow this evening. She loved winter, especially here, in the country, near all that she held dear.

Two days.

Ashby was in England, preparing. Months ago,

she'd delegated an array of tasks to him, relying on his supposed expertise. Now she wondered if that trust had been misplaced. A lot depended on what he was doing.

Everything, in fact.

She'd dodged Thorvaldsen's questions and not allowed him to read the papyri. He hadn't earned that right. None of the club members had, to this point. That knowledge was sacred to her family, obtained by Pozzo di Borgo himself when his agents stole the documents from shipments scheduled for St. Helena, part of Napoleon's personal effects sent into exile with him. Napoleon had noticed their omission and officially protested, but any improprieties had been imputed to his British captors.

Besides, no one cared.

By then, Napoleon was impotent. All European leaders wanted was for the once mighty emperor to die a quick, natural death. No foul play, no execution. He could not be allowed to become a martyr, so imprisoning him on a remote south Atlantic island seemed the best way to achieve the desired result.

And it worked.

Napoleon had, indeed, faded away.

Dead within five years.

She stood, approached the glass case, and studied the four ancient writings, safe in their cocoon. They'd long ago been translated and she'd committed every word to memory. Pozzo di Borgo had been quick to realize their potential, but he lived in a post-Napoleonic world, during a time when France stayed in constant upheaval, distrustful of monarchy, incapable of democracy.

So they'd been of little use.

She was truthful when she told Thorvaldsen that it was impossible to know who'd written them. All she knew was that the words made sense.

She slid open a drawer beneath the case. Inside lay translations of the original Coptic into French. Two days from now she'd share these words with the Paris Club. For now she shuffled through the typed pages, reacquainting herself with their wisdom, marveling at their simplicity.

War is a progressive force, naturally generating that which would not otherwise have taken place. Free thinking and innovation are but two of the many positive aspects that war creates. War is an active force for society, a stabilizing and dependable tool. The possibility of war forms the strongest foundation for any ruler's authority, the extent of which grows in direct relationship to the ever-increasing threat war poses. Subjects will willingly obey so long as there is at least the promise of protection granted them from invaders. Lose the threat of war, or breach the promise of protection, and all authority ends. War can bind the social allegiance of a people like no other institution.

Central authority simply would not exist without war and the extent of any ruler's ability to govern depends on the ability to wage war. Collective aggression is a positive force that both controls dissent and binds social allegiance. War is the best method for channeling collective aggression. Lasting peace is not in the best interest of maintaining central authority, nor is constant, never-ending war. Best is the mere possibility of war, since the perceived threat provides a sense of external necessity, without which no central authority can exist. Lasting stability can come simply from the organization of any society for war.

Amazing that an ancient mind possessed such modern thoughts.

A feared external menace is essential for any central authority to persevere. Such a menace must be believable and of a sufficient magnitude to instill absolute fear, and must affect society as a whole. Without such fear, central authority could well collapse. A societal transition from war to peace will fail if a ruler does not fill the sociological and political void created by the lack of war. Substitutions for the channeling of collective aggression must be found, but these surrogates must be both realistic and compelling.

She laid the translation atop the case.

In Pozzo di Borgo's time, the mid–19th century, there were no adequate substitutes, so war itself prevailed. First regional conflicts, then two world conflagrations. Today was different. Plenty of substitutes were available. In fact, too many. Had she chosen the right one?

Hard to say.

She returned to her chair.

There was something else she still must know.

After Thorvaldsen departed, she'd retrieved the oracle from her satchel. Now she reverently opened the book and prepared herself with a few deep breaths. From the list of questions she selected **Will the friend I most reckon upon prove faithful or treacherous?** For **friend** she substituted **Thorvaldsen** and then posed the question, out loud, to the burning fire.

She closed her eyes and concentrated.

Then she grasped a pen and slashed vertical lines in five rows, counting each set, determining the proper list of dots.

She quickly consulted the chart and saw that the answer to her question lay on page H. There the oracle proclaimed, **The friend will be unto thee a shield against danger.**

She shut her eyes.

She'd trusted Graham Ashby, allowed him into her confidence, knowing little about him except that he was of old money and an accomplished treasure hunter. She'd offered him a unique opportunity, and provided information that no one else in the world knew, clues passed down through her family starting with Pozzo di Borgo.

All of which might lead to Napoleon's lost cache.

Di Borgo spent the last two decades of his life searching, but to no avail. His failure eventually drove him mad. But he'd left notes, all of which she'd given to Graham Ashby.

Foolish?

She recalled what the oracle had just predicted about Thorvaldsen.

The friend will be unto thee a shield against danger.

Perhaps not.

THIRTY

PARIS

MALONE HEARD SHOTS. FIVE? SIX? THEN GLASS crashed onto something hard.

He passed through three rooms that displayed a thousand years of French history through elaborate art, colorful altarpieces, intricate metalwork, and tapestries. He turned right and approached another corridor. Twenty or so feet long. Hardwood floor. Coffered ceiling. Writing tools and brass instruments were displayed in two lighted cases built into the right side wall, a doorway opening between them into another lighted room. On the left wall he spied a stone archway and the balustrade where the woman had first shouted down her alarm.

A man appeared at the far end of the corridor.

Burly.

His attention was not on Malone but, when he turned and spotted someone carrying a sword and shield, he whirled his gun and fired.

Malone dove, keeping the shield pointed forward.

The bullet pinged off metal just as Malone released his grip on the shield and slammed into the hard floor. The shield clattered away. Malone rolled into the next room and quickly sprang to his feet.

Hard steps sounded his way. He was in a room that held several more bright cases and altarpieces.

No choice.

He couldn't go back the way he came, so he fled into the next room ahead.

SAM WATCHED THE WOMAN CATCH THE GUN——HER hands small but quick——then immediately ease herself forward. The doorway she occupied opened perpendicularly to the entrance into the red room, where the shooters had taken a stand, which gave her cover. She set her feet, aimed, and fired two rounds.

More glass shattered. One more display destroyed.

He risked a look and spotted one of the men as he darted across to the other side. The woman caught his escape, too, and fired another shot, trying to hit the target as he scurried behind another glass case.

The scene swam before him in a daze of uncertainty.

Where was security?

And the police?

MALONE SUDDENLY REALIZED THAT HE'D MADE A dangerous mistake. He recalled the museum brochure and knew that he was headed into the upper chapel, a small, compact space with only one way in and out.

He rushed inside the chapel and caught sight of its flamboyant Gothic style, highlighted by a central pillar rising to a rib vault that spread out like palm branches. Maybe twenty by thirty feet in size, devoid of all furnishings, nowhere to hide.

He still held the sword, but it was little use against a man with a gun.

Think.

SAM WONDERED WHAT THE WOMAN INTENDED. She'd obviously started the fight and now seemed intent on ending it.

Two more shots banged through the museum, but not from her gun, and not directed their way.

Keenly aware of bullets flying past, he carefully risked a glance and saw one of the attackers retreat behind an intact display case and fire his gun in another direction.

The woman saw this, too.

Someone else was firing at their attackers.

Three more rounds entered the red room and the shooter was caught in a crossfire, his attention more on the danger behind him than ahead. The woman seemed to be waiting for the right moment. When it came, she delivered another round.

The shooter lunged for cover, but another shot caught him in the chest. He staggered awkwardly. Sam heard a cry of pain, then watched as the man's twitching body collapsed to the floor.

MALONE BRACED HIMSELF. HIS SCALP TINGLED with fear. HE could only hope that his attacker approached the chapel with caution, unsure what lay beyond its unobstructed doorway. With a little luck the sword might prove enough of a weapon to grant him a few seconds of advantage, but this whole endeavor was turning into a nightmare—par for the course when Thorvaldsen was involved.

"Halt," he heard a male voice shout.

A moment passed.

"I said halt."

A gun exploded.

Flesh and bones thudded to a hard surface. Had the police, or museum security, finally acted? He waited, unsure.

"Mr. Malone, you can come out. He's down."

He wasn't that stupid. He inched his way to the doorway's edge and stole a peek. Burly lay on the floor, facedown, blood oozing from beneath him in a steady deluge. A few feet away a man in a dark suit stood with both feet planted, hands grasping a Sig Sauer .357 semi-automatic, pointed at the body. Malone noted the brush-cut hair, stern looks, and trim physique. He'd also caught the clear English, with a southern twang.

But the gun was the giveaway.

Model P229. Standard issue.

Secret Service.

The muzzle of the gun swung upward until it was aimed straight at Malone's chest.

"Drop the sword."

SAM WAS RELIEVED THAT THE THREAT SEEMED ELIMINATED.

"Malone," he called out, hoping that was who'd taken the man down.

MALONE HEARD SAM CALL HIS NAME. HE STILL HELD the sword, but the Sig remained pointed his way.

"Keep quiet," the man softly said. "And drop the damn sword."

SAM HEARD NOTHING IN RESPONSE TO HIS SHOUTS.

He faced the woman, only to see that her gun was now aimed straight at him.

"Time for you and me to go," she said.

THIRTY-ONE

MALONE WAS LED AT GUNPOINT THROUGH THE deserted museum. All of the patrons were gone, and apparently the interior had been locked down. There'd been a lot of shooting, which made him wonder about the lack of police or museum security.

"What's the Secret Service doing here?" As if he had to ask. "Did you happen to see one of your own? Young guy. Good looking. A bit eager. Name's Sam Collins."

But it won him only more silence.

They passed through an exhibit hall with dark red walls, more altarpieces, and three display cases in shambles. Somebody in an official capacity was really going to be pissed.

He spotted another bleeding body lying on the floor.

Flat Face.

At the room's other exit a stairway dropped down to his right and an open double doorway broke the wall to his left. A laminated placard announced that beyond was LA DAME À LA LICORNE.

Malone pointed. "In there?"

The man nodded, then lowered his gun and withdrew back into the red gallery. The agent's diffident way amused him.

He stepped into a dark space that displayed six colorful tapestries, each carefully illuminated with indirect light. Ordinarily he'd be impressed, as he recalled that these were among the museum's most prized possessions, 15th-century originals, but it was the solitary figure sitting on one of three benches in the center of the room that connected all the dots.

Stephanie Nelle.

His former boss.

"You managed to destroy another national treasure," she said, rising and facing him.

"Wasn't me this time."

"Who slammed a chair into a glass case to get a sword and shield?"

"I see you were watching."

"The French want you," she made clear.

"Which means I owe you—" He caught himself. "No. I probably owe President Daniels. Right?"

"He personally intervened, once I reported that all hell had broken loose."

"What about the museum guard who was shot?"

"On the way to the hospital. He should make it."

"The guy outside. Secret Service?"

She nodded. "On loan."

He'd known Stephanie a long time, having worked for her twelve years at the Justice Department in the Magellan Billet. They'd been through a lot together, especially over the past two years, ever since he'd supposedly retired.

"I'm sorry about your father," she told him.

He hadn't thought about the last two weeks in a few hours. "Thanks for what you did on your end."

"It needed to be done."

"Why are you here?

"Sam Collins. I understand you two have met."

He sat on one of the benches and allowed the tapestries to draw his gaze. Each comprised a dark blue rounded isle, strewn with flowery plants, in vibrant colors that ranged from deep red to bright pink. A noble lady with a unicorn and a lion was depicted on all six, in varying scenes. He knew the allegory—representations of the five senses, mythical enchantment. Subtle messages from long ago, which he'd had more than his share of lately.

"Is Sam in trouble?" he asked.

"He was in trouble the moment he connected with Thorvaldsen."

She told him about a meeting with Danny Daniels yesterday, in the Oval Office, where the president of the United States made clear that something important was happening in Copenhagen.

"Daniels knew about Sam. He'd been briefed by the Secret Service."

"Seems like a trivial matter for the president to be concerned with."

"Not once he was told that Thorvaldsen is involved."

Good point.

"Cotton, this Paris Club is real. Our people have been watching it for over a year. Nothing alarming, until lately. But I need to know what Thorvaldsen is doing."

"So is this about Sam? Or Henrik?"

"Both."

"How did we jump from the Paris Club to Henrik?"

"Like I'm an idiot. You're sitting there with the vacuum cleaner turned on, sucking in whatever info I'm willing to offer. That's not why I'm here. I need to know what that crazy Dane is doing."

He knew that Henrik and Stephanie enjoyed a relationship born of mutual distrust, though they'd been forced, on more than one occasion of late, to actually rely on each other. He decided that since he really didn't have a dog in this fight, other than helping his best friend, for once he'd tell the truth. "He's after Cai's killer."

Stephanie shook her head. "I knew it was probably something like that. He's about to screw up a major intelligence operation, along with compromising a critical source."

More dots instantly connected. His face tightened in speculation. "Graham Ashby works for our side?"

She nodded. "He's been providing a lot of vital intel."

A wave of unease broke over him. "Henrik's going to kill him."

"You have to stop him."

"That's not possible."

"Cotton, there's more happening here. The Paris Club is planning something spectacular. What? We don't know. At least not yet. A woman named Eliza Larocque heads the group. She's the brains. Ashby is part of the administrative arm. He does what she says, but he's been keeping our side informed. That club comprises seven of the wealthiest people in the world. Of course, we're not sure that the members all know what Larocque is planning."

"Why not tell them?"

"Because the decision has been made to take them all down at once. They're into corruption, bribery, extortion, and massive amounts of financial and securities fraud. They've disrupted currency exchanges and may be responsible for weakening the dollar internationally. We're going to send a message by taking them out in one swoop."

He knew the score. "They go down, while Ashby walks free."

"It's the price to be paid. We wouldn't have known about any of this without him."

He again focused on one of the tapestries. A young woman, surrounded by a lion and a unicorn, choosing a sweet from a dish while a parakeet held another in its claw.

"Do you have any idea the mess this is?" he asked.

"I do now. Our people recently learned that Thorvaldsen has Ashby under surveillance. He's even bugged the man's estate. That is probably only possible since Ashby's guard is down. He thinks he's okay with us **and** Eliza Larocque. He hasn't a clue Thorvaldsen is watching. But the president wants Thorvaldsen out of the picture."

"Henrik killed two men last night. One of them was involved with Cai's death."

"I can't blame him there. Nor am I going to interfere, except to the extent it jeopardizes Ashby."

He wanted to know, "What is the Paris Club planning?"

"That's the thing. Ashby hasn't told us yet. Just that it's coming, and soon. Within days. I assume it's his way to ensure a continued value."

"So who are the two dead men out there in the museum?"

"They work for Eliza Larocque. The other woman, the one in the blue smock, spooked them and they overreacted."

"How mad are the French?"

"It's not good."

"This is not my fault."

"The Secret Service has had this museum under watch for over a month." She hesitated. "With no problem."

"The girl in the blue smock started it."

"I learned on the flight over that Eliza Larocque

has been investigating the GreedWatch website. I assume that's what those two were doing following your man, Foddrell."

"Where's Sam?"

"He's been taken. I watched it happen on the security cameras."

"Police?"

She shook her head. "The girl in the blue smock."

"You think you should have helped him."

"It's not a problem."

He knew Stephanie well. They'd worked together a long time. He'd been one of the original twelve lawyer-agents at the Magellan Billet, personally hired by her. So his next question was easy, "You know all about her, don't you?"

"Not exactly. I had no idea what she was going to do, but I'm damn glad she did it."

THIRTY-TWO

SAM HAD BEEN LED FROM THE MUSEUM'S TOP floor, down the same stairway he'd initially climbed, to the ground. There he and the woman had descended another stairway into the closed **frigidarium,** where Jimmy Foddrell waited. Together they'd all passed through a stone archway, barred by an iron gate that the woman opened with a key.

He was a little unnerved by the gun. Never had one been pointed directly at him, so close, so direct, the threat of harm so immediate. Still, he sensed that he wasn't in danger. Instead, he may well be on the right trail.

He decided to follow it. He wanted to be a field agent. **So,** he told himself, **be one. Improvise. That's what Malone would do.**

Foddrell relocked the gate behind them.

Walls scabbed of brick and stone rose fifty feet around him. Light trickled in from windows high up, near a vaulted ceiling, the space chilly, with the look and feel of a dungeon. Some repair work was ongoing, as scaffolding had been erected against one of the rough-hewn walls.

"You can go or stay," the woman said to him. "But I really need you to stay."

"Who are you?"

"Meagan Morrison. GreedWatch is my website."

"Not his?" he asked, pointing at Foddrell.

She shook her head. "All mine."

"What's he doing here?"

She seemed to be deciding what—and how much—to say. "I wanted you to see that I'm not crazy. That there are people after me. They've been watching me for weeks. Michael works with me on the site. I made up the Foddrell name and used him as a decoy."

"So you led me and Malone here?" he asked the man she'd called Michael.

"It was pretty easy, actually."

Yes, it was.

"I work here, at the museum," she said. "When you emailed and said you wanted to meet, I was glad. Those two guys who were shot have been following Michael for two weeks. If I'd told you that, you wouldn't have believed me. So I showed you. There are some other men who also come nearly every day and check on me, but they think I don't notice."

"I have people who can help."

Her eyes flashed with anger. "I don't want **people.** In fact, it's probably some of **your** people doing that other watching. FBI. Secret Service. Who knows? I want to deal with **you.**" She paused. "You and I"—the anger had dropped form her voice—"see eye-to-eye."

He was transfixed by her earnestness, along with the attractive, wounded look on her face. But he had to say, "People were shot in there. One of the guards was hurt bad."

"And I hate that, but I didn't start this."

"Actually, you did. Yelling at those two guys."

She was petite, full-bosomed, slender-waisted, and feisty. Her fiery blue eyes sparkled with an almost fiendish delight—commanding and confident. He was actually the tense one, his palms moist, and he desperately didn't want to show his anxiety. So he assumed a casual pose and weighed his options.

"Sam," she said, her voice softer. "I need to talk with you. Privately. Those guys have been on Michael's trail. Not mine. The others, the Americans who watch me, we just avoided them by getting out of there."

"Are they the ones who shot those two?"

She shrugged. "Who else?"

"I want to know who sent those two we followed here. Who do they work for?"

She stared back with an expression of undisguised boldness. He felt himself being appraised. Part of him was repelled, another part hoped she was at least somewhat impressed.

"Come with me, and I'll show you."

MALONE LISTENED AS STEPHANIE EXPLAINED ABOUT GreedWatch.

"It's run by the woman who started this melee. Meagan Morrison. She's an American, educated here, at the Sorbonne, in economics. She set you up sending the other young man—Foddrell. That's a pseudonym Morrison uses to operate the web-site."

He shook his head. "Played by an idiot who eats kidneys for lunch. Story of my life."

She chuckled. "I'm glad you fell for it. Made it easy for us to connect. Daniels told me that Sam has been in contact with GreedWatch for over a year now. He was told to stop, but he didn't listen. The Secret Service, through its Paris field office, has been monitoring the site, and Morrison herself, for the past few months. She's a sly one. The guy who led you here is set up as the official webmaster. For the past two weeks, he's been under separate sur-veillance, which the Service traced back to Eliza Larocque."

"None of which tells me why you're here and know all this."

"We think that website is privy to some inside info, and apparently so does Larocque."

"You didn't come here just to tell me about a website. What's really going on?"

"Peter Lyon."

He knew about the South African. One of the world's most wanted men. Into illicit arms, political assassination, terrorism, whatever the client wanted. Billed himself as a broker of chaos. When Malone retired two years ago, at least a dozen bombings and hundreds of deaths were linked to Lyon.

"He's still in business?" he asked.

"More so than ever. Ashby has been meeting with him. Larocque is planning something that involves Lyon. Men like him don't surface often. This may be the best chance we ever have to nail him."

"And Ashby holding out information on that possible opportunity isn't a problem?"

"I know. I wasn't running this operation. I would have never allowed him to call those shots."

"It's obvious he's playing both ends against the middle. They sure as hell can't let him continue to hold back."

"He won't. Not anymore. This is now a Billet operation. As of twelve hours ago, I'm in charge. So I want the SOB squeezed."

"Before or after Henrik kills him?"

"Preferably before. Ashby met with Lyon in Westminister just a few hours ago. We had parabolic mikes on the conversation."

"I see somebody was thinking. What about Lyon?"

"They let him be. No tail, and I agreed with

that. If he gets spooked, he'll go to ground. Right now he's comfortable coming to Ashby."

He smiled at Lyon's cockiness. "Glad to know everyone screws up."

"Some keys were passed from Ashby to Lyon and a two-day time frame mentioned, but not much else. I have a tape of the conversation." She paused. "Now, where is the merry Dane? I need to talk to him."

"He went to see Eliza Larocque."

He knew that revelation would grab her attention.

"Please tell me Thorvaldsen's not going to spook her, too?"

He noticed a flash of anger in her eyes. Stephanie liked to run her operations her way.

"He's going to get his revenge," he made clear.

"Not as long as I'm here. Ashby is all we have, at the moment, to learn what Lyon is doing."

"Not necessarily. By now, Henrik's wiggled his way into the Paris Club. He could actually prove helpful."

They sat in silence while Stephanie pondered the situation.

"Meagan Morrison" she said, "took Sam off at gunpoint. I watched on the museum's closed-circuit TV. I decided to allow that to happen for a reason."

"That boy's no field operative."

"He's trained Secret Service. I expect him to act the part."

"What's his story?"

She shook her head. "You're as bad as Thorvald-sen. He's a big boy. He can handle himself."

"That doesn't answer my question."

"Another sad and sorry tale. Found abandoned as an infant and was raised in an orphanage."

"No adoption?"

She shrugged. "I have no idea why not."

"Where?"

"New Zealand, of all places. He came to America when he was eighteen on a student visa and eventually became a citizen. Attended Columbia University, graduated top third in his class. Worked hard for a few years as an accountant, then earned his way into the Secret Service. All in all, a good kid."

"Except he doesn't listen to his superiors."

"Hell, you and me both fit into that category."

He grinned. "I assume Meagan Morrison is harmless."

"More or less. It's Thorvaldsen who's the prob-lem. Sam Collins left Washington a couple of weeks ago, just after being questioned again about his website. The Secret Service tracked him straight to Copenhagen. They decided to leave him alone, but when they learned Thorvaldsen had Ashby under close watch, they went to the president. That's when Daniels dragged me in. He thought something big was happening, and he was right. He decided, considering my close personal relationship with Thorvaldsen, I was the best person to handle it."

He smiled at her sarcasm. "Does Eliza Larocque know Meagan Morrison is harmless?"

The tension that rose from her silence charged the room.

Finally, she said, "I don't know."

"She didn't send those men for the fun of it. We'd better find out. That could be a problem for Morrison and Sam, considering what just happened here."

"I'll deal with Sam. I need you to concentrate on Graham Ashby."

"How in the world did I get myself in the middle of this mess?"

"You tell me."

But they both knew the answer, so he simply asked, "What do you want me to do?"

THIRTY-THREE

THORVALDSEN WAS DROPPED OFF AT THE HÔTEL
Ritz by the private car that had brought him north,
from the Loire Valley, into central Paris. Along the
way he'd worked the phone, planning his next
move.

He fled the late-afternoon cold and entered the
hotel's famous lobby, adorned with a collection of
museum-caliber antiques. He especially loved the
tale of when Hemingway liberated the Ritz in
1944. Armed with machine guns, the writer and a
group of Allied soldiers stormed the hotel and
searched every nook and cranny. After discovering
that the Nazis had all fled, they retired to the bar
and ordered a round of dry martinis. In commem-
oration, management christened the place Bar
Hemingway, which Thorvaldsen now entered, the
place still warmed by wooden walls, leather armchairs, and an atmosphere redolent of a different

era. Photos taken by Hemingway himself adorned the paneling and some delicate piano music provided a measure of privacy.

He spotted his man at one of the tables, walked over, and sat.

Dr. Joseph Murad taught at the Sorbonne—a renowned expert on Napoleonic Europe. Thorvaldsen had kept Murad on retainer for the past year, ever since learning of Ashby's passionate interest.

"Single-malt whiskey?" he asked in French, noticing Murad's glass.

"I wanted to see what a twenty-two-euro drink tasted like."

He smiled.

"And besides, you're buying."

"That I am."

His investigators in Britain had telephoned him in the car and told him what they'd learned from the listening devices located in Caroline Dodd's study. Since it meant little to him, Thorvaldsen had promptly, by phone, provided that intelligence to Murad. The scholar had called back half an hour later and suggested this face-to-face.

"Napoleon's last will and testament definitely mentioned that book," Murad said. "I've always thought it an odd reference. Napoleon had some sixteen hundred books with him on St. Helena. Yet he went out of his way to leave four hundred to Saint-Denis and specifically name **The Merovingian**

Kingdoms 450–751 A.D. It's the maxim of 'what's missing' proven."

He waited for the academician to explain.

"There's a theory in archaeology. 'What's missing points to what's important.' For example, if three statues have square bases and a fourth a round one, it's the fourth that's usually important. It's been shown over and over that this maxim is true, especially when studying artifacts of a ceremonial or religious nature. This reference in the will, to a specific book, could well be equally significant."

He listened as Murad explained about Merovingians.

Their leaders, starting with Merovech, from whom they took their name, first unified the Franks, then swept east and conquered their German cousins. Clovis, in the 5th century, eliminated the Romans, claimed Aquitania, and drove the Visigoths into Spain. He also converted to Christianity and declared a little town on the Seine, Paris, his capital. The region in and around Paris, which was strategically located, defensible, and fertile, came to be called Francia. The Merovingians themselves were a strange lot—practicing odd customs, growing their hair and beards long, and burying their dead with golden bees. The ruling family evolved into a dynasty, but then declined with astonishing rapidity. By the 7th century real power in the Merovingian world was held by court administrators, the "mayors of the palace," Carolingians, who eventually seized control and eradicated the Merovingians.

"Rich in fable, short on history," Murad said. "That's the tale of the Merovingians. Napoleon, though, was fascinated by them. The golden bees on his coronation cloak were taken from them. Merovingians also believed strongly in hoarding booty. They stole at will from conquered lands, and their king was responsible for distributing the wealth among his followers. As leader, he was expected to fully support himself with the fruits of his conquests. This concept of royal self-sufficiency lasted from the 5th to the 15th centuries. Napoleon resurrected it in the 19th century."

"Considering the treasure Ashby is after, you think this Merovingian book may be a signpost?"

"We can't know that until we see it."

"Does it still exist?"

Caroline Dodd had not told Ashby the location while they were in her study. Instead, she'd teased Ashby with the information, making him wait until after their lovemaking. Unfortunately, Thorvaldsen's investigators had never been able to successfully wire Ashby's bedchamber.

Murad smiled. "The book exists. I checked a little while ago. It's at the Hôtel des Invalides, where Napoleon is buried, on display. Part of what Saint-Denis left to the city of Sens in 1856. Those books were eventually given by Sens to the French government. Most of the volumes burned in the Tuileries Palace fire of 1871. What remained made their way to the Invalides after World War II. Luckily, this book survived."

"Can we get a look at it?"

"Not without answering a multitude of questions that I'm sure you don't want to answer. The French are obsessively protective of their national treasures. I asked a colleague of mine, who told me the book is on display in the museum portion of the Invalides. But that wing is currently closed, under renovation."

He understood the obstacles—cameras, gates, security officers. But he knew Graham Ashby wanted the book.

"I'll need you available," he told Murad.

The professor sipped his whiskey. "This is evolving into something quite extraordinary. Napoleon definitely wanted his son to have his private cache. He carefully acquired that wealth, just like a Merovingian king. But then, unlike a Merovingian and more like a modern-day despot, he hid it away in a place only he knew."

Thorvaldsen could understand how such a treasure would lure people.

"After Napoleon was safely entrapped on St. Helena, English newspapers alleged that he'd salted away a vast fortune." Murad grinned. "Being Napoleon, he retaliated from his exile with a list of what he called the 'real treasure' of his reign. The Louvre, the **greniers publics,** the Banque of France, Paris' water supply, city drains, and all his other manifold improvements. He was bold, I'll give him that."

That he was.

"Can you imagine what might be in that lost repository?" Murad asked. "There are thousands of art objects Napoleon plundered that have never been seen since. Not to mention state treasuries and private fortunes looted. The gold and silver could be immense. He took the secret of the cache's location to his grave, but trusted four hundred books, including one he named specifically, to his most loyal servant, Louis Etienne Saint-Denis, though it's doubtful Saint-Denis had any knowledge of the significance. He was simply doing what his emperor wanted. Once Napoleon's son died, in 1832, the books became meaningless."

"Not to Pozzo di Borgo," Thorvaldsen declared.

Murad had taught him all about Eliza Larocque's esteemed ancestor and his lifelong **vendetta** against Napoleon.

"But he never solved the riddle," Murad said.

No, di Borgo hadn't. But a distant heir was working hard to reverse that failure.

And Ashby was coming to Paris.

So Thorvaldsen knew what had to be done.

"I'll get the book."

SAM ACCOMPANIED MEAGAN OUT A SIDE ENTRANCE of the Cluny that opened to a graveled walk bordered by tall trees. A break in the wrought-iron fence and wall that encircled the museum opened onto the sidewalk where he and Malone had first approached. They crossed the street, found a Métro station, then rode a series of trains to the Place de la Republique.

"This is the Marais," Meagan told him as they stepped back out into the cold. She had shed her blue smock and wore a canvas barn coat, jeans, and boots. "It was once a marsh, but it became prime real estate from the 15th to the 18th centuries, then fell into disrepair. It's making a comeback."

He followed her down a busy prospect lined with high, elegant houses far deeper than they were wide. Pink brick, white stone, gray slate, and black iron balustrades dominated. Trendy boutiques, perfumeries, tearooms, and glitzy art galleries pulsed with the holiday's vitality.

"A lot of the mansions are being restored," she said. "This is becoming **the** place to live once again."

He was trying to gauge this woman. Part of her seemed ready to risk anything to make a point, but she'd shown a cool head in the museum.

More so than he'd exhibited.

Which bothered him.

"The Templar's Paris headquarters was once here. Rousseau himself found sanctuary in some of these houses. Victor Hugo lived nearby. This is where Louis XVI and Marie Antoinette were imprisoned."

He stopped. "Why are **we** here?"

She halted, the top of her head level with his Adam's apple. "You're a smart guy, Sam. I could tell that from your website and your emails. I communicate with a lot of people who think like we do, and most are looney tunes. You're not."

"What about you?"

She grinned. "That's for you to decide."

He knew the gun was still nestled at the small of her back, beneath her jacket, where she'd tucked it before they'd left the museum. He wondered what would happen if he walked away right now. She'd fired on those two men in the museum with practiced skill.

"Lead on," he said.

They turned another corner and passed more buildings with entrances flush to the sidewalk. Not nearly as many people now, and much quieter. Traffic lay well beyond the warren of close-packed buildings.

"We would say, 'Old as the hills,' " she noted. "Parisians say 'Old as the streets.' "

He'd already noticed how street names were announced on blue enameled markers set into corner buildings.

"The names all have meaning," she said. "They honor someone or something specific, tell where the street leads, identify its most prominent tenant or what goes on there. It's always something."

They stopped at a corner. A blue-and-white enameled plate read RUE L'ARAIGNÉE.

"Spider Street," he said, translating.

"So you do speak French."

"I can hold my own."

A look of triumph flashed across her face. "I'm sure you can. But you're up against something you know little about." She pointed down the narrow way. "See the fourth house."

He did. Redbrick façade with diagonals of varnished black, stone-mullioned windows, iron balustrades. A wide archway, crowned by a sculpted pediment, was barred by a gilded gate.

"Built in 1395," she said. "Rebuilt in 1660. In 1777 it housed a swarm of lawyers. They were a front for the laundering of Spanish and French money to American revolutionists. Those same lawyers also sold arms to the Continental army against bills for future delivery of tobacco and colonial wares. The victorious Americans welshed on delivery, though. Aren't we a grand people?"

He didn't answer her, sensing she was about to make a point.

"Those lawyers sued the new nation and finally got paid in 1835. Determined bastards, weren't they?"

He still stayed silent.

"In the 13th century, Lombardian moneylenders

settled around here somewhere. A rapacious bunch, they loaned money at outrageous rates and demanded high returns."

She motioned again at the fourth house and cocked an eye his way.

"That's where the Paris Club meets."

THIRTY-FOUR

6:10 PM

MALONE LIGHTLY KNOCKED ON THE PANELED DOOR. He'd left the museum and taken a taxi across town to the Ritz. He hoped Thorvaldsen had returned from the Loire Valley and was relieved when his friend answered the door.

"Were you involved in what happened at the Cluny?" Thorvaldsen asked as he entered the suite. "It was on television."

"That was me. I managed to get out before getting caught."

"Where's Sam?"

He recapped everything that happened, including Sam's abduction, crocheting the facts while explaining about Jimmy Foddrell being Meagan Morrison, omitting any reference to Stephanie's appearance. He'd decided to keep that close. If he was to have any chance of stopping Thorvaldsen, or at least delaying him, he could not mention Washington's involvement.

Interesting how the tables had turned. Usually it was Thorvaldsen who held back, sucking Malone in deeper.

"Is Sam okay?" Thorvaldsen asked.

He decided to lie. "I don't know. But there's little I can do about it at the moment."

He listened as Thorvaldsen recapped his visit with Eliza Larocque, ending with, "She's a despicable bitch. I had to sit there, so polite, thinking the whole time about Cai."

"She didn't kill him."

"I don't relieve her of responsibility so easily. Ashby works with her. There's a close connection, and that's enough for me."

His friend was tired, the fatigue evident in weary eyes.

"Cotton, Ashby is going after a book."

He listened to more information about Napoleon's will and **The Merovingian Kingdoms 450–751, A.D.,** a volume supposedly on display in the Invalides.

"I need to get that book first," Thorvaldsen said.

Vague ideas floated through his brain. Stephanie wanted Thorvaldsen halted. To do that, Malone would have to take control of the situation, but that was a tall order considering who was currently in the driver's seat.

"You want me to steal it?" he asked.

"It won't be easy. The Invalides was once a national armory, a fortress."

"That's not an answer."

"I do."

"I'll get the book. Then what are you going to do? Find the lost cache? Humiliate Ashby? Kill him? Feel better?"

"All of the above."

"When my son was taken last year, you were there for me. I needed you, and you came through. I'm here now. But we have to use our heads. You can't simply murder a man."

An expression of profound sympathy came to the older man's face. "I did last night."

"Doesn't that bother you?"

"Not in the least. Cabral killed my son. He deserved to die. Ashby is as responsible as Cabral. And, not that it matters, I may not have to murder him. Larocque can do it for me."

"And that makes it easier?"

Stephanie had already told him that Ashby was coming to Paris, and had assured his American handler that tomorrow he would provide full details of what was about to happen. Malone despised the Brit for what he'd done to Thorvaldsen—but he understood the value of the intelligence Ashby could offer and the significance of taking down a man like Peter Lyon.

"Henrik, you've got to let me handle this. I can do it. But it has to be my way."

"I can get the book myself."

"Then what the hell am I doing here?"

A stubborn smile found the older man's lips. "I hope you're here to help."

He kept his eyes on Thorvaldsen. "My way."

"I want Ashby, Cotton. Do you understand that?"

"I get it. But let's find out what's going on before you kill him. That's the way you talked yesterday. Can we stick with that?"

"I'm beginning not to care about what's happening, Cotton."

"Then why screw with Larocque and the Paris Club? Just kill Ashby and be done with it."

His friend went silent.

"What about Sam?" Thorvaldsen finally asked. "I'm worried."

"I'll deal with that, too." He recalled what Stephanie had said. "But he's a big boy, so he's going to have to take care of himself. At least for a while."

SAM ENTERED THE APARTMENT, IN A SECTION OF town Morrision had called Montparnasse, not far from the Cluny Museum and Luxembourg Palace, in a building that offered a charm of days long gone. Darkness had swallowed them on the walk from the Métro station.

"Lenin once lived a few blocks over," she said. "It's now a museum, though I can't imagine who'd want to visit."

"Not a fan of communism?" he asked.

"Hardly. Worse than capitalism, in a multitude of ways."

The apartment was a spacious studio on the sixth floor with a kitchenette, bath, and the look of a student tenant. Unframed prints and travel posters brightened the walls. Improvised board-and-block shelving sagged under the weight of textbooks and paperbacks. He noticed a pair of men's boots beside a chair and wadded jeans on the floor, far too large for Morrison.

"This isn't my place," she said, catching his interest. "A friend's."

She removed her coat, slid the gun free, and casually laid it on a table.

He noticed three computers and a blade server in one corner.

She pointed. "That's GreedWatch. I run the site from here, but I let everyone think Jimmy Foddrell does."

"People were hurt at the museum," he told her again. "This isn't a game."

"Sure it is, Sam. A big, terrible game. But it's not mine. It's theirs, and people getting hurt is not my fault."

"You started it when you screamed at those two men."

"You had to see reality."

He decided, instead of arguing again about the obvious, he'd do what the Secret Service had taught him—keep her talking. "Tell me about the Paris Club."

"Curious?"

"You know I am."

"I thought you would be. Like I said, you and I think alike."

He wasn't so sure about that, but kept his mouth shut.

"As far as I can tell, the club is made up of six people. All obscenely wealthy. Typical greedy bastards. Five billion in assets isn't enough. They want six or seven. I know someone who works for one of the members—"

He pointed. "Same guy who wears those boots?"

Her grin widened into a crescent. "No. Another guy."

"You're a busy girl."

"You have to be to survive in this world."

"Who the hell are you?"

"I'm the gal who's going to save you, Sam Collins."

"I don't need saving."

"I think you do. What are you even doing here? You told me awhile back that your superiors had forbidden you to keep your website and talk to me. Yet it's still there and you're here, wanting to find me. Is this an official visit?"

He couldn't tell her the truth. "You haven't told me a thing about the Paris Club."

She sat sideways across one of the vinyl chairs, legs draped over one arm, her spine pressed to the other. "Sam, Sam, Sam. You don't get it, do you? These people are planning things. They're expert financial manipulators, and they intend to actually do all the things we've talked about. They're going to screw with economies. Cheat markets. Devalue currencies. You remember how oil prices were affected last year. Speculators, who artificially drove the market mad with greed, did that. These people are no different."

"That tells me nothing."

A knock on the door startled them both, the first time he'd seen a crack in her icy veneer. Her gaze locked on the gun, lying on the table.

"Why don't you just answer it?" he asked.

Another knock. Light. Friendly.

"Do you think bad guys knock?" he asked, invoking his own measure of cool. "And this isn't even your place, right?"

She threw him a discerning glance. "You learn fast."

"I did graduate college."

She stood and walked to the door.

When she opened it a petite woman in a beige overcoat appeared outside. Perhaps early sixties, with dark hair streaked by waves of silver, and intense brown eyes. A Burberry scarf draped her neck. One hand displayed a leather case with a badge and photo identification.

The other held a Beretta.

"Ms. Morrison," the woman said. "I'm Stephanie Nelle. U.S. Justice Department."

THIRTY-FIVE

LOIRE VALLEY
7:00 P.M.

ELIZA PACED THE LONG GALLERY AND EAVES-
dropped on a winter wind that battered the
château's windows. Her mind replayed all of what
she'd told Ashby over the past year, disturbed by
the possibility that she might have made a huge
mistake.

History noted how Napoleon Bonaparte had
looted Europe, stealing untold amounts of precious metals, jewels, antiquities, paintings, books,
sculptures—anything and everything of value. In-
ventories of that plunder existed, but no one
could vouch for their accuracy. Pozzo di Borgo
learned that Napoleon had secreted away portions
of the spoils in a place only the emperor knew.
Rumors during Napoleon's time hinted at a fabu-
lous cache, but nothing ever pointed the way
toward it.

Twenty years her ancestor searched.

She stopped before one of the windows and gazed out into the blackness. Below her, the River Cher surged past. She basked in the room's warmth and savored its homely perfume. She wore a thick robe over her nightclothes and sought comfort within them both. Finding that lost cache would be her way of vindicating Pozzo di Borgo. Validating her heritage. Making her family relevant.

A **vendetta** complete.

The di Borgo clan was one of long standing in Corsica. Pozzo, as a boy, had been a close friend of Napoleon. But the legendary revolutionary Pasquale Paoli drove a wedge between them when he favored the di Borgos over the Bonapartes, whom he found too ambitious for his liking.

A formal feud commenced when Napoleon, as a young man, sought election as a lieutenant colonel in the Corsican volunteers, with a brother of Pozzo di Borgo as his opponent. The high-handed methods Napoleon and his party used to secure a favorable result roused di Borgo's enmity. The breach became complete after 1792, when the di Borgos sided with Corsican independence and the Bonapartes teamed with France. Pozzo di Borgo was eventually named chief of the Corsican civil government. When France, under Napoleon, occupied Corsica, di Borgo fled and, for the next twenty-three years, skillfully worked to destroy his sworn enemy.

For all the attempts to restrict, suppress, and muffle me, it will be difficult to make me disappear from the public memory completely. French historians will have to deal with the Empire and will have to give me my rightful due.

Napoleon's arrogance. Burned into her memory. Clearly, the tyrant had forgotten the hundreds of villages he'd burned to the ground from Russia, to Poland, to Prussia, to Italy, and across the plains and mountains of Iberia. Thousands of prisoners executed, hundreds of thousands of refugees rendered homeless, countless women raped by his Grande Armée. And what of the three million or so dead soldiers left rotting across Europe. Millions more wounded or permanently handicapped. And the destroyed political institutions of a few hundred states and principalities. Shattered economies. Fear and dread everywhere, France itself included. She agreed with what the great French writer Émile Zola observed at the end of the 19th century: **What utter madness to believe that one can prevent the truth of history from eventually being written.**

And the truth on Napoleon?

His destruction of the Germanic states, and the reunifying of them, along with Prussia, Bavaria, and Saxony, facilitated German nationalism, which led to their consolidation a hundred years later, which stimulated the rise of Bismarck, Hitler, and two world wars.

Give me my rightful due.

Oh, yes.

That she would.

Leather heels clicked off the floor from the gallery. She turned and watched as her chamberlain walked her way. She'd been expecting the call and knew who was on the other end of the line.

Her acolyte handed her the phone, then withdrew.

"Good evening, Graham," she said into the unit.

"I have excellent news," Ashby said. "The research and investigation have paid off. I think I may have found a link, one that could lead us directly to the cache."

Her attention was piqued.

"I require some assistance, though," he said.

She listened, her mind cautious and suspicious, but stimulated by the possibilities his enthusiasm promised.

Finally, he said, "Some information on the Invalides would be helpful. Do you have a way to make that happen?"

Her mind raced through the possibilities. "I do."

"I thought you might. I'm coming in the morning."

She soaked in more details, then said, "Well done, Graham."

"This could be it."

"And what of our Christmas presentation?" she asked.

"On schedule, as you requested."

That was exactly what she wanted to hear. "Then I shall see you on Monday."

"I wouldn't miss it."

They said their goodbyes.

Thorvaldsen had teased her with the possibility that Ashby may be a traitor. But the Brit was doing everything she'd recruited him to do, and doing it rather well.

Still, doubt clouded her thoughts.

Two days.

She'd have to juggle these unstable balls, at least until then.

SAM CAME TO HIS FEET AS STEPHANIE NELLE entered the apartment and Meagan closed the door. Ice-cold perspiration burst out on his forehead.

"This isn't the United States," Meagan said, her passions clearly aroused. "You have no jurisdiction here."

"That's true. But at the moment, the only thing stopping the Paris police from arresting you is me. Would you prefer I leave, allow them to take you, so we can talk while you're in custody?"

"What did I do?"

"Carrying a weapon, discharging a firearm within

the municipal limits, inciting a riot, destruction of state property, kidnapping, assault. I leave anything out?"

Meagan shook her head. "You're all alike."

Stephanie smiled. "I'll take that as a compliment." She faced Sam. "Needless to say, you're in a world of trouble. But I understand part of the problem. I know Henrik Thorvaldsen. I assume he's at least partly to blame for why you're here."

He didn't know this woman, so he wasn't about to sell out the only person who'd treated him with a measure of respect. "What do you want?"

"I need you both to cooperate. If you do, Ms. Morrison, you'll stay out of jail. And you, Mr. Collins, you might still have a career."

He didn't like her condescending attitude. "What if I don't want a career?"

She threw him a look he'd seen from his superiors—people who enforced petty rules and imposed time-honored barriers that made it next to impossible for anyone to leap ahead.

"I thought you wanted to be a field agent. That's what the Secret Service told me. I'm simply offering you the chance."

"What is it you want me to do?" he asked.

"That all depends on Ms. Morrison here." The older woman stared at Meagan. "Whether you believe it or not, I'm here to help. So tell me, besides spouting off on your website about world conspiracies that may or may not exist, what tangible evidence do you have that I might find interesting?"

"Cocky bitch, aren't you?"

"You have no idea."

Meagan smiled. "You remind me of my mother. She was tough as nails, too."

"That just means I'm old. You're not endearing yourself to me."

"You're still the one holding a gun."

Stephanie stepped around them and approached the kitchen table, where Meagan's gun lay. She lifted the weapon. "Two men died at the Cluny. Another is in the hospital."

"The guard?" Sam asked.

Stephanie nodded. "He'll make it."

He was glad to hear that.

"How about you, Ms. Morrison? Glad to hear it, too?"

"It's not my problem," Meagan said.

"You started it."

"No. I exposed it."

"Do you have any idea who the two dead men worked for?"

Meagan nodded. "The Paris Club."

"That's not exactly correct. Actually, Eliza Larocque employed them to follow your decoy."

"You're a little behind the curve."

"So tell me something I don't know."

"All right, smart lady. How about this? I know what's going to happen in two days."

THORVALDSEN SAT ALONE IN HIS SUITE AT THE
Ritz, his head resting against the back of a chair.
Malone was gone, having assured him that tomorrow he'd retrieve the book from the Invalides. He
had confidence in his friend, more so at the moment than in himself.

He nursed a brandy, sipping from a crystal snifter,
trying to calm his nerves. Thankfully, all of the ban-
tering spirits clamoring within him had retreated for
the night. He'd been in a lot of fights, but this one
was different—beyond personal, clearly obsessive—
and that frightened him. He may come in contact
with Graham Ashby as soon as tomorrow, and he
knew that moment would be difficult. He must appear cordial, shaking the hand of the man who'd
murdered his son, extending every courtesy. Not a
hint could be revealed until the right moment.

He sipped more alcohol.

Cai's funeral flashed through his mind.

The casket had been closed because of the ir-
reparable damage the bullets had done, but he'd
seen what was left of his son's face. He'd insisted.
He needed that horrific image burned into his
memory because he knew that he'd never rest until
that death was fully explained.

Now, after two years, he knew the truth.

And he was within hours of revenge.

He'd lied to Malone. Even if he managed to incite Eliza Larocque into moving on Ashby, he'd still kill the bastard himself.

No one else would do it.

Just him.

Same as last night when he'd stopped Jesper and shot Amando Cabral and his cohort. What was he becoming? A murderer? No. An avenger. But was there really a difference?

He held his glass against the light and admired the alcohol's rich color. He savored another swallow of brandy, longer this time, more satisfying.

He closed his eyes.

Scattered recollections flickered through his mind, faded a moment, then reappeared. Each came in a smooth, silent process, like shifting images from a projector.

His lips quivered.

Memories he'd nearly forgotten—from a life he hadn't known for many years—swam into view, blurred, then disappeared.

He'd buried Cai on the estate, in the family cemetery, beside Lisette, among other Thorvaldsens who'd rested there for centuries, his son wearing a simple gray suit and a yellow rose. Cai had loved yellow roses, as had Lisette.

He remembered the peculiar smell from within the casket—a little acidic, a little dank—the smell of death.

His loneliness returned in a fresh surge.

He emptied the snifter of the remaining brandy.

A rush of sadness broke over him with an intolerable force.

No more doubts nagged him.

Yes, he'd kill Graham Ashby himself.

THIRTY-SIX

PARIS
MONDAY, DECEMBER 24
11:00 AM

MALONE ENTERED THE CHURCH OF THE DOME, attached like a stray appendage to the south end of the imposing Hôtel des Invalides. The baroque edifice, with a façade of Doric columns and a single pediment, was capped by an imposing gilded dome—the second tallest structure in Paris—crowned by a lantern and spire. Originally a royal place of worship, erected by Louis XIV to extol the glory of the French monarchy, it had been converted by Napoleon into a warriors' tomb. Three of the greatest names in French military history—Turene, Vaubon, Foch—rested here. In 1861 Napoleon himself was buried beneath the dome, and eventually his two brothers and son joined him.

Christmas Eve had not diminished the crowds.

The interior, though only open for the past hour, was packed with people. Though the place was no longer used for religious services, a placard reminded everyone to remove their hats and speak in a low voice.

He'd stayed last night at the Ritz, in a room Thorvaldsen had arranged, groping for sleep, but finding only disturbing thoughts. He was worried about Sam, but trusted that Stephanie had the situation under control. He was more concerned about Thorvaldsen. **Vendettas** could be expensive, in more ways than one—something he'd learned from personal experience. He still wasn't sure how to rein in Thorvaldsen, but he knew that it had to be done.

And fast.

He ambled toward a waist-high marble balustrade and glanced upward into the towering dome. Images of the Evangelists, the kings of France, and Apostles stared back. Glancing down, beneath the dome, past the banister, he studied Napoleon's sarcophagus.

He knew the particulars. Seven coffins held the imperial remains, one inside the other, two of lead, the rest in mahogany, iron, ebony, oak, and—the visible one—red porphyry, the stuff of Roman sepulchres. Nearly twelve feet long and six feet high, shaped like an ark adorned with laurel wreaths, it rested on an emerald granite base. Twelve colossal figures of victory, and the names of Napoleon's chief battles, etched into the floor, surrounded the tomb.

He stared across the busy church at Graham Ashby.

The Brit matched the description Stephanie had provided and stood on the far side, near the circular railing.

Thorvaldsen had told him an hour ago that his operatives had tracked Ashby from London to Paris to here. Beside him stood an attractive woman with long flowing hair. She brought to mind another blonde who'd consumed his attention the previous two weeks. One of those mistakes in judgment that had nearly cost him his life.

The blonde stood with her hips touching the railing, her back arched, pointing upward to the impressive entablature that circled the church, seemingly explaining something that Ashby found interesting. She had to be Caroline Dodd. Thorvaldsen had briefed him on her. Ashby's mistress, but also the holder of degrees in medieval history and literature. Her being here signified that Ashby believed there was something significant to find.

The level of noise surrounding him rose and he turned. A sea of people flooded in through the main doors. He watched as each new visitor paid the admission.

He glanced around and admired the collage of marble rising around him, the dome held aloft by majestic Corinthian columns. Symbols of the monarchy sprang from the sculpted décor, reminding the visitor that this was once a church of kings, now the home of an emperor.

"Napoleon died in 1821 on St. Helena," he heard one of the tour guides explain in German to a nearby group. "The British buried him there, with little honor, in a quiet hollow. But in his last will Napoleon wrote that he wanted his ashes **to rest by the banks of the Seine in the midst of the French people whom I loved so dearly.** So in 1840, King Louis Philippe decided to honor that wish and bring the emperor home. It was a move meant to both please the public and reconcile the French with their history. By then, Napoleon had evolved into a legend. So on December 15, 1840, in a grandiose ceremony, the king welcomed the remains of the emperor to the Invalides. Twenty years were needed, though, to modify this church and dig the crypt you see below."

He stepped away from the marble railing as the Germans pressed close and gazed down at the imposing sarcophagus. More groups in tight phalanxes swept across the floor. He noticed that another man had joined Ashby. Medium height. Blank face. Sparse gray hair. He wore an overcoat that sheathed a thin frame.

Guildhall.

Thorvaldsen had briefed him on this man as well.

The three turned from the railing to leave.

Improvise.

That's what he'd told Sam agents did.

He shook his head.

Yeah, right.

ASHBY EXITED THE CHURCH OF THE DOME AND rounded the exterior, finding a long arcade, lined with cannon, that led into the Invalides. The massive complex encompassed two churches, a Court of Honor, a military museum, garden, and an elegant esplanade that stretched from the north façade to the Seine, nearly a kilometer away. Founded in 1670 by Louis XIV to house and care for invalid soldiers, the connected multistory buildings were masterpieces of French classicism.

Similar to Westminister, history happened here. He imagined July 14, 1789, when a mob overwhelmed the posted sentries and raided the underground rifle house, confiscating weapons used later that day to storm the Bastille and begin the French Revolution. Seven thousand military veterans had once lived here, and now it was the haunt of tourists.

"Do we have a way to get inside the museum?" Caroline asked.

He'd spoken with Eliza Larocque three more

times since last night. Thankfully, she'd managed to obtain a great deal of relevant information.

"I don't think it is going to be a problem."

They entered the Court of Honor, a cobbled expanse enclosed on four sides with long two-story galleries. Maybe a hundred meters by sixty. A bronze statue of Napoleon guarded the massive courtyard, perched above the pedimented entrance to the Soldiers' Church. He knew that here was the spot where de Gaulle had kissed Churchill in thanks after World War II.

He pointed left at one of the stern classical façades, far more impressive than attractive.

"Former refectories. Where the pensioners took their meals. The army museum starts in there." He motioned right at another refectory. "And ends there. Our destination."

Scaffolding sheathed the left-hand building. Larocque had told him that half of the museum was undergoing a modernization. Mainly the historical exhibits, two entire floors closed until next spring. The work included exterior renovations and some extensive remodeling of the main entrance.

But not today. Christmas Eve.

A work holiday.

MALONE MARCHED DOWN ONE OF THE INVALIDES' long arcades, passing a closed wooden door every ten feet, flanked by cannon standing upright at attention. He made his way from the south to the east arcade, passing the Soliders' Church, turning a corner and hustling toward a temporary entrance into the east building. Ashby and his contingent stood on the opposite side of the Court of Honor, facing the closed portion of the east museum, which housed historical objects from the 17th and 18th centuries, along with artifacts dating from Louis XIV until Napoleon.

A gray-coated attendant with a slow pace and a supervisory eye staffed the makeshift entry that led to a stairway up to the third floor, where the relief map museum remained open, along with a bookstore.

He climbed the stairs, gripping a thick wooden banister.

On the second floor the elevator doors were blocked by two planks nailed together in an X. Work pallets held more disassembled scaffolding. White metal doors, clearly temporary, were shut and a sign taped to them read INTERDIT AU PUBLIC. ACCESS DENIED. Another sign affixed to the wall identified that past the closed doors lay SALLES NAPOLÉON 1ER. ROOMS OF NAPOLEON 1ST.

He approached and yanked the handle for the metal doors.

They opened.

No need to lock them, he'd been told, since the building itself was sealed each night and there was little of value in the galleries beyond.

He stepped into the dim space, drained of noise, allowed the door to close behind him, and hoped he wasn't going to regret the next few minutes.

THIRTY-SEVEN

NAPOLEON LAY PRONE IN THE BED AND STARED
into the fireplace. The tapers burned bright,
shedding a red luster on his face, and he
allowed the heat and silence to lull him into
sleep.

"Old seer. Do you at last come for me?" he
asked out loud, in a tender voice.

A joyous expression spread over Napoleon's
countenance, which immediately twisted into
a show of anger. "No," he yelled, "you are
mistaken. My luck does not resemble the
changing seasons. I am not yet in autumn.
Winter does not approach. What? You say my
family will leave and betray me? That can't be.
I have lavished kindness on them—" He
paused, and his face assumed the expression
of an attentive listener. "Ah, but that is too
much. Not possible. All Europe is unable to
overthrow me. My name is more powerful
than fate."

Awakened by the loud sound of his own voice, Napoleon opened his eyes and gazed around the room. His trembling hand found his moist forehead.

"What a terrible dream," he said to himself.

Saint-Denis drew close. Good and faithful, always at his side, sleeping on the floor beside the cot. Ready to listen.

"I am here, sire."

Napoleon found Saint-Denis' hand.

"Long ago, while in Egypt, a sorcerer spoke to me in the pyramid," Napoleon said. "He prophesied my ruin, cautioned me against my relatives and the ingratitude of my generals."

Absorbed by his reflections, in a voice made rough by fading sleep, he seemed to need to speak.

"He told me I would have two wives. The first would be empress and not death, but a woman would hurl her from the throne. The second wife would bear me a son, but all my misfortune would nevertheless begin with her. I would cease to be prosperous and powerful. All my hopes would be disappointed. I would be forcibly expelled and cast upon a foreign soil, hemmed in by mountains and the sea."

Napoleon gazed up from the bed with a look of undisguised fear.

"I had that sorcerer shot," he said. "I thought him a fool, and I never listen to fools."

Thorvaldsen listened as Eliza Larocque explained what her family had long known about Napoleon.

"Pozzo di Borgo thoroughly researched all that happened on St. Helena," she said. "What I just described occurred about two months before Napoleon died."

He listened with a false attentiveness.

"Napoleon was a superstitious man," she said. "A great believer in fate, but never one to bow to its inevitability. He liked to hear what he wanted to hear."

They sat in a private room at Le Grand Véfour, overlooking the Palais Royal gardens. The menu proudly proclaimed that the restaurant dated back to 1784, and guests then and now dined amid 18th-century gilded décor and delicate hand-painted panels. Not a place Thorvaldsen usually frequented, but Larocque had called earlier, suggested lunch, and selected the location.

"Reality is clear, though," she said. "Everything that Egyptian sorcerer predicted came to pass. Josephine did become empress and Napoleon divorced her because she could not produce an heir."

"I thought it was because she was unfaithful."

"That she was, but so was he. Marie Louise, the eighteen-year-old archduchess of Austria, eventually captured his imagination, so he married her. She gave him the son he wanted."

"The way of royalty, at the time," he mused.

"I think Napoleon would have taken offense at being compared to royalty."

Now he chuckled. "Then he was quite the fool. He was nothing but royalty."

"Just as predicted, it was after his second marriage, in 1809, that Napoleon's luck changed. The failed Russian campaign in 1812, where his retreating army was decimated. The 1813 coalition brought England, Prussia, Russia, and Austria against him. His defeats in Spain and at Leipzig, then the German collapse and the loss of Holland. Paris fell in 1814, and he abdicated. They sent him to Elba, but he escaped and tried to retake Paris from Louis XVIII. But his Waterloo finally came on June 18, 1815, and it was over. Off to St. Helena to die."

"You truly hate the man, don't you?"

"What galls me is we'll never know the man. He spent the five years of his exile on St. Helena burnishing his image, writing an autobiography that ended up being more fiction than fact, tailoring history to his advantage. In truth, he was a husband who dearly loved his wife, but quickly divorced her when she failed to produce an heir. A general who professed great love for his soldiers, yet sacrificed them by the hundreds of thousands. Supposedly fearless, he repeatedly abandoned his men when expedient. A leader who wanted nothing more than to strengthen France, yet kept the nation constantly embroiled in war. I think it's obvious why I detest him."

He thought a little aggravation might be good. "Did you know that Napoleon and Josephine dined here? I'm told this room remains much the same as it was in the early 19th century."

She smiled. "I was aware of that. Interesting, though, that you know such information."

"Did Napoleon really have that sorcerer killed in Egypt?"

"He ordered one of his **savants,** Monge, to do it."

"Do you adhere to the theory that Napoleon was poisoned?" He knew that, supposedly, arsenic had been slowly administered in his food and drink, enough to eventually kill him. Modern tests run of strands of hair that survived confirmed high levels of arsenic.

She laughed. "The British had no reason to kill him. In fact, it was quite the opposite. They wanted him alive."

Their entrées arrived. His was a pan-fried red mullet in oil and tomatoes, hers a young chicken in wine sauce, sprinkled with cheese. They both enjoyed a glass of merlot.

"Do you know the story of when they exhumed Napoleon in 1840, to return him to France?" she asked.

He shook his head.

"It's illustrative of why the British would never have poisoned him."

MALONE THREADED HIS WAY THROUGH THE deserted gallery. No lights burned, and the illumination provided by sunlight was diffused by plastic sheets that protected the windows. The air was warm and laced with the pall of fresh paint. Many of the display cases and exhibits were draped in crusty drop cloths. Ladders dotted the walls. More scaffolding rose at the far end. A section of the hardwood flooring had been removed, and messy repairs were being made to the stone subsurface.

He noticed no cameras, no sensors. He passed uniforms, armor, swords, daggers, harnesses, pistols, and rifles, all displayed in silk-lined cases. A steady and intentional procession of technology, each generation learning how to kill the next faster. Nothing at all suggested the horror of war. Instead, only its glory seemed emphasized.

He stepped around another gash in the floor and kept walking down the long gallery, his rubber soles not making a sound.

Behind him he heard the metal doors being tested.

ASHBY STOOD ON THE SECOND-FLOOR LANDING and watched as Mr. Guildhall pressed on the doors that led into the Napoleon galleries.

Something blocked them.

"I thought they were open," Caroline whispered.

That was exactly what Larocque had reported. Anything of value had been removed weeks ago. All that remained were minor historical artifacts, left inside since outside storage was limited. The contractor performing the remodeling had agreed to work around the exhibits, required to purchase liability insurance to guarantee their safety.

Yet something blocked the doors.

He did not want to attract the attention of the woman below, or employees one floor above in the relief map museum.

"Force them," he said. "But quietly."

THE FRENCH FRIGATE LA BELLE POULE arrived at St. Helena in October 1840 with a contingent led by Prince de Joinville, the third son of King Louis Philippe. The British governor, Middlemore, sent his son to greet the ship and Royal Naval shore batteries fired a twenty-one-gun salute in their honor. On October 15, twenty-five years to the day since Napoleon first arrived on St. Helena, the task of exhuming the emperor's body began. The French wanted the process managed by their sailors, but the British insisted that the job be done by their people. Local workmen and British soldiers toiled through the night in a pouring rain. Nineteen years had passed since Napoleon's coffin had been lowered into the earth, sealed with bricks and cement, and reversing that process proved challenging. Freeing the stones one by one, puncturing layers of masonry reinforced with metal bands, forcing off the four lids to finally confront the sight of the dead emperor had taken effort.

A number of people who'd lived with Napoleon on St. Helena had returned to witness the exhumation. General Gourgaud. General Bertrand. Pierron, the pastry cook. Archambault, the groom. Noverraz, the third valet. Marchand, and Saint-Denis, who'd never left the emperor's side.

The body of Napoleon was wrapped in fragments of white satin that had fallen from the coffin's lid. His black riding boots had split open to reveal pasty white toes. The legs remained covered in white britches, the hat still resting beside him where it had been placed years before. The silver dish containing his heart lay between the thighs. His hands—white, hard, and perfect—showed long nails. Three teeth were visible where the lip had drawn back, the face gray from the stubble of a beard, the eyelids firmly closed. The body was in remarkable condition, as if he were sleeping rather than decomposing.

All of the objects that had been included to keep him company were still there, crowded around his satin bed. A collection of French and Italian coins minted with his impassive face, a silver sauceboat, a plate, knives, forks, and spoons engraved with the imperial arms, a silver flask containing water from the Vale of Geranium, a cloak, a sword, a loaf of bread, and a bottle of water.

Everyone removed their hats and a French priest sprinkled holy water, reciting the words from Psalm 130. "Out of the depths have I cried unto thee, O Lord."

The British doctor wanted to examine the body in the name of science, but General Gourgaud, heavyset, red-faced with a gray beard, objected. "You shall not. Our emperor has suffered enough indignities."

Everyone there knew that London and Paris had agreed to this exhumation as a way to reconcile differences between the two nations. After all, as the French ambassador to England had made clear, "I do not know any honorable motive for refusal, as England cannot tell the world that she wishes to keep a corpse prisoner."

The British governor, Middlemore, stepped forward. "We have the right to examine the body."

"For what reason?" Marchand asked. "What purpose? The British were there when the coffin was sealed, the body subjected to autopsy by your doctors, though the emperor specifically left instructions for that not to occur."

Marchand himself had been there that day, and it was clear from his bitterness that he hadn't forgotten the violation.

Middlemore lifted his hands in mock surrender. "Very well. Would you object to an outer inspection? After all, the body is, would you not say, in remarkable condition for being entombed for so long. That demands some investigation."

Gourgaud relented, and the others agreed.

So the doctor felt the legs, the belly, the hands, an eyelid, then the chest.

"Napoleon was then sealed in his four coffins of wood and metal, the key to the sarcophagus turned, and everything made ready to return him to Paris," Eliza said.

"What was the doctor really after?" Thorvaldsen asked.

"Something the British had tried, in vain, to learn while Napoleon was their prisoner. The location of the lost cache."

"They thought it was in the grave?"

"They didn't know. A lot of odd items were placed in that coffin. Someone thought maybe the answer lay there. It's believed that was one of the reasons why the Brits agreed to the exhumation—to have another look."

"And did they find anything?"

She sipped her wine. "Nothing."

She watched as her words took root.

"They didn't look in the right place, did they?" he asked.

She was starting to like this Dane. "Not even close."

"And you, Madame Larocque, have you discovered the right place?"

"That, Herre Thorvaldsen, is a question that may well be answered before this day is completed."

THIRTY-EIGHT

MALONE FOUND THE NAPOLEONIC EXHIBITS AND examined relics of both the emperor's triumph and his fall. He saw the bullet that wounded the general at Ratisbon, his telescope, maps, pistols, a walking stick, dressing gown, even his death mask. One display depicted the room on St. Helena where Napoleon died, complete with folding cot and canopy.

A scraping sound echoed through the hall.

The metal doors a hundred feet behind him were being forced.

He'd settled one of the construction pallets against the doors, knowing that he would soon have company. He'd watched as Ashby had left the church and calmly walked into the Invalides. While Ashby and his entourage stopped to admire the Court of Honor, he'd hurried inside. He was assuming that Ashby was privy to the same sort of inside information Stephanie had provided him. He'd called her last night, after leaving Thorvaldsen, and formulated a plan that accommodated her needs while not compromising his friend.

A juggling act. But not impossible.

The pallet guarding the metal doors scraped louder across the floor.

He turned and spied light seeping into the dim hall.

Three shadows broke the illumination.

Before him, resting inside a partially opened glass case were some silver cutlery, a cup used by Napoleon at Waterloo, a tea box from St. Helena, and two books. A small placard informed the public that the books were from Napoleon's personal library on St. Helena, part of the 1,600 he'd maintained. One was **Memoirs and Correspondence of Joséphine** read, the placard informed, by Napoleon in 1821, shortly before he died. He'd supposedly questioned its veracity, upset by its content. The other was a small, leather-bound volume, opened to pages near its center that another placard identified as **The Merovingian Kingdoms 450–751 A.D.,** from the same personal library, though this book had the distinction of being specially identified in the emperor's last will and testament.

A click of urgent heels on hard floor echoed through the hall.

ASHBY LOVED THE CHASE.

He was always amused by books and movies that depicted treasure hunters as swashbucklers. In reality, most of the time was spent poring through old writings, whether they be books, wills, correspondence, personal notes, private diaries, or public records. Bits and pieces, here and there. Never some singular piece of proof that solved the puzzle in one quick swoop. Clues were generally either barely existent or undecipherable, and there were far more disappointments than successes.

This chase was a perfect example.

Yet they may actually be on to something this time.

Hard to say for sure until they examined **The Merovingian Kingdoms 450–751 A.D.**, which should be waiting for them a few meters ahead.

Eliza Larocque had advised him that today would be a perfect opportunity to sneak into this part of the museum. No construction crews should be on the job. Likewise, the Invalides staff would be anxious to be done with the day and go home for Christmas. Tomorrow was one of the few days the museum was closed.

Mr. Guildhall led the way through the cluttered gallery.

The tepid air smelled of paint and turpentine, further evidence of the obvious ongoing renovations.

He needed to leave Paris as soon as this errand was completed. The Americans would be waiting in London, anxious for a report. Which he would finally provide. No reason to delay any longer. Tomorrow would prove a most interesting day—a Christmas he'd certainly remember.

Mr. Guildhall stopped and Ashby caught sight of what his minion had already seen.

In the glass case where the assorted Napoleonic relics and books should be waiting, he saw one volume. But the second book was gone. Only a small card, angled on the wooden easel, remained.

A moment of silence seemed like an hour.

He quelled his dismay, stepped close, and read what was written on the card.

Lord Ashby, if you're a good boy, we'll give you the book.

"What does that mean?" Caroline asked.

"I assume it's Eliza Larocque's way of keeping me in line."

He smiled at the fervor of hope in his lie.

"It says **we'll**."

"She must mean the club."

"She gave you all the other information she had. She provided the intel on this place." The words were more question than statement.

"She's cautious. Perhaps she doesn't want us to have it all. Not just yet, anyway."

"You shouldn't have called her."

He caught the next question in her eyes and said, "We go back to England."

They retreated from the gallery and his mind clicked through the possibilities. Caroline knew nothing of his secret collaboration with Washington, which was why he'd blamed the missing book on Larocque and the Paris Club.

But the truth frightened him even more.

The Americans knew his business.

MALONE WATCHED FROM THE FAR END OF THE HALL as Ashby and company fled the gallery. He grinned at Ashby's dilemma, noticing how he'd deceived Caroline Dodd. He then departed through a rear stairway and escaped the Invalides out its north façade. He flagged a taxi, crossed the Seine, and found Le Grand Véfour.

He entered the restaurant and glanced around at a pleasant room, entirely French, with resplendent walls sheathed in gilt-edged mirrors. He scanned the clothed tables and caught sight of Thorvaldsen sitting with a handsome-looking woman, dressed in a gray business suit, her back to him.

He casually displayed the book and smiled.

THORVALDSEN NOW KNEW THAT THE BALANCE OF power had shifted. He was in total control, and neither Ashby nor Eliza Larocque realized it.

Not yet anyway.

So he placed one knee over the other, leaned back in his chair, and returned his attention to his hostess, confident that soon all his debts would be paid.

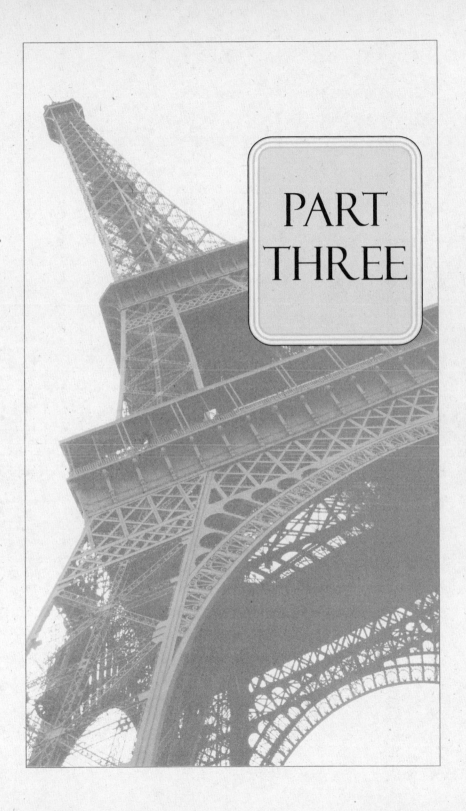

PART
THREE

THIRTY-NINE

12:15 PM

SAM FOLLOWED MEAGAN MORRISON AND Stephanie Nelle as they each paid admission to the Eiffel Tower. The lines at the other two entrances, with elevators to the first and second platforms, were massive, at least a two-hour wait. But the one here at the south pylon was much shorter, since the only way to the first platform was to climb 347 steps.

"We don't have time to wait in line," Stephanie Nelle had said.

Sam had spent the night at a Left Bank hotel in one room, Meagan Morrison in another, two Secret Service agents guarding their doors. Stephanie had listened to the information Meagan had to offer, then she'd made a few phone calls. After apparently confirming at least some of what she'd heard, she'd insisted on protective custody.

"Do field agents wear the same clothes all the

time?" he asked Stephanie as they climbed the stairs. He was going on three days with his current ensemble.

"Few tuxedos or designer digs," she said. "You make do, and get the job done."

They passed a riser marked 134. Four immense, lattice-girder piers, the space within them larger than a football field, supported the tower's first platform—189 feet high, as a sign at the bottom of the stairs had informed. The pylons tapered upward to a second platform, at 379 feet, then continued rising to the top level observation deck, at 905 feet. The tallest structure in Paris—a gangly network of exposed puddle iron, riveted together, painted a brownish gray, the image of which had evolved into one of the most recognizable in the world.

Meagan was handling the climb with easy effort, but his own calves ached. She'd said little last evening, after they were taken to the hotel. But he'd made the right choice going with her from the museum. Now he was working with the head of the Magellan Billet.

Ten more minutes of climbing and they tackled the final flight.

The first-floor platform was busy with visitors swarming through a souvenir shop, post office, exhibit hall, snack bar, and restaurant. Elevators on the far side led down to ground level. Another 330 or so steps right-angled upward to the second level. The first-level platform wound around an open center that offered a view down to the plaza.

Stephanie rested against the iron railing. He and Meagan joined her. Together they stared across at a glass wall and doors, above which lettering identified LA SALLE GUSTAV EIFFEL.

"The Paris Club meets in that room tomorrow," Meagan told Stephanie in a whisper.

"And how do you **really** know that?"

They'd had this same conversation yesterday. Obviously Stephanie was practicing the old adage, "Ask the same question enough and see if you get the same answer."

"Look, Ms. Justice Department," Meagan said. "I've played along with your show of authority. I've even tried to be helpful. But if you still don't believe me, then what are we doing here?"

Stephanie did not respond to the challenge. Instead, they continued to lean against the railing and kept their gazes focused on the far side.

"I know they will be here tomorrow," Meagan finally said. "It's a big to-do. The whole club coming together on Christmas."

"Odd time for a meeting," Sam said.

"Christmas here is a strange holiday. I learned that a long time ago. The French aren't all that big on yuletide cheer. Most leave town for the day, and the rest go to restaurants. They all like to eat this cake called a **bûche de Noël.** Looks like a log and tastes like wood with butter frosting on it. So it doesn't surprise me the club's meeting on Christmas."

"The Eiffel Tower is open?" Sam asked.

Meagan nodded. "At one PM."

"Tell me again what you know," Stephanie said.

Meagan appeared irritated, but complied. "Larocque rented the Gustav Eiffel Room, right over there. The shindig starts at eleven AM and goes to four PM. She's even catered lunch. I guess she thinks two hundred feet in the air gives her and her accomplices some privacy."

"Any security?" Stephanie asked.

"Now, how would I know that? But I'm betting you do."

Stephanie seemed to relish the crisp bite of Meagan's pronouncement. "The city owns the tower, but the Société Nouvelle d'Exploitation de la Tour Eiffel operates the site. They have a private firm that provides security, along with the Paris police and French military."

Sam had noticed a police station beneath the south tower entrance, along with some serious-looking men, dressed in combat fatigues, toting automatic rifles.

"I checked," Stephanie said. "There is a group scheduled in that room tomorrow, for that time frame, which contracted for some additional security. The meeting hall itself will be closed off. The tower is closed until one PM. After that, there should be as many people visiting then as today, which is a considerable number."

"Like I said," Meagan made clear. "It's the first time the club has ventured out of its house in the Marais. The one I showed Sam yesterday."

"And you think that's significant?" Stephanie asked Meagan.

"Has to be. This club is trouble."

MALONE LEFT LE GRAND VÉFOUR AND GRABBED A taxi outside the restaurant for a short hop south to the Louvre. He paid the driver and crossed beneath a grand archway into the Cour Napoleon, immediately spotting the signature geometric glass pyramid that served as a skylight for the museum's entrance below. The classical façade of the Louvre engulfed the massive parade ground on three sides, while the Arc du Carousel, a pastiche of a Roman arch with rose marble columns, stood guard at the open east end.

Seven triangular granite basins surrounded the glass pyramid. On the edge of one sat a slender man with thin features and thick sandy hair touched by gray at the temples. He wore a dark wool coat and black gloves. Though the afternoon air had warmed from the morning chill, Malone estimated it was maybe the high 40s at the most. Thorvaldsen had told him the man would be waiting here, once he obtained the book. So he walked over and sat on the cold edge.

"You must be Cotton Malone," Professor Murad said in English.

Taking a cue from Jimmy Foddrell, he'd been carrying the book out in the open, so he handed it over. "Fresh from the Invalides."

"Was it easy to steal?"

"Just sitting there waiting, like I was told it would be."

He watched as Murad thumbed through the brittle pages. He'd already studied them during the two cab rides and knew where the perusing would stop. The first halt came halfway through, where the manuscript divided itself into two parts. On a blank page, which acted as a divider, was written:

CXXXV II CXLII LII LXIII XVII
II VIII IV VIII IX II

He watched as the professor's forehead crinkled and a frown signaled reluctance. "I didn't expect that."

Malone blew warmth into his ungloved hands and watched the frenetic hustle and bustle in the courtyard as hundreds of tourists came and went from the Louvre.

"Care to explain?"

"It's a Moor's Knot. A code Napoleon was known to use. These Roman numerals refer to a specific text. Page and line, since there are only two sets. We would need to know the text he used in order to re-veal the specific words that form a message. But there's no third line of numerals. The ones that would identify the right word on the right line."

"How did I know this wasn't going to be easy?"

Murad grinned. "Nothing ever was with Napoleon. He loved drama. This museum is a perfect example. He exacted tributes from every place he conquered and brought them here, making this, at the time, the world's richest collection."

"Unfortunately, the Allies took it all back—at least what was here to find—after 1815."

"You know your history, Mr. Malone."

"I try. And it's Cotton. Please."

"Such an unusual name. How did you acquire it?"

"Like Napoleon, too much drama in that explanation. What about the Moor's Knot? Any way to solve it?"

"Not without knowing what text was used to generate the numbers. The idea was that the sender and receiver would have the same manuscript to compare. And that missing third set of numerals could be a real problem."

Thorvaldsen had fully briefed him on Napoleon's will and the relevance of the book that Murad held to that final testament. So he waited while the professor finished his appraisal of the remaining pages.

"Oh, my," Murad said when he reached the end flaps. The older man glanced up at him. "Fascinating."

He'd already studied the curiously twisted hand-writing, in faded black ink, same as the ink used to pen the Roman numerals.

"You happen to know what that is?" he asked.

Murad shook his head. "I have no idea."

Sam came to Meagan's defense. "Apparently, she doesn't need much proof of anything. I'd say you being here is more than enough."

"Well, well," Stephanie said. "Mr. Collins has finally started thinking like a Secret Service agent."

He did not appreciate her condescending attitude, but he wasn't in a position to protest. She was right—he did need to start using his brain. So he said, "You've been monitoring her website. Mine, too. God knows how many others. So there has to be something going on here. Something that has caught everyone's attention."

"It's simple," Stephanie said. "We want the members of this Paris Club in jail."

He didn't believe her. "There's more here than that, and you know it."

Stephanie Nelle did not answer him, which only reinforced what he believed. But he couldn't blame her. No need to tell them anything more than was necessary.

He watched as people bundled to the cold kept streaming up from below on the stairs. More paraded in and out of elevators that rose through the open ironworks to the second platform. A boisterous lunch crowd entered the nearby restaurant. A frigid breeze eased through the brownish gray metal that spiderwebbed up all around them.

"If you want to be privy to that meeting tomorrow," Meagan said, "I doubt you're going to get any listening devices installed. My source tells me that the club sweeps their rooms clean before, during, and after meetings."

"We won't need them," Stephanie made clear.

Sam stared at her, and she returned his glare with a grin he did not like.

"You two ever waited tables?"

FORTY

ELIZA WAS ACTUALLY ENJOYING HER LUNCH CONversation with Henrik Thorvaldsen. He was an intelligent, quick-witted man who did not waste time on small talk. He seemed an eager listener, a person who absorbed facts, cataloged them in proper order, then swiftly drew conclusions.

Just like herself.

"Napoleon realized," she said, "that war was good for society. Like nothing else, it mobilized his best thinkers to think better. He discovered that scientists were more creative when a threat was real. Manufacturing became more innovative and productive. The people more obedient. He discovered that the citizenry, if threatened, would allow just about any violation from government, so long as they were protected. But too much war is destructive. People will only tolerate so much, and his enemies made sure there was far more than he ever intended, and he ultimately lost all ability to govern."

"I can't see how war would ever be termed a good thing," Thorvaldsen said. "There are so many things wrong with it."

"There is death, destruction, devastation, waste. But war has always existed. How could something so utterly wrong continue to thrive? The answer is simple. War works. Man's greatest technological achievements have always come as the result of war. Look at the last world conflict. We learned to split the atom and fly in space, not to mention countless advances in electronics, science, medicine, engineering. All while we slaughtered one another on an unprecedented scale."

He nodded. "There is truth in what you say."

"It's even more dramatic than that, Herre Thorvaldsen. Look at American history. Its economy is as rhythmic as a clock—a cycle of boom, recession, and depression. But here's a fact. Every one of America's cyclical depressions has occurred during a period of inadequate military spending. There were depressions after the War of 1812, the Civil War in the 1860s, and the Spanish-American War at the turn of the 20th century. The Great Depression of the 1930s came at a time, after the First World War, when America went into isolationism and literally dismantled its military. It took another war to bring it out."

"Sounds like a subject you have studied."

"I did and the evidence is clear. War makes the stable governing of society possible. It provides a clear external necessity for society to accept political rule. End war and national sovereignty will eventually end as well—this was a concept Napoleon **understood.** He may actually have been the first modern leader to grasp its meaning."

The dining room at Le Grand Véfour was beginning to empty. Lunchtime was drawing to a close, and she watched as patrons said their goodbyes to each other and slowly departed.

"Napoleon planned to transition not only France," she said, "but all of his conquered territory from a war state to a peace-oriented society. But he recognized that to do it, he'd need adequate substitutes for war. Unfortunately for him, none existed in his day."

"What could possibly take war's place?"

She shrugged. "It's difficult to find, but not impossible. The idea would be to create an alternative enemy. A threat, either real or perceived, against which society rallies to defend itself. Mass destruction by nuclear weapons, for example. That was what the Cold War was all about. Neither side ever did much to the other, but both spent billions and billions in preparation. Government flourished during the Cold War. The American federal system expanded to unprecedented levels. Western civilization escalated to new heights from 1950 to 1990. Man made it to the moon thanks to the Cold War. **There's** an example of a worthy substitute to war."

"Your point is well taken."

"There are other examples, though less compelling. Global warming, perceived food shortages, control of fresh water. In recent years these have been tried. But they have not, as yet, either risen in actuality or been perceived as a sufficient threat.

"Massive programs that drastically expand health care, education, public housing, and transportation might work. But they would have to be all-encompassing, engrossing the entire population in their success, expending resources at obscene levels. It's doubtful that this could occur. Even a small war expends massive amounts of resources. Military spending and preparedness is wasteful beyond measure, and no social-welfare program could ever compare, though the various national health care and social security programs around the world do waste money at extraordinary levels. But in the end, they simply can't waste enough to make the venture a viable substitute for war."

Thorvaldsen chuckled. "Do you realize the absurdity of what you're saying?"

"Perfectly. But transitioning to world peace is a difficult endeavor. Ignoring the challenge of governing for a moment, there's the matter of channeling collective aggression."

"As the Romans did? In the Colosseum? With gladiators and games and sacrifice?"

"The Romans were smart. They recognized the concepts I'm explaining. In a peace-based society, if social disintegration is to be avoided, alternatives to war have to be created. The games offered that to the Roman people, and their society flourished for centuries."

She could see that he was interested in what she was saying.

"Herre Thorvaldsen, it was long ago realized, even by ancient monarchs, that their subjects would not tolerate in peace that which they would willingly accept in war. This concept is particularly true today, in modern democracies. Again, look at America. In the 1950s it allowed the trampling of its First Amendment when the threat of encroaching communism was thought real. Free speech became unimportant when compared with the imagined danger of the Soviet Union. Even more recently, after the September 11 attacks in 2001, laws were passed that, at any other time, Americans would have found repulsive. The Patriot Act suppressed liberties and invaded privacies on an unprecedented level. Surveillance laws curbed civil liberties and restricted established freedoms. Identification laws came into being that, heretofore, Americans found repugnant. But they allowed those violations so that they could be safe—"

"Or at least perceive themselves to be safe."

She smiled. "Precisely. That is exactly what I'm talking about. A credible external threat equals expanded political power—so long as the threat remains credible."

She paused.

"And within that formula, there exists the potential for great profit."

MALONE POINTED AT THE BOOK PROFESSOR Murad held and the curious lines of writing. "Henrik isn't going to like that we don't know what that is."

Murad continued to examine the anomaly. "I have an idea. Let's go inside the Louvre. I need to check something."

THORVALDSEN WAS ABSORBING ALL THAT ELIZA Larocque was explaining. She'd obviously invested a lot of thought into what she was planning. He decided to steer her back toward Ashby.

"You haven't asked me a thing about your security problem," he said in a kindly voice.

"I assumed you would tell me when ready."

He sipped his wine and arranged his thoughts. "Ashby is nearly thirty million euros in debt. Most of that is unsecured, high-interest personal loans."

"I have found Lord Ashby to be straightforward and quite dedicated. He's done everything I've requested of him."

"Lord Ashby is a thief. As you well know, a few

years back he was involved with a group of illicit art collectors. Many of the group ultimately faced justice—"

"Nothing was ever proven regarding Lord Ashby."

"Again, none of which exonerates him. I know he was involved. You know he was involved. That's why he's part of your club."

"And he's making excellent progress doing what I requested. In fact, he's here, right now, in Paris, following up on a promising lead. One that could lead straight to our goal. And for that, Herre Thorvaldsen, I might be willing to forgive a gracious plenty."

MALONE FOLLOWED PROFESSOR MURAD INTO THE glass pyramid and down a series of escalators. A low rumble of noise seeped from crowds waiting to enter the museum. He wondered where they were headed and was grateful when the professor bypassed the long lines at ticket counters and headed into the bookstore.

The two-story shop was packed with information—thousands of books for sale, all arranged by country and period. Murad headed for the expansive French section and several tables stacked with tomes relative to the Napoleonic Age.

"I come here all the time," the academician said. "It's a great store. They carry so many obscure texts that ordinary places never would stock."

He could understand that obsession. Bibliophiles were all alike.

Murad hastily searched the titles.

"Can I help?" he asked.

"I'm looking for a French volume." His eyes kept raking the table. "It's on St. Helena. I almost bought it a few weeks ago but—" He reached down and slid out one of the hardbacks. "Here it is. Too expensive. So I settled for admiring it from afar."

Malone smiled. He liked this man. Nothing pretentious about him.

Murad laid the volume down and thumbed through the pages. He seemingly found what he was searching for and asked Malone to open the book from the Invalides to the page with the curious lines of writing.

"Just what I thought," Murad said, pointing to the book they'd come to see. "This is a picture of some notes from St. Helena, written during Napoleon's exile. We know that his steward, Saint-Denis, rewrote many of Napoleon's drafts, since the emperor's penmanship was atrocious." Murad pointed. "See. The two samples we have here are nearly identical."

Malone compared the books and saw that the script was indeed similar. The same rounded **M**'s— *m*—and stilted **E**'s—*ε*. The flare at the base of the

F's—. The odd-shaped **A**'s——that looked like slanted **D**'s.

"So Saint-Denis wrote what's in this Merovingian book?" he asked.

"No, he didn't."

Malone was puzzled.

Murad pointed to the open Louvre book. "Read the caption beneath the photo."

He did—and now realized. "That's Napoleon's handwriting?"

Murad nodded and pointed to the Merovingian text. "He personally wrote what's in this book, then left it specifically in Saint-Denis' charge. That makes this writing significant."

He recalled what Henrik had told him about the conversation between Ashby and Caroline Dodd. A letter she'd located, also written in Napoleon's hand. Unusual to see the emperor's handwriting, she'd told Ashby.

He mentioned that to Murad.

"I was thinking the same thing," the professor said. "Henrik briefed me, too. Mighty curious."

He studied the fourteen lines of odd letters and other random markings written by Napoleon Bonaparte himself.

"There's a message here," Malone said. "There has to be."

THORVALDSEN DECIDED TO SINK THE KNIFE DEEPER into Eliza Larocque and asked, "What if Lord Ashby can't deliver that which you want?"

She shrugged. "Few, besides my ancestor, have ever searched for Napoleon's cache. It's generally regarded as myth. I'm hoping they are wrong. I don't think it will be Ashby's fault if he fails. He's at least trying."

"While deceiving you about his finances."

She fingered her wineglass. "I admit, that's a problem. I'm not happy about it." She paused. "But I've yet to see any proof."

"What if Ashby finds the cache and doesn't tell you?"

"How would I ever know?"

"You won't."

"Is there a point to your badgering?"

He saw that she'd heard the hint of an unspoken promise. "Whatever he's after, here, today, in Paris, seems important. You yourself said it might hold the key. If I'm right about him, he's going to tell you that he wasn't able to retrieve whatever it is—that it wasn't there or some other such excuse. It will be for you to judge whether that be truth or a lie."

FORTY-ONE

Malone left Dr. Murad at the Louvre, after photocopying the two pages in the Merovingian book with Napoleon's writing and leaving the copies with the professor. He needed to keep the book.

He grabbed a taxi, crossed the Seine, and headed to the Eiffel Tower. Beneath the ironworks, among a bustling crowd of visitors waiting in line to ascend the elevators, he spotted Stephanie, Sam, and another woman—Meagan Morrison.

"Good to see you're okay," he said to Sam. "Of course, you didn't listen to a thing I said in the museum."

"I couldn't just stand there and do nothing."

"Actually you could and should have."

Malone faced Morrison. She was exactly as Stephanie described—short, anxious, attractive, and interesting.

Meagan pointed at Stephanie. "Is she always so pushy?"

"Actually, she's mellowed over the years."

"How about you two excusing us a minute," Stephanie said. She grabbed Malone's arm and led him away, asking, "What did you find in the Invalides?"

He reached beneath his jacket and showed her the book. "Lord Ashby wasn't happy it was gone. I watched as he read my note. But I also noticed that he avoided Caroline Dodd's questions and blamed it all on Larocque."

"Which explains why Thorvaldsen doesn't know Ashby is working for us. He's kept his spying close. I didn't think Henrik could have the man followed twenty-four hours a day, or listen to every communication."

Malone knew intense surveillance, no matter how professionally done, was eventually noticed. Better to be selective and careful.

"Our handlers have done a poor job riding herd over Ashby," she said. "He's had a free rein, calling all the shots."

He watched Sam and Meagan Morrison as they stood a hundred feet away. "Is he doing all right?"

"He wants to be a field agent, so I'm going to give him a chance."

"Is he ready?"

"He's all I've got right now, so he's going to have to be."

"And her?"

"Hothead. Cocky. The balls of an alley cat."

"Easy to see how you two would butt heads."

She smiled. "I have French intelligence working with me. They've been told about Peter Lyon. They want him bad. He's linked to three bombings here a decade ago where four policemen died."

"They still pissed about the Cluny?"

She chuckled. "The **directeur générale de la sécurité extérieure** knows all about you. He told me about the abbey at Belém and Aachen's cathedral. But he's reasonable. That's how you and Ashby walked in and out of the Invalides with no problem. Believe me, they have better security than that."

"I need something else." He motioned with the book. "A press story on its theft. Nothing major— just enough to make tomorrow's paper. It would help."

"With Henrik?"

He nodded. "I need to keep him at bay. He has a plan to use the theft against Ashby with Larocque. I don't see the harm, so let's indulge him."

"Where is he?"

"Driving a wedge deeper between Eliza Larocque and Ashby. You realize, like him, I'm playing both ends against the middle."

"Played right, we may all get what we want."

He was tired, the strain from the past couple of weeks returning. He ran a hand through his hair. He also should call Gary. Christmas was tomorrow, a day when fathers should talk to their sons.

"What now?" he asked.

"You and I are headed to London."

SAM STUFFED HIS BARE HANDS INTO HIS COAT pockets and stood in the crowd with Meagan. The sun shone brightly in a cloudless winter sky.

"Why are you doing this?" he asked her.

"Your lady friend there said I'd be arrested if I didn't."

"That's not why."

Her pleasant face showed no apprehension, something he'd noticed often since yesterday. No negativity in this personality, or at least not any she allowed to surface.

"We're finally doing it," she said. "No more talking. We're here, Sam, doing something."

He'd felt some of the same ebullience.

"We can stop them. I knew it was real. So did you. We're not crazy, Sam."

"You realize what Stephanie wants us to do is dangerous."

She shrugged. "How bad could it be? Any worse than at the museum yesterday? What's wrong with being a little cavalier?"

"What's that word mean?" he asked Norstrum.

"Free. Offhand. Somewhat careless."

He allowed his fifteen-year-old brain to absorb the definition. He'd broken another rule and risked a free climb up the rock face.

Norstrum had told him to use a rope, but he hadn't obeyed.

"Sam, we all take chances. That's how you succeed. But never foolish ones. Success comes from minimizing risk, not making it greater."

"But the rope wasn't needed. I made it fine."

"And what would have happened if your grip had not held? Or your foot slipped? Or a muscle cramped?" Norstrum's terse questions were a clear indication that he was, if not displeased, certainly unhappy. "You would have fallen. Been maimed for life, maybe killed, and what would you have gained from taking such a risk?"

He tried to place the information into context, allowing the rebuke to float through his mind as he determined the right response. He did not like that he'd upset Norstrum. When he was younger he didn't care, but as he'd grown older he'd come to want not to disappoint this man.

"I'm sorry. It was foolish."

The older man grasped his shoulder. "Remember, Sam, foolishness will get you killed."

Norstrum's warning rang clear in his brain as he considered Meagan's three questions. Seventeen years ago, when he'd scaled the rock face with no safety rope, he'd learned that Norstrum had been right.

Foolishness will get you killed.

Yesterday, in the museum, he'd forgotten that lesson.

Not today.

Stephanie Nelle had drafted him for a job. Did it entail risks? Plenty. But they should be measured and calculated.

Nothing cavalier.

"I want to be careful, Meagan. You should be, too."

FORTY-TWO

ENGLAND
2:40 PM

ASHBY GLANCED AT HIS WATCH AND NOTED THAT IT had taken the Bentley a little over an hour to make the drive from Heathrow Airport to Salen Hall. He also noticed that his estate workers were busy maintaining the grounds, though the seahorse fountain, canal pond, and cascade were silent for winter. Except for an enlarged stable and a kitchen and servant wing, the main house had remained unchanged since the 18th century. The same clumps of forest and pasture also remained. The surrounding land all had once been ancient moors, driven back by Ashby ancestors who'd tamed the valley with grass and fence. He prided himself on both its beauty and its independence, one of the last privately owned British manors that did not depend on tourism for revenue.

And it never would.

The Bentley stopped at the crown of a graveled cul-de-sac. Orange brick and diamond-paned windows glistened in the bright sun. Gargoyles leered down from the roofline, their axes poised, as if to warn invaders.

"I'm going to do a little research," Caroline told him as they stepped inside the house.

Good. He needed to think. He and Mr. Guildhall headed straight for his study and Ashby sat behind the desk. This day had turned disastrous.

He'd kept quiet during the short flight back from Paris and delayed the inevitable. Now he lifted the phone and dialed Eliza Larocque's mobile number.

"I hope you have more good news," she said.

"Actually, no. The book wasn't there. Perhaps it's been moved during the renovation? I found the display case and the other items, but not the volume on the Merovingians."

"The information provided to me was quite specific."

"The book was not there. Can you check again?"

"Of course."

"In the morning, once I return to Paris for our gathering, perhaps we can speak privately beforehand?"

"I will be at the tower by ten thirty."

"Till then."

He hung up the phone and checked his watch.

Four hours to go. That was when he was scheduled to meet with his American contact. He'd
hoped that to be his last conversation, as he was
tired of the juggling act. He wanted Napoleon's
cache and had hoped the book in the Invalides held
the key. Now the bloody Americans controlled it.

He'd have to bargain tonight.

Tomorrow would be far too late.

ELIZA CLICKED OFF HER PHONE AND THOUGHT
back to what Henrik Thorvaldsen had predicted. **If
I'm right about him, he's going to tell you that
he wasn't able to retrieve whatever it is, that it
wasn't there, or some other such excuse.** And to
what he'd told her again, just before they concluded their lunch and he left the restaurant. **It will
be for you to judge whether that be truth or
a lie.**

She was safe inside her house in the Marais, not
far from where the Paris Club gathered. Her family
had owned the property since the mid–19th century. She'd grown up within these elegant walls and
now spent the majority of her time here. Her
sources within the French government had assured
her that the book she sought was there, in the museum. A minor relic, of little historical significance,
other than being from Napoleon's personal library

and mentioned in his will. Her sources had asked few questions, nor would they have once they learned the book was gone, since they'd learned long ago that to appreciate her generosity meant to keep their mouths shut.

She'd debated what to do about Thorvaldsen ever since leaving Le Grand Véfour. The Danish billionaire had appeared from nowhere with information that she simply could not ignore. He clearly knew her business, and the oracle had confirmed his intentions. Now Ashby himself had corroborated what Thorvaldsen predicted. She did not intend to ignore the warnings any longer.

She retrieved the telephone number Thorvaldsen had provided to her yesterday and dialed. When he answered, she told him, "I have decided to extend you an invitation to join our group."

"Most generous. I assume, then, Lord Ashby disappointed you."

"Let us say that he's aroused my curiosity. Are you free tomorrow? The club is gathering for an important session."

"I'm a Jew. Christmas is not a holiday for me."

"Nor me. We meet in the morning, in La Salle Gustav Eiffel, on the first platform of the tower, at eleven. They have a lovely banquet room, and we have a lunch planned after we talk."

"Sounds wonderful."

"I shall see you then."

She clicked off the phone.

Tomorrow.

A day she'd been anticipating for a long time. She planned to fully explain to her cohorts what the parchments had taught her family. Some of which she'd related to Thorvaldsen at lunch, but she'd intentionally not mentioned a caveat. In a peace-based society, with no war, stimulating mass fear through political, sociological, ecological, scientific, or cultural threats could prove nearly impossible. No attempt, so far, had ever carried sufficient credibility or magnitude to work for long. Something like black plague, which had threatened on a global scale, came close, but a threat such as that, conceived from unknown conditions, with little or no control, was impractical.

And any threat would have to be containable.

After all, that was the whole idea. Scare the people into obeying—then extract profit from their fear. The better solution was the simplest. Invent the threat. Such a plan came with a multitude of advantages. Like a dimmer switch on a chandelier that could be adjusted into infinite degrees of intensity. Thankfully, in today's world, a credible enemy existed and had already galvanized public sentiment.

Terrorism.

As she'd told Thorvaldsen, that precise threat had worked in America, so it should work anywhere.

Tomorrow she'd see if the parchments were correct.

What Napoleon had wanted to do, she would now do.

For two hundred years her family had profited from the political misfortunes of others. Pozzo di Borgo deciphered enough from the parchments to teach his children, as they'd taught theirs, that it truly did not matter who made the laws—control the money and you possess real power.

To do that, she needed to control events.

Tomorrow would be an experiment.

And if it worked?

There'd be more.

FORTY-THREE

LONDON
6:40 PM

ASHBY SEARCHED THE DARKNESS AND THE HUNDRED or so faces for a green-and-gold Harrods scarf. Most of the people surrounding him were clearly tourists, their guide yelling something about the **feel of gaslight and fog** and August 1888 when Jack the Ripper **struck terror into drink-sodden East End prostitutes.**

He grinned.

The Ripper seemed to interest only foreigners. He wondered if those same people would pay money in their own countries to be taken on a tour of a mass murderer's haunts.

He was on the city's east side, in Whitechapel, walking down a crowded sidewalk. To his left, across a busy street, rose the Tower of London, its taupe-colored stones awash in sodium vapor light. What was once an enormous moat was now a sea of emerald winter grass. A cold breeze eased inland off the nearby Thames, with the Tower Bridge lighted in the distance.

"Good evening, Lord Ashby."

The woman who appeared beside him was petite with short-cut hair, late fifties, early sixties, definitely American, and wearing a green-and-gold scarf. Exactly as he'd been told.

However.

"You are new," he said to her.

"I'm the one in charge."

That information caught his attention.

He'd met his regular contact with American intelligence on several of London's walking tours. They'd taken the British Museum stroll, Shakespeare's London, Old Mayfair, and now Jack the Ripper Haunts.

"And who are you?" he casually asked.

"Stephanie Nelle."

The group halted for the guide to spew out something about how the building just ahead was where the Ripper's first victim had been found. She grasped his arm and, as others focused on the guide, they drifted into the crowd's wake.

"Fitting we should meet on this tour," she said. "Jack the Ripper terrorized people and was never caught, either."

He didn't smile at her attempt toward irony. "I could end my involvement now and leave, if you no longer require my help."

The group again started forward.

"I realize the price we're going to have to pay is your freedom. But that doesn't mean I like it."

He told himself to stay calm. This woman, and who she represented, had to be stroked, at least for another twenty-four hours, and at least until he obtained the book.

"The last I was told we were in this endeavor together," he said.

"You promised to deliver information today. I came to personally hear what you have to offer."

The group stopped at another notable site.

"Peter Lyon will bomb the Church of the Dome, at the Invalides, tomorrow," he said in a low voice. "Christmas Day. As a demonstration."

"Of what?"

"Eliza Larocque is a fanatic. She has some ancient wisdom that her family has lived by for centuries. Quite complicated and, to me, generally irrelevant, but there is a French extremist group—isn't there always one?—that wants to make a statement."

"Who is it this time?"

"It involves immigrant discrimination under French law. North Africans, who flooded into France years ago, welcomed then as guest workers. Now they're ten percent of the population and tired of being held down. They want to make a statement. Larocque has the means and wants no credit, so Peter Lyon brokered a partnership."

"I want to understand the purpose of this partnership."

He sighed. "Can't you decipher it? France is in the middle of a demographic shift. Those Algerian and Moroccan immigrants are becoming a problem. They are now far more French than African, but the xenophobic right and the secularist left hate them. If birthrates continue as they are, within two decades those immigrants will outnumber the native French."

"And what does blowing up the Invalides have to do with that inevitability?"

"It's all a symbol. Those immigrants resent their second-class status. They want their mosques. Their freedom. Political expression. Influence. Power. What everyone else has. But the native French don't want them to have those. I'm told a great many laws have been passed trying to keep these people at a distance." He paused. "And anti-Semitism is also on a sharp rise throughout France. Jews are becoming afraid once again."

"And those immigrants are to blame for that?"

He shrugged. "Perhaps some. To me, if the truth be told, the radical French are more responsible. But the political right and the extreme left have done a good job blaming those immigrants for all the ills that befall the country."

"I'm still waiting for my answer."

The tour stopped at another point of interest, and the guide droned on.

"Eliza is conducting a test," he said. "A way to channel French national aggression onto something other than war. An attack by some perceived radical element against a French national monument, the grave of its beloved Napoleon—whom she despises, by the way—would, to her way of thinking, channel that collective aggression. At least that's her way of explaining it."

"Why does she hate Napoleon?"

He shrugged. "How would I know? Family tradition, I assume. One of her ancestors carried on a Corsican **vendetta** against Napoleon. I've never really understood."

"Does the Paris Club meet tomorrow at the Eiffel Tower?"

He nodded his head in appreciation. "You've been busy. Would it not have been more prudent to ask me a direct question to see if I would be truthful?"

"I'm in a hurry, and I don't necessarily believe a word you say anyway."

He shook his head. "Impertinent. And arrogant. Why? I've cooperated with your people—"

"When you wanted to. You deliberately held back this information on an attack."

"As you would have done, if in my place. But you now know, in plenty of time, so prepare accordingly."

"I don't know anything. How is it going to be done?"

"Good heavens, why would I be privy to that information?"

"You're the one who made the deal with Lyon."

"Believe me, that devil offers precious little in the way of details. He just wants to know when and if his money has been wired. Beyond that, he explains nothing."

"Is that all?"

"The Invalides is closed for Christmas Day. At least there will be no people to worry about."

She did not appear comforted. "You still haven't answered my question about the Paris Club."

"We meet tomorrow morning at the Eiffel Tower. Eliza has rented the banquet room on level one and plans to take everyone to the top around noon. As I said, Lyon likes timelines. Noon is when the explosion will occur, and the club will have the perfect vantage point."

"Do the members know what's going to happen?"

He shook his head. "Heavens, no. Only she and I, and our South African. I would assume most of them would be appalled."

"Though they won't mind profiting from it."

The tour headed farther into the bowels of London's darkened east side.

"Morality rarely plays into the quest for profit," he said.

"So tell me what I really want to know. How do we finally connect with Lyon?" she asked.

"The same way I did."

"Not good enough. I want him delivered."

He stopped walking. "How do you propose I

do that? I've only seen him once, and he was totally disguised. He communicates with me at his choosing."

They were keeping their voices down, walking behind the main group. Even though he'd worn his thickest wool coat and fur-lined gloves, he was cold. Each exhale vaporized before his eyes.

"Surely you can arrange something," she said. "Considering we won't be prosecuting you."

He caught the unspoken threat. "Is that why I'm honored tonight with your presence? You came to deliver an ultimatum? Your representative wasn't authoritative enough?"

"Game's over, Ashby. Your usefulness is rapidly diminishing. I'd suggest you do something to increase your value."

He'd actually already done just that, but he wasn't about to tell this woman anything. So he asked, "Why did your people take the book in the Invalides?"

She chuckled. "To show you that there's been a change in management on this end. New rules apply."

"Lucky for me that you're so dedicated to your profession."

"You really think that there's some lost treasure of Napoleon out there to find?"

"Eliza Larocque certainly does."

She reached beneath her coat, removed something, and handed it to him. "That's my show of good faith."

He gripped the volume through his gloves. In the ambient glow of a nearby street lamp he caught the title. **The Merovingian Kingdoms 450–751 A.D.**

The book from the Invalides.

"Now," she said, "give me what I want."

The tour approached Ten Bells pub and he heard the guide explain how the establishment had played host to many of Jack the Ripper's victims, perhaps even the Ripper himself. A fifteen-minute break was announced and drinks were available inside.

He should head back to Salen Hall and Caroline. "Are we finished?"

"Until tomorrow."

"I'll do everything possible to make sure you get what you want."

"I hope so," she said. "For your sake."

And with that the woman named Stephanie Nelle walked off into the night.

He stared down at the book. Things really were finally falling into place.

"Good evening, Lord Ashby."

The unexpected voice came near his right ear, low and throaty, below the rhythmic sound of soles slapping pavement around him. He turned and, in the glow of another street lamp, caught a reddish hue in thick hair and thin eyebrows. He noticed an aquiline nose, scarred face, and eyeglasses. The man was dressed, like the others around him, in thick winter wear, including scarf and gloves. One hand clutched the roped handles of a Selfridges shopping bag.

Then he saw the eyes.

A burnt amber.

"Do you ever look the same?" he asked Peter Lyon.

"Hardly."

"It must be difficult having no identity."

"I have no problem with my identity. I know exactly who and what I am." The voice this time seemed almost American.

He was concerned. Peter Lyon should not be here.

"You and I need to speak, Lord Ashby."

FORTY-FOUR

SAM FOLLOWED MEAGAN DOWN A SPIRAL STAIRCASE that cork screwed into the earth. They'd dined at a café in the Latin Quarter after being granted a temporary release from Stephanie Nelle's protective custody.

"Where are we going?" he asked her as they kept descending into pitch blackness.

"To Paris' basement," Meagan said.

She was ahead of him, her flashlight dissolving the darkness below. When he reached the bottom, she handed him another light. "They don't keep flashlights down here for trespassers like us."

"Trespassers?"

She motioned with her beam. "It's illegal to be here."

"What is **here**?"

"The quarries. A hundred and seventy miles of tunnels and galleries. Formed when limestone was torn from the ground, used for buildings, to make gypsum for plaster, clay for bricks, and roof tiles. Everything needed to build Paris, and this is what's left. The Paris underground."

"And the reason we're here?"

She shrugged. "I like this place. I thought you might, too."

She walked ahead, following a damp passage clearly hewn from solid rock and supported by a chalky framework. The air was cool but not cold, the floor uneven and unpredictable.

"Careful of the rats," she said. "They can pass leptospirosis."

He stopped. "Excuse me?"

"Bacterial infection. Fatal."

"Are you nuts?"

She stopped. "Unless you plan on letting one bite you or swishing your fingers in their urine, I'd say you're okay."

"What are we doing here?"

"Are you always so antsy? Just follow me. I want to show you something."

They started back down the corridor, the roof just above his head. Her light beam revealed about fifty feet of tunnel ahead of them.

"Norstrum," he called out to the blackness.

He wondered why he'd disobeyed and come, but the promise of an adventure had been too enticing to ignore. The caves were not far from the school, and everyone knew

about them. Funny how no one ever used the word orphanage. Always the school. Or the institute. Who were his parents? He had no idea. He'd been abandoned at birth, and how he arrived in Christchurch the police never determined. The school insisted students know all they could about themselves. No secrets—he actually appreciated that rule—but there was simply nothing for him to learn.

"Sam."

Norstrum's voice.

He'd been told that Norstrum, when he'd first arrived at the school, had named him Sam Collins, after a beloved uncle.

"Where are you?" he called out to the blackness.

"Not far."

He aimed his light and kept walking.

"It's just up here," Meagan said, as the tunnel ended in what appeared to be a spacious gallery, with multiple exits and a high ceiling. Stone pillars supported a curved roof. Meagan shone her light on the rough walls and he spied myriad graffiti, paintings, inscriptions, cartoons, mosaics, poetry, even musical lyrics.

"It's a collage of social history," she said. "These drawings date back to the time of the French Revolution, the Prussian siege in the late 19th century, and the German occupation in the 1940s. The

Paris underground has always been a refuge from war, death, and destruction."

One drawing caught his eye. A sketch of a guillotine.

"From the **Grande Terreur,**" she said, over his shoulder. "Two hundred years old. A testament to a time when bloody deaths were a part of everyday life here. That was made with black smoke. Quarrymen of that day carried candles and oil lamps, and they'd place the flame close against the wall, which baked carbon into the stone. Pretty smart."

He pointed with his light. "That's from the French Revolution?"

She nodded. "This is a time capsule, Sam. The entire underground is that way. See why I like it?"

He glanced around at the images. Most seemed conceived with sobriety, but humor and satire were also evident, along with several titillating pornographic additions.

"This is a pretty amazing place," she said to the darkness. "I come here a lot. It's peaceful and silent. Like a return to the womb. Going back to the surface, to me, can be like a rebirth."

He was taken aback by her frankness. Apparently cracks did exist in her tough veneer. Then he understood.

"You're scared, aren't you?"

She faced him and, in the glow from her light, he caught sincerity in her eyes. "You know I am."

"I am, too."

"It's okay to be scared," Norstrum had said when he finally found him in the cave. "But you should not have come here alone."

He knew that now.

"Fear can be an ally," Norstrum said. "Always take it with you, no matter what the fight. It's what keeps you sharp."

"But I don't want to be afraid. I hate being afraid."

Norstrum laid a hand on his shoulder. "There's no choice, Sam. It's the circumstances that create fear. How you respond is all you can control. Concentrate on that, and you'll always succeed."

He gently laid his hand on her shoulder. It was the first time they'd touched, and she did not pull away.

Surprising himself, he was glad.

"We'll be okay," he told her.

"Those men yesterday, in the museum, I think they would have eventually hurt me."

"That's really why you forced things, while I was there?"

A hesitation, then she nodded.

He appreciated her honesty. Finally. "Looks like we've both bit off a lot."

She grinned. "Apparently so."

He withdrew his hand and wondered about her show of vulnerability. Through emails, they'd communicated many times over the past year. He'd thought he was speaking to a man named Jimmy Foddrell. Instead, an intriguing woman had been on the other end of the Internet. Thinking back, she'd actually reached out in some of those communiqués. Never like this—but enough that he'd felt a connection.

She pointed with her light. "Down those corridors you'll eventually find the catacombs. The bones of six million people are stacked there. Ever been?"

He shook his head.

"Don't."

He kept silent.

"These drawings," she said, "were made by ordinary people. But they're a historical essay. The walls down here, for miles, are covered in pictures. They show people's life and times, fears, and superstitions. They are a record." She paused. "We have a chance, Sam, to do something real. Something that could make a difference."

They were so much alike. Both of them lived in a virtual world of paranoia and speculation. And both of them harbored good intentions.

"Then let's do it," he said.

She chuckled. "I wish it were that easy. I have a bad feeling about this."

She seemed to draw strength from this underground spectacle. Perhaps even some wisdom, too.

"Care to explain that one?"

She shook her head. "I can't, really. Just a feeling."

She came closer. Barely a few inches away. "Did you know that a kiss shortens life by three minutes?"

He considered her strange inquiry, then shook his head.

"Not a peck on the cheek. A real kiss, like you mean it, causes palpitations to such a degree that the heart works harder in four seconds than it normally would in three minutes."

"Really, now?"

"There was a study. Hell, Sam, there's a study for everything. 480 kisses—again, like you mean it—will shorten a person's life by one day. 2,300 will cost a week. 120,000? There goes a year."

She inched closer.

He smiled. "And the point?"

"I can spare three minutes of my life, if you can."

FORTY-FIVE

LONDON

MALONE WATCHED AS STEPHANIE DISAPPEARED
into the night and another man immediately approached Graham Ashby, toting a Selfridges shopping bag. Malone had immersed himself among
the walking tour, embracing the talkative crowd.
His task was to cover Stephanie's back, keep a close
eye on things, but now they may have finally
caught a break.

He noted the features of Ashby's companion.

Reddish hair, thin nose, medium build, about
160 to 170 pounds, dressed like everybody else in a
wool coat, scarf, and gloves. But something told
him that this was not just anybody else.

Many in the tour were making their way into
the Ten Bells pub, the rattle from a multitude of
conversations spilling out into the night. Entre-
preneurs were actively hawking Jack the Ripper
T-shirts and commemorative mugs. Ashby and

Red loitered on the sidewalk, and Malone crept to within thirty feet, a spate of boisterous people between them. Flashbulbs strobed the darkness as many in the group stole a picture before the pub's colorful façade.

He joined in the revelry and bought a T-shirt from one of the vendors.

ASHBY WAS CONCERNED.

"I thought it best we speak tonight," Peter Lyon said to him.

"How did you know I was here?"

"The woman. Is she an acquaintance?"

He thought back to his conversation with Stephanie Nelle. They'd kept their voices low and had stood apart from the crowd. No one had been nearby. Had Lyon heard anything?

"I have many female acquaintances."

Lyon chuckled. "I'm sure you do. Women provide the greatest of pleasures, the worst of problems."

"How did you find me?" he asked again.

"Did you think for one moment that I wouldn't discover what you are doing?"

His legs began to shake, and not from the cold.

Lyon motioned for them to drift across the street, away from the pub, where fewer people stood and no street lamps burned. Ashby walked with trepidation, but realized that Lyon wouldn't do anything here, with so many witnesses.

Or would he?

"I've been aware of your contacts with the Americans from the beginning," Lyon said to him, the voice low and controlled. "It's amusing you think yourself so clever."

No sense lying. "I had no choice."

Lyon shrugged. "We all have choices, but it matters not to me. I want your money, and you want a service. I assume you still want it?"

"More than ever."

Lyon pointed a finger at him. "Then it will cost triple my original fee. The first hundred percent for your treachery. The second for the trouble you've put me to."

He was in no position to argue. Besides, he was using club money anyway. "That can be arranged."

"She gave you a book. What is it?"

"Is that part of the new arrangement? You are to know all of my business?"

"You should know, Lord Ashby, that I've found it hard to resist the urge of placing a bullet between your eyes. I detest a man with no character and you, sir, have none."

Interesting attitude for a mass murderer, but he kept his opinion to himself.

"If not for your money—" Lyon paused. "Please, don't try my patience any further."

He accepted the advice and answered the man's question. "It's a project I've been working on. A lost treasure. The Americans confiscated a vital clue to keep me compliant. She returned it to me."

"A treasure? I learned that you were once an avid collector. Stealing objects already stolen. Keeping them for yourself. Quite the clever one, you are. But the police put a stop to that."

"Temporarily."

Lyon laughed. "All right, Lord Ashby, you go after your treasure. Just transfer my money. By dawn. I'll be checking, **before** events start to happen."

"It will be there."

He heard the guide draw the crowd together, telling them it was time to move on.

"I think I'll finish the tour," Lyon said. "Quite interesting, Jack the Ripper."

"What about tomorrow? You know the Americans are watching."

"That I do. It will be quite the show."

MALONE DISSOLVED INTO THE TOUR AS THE CROWD, including Red, drew into the guide's wake and they all ambled off into the darkness. He kept Red just inside his peripheral vision, deciding he was far more interesting than Ashby.

The tour continued another twenty minutes down coal-black streets, ending at an Underground station. Inside, Red used a travel card to pass through the turnstile. Malone hurried over to a token machine and quickly purchased four, making his way past the gate to the escalator just as his quarry stepped off at the bottom. He did not like the bright lights and the sparse crowd, but had no choice.

He stepped off the escalator onto the platform.

Red was standing twenty feet away, still holding his shopping bag.

An electronic billboard indicated the train was 75 seconds away. He studied a schematic of the London subway hanging on the wall and saw that this station serviced the District Line, which paralleled the Thames and ran east to west the city's full length. This platform was for a westbound train, the route taking them to Tower Hill, beneath Westminster, through Victoria Station, and eventually beyond Kensington.

More people filtered down from above as a train arrived.

He kept his distance, positioning himself well behind, and followed his quarry into the car. He stood, hugging one of the stainless-steel poles, Red doing the same thirty feet away. Enough people were crammed into the car that no one face should draw much attention.

As the train chugged beneath the city, Malone

studied his target, who seemed an older man, out for the evening, enjoying London.

But he spotted the eyes.

Amber.

He knew Peter Lyon possessed one anomaly. He loved disguise, but a genetic eye defect not only oddly colored his irises, but also made them overly susceptible to infection and prevented him from wearing contact lenses. Lyon preferred glasses to shield their distinctive amber tint, but had not worn any tonight.

He watched as Lyon engaged in a conversation with a dowager standing beside him. Malone noticed a copy of **The Times** lying on the floor. He asked if the paper belonged to anyone and, when no one claimed ownership, he grabbed and read the front page, allowing his gaze to periodically shift from the words.

He also kept track of the stations.

Fifteen came and went before Lyon exited at Earl's Court. The stop was shared by the District and Piccadilly lines, blue and green signs directing passengers to either route. Lyon followed the blue signs for the Piccadilly Line, headed west, which he boarded with Malone a car behind. He didn't think it prudent to share the same space again and was able to spy his quarry through windows in the car ahead.

A quick glance at a map over the doors confirmed they were headed straight for Heathrow Airport.

FORTY-SIX

PARIS

THORVALDSEN STUDIED THE TWO PAGES OF WRITING from the Merovingian book. He'd expected Malone to hand over the entire book to Murad when they'd met earlier at the Louvre but, for some reason, that had not occurred.

"He only made me copies of the two pages," Murad said to him. "He took the book with him."

They were again sitting at the Ritz, in the crowded Bar Hemingway.

"Cotton didn't happen to mention where he was going?"

Murad shook his head. "Not a word. I spent the day at the Louvre comparing more handwriting samples. This page, with the fourteen lines of letters, was definitely written by Napoleon. I can only assume that the Roman numerals are in his hand too."

He checked the clock on the wall behind the bar. Nearly eleven PM. He did not like being kept in the dark. God knows he'd done that enough to others, but it was a different matter when it was his turn.

"The letter you told me about," Murad said. "The one Ashby found on Corsica, with the raised letters coded to Psalm 31. Any letter written by Napoleon to his family would have been an excercise in futility. His second wife, Marie Louise, had by 1821 birthed a child with another man, while still legally married to Napoleon. The emperor surely never knew that since he kept a portrait of her in his house on St. Helena. He revered her. Of course, she was in Austria, back with her father, the king, who'd aligned himself with Tsar Alexander and helped defeat Napoleon. There's no evidence that the letter Napoleon wrote ever made it to her, or his son. In fact, after Napoleon died, an emissary traveled to Vienna with some last messages from him, and she refused to even see the messenger."

"Lucky for us."

Murad nodded. "Napoleon was a fool when it came to women. The one who could have really helped him, he discarded. Josephine. She was barren and he needed an heir. So he divorced her and married Marie Louise." The professor motioned with the two photocopies. "Yet here he is, sending secret messages to his second wife, thinking her still an ally."

"Any clue what the reference to Psalm 31 means from the letter Ashby found?" he asked.

The scholar shook his head. "Have you read that Psalm? Seems his way of feeling sorry for himself. I did come across something interesting, though, this afternoon in one of the texts for sale at the Louvre. After Napoleon abdicated in 1814, the new Paris government sent emissaries to Orleans to confiscate Marie Louise's clothing, imperial plate, diamonds, everything of value. They questioned her at length about Napoleon's wealth, but she told them she knew nothing, which was probably true."

"So the search for his cache started then?"

"It would seem so."

"And continues to this day."

Which made him think of Ashby.

Tomorrow they'd finally find themselves face-to-face.

And what about Malone.

What **was** he doing?

MALONE STEPPED FROM THE TRAIN AND FOLLOWED Lyon into Terminal Two at Heathrow. He was worried that his quarry was about to leave London, but the man ventured nowhere near any ticket counters or security screening. Instead he passed through the terminal, stopping at a checkpoint, displaying what appeared to be a picture identification. No way Malone could safely follow, as the corridor was empty, a solitary door at its far end. So he stepped into an alcove, removed the cell phone from his coat pocket, and dialed Stephanie's number.

"I'm at Heathrow Airport at a checkpoint marked 46-B. I need to get past it, and fast. There's a single guard with a radio."

"Sit tight. I have the right people here with me now."

He liked Stephanie's ability to instantaneously digest a problem, without questions or arguments, then fashion a solution.

He slipped from the alcove and approached the young guard. Lyon was gone, having exited the door at the far end of the corridor. He told the guard who he was, showed him his passport, and explained he needed to go through the door.

"No way," the man said. "You have to be marked on the list." A bony finger tapped a notebook open on the desk before him.

"Who was the man that just passed through?" he tried.

"Why would I tell you that? Who the bloody hell are you?"

The man's radio squawked and he unclipped the unit and replied. An ear fob prevented Malone from hearing, but from the way he was now being eyed he assumed the conversation concerned him.

The guard finished his conversation.

"I'm the guy who made that call happen," Malone said. "Now, who was the man who just passed through here?"

"Robert Pryce."

"What's his business?"

"No clue, but he's been here before. What is it you need, Mr. Malone?"

He had to admire the English respect for authority.

"Where is Pryce headed?"

"His credentials assign him to Hangar 56-R."

"Tell me how to get there."

The guard quickly sketched a map on a piece of paper and pointed to the door at the far end of the hall. "That leads onto the apron."

Malone trotted off and exited into the night.

He quickly found Hangar 56-R, three of its windows lit with orange and white light. Jet engines roared in the distance above a busy Heathrow. An array of buildings of varying sizes surrounded him. This area seemed the realm of private aviation companies and corporate jets.

He decided a quick view in one of the windows was the safest course. He rounded the building and passed the retracting door. On the other side he crept to a window and glanced in, spotting a single-engine Cessna Skyhawk. The man who called himself Robert Pryce, but who was surely Peter Lyon, was busy inspecting the wings and engine. The fuselage was white, striped blue and yellow, and

Malone memorized the tail identification numbers. No one else could be seen in the hangar and Lyon seemed focused on a visual inspection. The Selfridges bag rested on the concrete floor near an exit door.

He watched as Lyon climbed inside the plane, lingered for a few minutes, then slipped out, slamming the cabin door shut. Lyon grabbed the shopping bag and switched off the hangar lights.

He needed to beat a retreat while he still could. Exposure was a real possibility.

Malone heard a metal door open, then close.

He froze, hoping his prey was heading back toward the terminal. If he came this way, there'd be no escape.

He crept to the corner and stole a quick glance.

Lyon was making his way back toward the terminal, but not before he stepped to a dumpster between the darkened hangars and tossed the Selfridges bag inside.

Malone wanted that bag, but he also did not want to lose his target.

So he waited until Lyon reentered the terminal, then rushed to the trash bin. No time to climb inside, so he hustled to the door, hesitated a moment, then cautiously turned the knob.

Only the guard was visible, still sitting at his desk.

Malone entered and asked, "Where did he go?"

The guard pointed toward the main terminal.

"There's a Selfridges bag in a dumpster outside. Stash it somewhere safe. Don't open or disturb the contents in any way. I'll be back. Understand?"

"What's not to?"

He liked this young man's attitude.

In the heart of the terminal, Malone did not spot Peter Lyon. He raced for the Underground station and saw that a train was not scheduled to arrive for another ten minutes. He backtracked and scanned the assortment of rental car counters, shops, and currency exchange vendors. A good number of people milled about for nearly ten PM on Christmas Eve.

He drifted toward a men's room and entered.

The dozen or so urinals were unused, white tiles glistening under the glare of bright fluorescent lights. Warm air smelled of bleach. He used one of the urinals, then washed his hands, lathering soap and cleaning his face.

The cold water felt good.

He rinsed the suds away and reached for a paper towel, dabbing his cheeks and forehead dry, swiping soapy water from his eyes. When he opened them, in the mirror, he saw a man standing behind him.

"And who are you?" Lyon asked in a deep throaty voice, more American than European.

"Somebody who'd like to put a bullet in your head."

The deep amber color of the eyes drew his attention, their oily sheen casting a spell.

Lyon slowly removed his hand from his coat pocket, revealing a small-caliber pistol. "A shame you can't. Did you enjoy the tour? Jack the Ripper is fascinating."

"I can see how he would be to you."

Lyon gave a light chuckle. "I so enjoy dry wit. Now—"

A small boy rushed inside the restroom, rounding the open doorway that led back out to the terminal, calling after his dad. Malone used the unexpected distraction to slam his right elbow into Lyon's gun hand.

The weapon discharged with a loud retort, the bullet finding the ceiling.

Malone lunged forward and propelled both himself and Lyon into a marble partition. His left hand clamped onto Lyon's wrist and forced the gun upward.

He heard the boy yell, then other voices.

He brought a knee into Lyon's abdomen, but the man seemed to anticipate the move and pivoted away.

Lyon apparently realized the confines were tightening, so he darted for the door. Malone raced after him and wrapped his arm around Lyon's neck, one hand on the face, yanking back, but the gun butt suddenly slammed into Malone's forehead.

The room winked in and out.

His balance and grip failed.

Lyon broke free and disappeared out the door.

Malone staggered to his feet and tried to give pursuit, but a wave of dizziness forced him to the floor. Through a fog he saw a uniformed guard rush in. He rubbed his temples and tried to find his balance.

"A man was just here. Redhead, older looking, armed." He noticed that his hand held something. He'd felt it give way when he tried to halt Lyon's retreat. "He'll be easy to find."

He held up a shard of silicon, fashioned and colored like a thin human nose. The guard was dumbfounded.

"He's masked. I got a piece of it."

The guard rushed out and Malone slowly staggered out into the terminal. A crowd had formed and several other guards appeared. One of them was the young one from earlier.

Malone walked over and asked, "You get the shopping bag?"

"Follow me."

Two minutes later he and the guard were in a small interview room near the security office. The Selfridges bag lay on a laminated table.

He tested its weight. Light. He reached inside and removed a green plastic bag that apparently contained several odd-shaped objects.

Clanging together.

He laid the bundle on the table and unraveled it.

He wasn't necessarily concerned about explosives

since Lyon had clearly discarded what was inside. He allowed the contents to roll onto the table and was shocked to see four small metal replicas of the Eiffel Tower, the kind of souvenir easily bought anywhere in Paris.

"The bloody hell?" the young guard asked.

His thoughts exactly.

FORTY-SEVEN

ASHBY WATCHED AS CAROLINE EXAMINED THE book Stephanie Nelle had so conveniently provided. He'd lied and told Caroline that he'd spoken to Larocque and she'd finally agreed to give it to him, promptly ferrying it across the channel by personal courier.

"It's Napoleon's handwriting," she said, excitement in her voice. "No doubt."

"And this is significant?"

"It has to be. We have information that we didn't have before. Much more than Pozzo di Borgo ever amassed. I've been through every writing Eliza Larocque provided. Not much there, really. Di Borgo worked more off rumor and gossip than historical fact. I think his hatred of Napoleon clouded his ability to effectively study the problem for an answer."

Hate could well affect judgment. That was why he rarely allowed that emotion to overtake him. "It's getting late and I have to be in Paris tomorrow."

"Do I get to go along?"

"This is club business. And it is Christmas Day, so the shops will be closed."

He knew that one of her favorite pastimes was roaming down Avenue Montaigne and its parade of designer stores. Ordinarily, he'd indulge her, but not tomorrow.

She continued to study the Merovingian book. "I can't help but think that we have all the pieces."

But he was still unnerved by Peter Lyon. He'd already made the additional money transfer, as demanded, terrified of the consequences if he balked. Incredibly, the South African was completely aware of the Americans.

"I'm sure you will be able to join these pieces," he told her.

"Now you're just trying to get my clothes off."

He smiled. "The thought had occurred to me."

"Can I go with you tomorrow?"

He caught the mischief in her eye and knew he had no choice. "All right. Provided I'm . . . fully satisfied tonight."

"I think that can be arranged."

But he saw that her mind was still on the book and Napoleon's message. She pointed at the handwritten text. "It's Latin. From the Bible. It deals with the story of Jesus and the disciples eating on the Sabbath. There are three versions of that story, one each in Luke, Matthew, and Mark. I've written the fourteen lines out so we can read them.

ET FACTUM EST EUM IN
SABBATO SECUNDO PRIMO A
BIRE PER SCCETES DISCIPULI AUTEM ILLIRIS COE
PERUNT VELLER SPICAS ET FRINCANTES MANIBUS + MANDU
CABANT QUIDAM AUTEM DE FARISAEIS DI
CEBANT EI ECCE QUIA FACIUNT DISCIPULI TUI SAB
BATIS + QUOD NON LICET RESPONDENS AUTEM INS
SE IXIT AD EOS NUMQUAM HOC
LECISTIS QUOD FECIT DAVID QUANDO
ESURUT IPSE ET QUI CUM EO ERAI + INTROIBOT IN DOMUM
DEI EE PANES PROPOSITIONIS
MANDUCA VIT ET DEDIT ET QUI
CUM ERANT UXIIO QUIBOS NO
N LICEBAT MANDUCARE SI NON SOLIS SACERDOTIBUS

"There's a multitude of errors. **Discipuli** is spelled with a **c,** not a **g,** so I corrected that from the original here in the book. Napoleon also made a complete muddle of **ipse dixit.** And the letters **uxiio** make no sense at all. But given all that, here's what it means.

" 'And it came about that on the second Sabbath he walked through a cornfield. But his disciples began to pluck the ears and rubbing them in their hands ate them. Some of the Pharisees said to him, "Behold because your disciples are doing on the Sabbath that which is not lawful." Replying, he said to them, "Have you never read what David did when he was hungry? He and those who were with him entered into the house of God and ate the bread of the sacrament and gave it to those who were with him, for whom it was not lawful to eat, except only for priests." ' "

She glanced up at him. "Damn strange, wouldn't you say?"

"To say the least."

"It doesn't match any of the three biblical verses. More a composite. But there's something even stranger."

He waited.

"Napoleon knew no Latin."

THORVALDSEN SAID GOODBYE TO PROFESSOR Murad and retired upstairs to his suite. The time was approaching midnight, but Paris seemed never to sleep. The Ritz's lobby bustled with activity, people streaming in and out of the noisy salons. As he exited the elevator on his floor, he spotted a dour-faced man with a fleshy complexion and straight dark hair waiting on a settee.

He knew him well, having two years ago hired the man's Danish firm to investigate Cai's death. Their contacts were usually by phone, and he actually thought him in England, supervising Ashby's surveillance.

"I didn't expect to see you here," he said.

"I flew over from London earlier. But I've been monitoring what's happening there."

Something was wrong. "Walk with me."

They strolled down the quiet corridor.

"There's some information you should be aware of."

He stopped and faced his investigator.

"We followed Ashby from the time he left Paris. He went home for a few hours, then out, after dark. He took a walking tour about Jack the Ripper."

He realized the oddity of that for a Londoner.

He was handed a photo. "He met with this woman. We managed to snap a picture."

Only an instant was needed to recognize the face. Stephanie Nelle.

Alarm bells sounded in his brain, and he fought hard to keep his concern to himself.

"Malone was there, too."

Had he heard right? "Malone?"

His investigator nodded and showed him another photo. "In the crowd. He left when the woman did."

"Did Malone talk with Ashby?"

"No, he headed off following a man who did speak with Ashby. We decided to let them both go, so as not to cause a problem."

He did not like the look in the man's eye. "It gets worse?"

The investigator nodded.

"That woman in the photo, she gave Ashby a book."

FORTY-EIGHT

PARIS
TUESDAY, DECEMBER 25
10:30 AM

MALONE EXPLORED THE CHURCH OF THE DOME AT the Hôtel des Invalides. Six chapels jutted from a central core, each housing their respective military heroes and dedicated to either the Virgin Mary or one of the fathers of the Roman Catholic Church. He was patrolling downstairs, twenty feet below the main level, circling Napoleon's tomb. He still hadn't called Gary and was mad at himself for it, but last night had been long.

"Anything?" he heard Stephanie call down from above.

She was standing at a marble balustrade, staring at him.

"There's nowhere to hide anything, much less a bomb, in this mausoleum."

Dogs had already swept every niche. Nothing

had been found. The Invalides itself was now being searched. Nothing, so far. But since Ashby had said the church was the primary target, another careful sweep of every square inch was happening.

He stood at the entrance to a small gallery lit by antique brass lamps. Inside, a floor monument identified the crypt of Napoleon II, King of Rome, 1811–1832. Towering above the son's grave was a white marble statue of the father, decked out in coronation robes, bearing a scepter and globe with a cross.

Stephanie glanced at her watch. "It's approaching meeting time. This building is clean, Cotton. Something's wrong."

They'd entered the hangar at Heathrow last night, after Peter Lyon fled the terminal, and examined the plane. The Cessna's registration was to a nondescript Belgium corporation, owned by a fictitious Czech concern. Europol attempted to tag a human being, but all the names and addresses followed a trail to nowhere. The hangar itself was leased to the same Czech corporation, the rental paid three months in advance.

"Lyon confronted me for a reason," he said. "He wanted us to know that he knew we were there. He left those little Eiffel Towers for us. Hell, he didn't even shield his eyes with glasses. The question is, does Ashby know we know?"

She shook her head. "He's at the Eiffel Tower. Arrived a few minutes ago. We would have heard about it by now, if he did know. I'm told by his

handlers that he's never been bashful about expressing himself."

His mind rifled through the possibilities. Thorvaldsen had tried to call, three times, but he hadn't
answered or returned the calls. Malone had stayed
in London last night to avoid the many questions
about the book that he simply could not answer.
Not now. They'd talk later. The Paris Club had
gathered for its meeting. The Eiffel Tower was
closed until one PM. Only club members, serving
staff, and security would be on the first platform.
Malone knew that Stephanie had decided against
overly infecting the security detail with loaners
from French intelligence. Instead, she'd snuck two
sets of eyes and ears into the meeting room.

"Are Sam and Meagan in place?" he asked.

He saw her nod. "Both quite eager, I might
add."

"That's always a problem."

"I doubt they're in any danger there. Larocque
insisted that everyone be swept for weapons and
listening devices."

He stared at Napoleon's monstrous tomb. "You
know the thing isn't even made of red porphyry?
It's aventurine quartzite from Finland."

"Don't tell the French," she said. "But I guess it's
like the cherry tree and George Washington."

He heard a ding and watched as Stephanie answered her cell phone, listened a moment, then
ended the call.

"A new problem," she said.

He stared up at her.

"Henrik's at the Eiffel Tower, entering the club meeting."

SAM WORE THE SHORT JACKET AND BLACK TROUSERS of the serving staff, all courtesy of Stephanie Nelle. Meagan was similarly attired. They were part of the eleven who'd set up the banquet room with only two circular tables, each clothed in gold linen and adorned with fine china. The hall itself was maybe seventy-five by fifty feet, with a stage at one end. It could have easily accommodated a couple hundred diners, so the two tables seemed lonely.

He was busy preparing coffee cups and condiments and making sure a steaming samovar worked properly. He had no idea how the machine functioned, but it kept him near where members were making their way into the gathering. To his right, courtesy of a long wall of plate-glass windows, was a spectacular view of the Seine and the Right Bank.

Three older men and two middle-aged women had already arrived, each greeted by a stately-looking woman in a gray business suit.

Eliza Larocque.

Three hours ago Stephanie Nelle had shown him photographs of the seven club members, and he connected a face to each picture. Three controlled major lending institutions, one served in the European parliament. Each had paid 20 million euros to be a part of what was happening—which, according to Stephanie, had already netted them far more than 140 million in illicit profits.

Here was the living embodiment of all he'd long suspected existed.

He and Meagan were to look and listen. Above all, Stephanie had cautioned, take no unnecessary chances that could compromise their identities.

He finished fiddling with the coffee machine and turned to leave.

Another guest arrived.

Dressed similarly to the other men in an expensive charcoal-gray business suit, white shirt, and pale yellow tie.

Henrik Thorvaldsen.

THORVALDSEN ENTERED LA SALLE GUSTAV EIFFEL and was immediately greeted by Eliza Larocque. He extended his hand, which she lightly shook.

"I am so glad you are here," she said. "That suit looks quite elegant."

"I rarely wear one. But I thought it best for today's occasion."

She nodded in gratitude. "I appreciate the consideration. It is an important day."

He'd kept his gaze locked on Larocque. It was important for her to think him interested. He noted the small talk occurring elsewhere in the room as a few of the other members milled about. The serving staff were busy preparing the dining and refreshment stations. Long ago he'd taught himself a useful lesson. Within two minutes of entering any room, know if you are among friends or enemies.

He recognized at least half the faces. Men and women of business and finance. A couple were genuine surprises, as he'd never thought them conspiratorialists. They were all wealthy, but not enormously, certainly not in his league, so it made some sense they would latch on to a scheme that could possibly generate some fast, easy, and unaccounted-for profits.

Before he could fully assess his surroundings, a tall, swarthy man with a silver-streaked beard and intense gray eyes approached.

Larocque smiled and extended her arm, sweeping the newcomer close, and saying, "There's someone I'd like you to meet."

She faced him.

"Henrik, this is Lord Graham Ashby."

FORTY-NINE

MALONE ASCENDED FROM NAPOLEON'S CRYPT BY way of a marble staircase, flanked at the top by two bronze funerary spirits. One bore the crown and hand of justice, the other a sword and globe. Stephanie waited for him, standing before the church's great altar with its canopy of twisted columns reminiscent of Bernini's in St. Peter's Basilica.

"Seems Henrik's efforts were successful," she said. "He managed an invitation to the club."

"He's on a mission. You can understand that."

"That I can. But I'm on one too, and **you** can understand that. I want Peter Lyon."

He glanced around at the deserted church. "This whole thing feels wrong. Lyon knows we're on to him. That plane at Heathrow was useless to him from the start."

"But he also knows that we can't tip our hand."

Which was why the Church of the Dome was not surrounded by police. Why the Invalides' hospital and retirement center had not been evacuated. Its ultramodern surgical unit catered to veterans, and about a hundred lived there full-time in buildings that flanked the Church of the Dome. The search for explosives had started there quietly, last night. Nothing to alert anyone that there may be a problem. Just a calm search. A full-scale alarm would have ended any chance of nailing Lyon or the Paris Club.

But the task had proven daunting.

The Invalides comprised hundreds of thousands of square feet, spread over dozens of multistory buildings. Far too many places to hide an explosive.

The radio Stephanie carried crackled with her name, then a male voice said, "We have something."

"Where?" she answered.

"In the cupola."

"We're on our way."

THORVALDSEN SHOOK GRAHAM ASHBY'S HAND, forced his lips to smile, and said, "A pleasure to meet you."

"And you as well. I've known of your family for many years. I also admire your porcelain."

He nodded at the compliment.

He realized Eliza Larocque was watching his every move, performing her own assessment of both he and Ashby, so he summoned all of his charm and continued to play the role.

"Eliza tells me," Ashby said, "that you want to join."

"This seems like a worthwhile endeavor."

"I think you'll find us a good group. We are only beginning, but we have a grand time at these gatherings."

He surveyed the room again and counted seven members, including Ashby and Larocque. Serving staff wandered about like stray ghosts, finishing their tasks, one by one withdrawing through a far doorway.

Bright sunshine flooded in from a wall of windows and bathed the red carpet and plush surroundings in a mellow glow.

Larocque encouraged everyone to find a seat.

Ashby walked off.

Thorvaldsen made his way to the nearest of the two tables, but not before he caught sight of a young man, one of the servers, storing away extra chairs behind the stage to his right. He'd thought at first he was mistaken, but when the worker returned for one more load he was certain.

Sam Collins.

Here.

Malone and Stephanie climbed a cold metal ladder that led up into a space between the interior and exterior walls. The dome itself was not a single piece. Instead, only one of the two stories of windows visible on the drum's exterior could be seen from inside. A second cupola, completely enclosed by the first, visible through the open top of the lower cupola, captured daylight through a second level of windows and illuminated the inside. It was an ingenious nesting design, only evident once high above everything.

They found a platform that abutted the upper cupola, among the building's crisscrossing exoskeleton of wooden timbers and more recent steel beams. Another metal ladder angled toward the center, between the supports, to a second platform that anchored one last ladder leading up into the lantern. They were near the church's summit, nearly three hundred feet high. On the second platform, below the lantern, stood one of the French security personnel who'd slipped into the Invalides several hours ago.

He was pointing upward.

"There."

Eliza was pleased. All seven members, along with Henrik Thorvaldsen, had come. Everyone was finding a seat. She'd insisted on two tables so that no one would feel crowded. She hated to be crowded. Perhaps it came from living alone her entire adult life. Not that a man couldn't occasionally provide a delightful distraction. But the thought of a close personal relationship, someone who'd want to share her thoughts and feelings, and would want her to share his? That repulsed her.

She'd watched carefully as Thorvaldsen met Graham Ashby. Neither man showed any reaction. Clearly, two strangers meeting for the first time.

She checked her watch.

Time to begin.

Before she could attract everyone's attention, Thorvaldsen approached and quietly said, "Did you read this morning's **Le Parisien**?"

"It's waiting for me later today. The morning was busy."

She watched as he reached into his suit pocket and removed a newspaper clipping. "Then you should see this. From page 12A. Top right column."

She quickly scanned the piece, which reported a theft yesterday at the Hôtel des Invalides and its Musée de l'Armée. In one of the galleries being renovated, thieves had taken an item from the Napoleon exhibit.

A book.

The Merovingian Kingdoms 450–751 A.D.

Significant only since it was specifically mentioned in the emperor's will, but otherwise not all that valuable, which was one reason it had been left in the gallery. The museum staff was in the process of inventorying the remaining artifacts to ascertain if anything else had been stolen.

She stared at Thorvaldsen. "How could you possibly know that this may be relevant to me?"

"As I made clear at your château, I've studied you, and him, in great detail."

Thorvaldsen's warning from yesterday rang in her ears.

If I'm right about him, he's going to tell you that he wasn't able to retrieve whatever it is, that it wasn't there, or some other such excuse.

And that's exactly what Graham Ashby had told her.

FIFTY

MALONE CLIMBED THROUGH AN OPENING IN THE floor into the lantern. Frigid air and sunshine greeted him as he stood out in the bright midday, at the top of the church. The view in all directions was stunning. The Seine wound a path through the city to his north, the Louvre rose toward the northeast, the Eiffel Tower less than two miles to the west.

Stephanie followed him up. The security man climbed up last, but remained on the ladder, only his head and shoulders visible.

"I decided to examine the cupola myself," the man said. "Nothing was there, but I wanted a cigarette, so I climbed up here and saw that."

Malone followed the man's pointing finger and spotted a blue box, maybe four inches square, affixed to the lantern's ceiling. A decorative brass railing guarded each of the cupola's four archways. Carefully, he hoisted himself onto one of the railings and stood within a few inches of the box. He spotted a thin wire, perhaps a foot long, extending from one side, dangling in the breeze.

He stared down at Stephanie. "It's a transponder. A beacon to draw that plane here." He wrenched the unit free, held in place with strong adhesive. "Remote-activated. Has to be. But placing it up here took effort."

"Not a problem for Peter Lyon. He's accomplished tougher things than this."

He hopped down, still holding the transponder, and clicked the unit off with a switch on its side. "That should complicate the matter for him." He handed the device to Stephanie. "You realize this is way too easy."

He saw that she agreed.

He stepped to another railing and gazed down to where streets converged at an empty plaza before the church's southern façade. Christmas Day had siphoned away the vast majority of the daily traffic. So as not to alert anyone on the nearby Eiffel Tower, which offered an unobstructed view of the Invalides, no police had cordoned off the streets.

He spotted a light-colored van, speeding northward, down the Boulevard des Invalides. Moving unusually fast. The van whipped left onto Avenue de Tourville, which ran perpendicular to the Church of the Dome's main entrance.

Stephanie noticed his interest.

The van slowed, veered right, then abandoned the street and clunked its way up a short set of stone steps toward the church's main doors.

Stephanie found her radio.

The van cleared the steps and sped forward on a walkway between patches of winter grass. It skidded to a halt at the base of more steps.

The driver's-side door opened.

Stephanie activated her radio, calling for attention, but before she could utter a word a man fled the vehicle and raced toward a car that had appeared on the street.

He jumped in and the car accelerated away.

Then the van exploded.

"LET ME WISH EACH OF YOU A HAPPY CHRISTMAS," Eliza said, standing before the group. "So glad to have everyone here. I thought this locale would be excellent for today's gathering. A little different for us. The tower itself does not open until one, so we have privacy until then." She paused. "And we have a delicious lunch prepared."

She was especially pleased that Robert Mastroianni had come, keeping the pledge he'd made on the plane.

"We have about an hour of business, then I thought a short trip to the top, before the crowds arrive, would be wonderful. It's not often that one has the opportunity to be at the summit of the Eiffel Tower with so few people. I made sure that was included in our lease."

Her suggestion met with a clear approval.

"We're also privileged to have our final two members present."

And she introduced Mastroianni and Thorvaldsen.

"It's wonderful to have you both involved with our group. That brings us to eight, and I believe we'll keep it at that number. Any objections?"

No one voiced a word.

"Excellent."

She glanced around at the eager and attentive faces. Even Graham Ashby seemed exuberant. Had he lied to her about the Merovingian book?

Apparently so.

They'd met earlier, before the others arrived, and Ashby had again told her that the book had not been in its display case. She'd listened carefully, watched his every nuance, and concluded that either he was telling the truth or he was one of the finest liars she'd ever known.

But the book **had** been stolen. Paris' leading newspaper had reported the theft. How did Thorvaldsen know so much? Was Ashby, indeed, a security leak? No time to answer those inquiries at the moment. She had to focus on the task at hand.

"I thought I would begin by telling you a story. Signore Mastroianni will have to excuse the repetition. I told him this same story a couple of days ago, but for the remainder of you it will be instructive. It's about what happened to Napoleon while in Egypt."

MALONE RUSHED FROM THE CHURCH OF THE Dome, through its shattered main entrance. Stephanie followed. The van continued to burn at the foot of the stairs. Besides the glass doors of the entrance itself, little damage had occurred to the church. He realized that a van loaded with explosives this close should have obliterated the entire south façade, not to mention the nearby buildings housing the hospital and veterans' center.

"That wasn't much of a bomb," he said. "More flash in the pan."

Sirens blared in the distance. Fire and police were headed this way. Heat from the smoldering van warmed the chilly midday air.

"Could have been a malfunction?" she said.

"I don't think so."

Sirens grew louder.

Stephanie's radio came to life. She answered the call, and Malone heard what the man on the other end reported.

"We have a live bomber in the Court of Honor."

THORVALDSEN LISTENED AS LAROCQUE FINISHED her Egyptian tale, explained Napoleon's original concept of a Paris Club, and provided an overview of the four papyri. He noticed she hadn't mentioned that he, too, had been previously told much of the information. Clearly, she wanted their conversations private. Her reading of the newspaper clipping had surely affected her.

How could it not?

Her reaction also told him something else. Ashby had not reported that, thanks to Stephanie and Cotton, he now possessed the book.

But what was the Magellan Billet doing in this business?

He'd tried to make contact with Malone during the night and all morning, but his friend had not answered his phone. He'd left messages, and none had been returned. Malone's room at the Ritz went unused last night. And though his investigators had not spied the title of the book Stephanie gave to Ashby, he knew that it was the one from the Invalides.

What else could it be?

There had to be a good reason why Malone handed the book over to Stephanie, but he could not conceive of one.

Ashby sat calmly across the table, watching Larocque with attentive eyes. Thorvaldsen wondered if the other men and women sitting in this room realized what they'd actually signed on for. He doubted Eliza Larocque was solely interested in illicit profits. He sensed from their two meetings that she was a woman on a mission—determined to prove something, perhaps justify her family's denied heritage. Or maybe rewrite history? Whatever **it** may be, it was more than simply making money. She'd assembled this group here, at the Eiffel Tower, on Christmas Day, for a reason.

So he told himself, for the moment, to forget about Malone and concentrate on the problem at hand.

———— A ————

MALONE AND STEPHANIE RACED INTO THE COURT of Honor and stared out into the elegant square. In the center stood a young woman. Maybe early thirties, long dark hair, wearing corduroy trousers and a faded red shirt beneath a black coat. One hand held an object.

Two security men, guns aimed, were positioned in the shadows of the opposite arcade, near the scaffolding where Malone had entered the museum yesterday. Another armed man stood to the left, at the archway that led out through the Invalides' north façade, the iron gates closed.

"What the hell?" Stephanie muttered.

A man appeared behind them, entering the arcade from glass doors that led into the museum. He wore the protective vest and uniform of the French police.

"She appeared a few moments ago," the man informed them.

"I thought you searched these buildings," Stephanie said.

"Madame, there are hundreds of thousands of square meters of buildings here. We have been going as fast as we can, without drawing attention, per your instructions. If someone wanted to evade us, it would not be hard."

He was right.

"What does she want?" Stephanie asked.

"She told the men she controlled a bomb and told them to stand their ground. I radioed you."

Malone wanted to know, "Did she appear before or after the van exploded in front of the church."

"Just after."

"What are you thinking?" Stephanie asked him.

He stared at the woman. She swung around, looking at the various men who continued to train their weapons on her. Wisely, she kept the hand with the controller moving, too.

"**Gardez vos distances et baissez les armes,**" she screamed.

Malone silently translated. Keep your distance and lower your weapons.

None of the men complied.

"**Il se pourrait que la bombe soit à l'hôpital. Ou à l'hospice. Fautil prendre le risque?**" she yelled, displaying the controller. The bomb could well be in the hospital. Or the pensioners' home. Do you risk it?

The policeman standing beside them whispered,

"We searched both of those buildings first. Carefully. There is nothing there."

"**Je ne le redirai pas,**" the woman called out. I shall not say it again.

Malone realized that it was Stephanie's call on what the French would do, and she was not one to be bluffed.

Still.

"Lower the weapons," she ordered.

FIFTY-ONE

ELIZA STROLLED TOWARD THE STAGE AT ONE END OF the hall. A quick glance at her watch confirmed the time. 11:35 AM.

Twenty-five minutes left.

"We will take our trip to the top soon. First, though, I want to explain what I am proposing for our near future."

She faced the group.

"Over the past decade we've seen a great deal of change in world financial markets. Futures, once a way for producers to hedge their products, are now simply a game of chance, where commodities that don't exist are traded at prices that bear no relation to reality. We saw this a few years ago when oil topped off at more than $150 a barrel. That price had no relation to supply, which was, at the time, at an all-time high. Eventually, that market imploded and prices plummeted."

She saw that many in the room agreed with her assessment.

"America is mainly to blame for this," she made clear. "In 1999 and 2000 legislation was passed that paved the way for a speculative onslaught. That legislation actually repealed older statutes, passed in the 1930s, designed to prevent another stock market crash. With the safeguards gone, the same problems from the 1930s recurred. The global stock market devaluations that ensued should have been no surprise."

She caught the curious expressions of a few faces.

"It's elementary. Laws that place greed and irresponsibility before hard work and sacrifice come with a price." She paused. "But they also create opportunities."

The room was silent.

"Between August 26 and September 11, 2001, a group of covert speculators sold short a list of thirty-eight stocks that could reasonably be expected to fall in value as the result of any attack on America. They operated out of the Canadian and German stock exchanges. The companies included United Airlines, American Airlines, Boeing, Lockheed Martin, Bank of America, Morgan Stanley Dean Witter, Merrill Lynch. In Europe, they targeted insurance companies. Munich Re, Swiss Re, and AXA. On the Friday before the attacks, ten million shares of Merrill Lynch were sold. No more than four million are sold on a normal day. Both United and American Airlines saw an unusual amount of speculative activity in the days prior to the attack. No other airline company experienced this."

"What are you suggesting?" one of the group asked.

"Only what an Israeli counterterrorism think tank concluded when it studied Osama bin Laden's financial portfolio. Nearly twenty million U.S. dollars in profits were realized by bin Laden from the September 11 attacks."

MALONE HEARD THE ROAR OF A HELICOPTER OVERhead and glanced up to see a Royal Navy Westland Lynx sweep past at low altitude.

"NATO," Stephanie said to him.

At Stephanie's instruction, the men encircling the woman in the courtyard had lowered their weapons.

"I did as you wanted," Stephanie called out in French.

The bomber did not reply. She stood fifty feet away and kept her gaze on the arcades that surrounded the Court of Honor. She remained edgy, unsteady, keeping her hands in constant movement.

"What do you want?" Stephanie asked her.

Malone kept his eyes locked on the woman and

used the few seconds when her gaze drifted away to ease his hand beneath his jacket, his fingers finding the Beretta that Stephanie had provided a few hours ago.

"I came to prove a point," the woman yelled in French. "To all those who want to treat us with hate."

He clamped his hand tight on the gun.

Her hands kept moving, the bomb controller in constant flight, her head flitting from one point to another.

"Who is **us**?" Stephanie asked.

Malone knew his former boss was playing the scenario by the manual. Keep the attacker occupied. Be patient. Play for a fumble.

The woman's eyes met Stephanie's. "France must know that we are not to be ignored."

Malone waited for her to resume her visual reconnoiter of the cobbled pavement, just as she'd done before.

"Who is—" Stephanie said

The hand with the controller swung left.

As her head pivoted toward the opposite arcade, Malone freed his gun and leveled his aim.

SAM HAD SECRETED HIMSELF JUST BEYOND THE meeting room's stage, out of sight. He'd managed to remain inside the room, undetected, as the rest of the staff vacated. The idea had been to maneuver one of them within earshot. He'd watched as Meagan had tried, but was corralled by the other servers to help remove some serving carts. Her frustrated eyes had told him that it was up to him, and he'd made his move.

No security personnel remained inside. All of them had been stationed outside. No danger existed of anyone entering from the doors that led out to the observation balcony, since it was nearly two hundred feet above the ground.

He'd listened to Eliza Larocque's speech and understood exactly what she was describing. Short selling happened when someone sold a stock they did not own in the hope of repurchasing it later, at a lower price. The idea was to profit from an expected decline in price.

A risky venture in a multitude of ways.

First, the potentially shorted securities have to be borrowed from their owner, then sold for the current price. Once the price dropped, they would be repurchased at the lower value, returned to the owner, the profit kept by the short seller. If the price climbed, as opposed to falling, the stocks would have to be repurchased at the higher price, generating a loss. Of course, if the short seller knew that the price of a given security would drop, and even the exact moment when that would happen, any risk of loss would be nonexistent.

And the profit potential would be enormous.

One of the financial manipulations his and Meagan's websites had warned about.

He'd heard rumors within the Secret Service about bin Laden's possible manipulation, but those investigations were classified, handled many levels above him. Perhaps his postings on the subject were what had caused his superiors to apply pressure. Hearing Eliza Larocque say many of the same things he'd publicly speculated about only confirmed what he'd long suspected.

He'd been closer to the truth than he'd ever realized.

ASHBY LISTENED WITH GREAT INTEREST TO WHAT Larocque was saying, beginning to piece together what she may be planning. Though he'd been charged with arranging for Peter Lyon, she hadn't shared the substance of her entire plan.

"The problem with what bin Laden set in motion," she said, "was that he failed to anticipate two things. First, the American stock market was completely closed for four full days after the attacks. And second, there are automatic procedures in place to detect short selling. One of those, 'blue sheeting,' analyzes trade volumes and identifies potential threats. Those four down days gave market authorities time to notice. At least in America. But overseas the markets continued to function, and profits were quickly extracted before anyone could detect the manipulation."

Ashby's mind recalled the aftermath of September 11, 2001. Larocque was right. Munich Re, Europe's second largest reinsurer, lost nearly two billion dollars from the destruction of the World Trade Center, and its stock plummeted after the attacks. A knowledgeable short seller could have made millions.

He also recalled what happened to other markets.

Dow Jones down 14%, Standard & Poor's 500 Index reduced 12%, NASDAQ Composite down 16%—those same results mirrored in nearly every overseas market for weeks after the attacks. His own portfolio had taken a beating—actually the beginning of a downturn that progressively worsened.

And what she said about derivatives. All true. Nothing more than wild bets placed with borrowed money. Interest rates, foreign currencies, stocks, corporate failures—all of them were gambled upon by investors, banks, and brokerages. His financial analysts once told him that more than 800 trillion euros, worldwide, stayed at risk on any given day.

Now he was learning that there may be a way to profit from all that risk.

If he'd only known.

MALONE WATCHED AS THE WOMAN SPOTTED HIS gun. Her eyes locked on his.

"Go ahead," he yelled in French. "Do it."

She pressed the controller.

Nothing happened.

Again.

No explosion.

Bewilderment swept across her face.

FIFTY-TWO

THORVALDSEN SAT RIGID IN HIS CHAIR, BUT HE WAS finding it hard to maintain his composure. Here was a woman calmly discussing how a terrorist profited from murdering thousands of innocent people. No outrage, no disgust. Instead, Eliza Larocque was clearly in awe of the achievement.

Likewise, Graham Ashby seemed impressed. No surprise there. His amoral personality would have no problem profiting from other people's misery. He wondered if Ashby had ever given a thought to those seven dead in Mexico City. Or had he simply heaved a sigh of relief that **his** troubles were finally resolved? He clearly did not know the names of the dead. If he had, Ashby would have reacted when they were introduced earlier. But not a hint of recognition. Why would he know the victims? Or care? Amando Cabral had been charged with cleaning up the mess, and the less Ashby knew of the details, the better.

"Why have we never heard of this before?" Ashby asked.

"The Internet has been alive with rumors for years," Larocque said. "**Les Echos,** a quite reputable French financial periodical, published an article on the subject in 2007. Several American newspapers have hinted at the story. People whom I know close to the U.S. government tell me that the entire matter has been stamped classified. I don't imagine the Americans want those rumors confirmed. Officially, the Securities and Exchange Commission has stated that there was no insider trading."

Ashby chuckled. "Typical Yanks. Slam a lid on things and hope it goes away."

"Which this did," another in the group said.

"But we can learn from that effort," Larocque said. "In fact, I've been studying it for some time."

MALONE LOWERED HIS WEAPON AS THE SECURITY men swarmed over the woman. Her arms and hands were restrained and she was hauled from the Court of Honor.

"How did you know to call her bluff?" Stephanie asked.

"That bomb out front was nothing. They could have blown the entire church away. Lyon was counting on a loose net and took advantage of it." He motioned with the Beretta at the controller on the pavement. "That thing activates nothing."

"And what if you'd been wrong?"

"I wasn't."

Stephanie shook her head.

"Lyon didn't lead us here to kill us," he said. "He knew Ashby was playing both sides. He led us here because he wanted us **here.**"

"That woman had no idea. The look on her face said it all. She was ready to blow something up."

"There's a fool for every job. Lyon used her to buy more time. He wants us busy, at least until he's ready for us."

Inside the courtyard, surrounded by the Invalides' four-story buildings, they could not see the Eiffel Tower. What was happening there with Sam and Henrik. He thought back to the dome and the transponder. "My guess is, when we shut that homing device off we signaled for the show to begin."

Stephanie's radio sprang to life.

"Are you there?" The voice was a deep baritone and instantly recognizable. President Danny Daniels.

Surprise filled her face.

"Yes, sir. I'm here," she answered.

"Cotton there, too?"

"He is."

"Staff wanted to handle this communication, but I thought it better that I speak to you myself. We don't have time for translations and interpretations. We've been monitoring things here and you've got one squirrelly mess over there. Here's a new wrinkle. Six minutes ago a small plane diverted off its flight path and bypassed a scheduled landing at Aéroport de Paris—Le Bourget."

Malone knew the field, located about seven miles northeast. For decades it was Paris' only airport, famous as the landing site for Charles Lindbergh's transatlantic crossing in 1927.

"That plane is now headed your way," Daniels said.

All of the dots connected in Malone's brain and he said, "That's what Lyon had been buying time for."

"What do you want us to do?" Stephanie asked.

"There's a NATO helicopter landing, as we speak, to the north of the Invalides. Climb aboard. I'll contact you there."

ELIZA WAS ENJOYING THE MOMENT. THE EXPRESSions her words inspired on the faces of her audience confirmed that she'd chosen this group correctly. Each one was a bold, intrepid entrepreneur.

"Bin Laden failed because he allowed fanaticism to overtake good judgment. He wasn't careful. He wanted to make a statement and he wanted the world to know he made it." She shook her head. "You can't generate long-term profits from such foolishness."

"I'm not interested in killing people," Robert Mastroianni said.

"Neither am I. And it's not necessary. All you need is a credible threat that the public fears. Within that fear is where we will operate."

"Isn't the world scared enough?" one of the others asked.

"Indeed it is," she said. "All we have to do is use it to our advantage."

She reminded herself of something her mother had taught her. **The best way to gain listeners' confidence is make them think you have trusted them with a secret.**

"We have the wisdom of the papyri. They taught Napoleon a great deal and, believe me, they can guide us as well."

She settled her face into a thoughtful expression.

"The world is already scared. Terrorism is real. None of us can alter that. The issue is how that reality can be used."

"**Cui bono,**" one of them said.

She smiled. "That's right. Who benefits. That Latin principle describes this endeavor perfectly." She raised a finger to add emphasis. "Have you ever considered who does benefit from terrorism? There's an immediate increase in airport and building security. Who controls all those facilities? The flow of air traffic—not to mention data. Profits are made by those who provide these essential services. The economics of the insurance business is directly affected. The militarization of our air, land, water, oceans, and space is occurring at increased levels. Nothing is too expensive to protect us from a threat. The business of logistical support, engineering, and construction services related to the **war** on terror is staggering. This war is fought more by private contractors than the military itself. Profits made there are almost beyond comprehension. We've seen shares in companies that supply war-support services increase in value by five to eight hundred percent since 2001."

She smiled, offering a lift of her brow.

"Some of that is obvious, I realize. But there are other, more subtle ways to profit. These I want to speak with you about after lunch."

"What are you planning?" Ashby asked her. "I'm bloody curious."

She did not doubt that observation. She was curious, too. Wondering if Ashby was a friend or foe.

"Let me explain it this way. In the late 1990s South Korea, Thailand, and Indonesia all experienced near financial collapse. The International Monetary Fund eventually bailed them out. Our own Robert Mastroianni was working with the IMF then, so he knows what I'm referring to."

Mastroianni nodded in assent.

"While that bailout occurred, investors ransacked all three economies, reaping huge profits. If you possess the right information, at the right time, even in the risky derivatives and futures markets, millions in profits can be made. I've made some preliminary projections. With the nearly three hundred million euros we currently have on hand, a return of between four point four and eight billion euros can reasonably be expected over the next twenty-four months. And I'm being conservative. All of those amounts would accrue tax-free, of course."

She saw that the group liked that prediction. Nothing appealed to a person with money more than the opportunity to make more money. Her grandfather had been right when he said, **Make all the money possible and spend it, for there is much more to be made.**

"How would we be allowed to get away with this?" one of them asked.

She shrugged. "How can we not? Government is incapable of managing the system. Few within government even understand the problem, much less how to fashion a solution. And the general public is totally ignorant. Just look at what the Nigerians do every day. They send out millions of emails to unsuspecting people, claiming that a huge return can be made on some sort of unclaimed funds, provided you forward a small administrative fee. Countless people around the globe have been bilked. When it comes to money, few think clearly. I propose that we think with crystal clarity."

"And how are we to do that?"

"I'll explain all of that after lunch. Suffice it to say that we are in the process of securing a source of financing that should provide us many more billions in untraced resources. It's a cache of unrecorded wealth that can be invested and used to our collective advantage. Right now, it's time for us to venture to the top of the tower for our few minutes of viewing."

The group stood.

"I assure you," she said, "the trip will be worth it."

FIFTY-THREE

MALONE LISTENED AS THE ROLLS-ROYCE TUR-boshafts drove the blades of the Westland Lynx. The navy had taught him how to fly fighters and he'd logged a respectable amount of time in jets, but he'd never flown a helicopter. He settled back in the rear compartment as the chopper arched up into a cold midday sky.

Stephanie sat beside him.

A rap from the cockpit door window caught his attention. The pilot was pointing to his headset and motioning to two sets that hung on the wall. A corpsman handed the earphones over to both he and Stephanie.

"There's an encrypted communication coming in for you," the pilot's voice said in his ears.

He twisted the microphone close to his mouth. "Let's hear it."

A few clicks and a voice said, "I'm back."

"Care to tell us what's going on?" Malone asked Danny Daniels.

"The plane deviated off course. First it headed north, away from the city, and now it's turned back south. No radio contact can be made. I want you two to check it out before we blow it from the sky. I have the French president on the other line. He's scrambled a fighter. Right now the target's not over any populated areas, so we can take it down. But we don't want to do that, obviously, unless absolutely necessary. Too much explaining to do."

"You sure this threat is real?" he asked.

"Hell, Cotton, I'm not sure of crap. But Lyon had a plane at Heathrow. You found it. Which, I might add, seems like he wanted us to find—"

"So you know what happened last night?"

"Every detail. I want this son of a bitch. I had friends die when he bombed our embassy in Greece, and they are only a few of the many he's killed. We're going to punch this guy's ticket."

One of the pilots slid the panel door to the cockpit open and motioned ahead. Malone searched the sky. Clouds lay like tracks above the French landscape. The outskirts of Paris rolled past beneath the chopper's undercarriage. He spotted a blue-and-yellow-striped fuselage in the distance—another Cessna Skyhawk, identical to the one seen last night—cruising at about five thousand feet.

"Close the gap," he told the pilot through his headset.

"You see it?" Daniels asked.

He felt power seep from the rotors as the helicopter knifed its way forward.

The plane's metal sheeting sparkled in the sunshine.

"Stay behind him, out of his vision field," Malone told the pilot.

He spied red identification numbers on the tail that matched the ones from last night.

"That plane's ID is the same as the one in Heathrow," he said into the headset.

"You think Lyon is in the plane?" Daniels asked.

"I'd be surprised," Malone answered. "He's more the conductor than a member of the orchestra."

"It's turning," the pilot said.

He stared out the window and saw the Skyhawk bank east.

"Where are we?" he asked the pilot.

"North of Paris, maybe four miles. With that vector the plane has turned away from the city center, which will take us beyond the town proper."

He was trying to make sense of all that he knew. Scattered pieces. Random, yet connected.

"It's turning again," the pilot said. "Now on a westerly course. That's completely away from Paris, toward Versailles."

He wrenched the earphones off. "Did he spot us?"

"Not likely," the pilot said. "His maneuver was casual."

"Can we approach from above?"

The pilot nodded. "As long as he doesn't decide to climb."

"Do it."

The rudder control angled forward and the chopper's airspeed increased. The gap to the Skyhawk began to close.

The copilot motioned to the headset. "That same bloke again on the radio."

He snapped the headphones back on. "What is it?"

"The French want to take that plane down," Daniels said. "What do I tell them?"

He felt Stephanie's grip on his right arm. She was motioning forward, out the windshield. He turned just as the cabin door on the Skyhawk's left side sprang fully open.

"What the—"

The pilot jumped from the plane.

ASHBY WAS THE LAST TO CLIMB ABOARD THE ELEVATOR. The eight members of the Paris Club filled three glass-walled cars that rose from the second platform another 175 meters to the Eiffel Tower's summit. The giddy ascent, within the open ironwork, was a bit harrowing.

A bright sun set the world below glittering. He spied the Seine and thought its name apt—it meant "winding," and that was exactly what the river did through central Paris with three sharp curves. Usually car-jammed avenues that paralleled and crisscrossed the waterway were short on traffic for Christmas. In the distance rose the hulk of Notre Dame, engulfed by more church domes, zinc roofs, and a forest of chimney thickets. He caught a quick glimpse of La Défense and its avenues of high-rise towers. He also noticed lights affixed to the Eiffel Tower's girders—the source, he surmised, of the electric shimmy that illuminated the thing each night.

He checked his watch.

11:43 AM.

Not long now.

MALONE WATCHED AS A PARACHUTE SPRANG OPEN and the canopy caught air. The Skyhawk continued its westerly course, holding altitude and speed. Below was a vast expanse of field, forest, villages, and roads that dotted the rural landscape outside Paris.

He pointed to the plane and told the pilot, "Head in for a closer look."

The chopper eased forward and approached the Skyhawk. Malone shifted his position to the port side of the helicopter and stared out at the single-engine plane.

"No one inside," he said into the microphone.

He didn't like any of this. He turned to the corpsman. "Do you have binoculars?"

The young man quickly produced a pair. Malone focused across the bright sky at the Skyhawk.

"Ease forward some," he told the pilot.

Their parallel course changed, the chopper now slightly ahead of the plane. Through the binoculars he zeroed his gaze past the tinted windshield into the cockpit. The two seats were empty, yet the steering column moved in calculated jerks. Something lay on the copilot's seat, but a glare made it difficult to make out. Beyond, the aft seat was packed with packages wrapped in newspaper.

He lowered the binoculars.

"That plane's carrying something," he said. "I can't tell what, but there's an awful lot of it."

The Skyhawk's wings dipped and the plane banked south. The turn was controlled, as if someone was flying.

"Cotton," Daniels said in his ear. "What's your assessment?"

He wasn't sure. They were being led—no question—and he'd thought this plane to be the end. But—

"This is not our problem," he said into the microphone.

"Do you agree, Stephanie?" Daniels asked.

"I do."

Good to see that she still trusted his judgment, since her expression contradicted her words.

"Then where's our problem?" the president asked.

He played a hunch. "Have French air traffic control scan the area. We need to know about every plane in the sky."

"Hold on."

ELIZA STEPPED FROM THE ELEVATOR INTO THE empty summit-level observation area, seventy-five stories above the ground. "A bit unnerving to be here with no one else," she said to the group. "This platform is usually packed."

She pointed to metal stairs that led up through the ceiling, outside, to the uppermost deck.

"Shall we?" she said.

She watched as the group climbed the stairs. Ashby stood with her. When the last of them exited through the doorway at the top, she turned to him and asked, "Will it happen?"

He nodded. "In exactly fifteen minutes."

FIFTY-FOUR

MALONE KEPT HIS EYES ON THE SKYHAWK AND SAW the plane alter course once again. More southerly, as if seeking something.

"Is that fighter here?" he asked into the headset, wondering if anybody was still there.

"It's in position," Daniels said.

He made a decision. "Take it down while we still can. Nothing but fields below, but the city is coming up fast."

He banged on the window and told the pilot, "Back us off, and fast."

The Skyhawk accelerated away as the helicopter slowed.

"The order's been given," Daniels said.

THORVALDSEN STEPPED OUT INTO COLD DECEMBER air. He'd never visited the top of the Eiffel Tower.

No particular reason why he hadn't. Lisette had wanted to come once years ago, but business had prevented the trip. **We'll go next summer,** he'd told her. But next summer had come and gone, and more summers thereafter, until Lisette lay dying and there were no more. Cai had visited several times and liked to tell him about the view—which, he had to admit, was stunning. A placard affixed to the railing, beneath a cage that encased the observation deck, noted that on a clear day the view extended for sixty kilometers.

And today certainly qualified as clear. One of those sparkling winter days, capped by a cloudless, azure sky. He was glad he'd wore his thickest wool coat, gloves, and scarf, but French winters had nothing on their Danish counterpart.

Paris had always mystified him. He'd never been impressed. He actually liked a line from **Pulp Fiction,** one John Travolta's character had casually uttered. **Things are the same there as here, just a little bit different.** He and Jesper had watched the movie a few years ago, intrigued by its premise, but ultimately repulsed by the violence. Until a couple of days ago, he'd never considered violence except in self-defense. But he'd gunned down Amando Cabral and his armed accomplice with not a single speck of remorse.

And that worried him.

Malone was right.

He couldn't just murder people.

But staring across the chilly observation deck at Graham Ashby, who stood near Larocque, gazing out at Paris, he realized that murdering this man would be a pleasure. Interesting how his world had become so defined by hate. He told himself to think pleasant thoughts. His face and mood must not reveal what he was thinking.

He'd come this far.

Now finish.

ASHBY KNEW WHAT ELIZA LAROCQUE EXPECTED. She wanted a small plane, loaded with explosives, to crash into the Church of the Dome at the south end of the Invalides.

A grand spectacle.

The particular fanatics who'd volunteered to accept complete responsibility loved the idea. The gesture had a ghoulish 9/11 feel, albeit on a smaller scale, with no loss of life. That was why Christmas Day had been chosen: The Invalides and the church both were closed.

Simultaneous with the attack in Paris, two other national monuments, the Musée d'Aquitaine in Bordeaux, and the Palais des Papes in Avignon, would be bombed. Both closed, too.

Each act purely symbolic.

As they'd circled the observation platform, taking in the sights, he'd noticed a vehicle burning, smoke drifting into the cold air, from the front of the church at the Invalides. Police, fire, and emergency vehicles seemed abundant. Some of the others saw it, too. He caught a few comments, but nothing of dire concern. The situation seemed in hand. Surely the flames were related to Lyon, but he had no idea what the South African had actually planned. No details had been shared, nor had he wanted to know.

The only requirement was that it happen at noon.

He glanced at his watch.

Time to go.

He'd purposely drifted away from the others as Larocque led them on a visual tour. He'd noticed that she'd started with the view facing north, then walked to the west platform. As the group rounded to the south, he quickly stepped through the exit doorway that led down to the enclosed observation room. Slowly, he slid the glass panel shut, engaging the keyed lock at its bottom. Mr. Guildhall had thoroughly reconnoitered the summit platform and discovered that the two doors that lead up from the enclosed portion were equipped with bolts that engaged with a simple push and opened with a key that only security people carried.

But not today.

Larocque had bargained for the club to have an hour alone at the top, ending around twelve forty

PM, twenty minutes before ticket booths opened 275 meters below and visitors flooded upward.

Quickly, he descended fourteen metal risers and crossed to the east side. Larocque and the others were still on the south side, taking in the sights. He climbed the metal stairs to the second door and quietly slid the thick glass panel closed, engaging its lock.

The Paris Club was trapped at the top.

He descended the stairs, entered one of the elevators that waited, and sent the car downward.

"I HAVE THE INFORMATION," DANIELS SAID IN MAlone's headphones. "Six planes currently in Parisian airspace. Four are commercial jetliners on approach to Orly and Charles de Gaulle. Two are private." The president paused. "Both acting strange."

"Define that," Stephanie asked.

"One is not responding to radio commands. The other responded then did something different than was indicated."

"And they're both headed this way," Malone guessed, knowing the answer.

"One from the southeast, the other from southwest. We have a visual on the one from the southwest. It's a Beechcraft."

Malone banged on the cockpit window. "Head

southeast," he ordered the pilot, who'd been listening to the exchange.

"You sure?" Daniels said.

"He's sure," Stephanie answered.

He caught an aerial explosion off to their right, maybe five miles away.

The Skyhawk had been destroyed.

"I'm just told that the first plane is gone," Daniels said.

"And I'm betting there's another Skyhawk," Malone said. "To the southeast, headed this way."

"You're right, Cotton," Daniels said. "Just received a visual. Same colors and insignia as the one we just took down."

"That's the target," he said. "The one Lyon's protecting."

"And you have one more problem," the president said.

"I already know," Malone said. "We can't blow this one up. It's well over the city."

He heard Daniels sigh. "Seems the son of a bitch plans well."

ELIZA HEARD A BOOM IN THE DISTANCE, FROM THE tower's opposite side. She stood on the south portion of the observation deck, gazing out toward the Champ de Mars. Private houses and blocks of luxury flats lined both sides of the former parade ground, wide avenues paralleling both sides.

A quick glance to her left and she saw the Invalides, the gilded dome of the church still intact. She wondered about the noise, knowing that what she'd planned for so long was still a few minutes away. Ashby had told her that the plane would come from the north, swooping in over the Seine, following a locator beacon that had been hidden inside the dome a few days ago.

The plane would be loaded with explosives and, combined with its nearly full tanks of fuel, the resulting explosion promised to be quite a spectacle. She and the others would have an unobstructed view from nearly three hundred meters in the air.

"Shall we move to the east side for a final look before heading down?" she said.

They all rounded a corner.

She'd purposefully orchestrated their route around the platform, slowly gazing at the sights and the delightful day, so that they would end facing east, toward the Invalides.

She glanced around. "Has anyone seen Lord Ashby?"

A few shook their heads.

"I'll take a look," Thorvaldsen said.

THE WESTLAND LYNX SLICED ITS WAY THROUGH THE air, heading toward the Skyhawk. Malone kept his eyes locked outside the windows and spotted the plane.

"Eleven o'clock," he told the pilot. "Swing in close."

The chopper swooped around and quickly overcame the single-engine plane. Malone spied the cockpit through binoculars and saw that the two seats were empty, the steering column moving, as in the other plane, with calculated strokes. Just as before, something lay on the copilot's seat. Beyond, the aft area was packed tight with more packages wrapped in newspaper.

"It's just like the other one," he said, lowering the binoculars. "Flying automatically. But this one's for real. Lyon timed it so that there'd be little opportunity to deal with the problem." He glanced toward the ground. Nothing but streets and buildings stretched for miles. "And few options."

"So much for him telegraphing messages to us," Stephanie said.

"He didn't make it easy."

Outside the helicopter's window he spied a rescue hoist with steel cable.

What had to be done was clear, but he wasn't looking forward to it. He turned to the corpsman. "You have a body harness for that winch?"

The man nodded.

"Get it."

"What are you thinking?" Stephanie asked.

"Somebody has to go down to that plane."

"How do you plan to do that?"

He motioned outside. "A gentle drop."

"I can't allow that."

"You have a better idea?"

She shook her head. "No, but I'm the senior officer here. And that's final."

"Cotton's right," Daniels said into their ears. "It's the only play. You have to get control of that plane. We can't shoot it down."

"You wanted my help," he said to her. "So let me help."

Stephanie stared at him with a look that said **Do you really think this is necessary?**

"It's the only way," he said.

She nodded her assent.

He wrenched the headset off and slipped on an insulated flight suit that the corpsman handed him. He zipped it closed, then tightened a harness around his chest. The corpsman tested the fit with a few stiff tugs.

"There's big wind out there," the younger man said. "You're going to be swept back on the cable. The pilot'll keep the distance tight to minimize drift." The corpsman handed him a parachute, which he slipped on over the harness.

"Glad to see you have some sense," Stephanie yelled over the turbines.

"Don't worry. I've done this before."

"You don't lie well," she said.

He donned a wool cap that, thankfully, shielded his entire face like a bank robber. A pair of yellow-tinted goggles protected his eyes.

The corpsman motioned, asking if he was ready.

He nodded.

The compartment door was slid open. Frigid air flooded in. He slipped on a pair of thick insulated gloves. He heard a snap as the steel hook of the hoist was affixed to the harness.

He counted to five, then stepped outside.

FIFTY-FIVE

THORVALDSEN MADE HIS WAY AROUND FROM THE north to the west side of the caged deck. He passed windows on his right that exhibited wax figures of Gustave Eiffel and Thomas Edison, made to look like they were chatting in Eiffel's former quarters. Everything loomed still and quiet, and only the wind accompanied him.

Ashby was nowhere to be seen.

Halfway, he stopped and noticed that the glass door for the exit was closed. When the group had passed here a few minutes ago, the door had been open. He gripped the handle and tested.

Locked.

Perhaps one of the staff had secured it? But why? The tower would soon be open to visitors. Why lock one of only two ways to the top deck?

He walked back to the east side, where the others stood gazing out at the panorama. The second exit door was closed, too. He tested its handle.

Locked.

He listened as Eliza Larocque pointed out some landmarks. "That's the Invalides, there. Maybe three kilometers away. It's where Napoleon is entombed. Seems some sort of disturbance has occurred."

He saw a vehicle smoldering in front of the church, a multitude of fire trucks and police dotting the avenues that stretched away from the monument. He wondered if what was happening there was connected to the two locked doors. Coincidence rarely was coincidental.

"Madame Larocque," he said, trying to catch her attention.

She faced him.

"Both exits leading down are locked shut."

He caught the puzzled look on her face. "How is that possible?"

He decided to answer her question in another way. "And there's one other disturbing piece of news."

She stared at him with an intense glare.

"Lord Ashby is gone."

SAM WAITED ON THE FIRST-LEVEL PLATFORM AND wondered what was happening five hundred feet overhead. When the Paris Club had vacated the meeting room, and the staff had returned to prepare for lunch, he'd blended into the commotion.

"How'd it go?" Meagan whispered to him as they adjusted the silverware and plates at the dining tables.

"These people have some big plans," he murmured.

"Care to enlighten me?"

"Not now. Let's just say we were right."

They finished preparing the two tables. He caught an enticing waft of steaming vegetables and grilled beef. He was hungry, but there was no time to eat at the moment.

He readjusted the chairs before each place setting.

"They've been at the top about half an hour now," Meagan said as they worked.

Three security men kept watch on the attendants. He knew that this time he could not remain inside. He'd also seen Henrik Thorvaldsen's reaction as the Dane realized Sam was there. Surely he had to be wondering what was happening. He'd been told that Thorvaldsen was unaware of the American presence, and Stephanie had made it clear that she wanted to keep it a secret. He'd wondered why, but had decided to stop arguing with his superiors.

The chief steward signaled that everyone should withdraw.

He and Meagan left through the main doors with everyone else. They would wait in the nearby restaurant for the signal to return and clear away the dishes. He stared upward into the latticework of brown-gray pig iron. An elevator descended from the second level above.

He noticed that Meagan saw it, too.

They both hesitated at the central railing, near the restaurant's entrance, as other attendants hustled inside from the cold.

The elevator stopped at their level.

The car would open on the far side of the platform, beyond the meeting room, out of sight from where he and Meagan stood. Sam realized they could only hesitate a few moments longer before drawing the suspicion of either the head steward or the security men, who'd retaken their positions outside the meeting room doors.

Graham Ashby appeared.

Alone.

He hustled to the staircase that led down to ground level and disappeared.

"He was in a hurry," Meagan said.

He agreed. Something was wrong.

"Follow him," he ordered. "But don't get caught."

She flashed him a quizzical look, clearly caught off guard by the sudden harshness in his voice. "Why?"

"Just do it."

He had no time to argue and started off.

"Where are **you** going?" she asked.

"To the top."

MALONE NEVER HEARD THE HELICOPTER DOOR slam closed behind him, but he felt when the winch began to unwind. He positioned his arms at his side and lay prone with his legs extended outward. The sensation of falling was negated by the cable's firm grip.

He descended and, as the corpsman predicted, was swept back. The Skyhawk was flying fifty feet below him. The winch continued to slacken the cable and he slowly eased himself toward the wing top.

Bitter-cold air washed his body. The suit and wool face cap offered some protection, but his nose and lips began to chap in the arid air.

His feet found the wing.

The Skyhawk shivered at his violation, but quickly stabilized. He gently pushed off and motioned for more slack as he maneuvered toward the cabin door on the pilot's side.

A gust of cold air rushed past, disrupting his equilibrium, and his body swung out on the cable.

He clung to the line and managed to swing himself back toward the plane.

He again motioned and felt the cable lengthen.

The Skyhawk was a high-wing craft, its ailerons mounted to the top of the fuselage, supported by diagonal struts. To get inside he was going to have to slip below the wing. He motioned for the chopper to fall back so he could be lowered farther. The pilot seemed to know intuitively what Malone was thinking and easily slipped down so he was level with the cabin windows.

He peered inside.

The rear seats had been removed and the newspaper-wrapped bundles were indeed stacked ceiling-to-floor. His body was being buffeted and, despite the goggles, dry air sapped the moisture from his eyes.

He motioned for more slack and, as the cable loosened, he grabbed the flap's leading edge and maneuvered himself over to the strut, planting his feet onto the landing gear housing, wedging his body between the strut and wing. His weight disrupted the plane's aerodynamics and he watched as elevators and flaps compensated.

The cable continued to unwind, looping down below the plane, then stopped. Apparently, the corpsman had realized that there was no longer any tension.

He pressed his face close to the cabin window and stared inside.

A small gray box lay on the passenger's seat. Cables snaked to the instrument panel. He focused again on the wrapped packages. Toward the bottom, in the space between the two front seats, the bundles were bare, revealing a lavender-colored material.

Plastique explosives.

C-83, possibly, he figured.

Powerful stuff.

He should to get inside the Skyhawk, but before he could decide what to do, he noticed the cable slack receding. They were winching him back to the chopper and the wing blocked his ability to signal **no.**

He couldn't go back now.

So before the cable yanked him from his perch, he released the D-clamp and tossed the hook out, which continued a steady climb upward.

He clung to the strut and reached for the door latch.

The door opened.

The problem was the angle. He was positioned ahead, the hinges to his left, the door opening toward the front of the plane. Air sweeping from the prop beneath the wing was working against him, forcing the door closed.

He wrapped the gloved fingers of his left hand around the door's outer edge, his right hand still gripping the strut. At the limit of his peripheral vision he spied the chopper easing down to have a look. He managed to open the door against the wind but found that its hinges stopped at ninety degrees, which left not nearly enough space for him to slip inside.

Only one way left.

He released his grip on the strut, grabbed the

door with both hands, and swung his body inward toward the cockpit. Airspeed instantly worked the door hinges closed and his parachute pounded into the fuselage, the metal panel lodging him against the open doorway. His grip held and he slowly worked his right leg inside, then folded the rest of his body into the cockpit. Luckily the pilot's seat was fully extended.

He snapped the door shut and breathed a sigh of relief.

The plane's yoke steadily gyrated right and left.

On the instrument panel he located the direction finder. The plane was still on a northwesterly course. A full moving map GPS, which he assumed was coupled to the autopilot, seemed to be providing flight control but, strangely, the autopilot was disengaged.

He caught movement out of the corner of his eye and turned to see the chopper now snuggled close to the left wing tip. In the cabin window was a sign with numbers on it. Stephanie was pointing to her headset and motioning to the numbers.

He understood.

The Skyhawk's radio stack was to his right. He switched the unit on and found the frequency for the numbers she'd indicated. He yanked off the wool cap, snapped an ear-and-microphone set to his head, and said, "This plane is full of explosives."

"Just what I needed to hear," she said.

"Let's get it on the ground," Daniels added in his ear.

"The autopilot is off—"

Suddenly the Skyhawk angled right. Not a cursory move, but a full course change. He watched the yoke pivot forward, then back, foot pedals working on their own, controlling the rudder in a steep banked maneuver.

Another sharp turn and the GPS readout indicated that the plane's course had altered more westerly and rose in altitude to eight thousand feet, airspeed a little under a hundred knots.

"What's happening?" Stephanie asked.

"This thing has a mind of its own. That was a tight sixty-degree turn."

"Cotton," Daniels said. "The French have calculated your course. It's straight for the Invalides."

No way. They were wrong. He'd already determined the end point of this venture, recalling what had fallen from the Selfridges bag last night.

He stared out the windshield and spotted the true target in the distance.

"That's not where we're headed. This plane is going to the Eiffel Tower."

FIFTY-SIX

ELIZA APPROACHED THE GLASS DOOR AND TRIED the latch.

She stared down through the thick glass panel and saw that an inside lock had been engaged. No way that could have happened accidentally.

"The one on the other side is the same," Thorvaldsen said.

She did not like the Dane's calculated tone, which conveyed that this should be no surprise.

One of the other members turned the corner to her left. "There's no other way down from this platform, and I saw no call box or telephone."

Overhead, near the top of the caged enclosure, she spotted the solution to the problem. A closed-circuit television camera that angled its lens toward them. "Someone in security is surely watching. We simply have to gain their attention."

"I'm afraid it's not going to be that easy," Thorvaldsen said.

She faced him, afraid of what he might say, but knowing what was coming.

"Whatever Lord Ashby planned," he said, "he surely took that into account, along with the fact that some of us would be carrying our own phones. It will take a few minutes for someone to get here. So whatever is going to happen, will happen soon."

MALONE FELT THE PLANE DESCEND. HIS GAZE locked on THE altimeter.

7,000 feet and falling.

"What the—"

The drop halted at 5,600 feet.

"I suggest that fighter be sent this way," he said into the headset. "This plane may need to be blown out of the sky." He glanced down at the buildings, roads, and people. "I'm going to do what I can to change course."

"I'm told you'll have a fighter escort in less than three minutes," Daniels said.

"Thought you said that wasn't an option over populated areas?"

"The French are a bit partial to the Eiffel Tower. And they don't really care—"

"About me?"

"You said it. I didn't."

He reached over to the passenger seat, grabbed the gray box, and studied its exterior. Some sort of electronic device, like a laptop that didn't open. No control switches were visible. He yanked on a cable leading out, but it would not release. He tossed the box down and, with both hands, wrenched the connection free of the instrument panel. An electrical spark was followed by a violent buck as the plane rocked right, then left.

He threw the cable aside and reached for the yoke.

His feet went to the pedals and he tried to regain control, but the aileron trim and rudder were sluggish and the Skyhawk continued on a northwest vector.

"What happened?" Stephanie asked.

"I killed the brain, or at least one of them, but this thing is still on course and the controls don't seem to work."

He grabbed the column again and tried to veer left.

The plane buffeted as it fought his command. He heard a noticeable change in the prop's timbre. He'd flown enough single-engines to know that an altered pitch signaled trouble.

Suddenly the nose jerked and the Skyhawk started to climb.

He reached for the throttle and tried to close it down, but the plane continued to rise. The altimeter read 8,000 feet when the nose finally came down. He didn't like what was happening. Airspeed was shifting at unpredictable rates. Control surfaces were erratic. He could easily stall, and that was the last thing he needed with a cabinful of explosives over Paris.

He stared ahead.

On present course and speed, he was two minutes, at most, from the tower.

"Where's that fighter?" he asked either of his listeners.

"Look to your right," Stephanie said.

A Tornado air interceptor, its wings swept back, was just beyond his wing, two air-to-air missiles nestled to its underside.

"You in communication with him?" he asked.

"He's at our beck and call."

"Tell him to fall off and stand ready."

The Tornado dropped back and he returned his attention to the possessed plane.

"Get that chopper out of here," he said to Stephanie.

He grabbed the yoke.

"Okay, darling," he whispered, "this is going to hurt you far more than me."

THORVALDSEN SEARCHED THE PARISIAN SKY. Graham Ashby had gone to a lot of trouble to trap the entire Paris Club. To the east, police and firefighters still battled the flames at the Invalides.

He walked around the platform, toward the west and south.

And saw them.

A single-engine plane, followed by a military

helicopter, in close proximity, and a fighter jet veering off and climbing.

All three aircraft were close enough to signal trouble.

The helicopter drifted away, giving the single-engine plane room as it rocked on its wings.

He heard the others approach from behind him, Larocque included.

He pointed. "Our fate arrives."

She gazed out into the clear sky. The plane was descending, its prop pointed straight for the deck upon which they stood. He caught a shimmer of sunshine off metal, above and behind the chopper and plane.

The military jet.

"Seems somebody is dealing with the problem," he calmly noted.

But he realized that shooting down the plane was not a viable option.

So he wondered.

How was their fate to be determined?

MALONE WRENCHED THE COLUMN HARD LEFT AND held it in position against a surprisingly intense force compelling a return to center. He'd thought the gray box was flying the plane, but apparently the Skyhawk had been extensively altered. Somewhere there was another brain controlling things, since no matter what he did the plane stayed on course.

He worked the rudder pedals and tried to regain some measure of control, but the plane refused to respond.

He was now clearly on course for the Eiffel Tower. He assumed another homing device had been secreted there, just as in the Invalides, the signal irresistible to the Skyhawk.

"Tell the Tornado to arm his missile," he said. "And back that damn chopper farther off."

"I'm not going to destroy that plane with you in it," Stephanie said.

"Didn't know you cared so much."

"There are a lot of people below you."

He smiled, knowing better. Then a thought occurred to him. If the electronics controlling the plane couldn't be physically overcome, maybe they could be fooled into releasing their hold.

He reached for the engine cutoff and killed the prop.

The propeller spun to a standstill.

"What the hell happened?" Stephanie asked in his ear.

"I decided to cut blood to the brain."

"You think the computers might disengage?"

"If they don't, we have a serious problem."

He gazed below at the brown-gray Seine. He was losing altitude. Without the engine powering the controls, the column was looser, but still tight. The altimeter registered 5,000 feet.

"This is going to be close."

SAM RACED OFF THE ELEVATOR AT THE TOP OF THE tower. No one was inside the enclosed observation platform. He decided to slow down, be cautious. If he was wrong about Ashby, he'd have some impossible explaining to do. He was risking exposure. But something told him that the risk needed to be taken.

He scanned outside, past the windows, first east, then north, and finally south.

And saw a plane.

Closing fast.

Along with a military chopper.

To hell with caution.

He bolted up one of two metal stairways that led to the uppermost observation deck. A glass door at the top was closed and locked. He spied the bolt at the bottom. No way to release it without a key. He leaped down metal grates three at a time, ran across the room, and tried the other route up.

Same thing.

He banged a closed fist on the thick glass door.

Henrik was out there.

And there was nothing he could do.

ELIZA WATCHED AS THE PROP STOPPED TURNING and the plane lost altitude. The craft was less than a kilometer away and still closing on a direct path.

"The pilot is a maniac," one of the club members said.

"That remains to be seen," Thorvaldsen calmly said.

She was impressed by the Dane's nerve. He seemed totally at ease, despite the seriousness of the situation.

"What's happening here?" Robert Mastroianni asked her. "This is not what I joined to experience."

Thorvaldsen turned to face the Italian. "Apparently, we're meant to die."

MALONE FOUGHT THE CONTROLS.

"Get that engine back online," Stephanie said over the radio.

"I'm trying."

He reached for the switch. The motor sputtered, but did not catch. He tried again and was rewarded with a backfire.

He was descending, the summit of the Eiffel Tower less than a mile away.

One more time and, with a bang, the engine roared to life, the spinning prop quickly generating airspeed. He did not give the electronics time to react, quickly ramming the throttle to full speed. He banked the wings, angled the plane into the wind, and flew past the tower, spotting people standing at the top, pointing his way.

FIFTY-SEVEN

SAM WATCHED AS A SMALL PLANE APPROACHED. HE fled the locked glass door and leaped down the stairs, then rushed across to the southern observation windows. The plane roared past, a helicopter in close pursuit.

Elevator doors opened and uniformed men rushed out.

One was the head of security he'd met earlier.

"The doors leading upstairs are locked," he told them. "We need a key."

THORVALDSEN FOCUSED ON THE COCKPIT OF THE Cessna that skirted past, within a few hundred meters. Only an instant was needed for him to spot the face of the pilot.

Cotton Malone.

"I HAVE CONTROL," MALONE SAID.

His altitude was climbing. He decided to level off at 3,000 feet.

"That was close," he said.

"An understatement," Stephanie said. "Is it responding?"

"I need an airport."

"We're looking."

He didn't want to risk landing at Orly or Charles de Gaulle. "Find a smaller field somewhere. What's ahead of me?"

"Once past the city, which is only a few more miles, I'm told there's a wood and a marsh. There's a field at Créteil, another at Lagney, and one at Tournan."

"How far to open pastureland?"

"Twenty miles."

He checked his fuel. The gauge showed fifty liters, the tanks nearly full. Apparently, whoever planned this wanted a load of gasoline to aid the C-83.

"Find me a runway," he told Stephanie. "We need this plane on the ground."

"There's a private strip thirty miles ahead at Evry. Isolated, nothing there. We're alerting them to clear the area. How's the plane?"

"Like a woman tamed."

"You wish."

The prop suddenly sputtered.

He focused out the windshield, beyond the engine cowling, and watched as the propeller wound to a stop.

The engine, on its own, refired and started again.

The control column wrenched from his grip as the plane banked hard right. The engine roared to nearly full throttle and flaps deployed. Something, or somebody, was trying to regain control.

"What's happening?" Stephanie asked.

"I assume this thing didn't like my derogatory remark. It has a mind of its own."

He twisted in the seat as the cockpit leveled, then the plane hooked left. Perhaps its electronics were confused, the transceiver searching for the signal it had previously been following to the Eiffel Tower.

The Skyhawk sought altitude and started a climb, but just as quickly stopped. The airframe bucked like a horse. The yoke vibrated hard. Rudder pedals pounded in and out.

"This isn't going to work. Tell that fighter to stand ready to fire. I'm going to take this thing as high as I can then bail out. Tell him to give me a little clearance, then let loose."

For once Stephanie did not argue.

He angled the nose straight up. He forced the flaps to retract and held on tight, compelling the

Skyhawk to climb against its will. The engine started to labor, like a car struggling up a steep incline.

His eyes focused on the altimeter.

4,000 feet. 5,000. 6,000.

His ears popped.

He decided 8,000 should be enough and, when the gauge passed that mark, he released his grip. While he waited for the plane to level, he yanked off the headset and slipped the wool cap back over his face. He wasn't looking forward to the next few minutes.

He reached for the latch and opened the door.

Cold air rushed in as he forced the panel open. Not giving himself time to be scared, he rolled out, making sure to push off with his feet so momentum would send him clear of the fuselage.

He'd only jumped from a plane twice, once in flight school, and a second time last year over the Sinai, but he remembered what the navy taught him about a punch-out. Arch the back. Spread the arms and legs. Don't let the body roll out of control. He carried no altimeter and decided to estimate his free fall by counting. He needed to open the chute around 5,000 feet. His right hand reached to his chest and searched for the rip cord. **Never wait,** his flight instructor had always cautioned, and for one frightening moment he could not find the handle, but then his fingers wrapped around the D-ring.

He glanced up and watched the Skyhawk continue its erratic journey, searching for its target, engine sputtering, altitude ever changing.

Time seemed to slow as he fell through the winter air.

A collage of fields and forest extended below. He caught sight of the helicopter to his right as it kept him in view.

He reached ten in his count and yanked the rip cord.

ELIZA HEARD FOOTSTEPS AND TURNED TO SEE SECU-rity men rushing their way from around the deck's corner.

"Everyone here okay?' " the lead man asked in French.

She nodded. "We're fine. What is happening?"

"We're not sure. It appears that someone locked the doors to this upper platform and that a small plane almost crashed into this location."

Everything she heard simply confirmed what Thorvaldsen had already made clear.

She stared over at the Dane.

But he was not paying any attention. Instead, the older man simply stood at the platform's edge, hands inside his coat pockets, and gazed past the enclosure, toward the south, where the plane had exploded in the sky. The pilot had bailed out just prior, and was now descending on a chute, a helicopter keeping a watchful eye, circling.

Something was wrong here.

Way beyond Graham Ashby's treachery.

THE CHUTE EXPLODED OUTWARD AND MALONE'S gaze went up to the cords hoping none tangled. A mad rush of wind was instantly replaced by the flap of cloth as the chute grabbed air. He was still high, probably above 5,000 feet, but he didn't care, the thing opened and he was now gently falling toward the ground.

About a quarter mile away he spied a rocket trail and followed the missile on its trajectory. A moment later a huge fireball ignited in the sky, like a star going supernova, as the C-83 obliterated the Skyhawk.

The greater explosion confirmed what he'd suspected.

This plane was the problem.

The Tornado streaked by overhead, the helicopter remaining about half a mile away, following him down.

He tried to decide on the best place to land. He gripped the toggles and forced the rectangular canopy downward, like flaps closing on wings, which spiraled his descent and increased speed.

Thirty seconds later his feet found a plowed field and he folded to the ground. His nostrils filled with the musty smell of turned earth.

But the stench didn't matter.

He was alive.

THORVALDSEN STARED AT THE DISTANT PARACHUTE. No need to continue appearances any longer. Graham Ashby had shown his true colors. But so had Malone. What just happened involved governments. Which meant Malone was working with either Stephanie, the French, or both.

And that betrayal would not go unanswered.

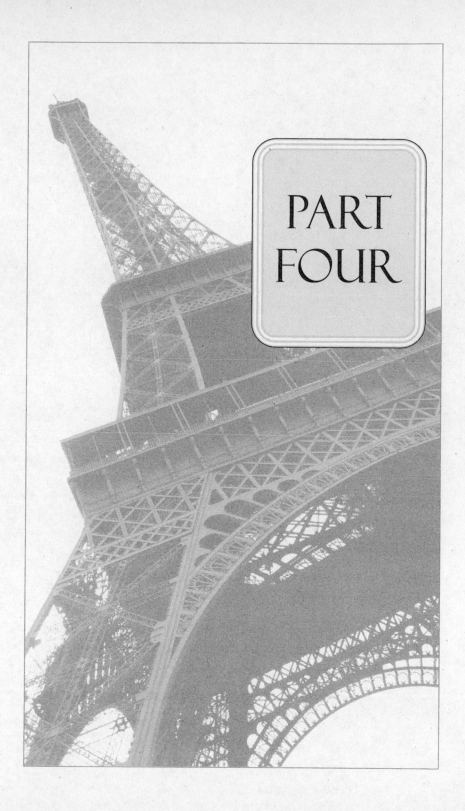

PART
FOUR

FIFTY-EIGHT

ASHBY HUSTLED DOWN THE STAIRS TOWARD GROUND level. He'd timed his escape closely, knowing that he'd have only a precious few minutes. The plan was to cross the Avenue Gustave Eiffel and make his way through the Champ de Mars, toward the Place Jacques Rueff, the nucleus of the former parade ground. Just east, a car with Caroline inside was waiting on the Avenue J. Bouvard. He'd have to finally explain a few things, considering what she was about to see, but his lies were ready.

He kept descending the stairs.

His deal with Peter Lyon had been clear. Never had Lyon been contracted to do what Larocque had wanted—crash a plane into the Church of the Dome and carry out two other simultaneous attacks in Avignon and Bordeaux. Instead, Ashby had confined their arrangement to Paris only, modifying the target to the Eiffel Tower. He'd never understood what Larocque intended, though after listening to her presentation earlier he now appreciated at least some of it.

Terror apparently could be profitable.

He came to the last flight of stairs. He was winded, but glad to be on solid earth. He told himself to calm down and walk slow. Several virile-looking males dressed in camouflage fatigues and toting automatic rifles patrolled the pavement. Beneath the iron base hundreds of people, in long lines, awaited the elevators opening at one PM.

Unfortunately, that would not happen today.

The Eiffel Tower was about to be no more.

In his altered version of Eliza Larocque's plan, he'd arranged with Lyon for the Invalides to be a diversion, a way to create as much confusion as possible. Lyon had always been told the tower was his primary target. He didn't need to know that he'd be killing the entire Paris Club—Larocque included. Not important. And what would Lyon care? He only provided the services a client requested. And to Lyon, Ashby was the client. It should be an easy matter to blame Lyon for everything that was about to happen. His explanation to the Americans as to why he hadn't been with the others on the summit was simple. Larocque had excused him from the rest of the day's gathering. Sent him on a mission.

Who would contradict him?

He passed beneath the southeast arch and cleared the tower. He kept walking, ticking off the seconds in his head. He checked his watch. Noon.

He had no idea where the plane was coming from, only that it should be here any moment.

He crossed the Avenue Gustave Eiffel and entered the Champs de Mars.

He was well clear, so he told himself to relax. Peter Lyon was one of the most experienced murderers in the world. Sure, the Americans were involved, but they'd never get near Lyon. And now, with the tragedy that was about to unfold, they'd have plenty extra to deal with. He'd reported about the Invalides, kept his part of the bargain. The burning vehicle he'd seen earlier in front of the Church of the Dome was surely part of Lyon's show, which should also provide him the perfect excuse for the Americans. Lyon had changed the plan. Apparently, the South African deceived everyone, himself included.

And the end result?

He'd be free of the Americans and Eliza Larocque, and, if all went well, he'd retain all of the club's deposits and find Napoleon's lost cache, which he could also now keep for himself.

Quite a payout.

His father and grandfather would both be proud.

He kept walking, waiting for the explosion, prepared to react as any shocked bystander would.

He heard the drone of a plane, growing louder.

And the dull thump of rotors.

A helicopter?

He stopped, turned, and gazed skyward just as a

single-engine plane, its wings banked nearly perpendicular to the ground, missed the third-level
platform by a few hundred meters.

A military chopper followed, in hot pursuit.

His eyes widened in alarm.

THORVALDSEN EXITED THE ELEVATOR WITH THE
other Paris Club members. Everyone was now back
on the first-level platform. The security men who'd
opened the glass doors high above had offered no
explanation as to how they became locked. But he
knew the answer. Graham Ashby had planned another mass murder.

He watched as the others made their way into
the meeting room. Most of the members were
shaken, but maintaining a confident façade. He'd
purposefully not kept his comments at the summit to himself and had seen the reaction of the
others to his observations about Graham Ashby.
He'd also noted Larocque's anger—at both he and
Ashby.

He stood near the outer railing, gloved hands in
his coat pockets, and watched as Larocque marched
toward him.

"The time for pretense between us is over," he
said to her. "I have no more patience to humor you."

"Is that what you've been doing?"

"Graham Ashby tried to kill us all."

"I'm aware of that. Was it necessary to share those thoughts with everyone?"

He shrugged. "They should know what's in store for them. But I wonder, what were you planning? We weren't up there to simply enjoy the view."

She threw him a quizzical look.

"You can't seriously think that I would have been a party to your madness. Those ideas you tossed out earlier. Insanity, all of it."

She seemed at once amazed, appalled, repelled, and fascinated by his indignation.

"I came for Graham Ashby," he made clear. "I used you to get close to him. At first, I thought what you were concocting was worth stopping. Maybe it is. But I don't care any longer. Not after what Ashby just tried."

"I assure you, Herre Thorvaldsen, I am not one to be trifled with. As Lord Ashby will soon learn."

He allowed his voice to assume an icy determination. "Madame, let me make something clear. You should be grateful that I no longer have any interest in your mischief. If I did, I'd stop you. But I could not give a damn. It's not my concern. You, though, have several problems. The first is Ashby. The second is the American government. That plane was being flown by a former Justice Department agent named Cotton Malone. His boss, from that same department, is here and, I assume, knows exactly what you're doing. Your plans are no longer secret."

He turned to leave.

She grabbed him by the arm. "Who do you think you are? I am not a person to be lightly dismissed."

He clung to the anger that coursed through him. The enormity of all that had happened struck him hard. As he'd watched the plane draw closer to the tower summit, he'd realized that his lack of focus could have cost him his ultimate goal. In one respect, he was glad Malone had stopped the plane. On the other hand, the sick, numbing realization that his friend had betrayed him hurt more than he'd ever imagined.

He needed to find Malone, Stephanie, and Ashby and finish things. The Paris Club was no longer part of the equation. Neither was this ridiculous woman who glared at him with eyes full of hate.

"Let go of my arm," he said through clenched teeth.

She did not release her grip.

He wrenched himself free.

"Stay out of my way," he ordered.

"As if I take orders from you."

"If you want to stay alive, you had better. Because if you interfere with me, in any way, I'll shoot you dead."

And he walked away.

———Δ———

ASHBY SPOTTED THE CAR WITH CAROLINE INSIDE waiting at the curb. Traffic was beginning to congeal on the boulevards that paralleled the Champs de Mars. Car doors had opened and people pointed skyward.

Ripples of concern ebbed through him.

He needed to be away.

The plane had not destroyed the Eiffel Tower. Worse, Eliza Larocque now realized that he'd tried to murder them all.

How could she not?

What happened? Had Lyon double-crossed him? He'd paid the first half of the extorted fee. The South African had to know that. Why would he have not performed? Especially considering that something clearly had happened at the Church of the Dome, smoke curling up from the east confirming that the fire there still raged.

And there was the matter of the remaining payment.

Three times the usual fee. A bloody well lot of money.

He entered the car.

Caroline sat in the rear seat across from him, Mr. Guildhall in the front, driving. He'd need to keep Guildhall near him.

"Did you see how close that plane came to the tower?" Caroline asked.

"I did." He was glad that he did not have to explain anything further.

"Is your business finished?"

He wished. "For now." He stared at her smiling face. "What is it?

"I solved Napoleon's riddle."

FIFTY-NINE

MALONE LAY ON GRASS THAT WINTER HAD CHILLED into brown hay and watched the helicopter land. The rear compartment door slid open and Stephanie leaped out, followed by the corpsman. He released the parachute's harness and came to his feet. He caught the worry, plain in her eyes, hoping he was okay.

He freed himself from the chute. "Tell the French that we're even."

She smiled.

"Better yet," he said. "Tell them they owe me."

He watched as the corpsman gathered up the billowing chute.

"Lyon's arrogant as hell," he said, "flaunting it in our faces. He was ready with the little towers in London, and he made no effort to conceal his amber eyes. He actually went out of his way to confront me. Either way was a win–win for him. We stop the plane, he sticks it to Ashby. We miss the plane, he makes the client happy. I doubt he really cared which was the ultimate outcome." Which, he knew, explained the diversions at the Invalides and the other planes. "We need to find Ashby."

"There's a bigger problem," she said. "When we passed the top of the tower, I saw Henrik."

"He had to have seen me in that cockpit."

"My thought exactly."

The corpsman grabbed Stephanie's attention and pointed to her handheld radio. She stepped away and spoke into the unit, then quickly returned.

"We caught a break," she said, motioning for the chopper. "They triangulated the signals being sent to those planes. We have a ground location."

—A—

SAM HAD FLED THE SUMMIT AS A SECURITY DETAIL unlocked the exit doors for the observation deck, mindful of Stephanie's instruction that he must not be compromised. He'd made it back to the first platform long before the Paris Club descended and the members reentered the meeting room. He'd watched as Eliza Larocque and Henrik confronted each other. Though he could not hear what they were saying it wasn't hard to sense the tension, especially when Henrik yanked himself free of her grip. He'd heard nothing from Stephanie and there was no way he could sneak himself back into the meeting room, so he decided to leave.

Somebody had tried to crash a plane into the

Eiffel Tower, and nearly succeeded. The military was obviously aware, as the chopper riding herd over the plane proved.

He needed to contact Stephanie.

He freed the tie from around his neck and released the top button of his shirt. His clothes and coat were below in the police station, beneath the south pylon, where he and Meagan had changed.

He paused at the first-level platform's open center and gazed down at the people below. Hundreds were waiting in line. An explosive crash nine hundred feet above them would have been horrific. Interesting that the authorities were not evacuating the site. In fact, the chaos from above had been replaced with utter calm. As if nothing had happened. He sensed Stephanie Nelle's involvement with that decision.

He fled the railing and started down the metal risers for the ground. Henrik Thorvaldsen was gone. Sam had decided not to confront him. He couldn't, not here.

Halfway down, the cell phone in his pocket vibrated.

Stephanie had given one to both him and Meagan, programming the numbers of each, along with hers, into the memory.

He found the unit and answered.

"I'm in a cab," Meagan said. "Following Ashby. I was lucky to snag one. He ran, but stopped long enough to watch the plane fly by. He was shocked, Sam."

"We all were."

"That's not what I mean." Surprise laced her voice. "He was shocked it missed."

ELIZA FACED THE GROUP, BUT HER MIND SWIRLED with so many conflicting thoughts it was hard to concentrate.

"What happened up there?" one of the members asked.

"The security people are investigating, but it appears the plane malfunctioned. Thankfully, the problem was rectified in time."

"Why were the exit doors locked?"

She could not tell them the truth. "We should soon know the answer to that as well."

"What did Herre Thorvaldsen mean when he said that plane was our fate—we were meant to die—and Lord Ashby was involved?"

She'd been dreading the inquiry. "There is apparently a private feud between Lord Ashby and Herre Thorvaldsen. One I was unaware of until a few moments ago. Because of that animosity, I've asked Herre Thorvaldsen to withdraw his membership, and he agreed. He apologized for any fear or inconvenience he may have caused."

"That doesn't explain what he said on that deck," Robert Mastroianni said.

"I think it was more his imagination talking. He has a personal dislike for Lord Ashby."

Her newest recruit did not seem satisfied. "Where is Ashby?"

She manufactured another lie. "He left, at my request, to handle another matter of vital importance. He may or may not make it back for the rest of the meeting."

"That's not what you said at the top of the tower," one of them noted. "You wanted to know where he was."

She told herself that these men and women were not stupid. **Don't treat them as so.** "I knew he would be leaving, I was simply unaware that he'd already left."

"Where did he go?"

"That cache of unaccounted-for wealth I told you about. Lord Ashby is searching for it, and he has located a new lead. Earlier, he asked to be excused so he could explore its possibilities."

She kept her voice calm and firm, having learned long ago that it was not only what you said, but how you said it that mattered.

"We're going to continue on?" one of the others asked.

She caught the surprise in the question. "Of course. Why not?"

"How about that we were all nearly killed?" Mastroianni said.

She had to alleviate their fears, and the best way

to quell speculation was focus on the future. "I'm sure that each of you experience risk every day. But that's precisely why we're all here. To minimize that risk. We still have much to discuss, and many millions of euros to realize. How about we focus our efforts and prepare for a new day?"

MALONE SAT IN THE CHOPPER'S REAR COMPARTMENT and enjoyed the heater's blast.

"The signal to the planes originated from a rooftop near Notre Dame," Stephanie said through his headphones. "On the Île St. Louis, one island behind the cathedral. Paris police have the building under surveillance. We used NATO monitoring posts to pinpoint the location."

"Which begs the question."

He saw she understood.

"I know," she said. "Too damn easy. Lyon is two full steps ahead of us. We're chasing his shadows."

"No. Worse. We're being led by shadows."

"I understand. But it's all we have."

SAM STEPPED FROM THE CAB AND PAID THE DRIVER. He was a block from the Champs-Elysées, in the heart of an upscale shopping district that played host to the likes of Louis Vuitton, Hermès, Dior, and Chanel. He'd followed directions that Meagan had called in to him, and was now standing before the Four Seasons, an eight-story hotel marked by 1920s architecture.

He glanced around and spotted Meagan across the street. He hadn't taken the time to change, though he had retrieved his coat and clothes before fleeing the Eiffel Tower. She was still dressed in the shirt and slacks of their serving uniform. He'd also brought her clothes.

"Thanks," she said, as she donned the coat.

She was shaking. True, the air was cold, but he wondered if it was more. He placed a hand on her back, steadying her, which she seemed to appreciate.

"You were at the top?" she asked.

He nodded.

"That was damn close, Sam."

He agreed. But it was over. "What's happening here?"

"Ashby and his entourage went inside the hotel."

"I wonder what we're supposed to do now."

She seemed to steel herself and walked toward a narrow alley between two buildings. "You think about it, Sherlock, while I change."

He smiled at her confidence, searching for some of his own. Calling Stephanie or Malone could prove problematic. His instructions had not been to follow anyone. Of course, Stephanie Nelle had not anticipated that a plane would be flown into the Eiffel Tower, either. He'd done what he thought best and, so far, had remained undetected.

Or maybe not.

Thorvaldsen may have seen him in the meeting room. But no one had mentioned that the Dane would be there.

So he made a decision.

To seek guidance from the one man who'd actually sought guidance from him.

MALONE SPRANG FROM THE CHOPPER AS IT LANDED behind Notre Dame on a leafy green. A uniformed police captain waited for them as they cleared the rotor blades' downwash.

"You were right," the policeman told Stephanie. "The landlord of the building confirmed that a man with amber eyes let an apartment on the fourth floor, a week ago. He paid three months in advance."

"Is the building secure?" she asked.

"We have it surrounded. Discreetly. As you requested."

Malone again sensed the uneasy restraint that seemed to bind him and Stephanie. Nothing about this was good. Once again, Lyon had made no effort to mask his tracks.

He no longer wore the dirty flight suit, having redonned his leather jacket and reacquired his Beretta.

With little choice, he started off.

"Let's see what the SOB has in store this time."

SIXTY

Ashby sat in one of the Four Seasons' royal suites.

"Get the Murrays over here," he ordered Guildhall. "I want them in France by nightfall."

Caroline watched him with eyes that seemed to pry into his thoughts. His face was red and puffy from both the cold and his frayed nerves, his voice tired and throaty.

"What's the problem, Graham?" she asked.

He wanted this woman as an ally, so he answered her with some truth. "A business arrangement has turned sour. I'm afraid Madame Larocque is going to be quite upset with me. Enough that she may want to do me harm."

Caroline shook her head. "What have you done?"

He smiled. "Simply trying to rid myself of the incessant grasp of others."

He allowed his eyes to play over her well-formed legs and the curve of her hips. Just watching those faultless lines freed his mind of the problem, if only for a moment.

"You can't blame me for that," he added. "We're finally back in shallow water. I simply wanted to be done with Eliza. She's mad, you know."

"So we need the Murrays? And Mr. Guildhall?"

"And even more men possibly. That bitch is going to be angry."

"Then let's give her something to be totally irritated about."

He'd been waiting for her to explain what she'd found.

She stood and retrieved a leather satchel from a nearby chair. Inside, she located a sheet of paper upon which was written the fourteen lines of letters from the Merovingian book, penned by Napoleon himself.

"It's just like the one we found in Corsica," she said. "The one with raised lettering that revealed

Psalm 31, written by Napoleon, too. When I laid a straightedge beneath the lines it became obvious."

She produced a ruler and showed him.

He immediately noticed letters higher than the others.

"What does it say?"

She handed him another piece of paper, and he saw all of the raised letters.

ADOGOBERTROIETASIONESTCETRESORETILESTLAMORT

"It wasn't hard to form the words," she said. "All you need to add is a few spaces."

She displayed another sheet.

A DOGOBERT ROI ET A SION EST CE TRESOR ET IL EST LA MORT

He translated the French. " 'To King Dagobert and to Sion belongs the treasure and he is there dead.' " He gave a pessimistic shrug. "What does it mean?"

A malicious grin formed on her inviting lips.

"A great deal."

MALONE ENTERED THE BUILDING, GUN IN HAND, and climbed the stairs.

Stephanie followed.

The Paris police waited outside.

Neither one of them was sure what was waiting,

so the fewer people involved, the better. Containment was rapidly becoming a problem, particularly considering that two national landmarks had been attacked and planes had been shot from the sky. President Daniels had assured them that the French would deal with the press. Just concentrate on finding Lyon, he'd ordered.

They reached the fourth floor and found the door for the apartment that the amber-eyed man had let, the landlord having provided a passkey.

Stephanie positioned herself to one side, gun in hand. Malone angled his body against the opposite and banged on the door. He didn't expect anyone to answer, so he inserted the key into the lock, turned the knob, and swung the door inward.

He waited a few seconds, then peered around the jamb.

The apartment was utterly bare, except for one item.

A laptop lying on the wood floor, the screen facing their way, a counter ticking down.

2:00 minutes.

1:59.

1:58.

THORVALDSEN HAD CALLED MALONE'S CELL PHONE seven times, each try diverting to voice mail, each failure escalating his anguish.

He needed to speak with Malone.

More important, he needed to find Graham Ashby. He hadn't ordered his investigators to tail the Brit after he left England earlier this morning. He assumed that Ashby would be within his sight at the Eiffel Tower, until late afternoon. By then, his men would be in France ready to go.

But Ashby had formulated a different plan.

Thorvaldsen sat alone in his room at the Ritz. What to do now? He was at a loss. He'd planned carefully, anticipating nearly everything—except the mass murder of the Paris Club. Innovative, he'd give Ashby that. Eliza Larocque had to be in turmoil. Her well-ordered plans were in shambles. At least she realized that he'd been telling the truth about her supposedly trustworthy British lord. Now Ashby had two people intent on his demise.

Which made him think again about Malone, the book, and Murad.

Perhaps the professor knew something?

His cell phone rang.

The screen displayed BLOCKED NUMBER but he answered anyway.

"Henrik," Sam Collins said, "I need your help."

He wanted to know if everyone around him was a liar. "What have you been doing?"

The other end of the phone stayed silent. Finally, Sam said, "I've been recruited by the Justice Department."

He was pleased that the young man had told him the truth. So he reciprocated. "I saw you at the Eiffel Tower. In the meeting hall."

"I thought you might."

"What's happening Sam?"

"I'm following Ashby."

The best news he'd heard. "For Stephanie Nelle?"

"Not really. But I had no choice."

"Do you have a way to contact her?"

"She gave me a direct number, but I've been hesitant to call. I wanted to talk to you first."

"Tell me where you are."

MALONE APPROACHED THE LAPTOP AS STEPHANIE searched the apartment's two remaining rooms.

"Empty," she called out.

He knelt. The screen continued to count down, approaching one minute. He noticed a data card inserted into a side USB port—the source of the wireless connection. At the screen's top right portion, the battery indicator read 80 percent. The machine had not been on long.

41 seconds.

"Shouldn't we be leaving?" Stephanie asked.

"Lyon knew we'd come. Just like at the Invalides, if he wanted to kill us there are easier ways."

28 seconds.

"You realize Peter Lyon is an amoral bastard."

19 seconds.

"Henrik called seven times," he said to her as they both watched the screen.

"He's got to be dealt with," she said.

"I know."

12 seconds.

"You could be wrong about there not being a bomb here," she muttered.

9 seconds.

"I've been wrong before."

6 seconds.

"That's not what you said back in the Court of Honor."

A 5 appeared, then 4, 3, 2, 1.

SIXTY-ONE

Ashby waited for Caroline to explain. She was clearly enjoying herself.

"If the legend is to be believed," she said, "only Napoleon knew the location of his cache. He trusted that information to no one we know of. Once he realized that he was going to die on St. Helena, he had to communicate the location to his son."

She pointed to the fourteen lines of writing. "'To King Dagobert and to Sion belongs the treasure and he is there dead.' It's quite simple."

Perhaps to someone with multiple degrees in history, but not to him.

"Dagobert was a Merovingian who ruled in the early part of the 7th century. He unified the Franks and made Paris his capital. He was the last Merovingian to wield any real power. After that, the Merovingian kings became ineffective rulers who inherited the throne as young children and lived only long enough to produce a male heir. Real power lay in the hands of the noble families."

His mind was still on Peter Lyon and Eliza

Larocque and the threat they posed. He wanted to be acting, not listening. But he told himself to remain patient. She'd never disappointed him before.

"Dagobert built the basilica at Saint-Denis, north of Paris. He was the first king to be buried there." She paused. "He's still there."

He tried to recall what he could about the cathedral. The building had first been constructed over the tomb of St. Denis, a local bishop martyred by the Romans in the 3rd century, and revered by Parisians. An exceptional building in both construction and design, regarded as one of the first examples of Gothic architecture on the planet. He remembered a French acquaintance once boasting that the world's greatest assembly of royal funerary monuments lay there. Like he cared. But maybe he should. Especially about one particular royal tomb.

"Nobody knows if Dagobert is actually buried there," she made clear. "The building was first erected in the 5th century. Dagobert ruled in the mid–7th century. He donated so much wealth to the basilica's enhancement that, by the 9th century, he was credited as its founder. In the 13th century, the monks there dedicated a funerary niche in his honor."

"Is Dagobert there or not?"

She shrugged. "What does it matter? That niche is still regarded as the tomb of Dagobert. Where he is. Dead."

He caught the significance of what she was saying. "That's what Napoleon would have believed?"

"I can't see how he would have thought anything else."

MALONE STARED AT THE LAPTOP AND THE SINGLE word, displayed in all caps, emphasized by three exclamation points.

BOOM!!!

"That's interesting," Stephanie said.

"Lyon has a bomb fetish."

The screen changed and a new message appeared.

WHAT IS IT AMERICANS SAY?
A DAY LATE AND A DOLLAR SHORT.
MAYBE NEXT TIME.

"Now, that's aggravating," he said, but he saw more than frustration in Stephanie's eyes and knew what she was thinking.

No Paris Club. No Lyon. Nothing.

"It's not all that bad," he said.

She seemed to catch the twinkle in his eye. "You have something in mind?"

He nodded. "A way for us to finally catch this shadow."

ASHBY STARED AT A PHOTO OF DAGOBERT'S FUNER-
ary monument that Caroline found online. A
Gothic flair dominated its busy design.

"It depicts the legend of John the Hermit," she
said. "He dreamed that the soul of Dagobert was
stolen away by demons, eventually snatched from
their clutches by Saints Denis, Maurice, and
Martin."

"And this sits inside the basilica at Saint-Denis?"

She nodded. "Adjacent to the main altar. It
somehow escaped the wrath of the French Revolution. Prior to 1800, just about every French
monarch was buried in Saint-Denis. But most of
the bronze tombs were melted down during the
French Revolution, the rest shattered and piled in a
garden behind the building. The remains of every
Bourbon king were dumped into a nearby cemetery pit."

That wild vengeance made him think of Eliza
Larocque. "The French take their anger quite to
heart."

"Napoleon stopped the vandalism and restored
the church," she said. "He again made it an imperial burying place."

He caught the significance. "So he **was** familiar
with the basilica?"

"The Merovingian connection surely attracted
his interest. Several Merovingians are buried there.
Including, to his mind, Dagobert."

The suite's door opened and Guildhall reappeared. A discreet nod told Ashby that the Murrays were on their way. He'd feel better when surrounded by loyalists. Something would have to be done about Eliza Larocque. He could not be constantly glancing over his shoulder, wondering if today was the day she finally caught up to him. Perhaps he could make a deal? She was negotiable. But he'd tried to kill her, a fact she certainly now knew. No matter. He'd deal with her later. Right now— "All right, my dear. Tell me. What happens when we visit Saint-Denis?"

"How about I answer that question once we're there."

"Do you have the answer?"

"I think I do."

THORVALDSEN EXITED THE CAB AND SPOTTED SAM and a woman standing across the street. He stuffed his bare hands into his coat pockets and crossed. Little traffic filled the tree-lined boulevard, all of the nearby upscale boutiques closed for Christmas.

Sam seemed anxious. He immediately introduced the woman and explained who she was.

"You two seem to have been drafted into quite a mess," he said.

"We didn't have a whole lot of choice," Meagan Morrison said.

"Is Ashby still inside?" he asked, motioning toward the hotel.

Sam nodded. "As long as he decided not to leave by another exit."

He stared across at the Four Seasons and wondered what his schemer was planning next.

"Henrik, I was on top of the tower," Sam said. "I came up after Ashby came down. That plane—was coming for the club, wasn't it?"

He nodded. "Indeed it was. What were you doing up there?"

"I came to see about you."

The words made him think of Cai. Sam was near the age Cai would have been, if he'd lived. Lots about this young American reminded him of his son. Perhaps that's why he'd gravitated toward him. Misplaced love and all that other psychological nonsense that, prior to two years ago, meant nothing to him.

Now it consumed him.

But through the dense cloud of bitterness that seemed to envelop his every thought, a faint voice of reason could still be heard. One that told him to slow down and think. So he faced Sam and said, "Cotton stopped that disaster from happening. He was flying the plane."

He caught the incredulous look in the younger man's eyes.

"You'll learn that both he and Stephanie are most resourceful. Luckily, they were on top of the matter." He paused. "As were you, apparently. That was a brave thing you did. I appreciate it." He came to the point of his visit. "You said you have a way of contacting Stephanie Nelle?"

Sam nodded.

"You know her?" Meagan asked him.

"She and I have worked together several times. We're—acquaintances."

The younger woman clearly was not impressed. "She's a bitch."

"That she can be."

"I've been reluctant to call her," Sam said.

"You shouldn't be. She must know about Ashby. Dial the phone and we'll talk with her together."

SIXTY-TWO

ELIZA SAID HER GOODBYES TO THE LAST OF THE Paris Club AS the members exited La Salle Gustav Eiffel. She'd managed to contain herself during the afternoon and alleviate the tidal wave of anxiety that had swept through the room. Thorvaldsen's accusations had seemed forgotten, or at least addressed, by the time the session finished.

Her own fears, though, were another matter.

So two hours ago, during a break, she'd made a call.

The man she'd sought was pleased to hear from her. His flat tone conveyed no emotion, only the fact that he was available and ready to do business with her. She'd stumbled on to him a few years ago when she'd required some unorthodox assistance with a debtor—someone who thought friendship made defaulting on his obligation an option. She'd asked around, learned of the man's abilities, met him, and four days later the debtor paid the several million euros owed, in full. She'd never asked how that was accomplished, simply pleased that it occurred. Since then there had been three other "situations." Each time she'd made contact. Each time the task had been accomplished.

She hoped today would be no exception.

He lived in the Montmartre, within the shadow of the domes and campaniles that rose from Paris' highest point. She found the building on the Rue Chappe, a shaded avenue of Second Empire homes, populated now with trendy shops, cafés, and expensive, upper-story flats.

She climbed the stairs to the third floor and knocked lightly on the door marked with a brass 5. The man who answered was short and slender, with straw-thin gray hair. The crook of his nose and the cut of his jaw reminded her of a hawk, which seemed a fitting symbol for Paolo Ambrosi.

She was invited inside.

"What may I do for you today?" Ambrosi asked in a calm voice.

"Always straight to the point."

"You are an important person. Time is valuable. I assume that you did not come here, on Christmas Day, for something trivial."

She caught what was unspoken. "And pay the fees you command?"

He gave a slight nod of his head, which was at least a size too small for his frame.

"This one is special," she said. "It must be done quickly."

"Define **quickly**."

"Today."

"I assume you have the information needed for a proper preparation."

"I'll lead you straight to the target."

Ambrosi wore a black turtleneck, a black-and-gray-tweed coat, and dark corduroy trousers that sharply contrasted with his pale complexion. She wondered what drove the grim man but realized that this was, most likely, a long story.

"Is there a preference as to the method?" he asked.

"Only that it be painful and slow."

His cool eyes were bereft of humor. "His betrayal must have been unexpected."

She appreciated his ability to peer into her thoughts. "To say the least."

"Your need for satisfaction is that great?"

"Beyond measure."

"Then we shall obtain a full absolution."

SAM DIALED HIS CELL PHONE. THE OTHER END OF the line was answered quickly.

"What is it, Sam?" Stephanie said.

"I have Ashby."

He told her exactly what happened since leaving the Eiffel Tower.

"You weren't supposed to follow him," she made clear.

"And a plane wasn't supposed to fly into us, either."

"I appreciate your ingenuity. Stay where you are—"

Henrik relieved him of the phone. Clearly his friend wanted to speak with Stephanie Nelle, and he wanted to know why, so Sam stepped back and listened.

"IT'S GOOD TO KNOW THAT THE AMERICAN GOV-ernment is directly atop things," Thorvaldsen said.

"And it's good to talk to you, too, Henrik," Stephanie replied, in a tone that signaled she was ready for battle.

"You interfered in my business," he said.

"On the contrary. You interfered in ours."

"How is that possible? None of this concerns America."

"Don't be so sure. You're not the only one who's interested in Ashby."

His stomach went hollow. He'd suspected as much, hoping he was wrong. "He's valuable to you?"

"You realize I can neither confirm nor deny that."

He didn't require any admissions from her.

What just happened at the Eiffel Tower explained everything. "It's not hard to imagine what's happening here."

"Let's just say that there's more at stake here than your revenge."

"Not to me."

"Would it do any good if I said I understand? That I'd do the same, if the roles were reversed?"

"You still interfered."

"We saved your life."

"You gave Ashby the book."

"Which was a good idea. It rocked him to sleep. Lucky for you, I might add, or you'd be dead right now."

He wasn't in the mood to be grateful. "Cotton betrayed me. I have not the time, at the moment, to deal with that disappointment. But I will."

"Cotton used his brain. You should, too, Henrik."

"My son is dead."

"I don't need a reminder."

"Apparently, you do." He paused, grabbed a breath, and steadied himself. "This is my affair, not yours, not Cotton's, not the U.S. government's."

"Henrik, listen to me. This is not about you. There's a terrorist involved here. A man named Peter Lyon. We've been trying to nail him for a decade. He's finally out in the open where we can see him. You have to let us finish this. But we need Ashby in order to do that."

"And when it's over? What of my son's murderer?"

The other end of the phone remained silent. Which told him what he already knew. "That's what I thought. Goodbye, Stephanie."

"What are you going to do?"

He switched off the phone and handed it to Sam. The younger man and Meagan Morrison had stood silent, watching him through concerned eyes.

"Will you betray me, too?" he asked Sam.

"No."

The answer came quick. Perhaps too quick. But this eager soul was anxious to prove himself.

"Something's happening," Meagan said.

He turned and focused across the boulevard at the hotel.

Ashby appeared out front and spoke to the doorman, who quickly motioned for a cab. Thorvaldsen turned away and faced the buildings behind them. His face might be seen.

"He's in the cab," Sam said.

"Flag us one, too."

SIXTY-THREE

ASHBY STEPPED OFF THE DOCK AT PONT DE L'ALMA and onto the tour boat. Off to the east a carillon of bells pealed for three PM. He'd never toured the Seine by boat, though he assumed the cruises were quite popular. Today only about twenty strangers filled the seats under a sooty Plexiglas canopy, the boat not quite half full. He wondered why Peter Lyon insisted on meeting in such tacky surroundings. The call had come an hour ago, a gruff voice instructing him on the time and place. He'd told Caroline to keep working on what she'd discovered and that he'd return shortly. He'd debated ignoring Lyon's summons, but knew better. Besides, Lyon had been the one who failed, not him. And there was the matter of the fee already paid, and the balance owed.

He settled into a seat on the last row and waited ten minutes until the engines revved and the flat hull glided out into the river, heading east toward the Île de la Cité. Through a loudspeaker a woman's voice described, in English, the two banks and the sights while cameras clicked.

A tap on the shoulder diverted his attention and he turned to see a tall, urbane-looking man with blond hair. He appeared to be midsixties, the face drawn and shielded by a bushy beard and mustache. A vastly different look from the other day, yet the eyes remained the same amber color. The man was dressed in a tweed coat and corduroy slacks, appearing, as usual, quite European.

Ashby followed him toward the stern, outside the Plexiglas enclosure, where they stood in the cold. The tour guide inside continued to hold the crowd's attention.

"What do I call you today?" he asked.

"How about Napoleon?" The voice was husky, throaty, more American this time.

The boat eased past the Grand Palais on the Right Bank.

"May I ask what happened?"

"No, you may not," Lyon said.

He wasn't about to accept that rebuke. "You are the one who failed. Not only that, you caused me to be exposed. The Americans are applying pressure. Do you have any idea the situation you have generated?"

"The Americans are the ones who interfered."

"And that was a surprise? You knew they were involved. I paid three times your fee to compensate for their involvement." His exasperation showed, but he did not care. "You said it would be quite a show."

"I don't know, as yet, who to blame," Lyon said. "My planning was precise."

He registered the same condescending tone he'd grown to hate. Since he could not reveal that he'd been using Lyon to do his dirty work, he asked, "What can be done to rectify the situation?"

"That will be your problem. I'm done."

He could not believe what he was hearing. "You're—"

"I want to know," Lyon said, interrupting. "What did you hope to gain from killing those people at the tower?"

"How do you know I wanted to kill them?"

"The same way I know about the Americans."

This man knew an awful lot. But he sensed that Lyon was not nearly as confident today. Good to know that even the devil failed occasionally. He decided not to rub the disaster in the man's face. He still needed Lyon.

"I would have never been rid of them," he said. "Larocque, especially. So I decided to terminate the relationship, in a way she would appreciate."

"And how much money was involved?"

He chuckled. "You like to come to the point, don't you?"

Lyon shifted on his feet as he stood, propped against the aft railing. "It's always about money."

"I have access to millions in club funds deposited

in my bank. That's how you were paid. I could not have cared less what you charge. Of course, that money, or what's left of it, would have been mine, if your flight had been successful." He allowed his words to linger, conveying again who was responsible for the botched attack. He was tiring of theatrics, gaining courage by the second, annoyed with this man's arrogance.

"What was really at stake, Lord Ashby?"

That he was not going to share. "More than you could ever imagine. Plenty to compensate for the risks involved in killing those people."

Lyon said nothing.

"You've been paid," Ashby made clear, "but I did not receive the service, as promised. You like to talk about character and how almighty important that is to you. Do you fail, then keep a person's money?"

"You still want them dead?" Lyon paused. "Assuming I'm interested in continuing our association."

"You don't have to kill them all. How about just Larocque. For what you've already been paid, and for the remaining payment owed to you."

THORVALDSEN HAD NOT BEEN ABLE TO BOARD THE tour boat with Ashby. His operatives were on the way from England and should arrive within the next few hours, so they were of no help. Instead, he'd opted to follow the slow-moving vessel, paralleling the Seine in a taxi, on a busy boulevard.

He'd first considered sending Sam or Meagan, but was concerned Ashby might recognize their faces from the meeting. Now he realized there was no choice. He faced Sam. "I want you to get aboard at the next stop and see what Ashby is doing. Also, find out the route and call that to me immediately."

"Why me?"

"You were able to masquerade for Stephanie Nelle, surely you can do this for me."

He saw that his rebuke bit into the young man, as intended.

Sam nodded. "I can do it. But Ashby may have seen me in the meeting room."

"It's a chance we have to take. But I doubt if he pays much attention to hired help."

The road ahead passed between the Louvre on the left and the Seine on the right. He saw the tour boat ease toward a dock just below the roadway. He signaled for the driver to stop at the curb.

He opened the door and Sam jumped out into the cold afternoon.

"Be safe," he said, then he slammed the door and told the driver to go, but slowly, and not to lose the boat.

"You still haven't answered my question," Lyon said to Ashby. "What's at stake here?"

He decided that to secure Lyon's continued help he was going to have to give a little. "A treasure beyond measure. One far greater than the fee you extorted from me." He wanted this demon to know that he wasn't intimidated any longer.

"And you needed Larocque and the others gone to acquire it?"

He shrugged. "Just her. But I decided that since you were killing people, why not kill them all."

"I so underestimated you, Lord Ashby."

No kidding.

"And what of the Americans? You deceived them, too?"

"I told them what I had to and, I might add, I never would have sacrificed you. If things had evolved properly, I would have had my freedom, the treasure, the club's money, and you would have been on to the next client—richer by three times your usual fee."

"The Americans were smarter than I anticipated."

"Seems that was your mistake. I performed my part, and I'm ready to pay the remainder of the fee. Provided—"

The boat eased to a stop at the Louvre. New riders stepped aboard and dutifully took their seats beneath the canopy. Ashby kept silent until the engines revved and they motored back into the swift Seine.

"I'm waiting," he said.

SAM DECIDED AGAINST SITTING TOO FAR AFT. HE chose instead to merge himself into the sparse camera-toting crowd. Beneath the canopy there was a measure of comfort provided by warm air from the boat's heaters. Ashby and the other man—the stranger dressed in English tweeds and sporting imperiously coiffed blond hair—stood beyond the enclosure where, he imagined, it was downright cold.

He focused his attention on the riverbanks as a tour guide spouted over a loudspeaker about the Île de la Cité and its many attractions, which lay directly ahead. He feigned sightseeing as a way to keep an eye on what was happening. The guide mentioned that they would be taking the Left Bank route around the Île, past Notre Dame, then on to the Bibliothèque François Mitterand.

He dialed his phone and quickly reported the route.

THORVALDSEN LISTENED, CLICKED OFF, AND STUDied the road ahead.

"Cross the river," he told the driver, "then go left, toward the Latin Quarter. But stay close."

He did not want to lose sight of the tour boat.

"What are you doing?" Meagan Morrison asked.

"How long have you lived in Paris?"

She seemed taken aback by his question, realizing he was ignoring hers.

"Years."

"Then tell me, are there any bridges across the river past Notre Dame, leading to and from the Left Bank?"

She hesitated, considering his inquiry. He realized that it wasn't that she didn't know the answer, she just wanted to know why the information was important.

"There's a bridge just past. The Pont de l'Archevêché."

"Crowded?"

She shook here head. "Mainly pedestrians. A few cars traveling over to the Île St. Louis, behind the cathedral."

"Go there," he told the driver.

"What are you going to do, old man?"

He ignored her goad and coolly said, "What must be done."

SIXTY-FOUR

ASHBY WAITED FOR PETER LYON TO TELL HIM WHAT he wanted to hear.

"I can eliminate Larocque," the South African made clear, in a hushed tone.

They stood facing the river, watching the boat's foamy wake dissolve into the brown-gray water. Two more canopied tourist boats and a handful of private craft followed.

"That needs to happen," Ashby made clear, "today. Tomorrow at the latest. She's going to be most disagreeable."

"She wants the treasure, too?"

He decided to be blunt. "More than you can imagine. It's a matter of family honor."

"This treasure. I want to know more."

He did not want to answer, but had no choice. "It's Napoleon's lost wealth. An incredible cache. Gone for two hundred years. But I think I've found it."

"Lucky for you treasure doesn't interest me. I prefer modern legal tender."

They motored past the Palais de Justice and passed beneath a bridge busy with traffic.

"I assume I don't have to pay the balance," he said, "until you fully perform on Larocque."

"To show you that I am a man of character, that will be fine. But she'll be dead by tomorrow." Lyon paused. "And know this, Lord Ashby. I don't fail often. So I don't appreciate reminders."

He caught the message. But he had something he wanted to emphasize, too.

"Just kill her."

SAM DECIDED TO EASE INTO THE LAST ROW OF SEATS beneath the canopy. He spied the familiar shape of Notre Dame approaching ahead on the left. On his right, the Latin Quarter and Shakespeare & Company, where yesterday all this had begun. The tour guide, not seen, only heard over the loudspeaker, droned bilingually about the Conciergerie, on the far Right Bank, where Marie Antionette was imprisoned before her execution.

He stood and casually walked toward the rear row, gazing out at the sights. He caught the chatter, picture taking, and pointing among the tourists aboard. Except for one man. Who sat at the end of an aisle, three rows from the end. Withered mushy face, long-eared, nearly chinless, he wore a pea-green coat over black jeans and boots. Blue-black hair was tied in a ponytail. He sat with both hands in his pockets, eyes ahead, disinterested, seemingly enjoying the ride.

Sam hugged the outer wall and crossed an invisible barrier where cold seeping in from the rear overcame warm air beneath the enclosure. He stared ahead and spotted another bridge spanning the Seine, coming closer.

Something rolled across the deck and clanged against the boat's side.

He gazed down at a metal canister.

He'd been taught about armaments during his Secret Service training, enough to recognize that this was not a grenade.

No.

A smoke bomb.

His gaze shot toward Green Coat, who was staring straight at him, lips curled into a smile.

Purple smoke escaped from the canister.

AN ODOR FILLED ASHBY'S NOSTRILS.

He whirled around and saw that the space beneath the Plexiglas canopy had filled with smoke.

Shouts. Screams.

People escaped the foggy shroud, fleeing toward him, onto the open portion of the deck, coughing away the remnants from inside.

"What in the world?" he muttered.

THORVALDSEN PAID THE CABDRIVER AND STEPPED out on the Pont de l'Archevêché. Meagan Morrison was right. Not much traffic on the two-lane stone bridge, and only a handful of pedestrians had paused to enjoy a picturesque view of Notre Dame's backside.

He included an extra fifty euros to the driver and said, "Take this young lady wherever she wants to go." He stared into the rear seat though the open door. "Good luck to you. Farewell."

He slammed the door closed.

The cab eased back into the road, and he approached an iron railing that guarded the sidewalk from a ten-meter drop to the river. Inside his coat pocket he fingered the gun, shipped by Jesper yesterday from Christiangade, along with spare magazines.

He'd watched as Graham Ashby and another man had stood outside the tour boat enclosure, propped against the aft railing, just as Sam had reported. The boat was two hundred meters away, cruising toward him against the current. He should be able to shoot Ashby, drop the gun into the Seine, then walk away before anyone realized what happened.

Weapons were no stranger. He could make this kill.

He heard a car brake and turned.

The cab had stopped.

Its rear door opened and Meagan Morrison popped out. She buttoned her coat and trotted straight toward him.

"Old man," she called out. "You're about to do something really stupid, aren't you?"

"Not to me it isn't."

"If you're hell-bent, at least let me help."

SAM RUSHED AFT WITH EVERYONE ELSE, SMOKE BIL-lowing from the boat as if it were ablaze.

But it wasn't.

He fought his way clear of the enclosure and spotted Green Coat, elbowing his way through the panic, toward the railing where Ashby and Tweed still stood.

THORVALDSEN GRIPPED THE GUN IN HIS POCKET and spotted smoke rushing from the tour boat.

Meagan saw it, too. "Now, that's not something you see every day."

He heard more brakes squeal and turned to see a car block traffic at each end of the bridge on which he stood.

Another car roared past and skidded to a stop in the center of the bridge.

The passenger-side door opened
Stephanie Nelle emerged.

ASHBY WATCHED AS A MAN IN A GREEN COAT LUNGED
from the crowd and jammed a fist into Peter Lyon's
gut. He heard the breath leave the South African, as
he crumbled to the deck.

A gun appeared in Green Coat's hand, and the
man said to Ashby, "Over the side."

"You must be joking."

"Over the side." The man motioned toward the
water.

Ashby turned to see a small craft, outfitted with
a single outboard, nestled close to the tour boat, a
driver at its helm.

He turned back and stared hard at Green Coat.

"I won't say it again."

Ashby pivoted over the railing, then dropped a
meter or so from the side into the second boat.

Green Coat hoisted himself up to follow, but
never made it down.

Instead his body was yanked backward.

SIXTY-FIVE

SAM WATCHED AS TWEED SPRANG TO HIS FEET AND yanked the man in the pea-green coat from the railing. Ashby had already leaped over the side. He wondered what was down there. The river would be nearly freezing. Certainly the fool had not plunged into the water.

Tweed and Green Coat slammed onto the deck.

Frightened passengers gave them room.

He decided to do something about the smoke. He stole a breath and rushed back beneath the enclosure. He found the smoke canister, lifted it from the deck, and, just past the last row of seats where the canopy ended, tossed it overboard.

The two men were still scuffling on the deck, the remaining smoke dissipating quickly in the cold, dry air.

He wanted to do something, but he was at a loss.

Engines dimmed. A door in the forward compartment opened and a crewman rushed out. Tweed and Green Coat continued to wrestle, neither man gaining an advantage. Tweed broke free, rolled away, and pushed himself up from the deck. Green Coat, too, was coming to his feet. But instead of rushing his opponent, the man in the green coat pushed through the surrounding onlookers and leaped over the side.

Tweed lunged after him, but the other man was gone.

Sam crossed the deck and spotted a small boat losing speed, drifting to their stern, then motoring away in the opposite direction.

Tweed watched, too.

Then the man peeled off a wig and ripped facial hair from his cheeks and chin.

He instantly recognized the face beneath.

Cotton Malone.

THORVALDSEN ALLOWED HIS GRIP ON THE GUN IN his pocket to relax. He casually withdrew his hand and watched as Stephanie Nelle stepped toward him.

"This can't be good," Meagan muttered.

He agreed.

The tour boat was approaching the bridge. He'd watched as the source of the smoke had been tossed overboard, then two men had jumped into a smaller craft—one of them had been Ashby—which roared away in the opposite direction, following the current, as the Seine wound deeper into Paris.

The tour boat glided past beneath the bridge and he caught sight of Sam and Cotton Malone standing at the aft railing, surrounded by people. The upward angle and the fact that Sam and Malone were facing away, watching the retreating motorboat, made it impossible for them to see him.

Meagan and Stephanie saw them, too.

"Now do you see what you're interfering with?" Stephanie asked as she stopped a meter away.

"How did you know we were here?" Meagan asked.

"Your cell phones," Stephanie said. "They have embedded trackers. When Henrik came on the line earlier, I realized there'd be trouble. We've been watching."

Stephanie faced him. "What were you going to do? Shoot Ashby from here?"

He threw her a fierce, indignant stare. "Seemed like a simple thing to do."

"You're not going to allow us to handle this, are you?"

He knew exactly what was meant by **us.** "Cotton seems not to have the time to answer my calls, but plenty of time to be a part of your operation."

"He's trying to solve all of our problems. Yours included."

"I don't require his assistance."

"Then why did you involve him?"

Because, at the time, he'd thought him a friend. One who'd be there for him. As he'd been for Malone.

"What was happening on that boat?" he asked.

Stephanie shook her head. "As if I'm going to explain that to you. And you," she added, pointing at Meagan. "Were you going to just let him kill a man?"

"I don't work for you."

"You're right." She motioned to one of the French policemen standing beside the car. "Get her out of here."

"That won't be necessary," Thorvaldsen made clear. "We'll leave together."

"You're coming with me."

He'd already anticipated that response, which was why he'd slipped his right hand back into his pocket and regripped the gun.

He withdrew the weapon.

"What do you plan to do? Shoot me?" Stephanie quietly asked.

"I wouldn't recommend you push me. At the moment, I seem nothing more than an obedient participant in my own humiliation, but it's my problem, Stephanie, not yours, and I intend to finish what I started."

She did not reply.

"Get us a cab," he ordered Meagan.

She ran to the bridge's end and flagged down the

first one that passed on the busy boulevard. Stephanie remained silent, but he saw it in her eyes. An introspective yet alert defensiveness. And something else. She had no intention of halting him.

He was acting on impulse, more panic than design, and she seemed to sympathize with his quandary. This woman, full of expertise and caution, could not help him, but in her heart she did not want to stop him, either.

"Just go," she whispered.

He scampered toward the waiting cab, as fast as his crooked spine would allow. Once inside he asked Meagan, "Your cell phone."

She handed the unit over.

He lowered the window and tossed it away.

ASHBY WAS TERRIFIED.

The motorboat was making its escape past the Île de la Cité, threading a quick path around other boats coming their way.

Everything had happened so fast.

He was talking to Peter Lyon, then a tidal wave of smoke had burst over him. The man in the green coat now held a gun, quickly displaying it the instant he'd leaped from the tour boat. Who was he? One of the Americans?

"You are truly a fool," the man said to him.

"Who are you?"

The gun came level.

Then he saw amber eyes.

"The man you owe a great deal of money."

MALONE PEELED THE REMAINING HAIR AND ADHE-
sive from his face. He held open each eyelid and
plucked out amber-colored contacts.

The tour boat had stopped at the nearest dock
and allowed frightened patrons to leave. Malone
and Sam debarked last, Stephanie waiting ashore,
up a stone stairway, at street level.

"What was that all about?" she asked.

"A royal mess," Malone said. "Didn't go as
planned."

Sam seemed perplexed.

"We had to corner Ashby," Malone said. "So I
called, as Lyon, and arranged a meeting."

"And the getup?"

"The French helped us out there. Their intelligence people found us a makeup artist. I was also
wired, getting admissions on tape. Peter Lyon,
though, had other ideas."

"That was him?" Sam asked. "In the green
coat?"

Malone nodded. "Apparently he wants Ashby,
too. And good job clearing the smoke bomb."

"Henrik was here," she said to him.

"How pissed is he?"

"He's hurt, Cotton. He's not thinking clearly."

He should talk with his friend, but there hadn't been a free moment all day. He found his cell phone, which he'd silenced before boarding the tour boat, and noted more missed calls from Henrik and three from a number he recognized.

Dr. Joseph Murad.

He punched REDIAL. The professor answered on the first ring.

"I did it," Murad said. "I figured it out."

"You know the location?"

"I think so."

"Have you called Henrik?"

"I just did. I couldn't reach you, so I called him. He wants me to meet him."

"You can't do that, Professor. Just tell me where and I'll handle it."

SIXTY-SIX

3:40 PM

ASHBY WAS LED FROM THE BOAT AT GUNPOINT, NEAR the Île Saint Germain, south of the old city center. He now knew that the man who held him was Peter Lyon and the man on the tour boat had most likely been an American agent. A car waited up from the river, at street level. Two men sat inside. Lyon signaled and they exited. One opened the rear door and yanked Caroline out into the afternoon.

"Your Mr. Guildhall won't be joining us," Lyon said. "I'm afraid he's been permanently detained."

He knew what that meant. "There was no need to kill him."

Lyon chuckled. "On the contrary. It was the only option."

The situation had just gravitated from serious to desperate. Obviously, Lyon had been monitoring everything Ashby had been doing, since he knew exactly where Caroline and Guildhall could be found.

He spied unrestrained fear on Caroline's lovely face.

He was scared, too.

Lyon led him forward and whispered, "I thought you might need Miss Dodd. That's the only reason she's still alive. I would suggest that you don't waste the opportunity I've offered her."

"You want the treasure?"

"Who wouldn't?"

"You told me last night in London that things like that didn't interest you."

"A source of wealth unknown to any government, with no accounting. There's so much I could do with that at my disposal—and I wouldn't have to deal with cheats like you."

They stood beyond a busy street, the car parked among a patch of trees bleached from winter. No one was in sight, the area largely a commercial center and boat repair facility, closed for the holiday. Lyon again withdrew the gun from beneath his coat and screwed a sound suppressor to the short barrel.

"Set her back in the car," Lyon directed as they approached.

Caroline was shoved across the rear seat. Lyon stepped to the open door and thrust his arm inside, aiming the gun directly at her.

She gasped. "Oh, God. No."

"Shut up," Lyon said.

Caroline started to cry.

"Lord Ashby," Lyon said. "And you, too, Miss Dodd. I'm only going to ask this once. If a truthful answer is not immediately forthcoming, clear and concise, then I will fire. Does everyone understand?"

Ashby said nothing.

Lyon stared straight at him. "I didn't hear you, Lord Ashby."

"What's not to understand?"

"Tell me where the treasure is located," Lyon said.

When Ashby had left Caroline earlier she was still developing the particulars, though she'd at least determined an initial starting point. He hoped, for both their sakes, she knew a lot more now.

"It's in the cathedral, at Saint-Denis," Caroline quickly said.

"You know where?" Lyon asked, his eyes locked on Ashby, the gun inside the car, still aimed.

"I believe so. But I need to go there to be sure. I have to see. I just figured all this out—"

Lyon withdrew his arm and lowered the weapon. "I hope, for your sake, you can determine the location."

Ashby stood still.

Lyon aimed the gun his way. "Your turn. Two questions, and I want simple answers. Do you have a direct line of communication to the Americans?"

That was easy. He nodded.

"Do you have a phone with you?"

He nodded again.

"Give me the phone and the number."

MALONE STOOD WITH SAM, TRYING TO DECIDE ON the next course of action, when Stephanie's cell phone sprang to life. She checked the display and said, "Ashby."

He knew better. "Apparently Lyon wants to talk to you."

She hit SPEAKER.

"I understand that you are the person in charge," a male voice said.

"The last time I looked," Stephanie said.

"You were in London last night?"

"That was me."

"Did you enjoy the show today?"

"We've had great fun chasing after you."

Lyon chuckled. "It kept you sufficiently occupied so I could deal with Lord Ashby. He is untrustworthy, as I'm sure you've discovered."

"He's probably thinking the same thing about you at the moment."

"You should be grateful. I did you a favor. I allowed you to monitor my conversation with Ashby at Westminster. I appeared at the Ripper tour so you could follow. I left the little towers for you to find. I even attacked your agent. What else did you need? But for me, you would have never known that the tower was Ashby's true target. I assumed you'd find a way to stop it."

"And if we hadn't, what would it have mattered? You'd still have your money, off to the next job."

"I had faith in you."

"I hope you don't expect anything for it."

"Heavens, no. I just didn't want to see that fool Ashby succeed."

Malone realized they were witnessing Peter Lyon's infamous arrogance. It wasn't enough that he was two steps ahead of his pursuers, he needed to rub that fact in their faces.

"I have another piece of information for you," Lyon said. "And this one is quite real. No distraction. You see, the French fanatics whom this entire endeavor was to be blamed on had a condition to their involvement. One I never mentioned to Lord Ashby. They are separatists, upset over the unfair treatment they have received at the hands of the French government. They loathe the many oppressive regulations, which they regard as racist. They're also tired of protesting. Seems it accomplishes little, and several of their mosques have been closed in Paris over the past few years as punishment for their activism. In return for assisting me at the Invalides, they want to make a more poignant statement."

Malone did not like what he was hearing.

"A suicide bombing is about to occur," Lyon said.

Chilly fingers caressed Malone's spine.

"During Christmas services in a Paris church. They thought this fitting, since **their** houses of worship are being closed every day."

There were literally hundreds of churches in Paris.

"After three duds, it's hard to take you seriously," she made clear.

"I see your point, but this one is real. And you can't rush there with police. The attack would occur before anyone could stop it. In fact, it's nearly imminent. Only **you** can prevent it."

"Bullshit," Stephanie said. "You're just buying more time for yourself."

"Of course I am. But can you afford to gamble that what I'm saying is a lie?"

Malone saw in Stephanie's eyes what he was thinking, too.

We have no choice.

"Where?" she asked.

Lyon laughed. "Not that easy. It's going to be a bit of a hunt. Of course, a churchful of people are counting on you making it there in time. Do you have ground transportation?"

"We do."

"I'll be in touch shortly."

She clicked the phone off.

Exasperation swept across her face, then vanished into the confidence that twenty-five years in the intelligence business had bestowed.

She faced Sam. "Go after Henrik."

Professor Murad had already told them that the Cathédrale de Saint-Denis was Thorvaldsen's destination.

"Try to keep him under control until we can get there."

"How?"

"I don't know. Figure it out."

"Yes, ma'am."

Malone smiled at his sarcasm. "That's how I used to say it, too, when she'd cut my tail. You can handle him. Just hold the line, keep things under control."

"That's easier said than done with Henrik."

He laid a hand on the younger man's shoulder. "He likes you. He's in trouble. Help him."

SIXTY-SEVEN

Eliza Larocque wandered around her Paris apartment and tried to restore order to her chaotic thoughts. She'd already consulted the oracle, asking the specific question, **Will my enemies succeed?** The answer that her slashes had produced seemed baffling. **The prisoner will soon be welcomed home, although he now smarts under the power of his enemies.**

What in the world?

Paolo Ambrosi was waiting for her call, ready to act. She wanted Graham Ashby dead, but not before she obtained answers to her many questions. She had to know the extent of Ashby's betrayal. Only then could she assess the potential damage. Things had changed. The sight of that airplane, powering toward her atop the Eiffel Tower, remained fresh in her thoughts. She also needed to wrestle back control of the hundreds of millions of Paris Club euros that Ashby maintained in his bank.

But today was a holiday. No way to make that

happen. She would handle it first thing in the morning.

Way too much trust had been placed in Ashby. And what of Henrik Thorvaldsen? He'd told her that the Americans were aware of all that had happened. Did that mean complete exposure? Was everything in jeopardy? If a connection had been established to Ashby, surely it reached to her?

The phone on the side table rang. Her landline. Few possessed the number besides some friends and senior staff.

And Ashby.

She answered.

"Madame Larocque, I am the man Lord Ashby hired to handle your exhibition this morning."

She said nothing.

"I'd be cautious, too," the voice said. "I called to tell you that I have Lord Ashby in my custody. He and I have some unfinished business. After that is completed, I plan to kill him. So rest assured that your debt to him will be satisfied."

"Why are you telling me this?"

"I'd like to be able to offer my services to you in the future. I'm aware of who was actually paying the bill. Ashby was merely your agent. This is my way of apologizing for the unfortunate occurrence. Suffice it to say that our British acquaintance lied to me as well. He meant to kill you and your associates, and lay the blame on me. Luckily, no harm came to anyone."

Not physically, she thought. But there'd been harm.

"No need to speak, madame. Know that the problem will be handled."

The phone went silent.

ASHBY LISTENED AS PETER LYON TAUNTED Larocque, chilled by the words **I plan to kill him.** Caroline heard the pronouncement, too. Her fear instantly evolved into terror, but he silenced her with a look that seemed to reassure.

Lyon closed the cell phone and smiled. "You wanted her off your back. She's off. There's nothing she can do, and she knows it."

"You underestimate her."

"Not really. I underestimated you. And that mistake I won't make again."

"You don't have to kill us," Caroline blurted out.

"That all depends on your level of cooperation."

"And what's to stop you from killing us once we fully cooperate?" Ashby asked.

Lyon's face seemed like that of a chess master, waiting coolly for his opponent's next move, already knowing his own. "Not a thing. But unfortunately for you both, cooperation is your only option."

HENRIK STEPPED FROM THE CAB BEFORE THE BASIL-ica of Saint-Denis and stared up at the church's single lateral tower, its twin missing, the building looking like an amputee, missing an appendage.

"The other tower burned in the 19th century," Meagan told him. "Struck by lightning. It was never replaced."

She'd explained on the ride north that this was where French kings had been buried for centuries. Begun in the 12th century, fifty years before Notre Dame, the church was a national landmark. Gothic architecture had been born here. During the French Revolution many of the tombs were destroyed, but they'd been restored. Now it was owned by the government.

Scaffolding clung to the outer walls, wrapping what appeared to be the north and west façades at least three-quarters of the way up. A hastily erected plywood barrier encircled the base, which blocked access to the main doors. Two construction trailers were parked on either side of the makeshift fence.

"Seems they're working on the place," he said.

"They're always working on something in this city."

He glanced at the sky. Gunmetal-gray clouds now shielded the sun, creating dense shadows and lowering the temperature.

A winter storm was coming.

The neighborhood lay about ten kilometers from Paris, traversed by both the Seine and a canal. The suburb was apparently an industrial center, as they'd passed several manufacturing facilities.

A mist began to build.

"The weather is about to get nasty," Meagan said.

People in the paved plaza before the church hurried off.

"This is a blue-collar area," Meagan noted. "Not a section of town where the tourists like to come. That's why you don't hear much about Saint-Denis, though I think it's more interesting than Notre Dame."

He wasn't interested in history, except as it related to Ashby's search. Professor Murad had told him some of what he'd deciphered—what Ashby surely knew by now as well, considering that Caroline Dodd was every bit the expert Murad was.

Mist turned to rain.

"What do we do now?" Meagan asked. "The basilica is closed."

He wondered why Murad wasn't already here. The professor had called nearly an hour ago and said he was leaving then.

He reached for his phone but, before he could place a call, the unit rang. Thinking it might be Murad, he studied the screen. COTTON MALONE.

He answered.

"Henrik, you've got to listen to what I have to say."

"Why would I have to do that?"

"I'm trying to help."

"You have an odd way of doing that. Giving that book to Stephanie was uncalled for. All you did was aid Ashby."

"You know better than that."

"No, I don't."

His voice rose, which startled Meagan. He told himself to remain composed. "All I know is that you gave her the book. Then you were on the boat, with Ashby, doing whatever it is you and your old boss think is right. None of which included me. I'm done with what's right, Cotton."

"Henrik, let us handle it."

"Cotton, I thought you my friend. Actually, I thought you were my best friend. I've always been there for you, no matter what. I owed you that." He fought a wave of emotion. "For Cai. You were there. You stopped his murderers. I admired and respected you. I went to Atlanta two years ago to thank you, and found a friend." He paused again. "But you haven't treated me with the same respect. You betrayed me."

"I did what I had to."

He didn't want to hear rationalizations. "Is there anything else you want?"

"Murad's not coming."

The full extent of Malone's duplicity struck hard.

"Whatever is at Saint-Denis, you're going to have to find it without him," Malone made clear.

He grabbed hold of his emotions. "Goodbye, Cotton. We shall never speak again."

He clicked off the phone.

MALONE CLOSED HIS EYES.

The acid declaration—**we shall never speak again**—burned his gut. A man like Henrik Thorvaldsen did not make statements like that lightly.

He'd just lost a friend.

Stephanie watched from the other side of the car's rear seat. They were headed away from Notre Dame, toward Gare du Nord, a busy rail terminal, following the first set of instructions Lyon had called back to them after his initial contact.

Rain peppered the windshield.

"He'll get over it," she said. "We can't be concerned with his feelings. You know the rules. We have a job to do."

"He's my friend. And besides, I hate rules."

"You're helping him."

"He doesn't see it that way."

Traffic was thick, the rain compounding the confusion. His eyes drifted from railings to balconies to roofs, the stately façades on both sides of the street receding upward into a graying sky. He noticed several secondhand-book shops, their stock displayed in windows of advertising posters, hackneyed prints, and arcane volumes.

He thought of his own business.

Which he'd bought from Thorvaldsen—his landlord, his friend. Their Thursday-evening dinners in Copenhagen. His many trips to Christiangade. Their adventures. They'd spent a lot of time together.

"Sam's going to have his hands full," he muttered.

A spate of taxis signaled the approach of the Gare du Nord. Lyon's instructions had been to call when they were in sight of the train station.

Stephanie dialed her phone.

SAM STEPPED FROM THE MÉTRO STATION AND trotted through the rain, using the overhangs from the closed shops as an umbrella, racing toward a plaza identified as PL. JEAN JAURÈS. To his left rose Saint-Denis basilica, its medieval aesthetic harmony marred by a curiously missing spire. He'd taken advantage of the Métro as the fastest way north, avoiding the late-afternoon holiday traffic.

He searched the frigid plaza for Thorvaldsen.

Wet pavement, like black patent leather, reflected street lamps in javelins of yellow light.

Had he gone inside the church?

He stopped a young couple, passing on their way to the Métro, and asked about the basilica, learning that the building had been closed since summer for extensive repairs, that fact confirmed by scaffolding braced against the exterior.

Then he saw Thorvaldsen and Meagan, near one of the trailers parked off to the left, maybe two hundred feet away.

He headed their way.

ASHBY FOLDED HIS COAT COLLAR UP AGAINST THE rain and walked down the deserted street with Caroline and Peter Lyon. An overcast sky draped the world in a pewter cloth. They'd used the boat and motored west on the Seine until the river started its wind north, out of Paris. Eventually, they'd veered onto a canal, stopping at a concrete dock near a highway overpass, a few blocks south of Saint-Denis basilica.

They'd passed a columned building identified as LE MUSÉE D'ART ET D'HISTOIRE, and Lyon led them beneath the portico.

Their captor's phone rang.

Lyon answered, listened a moment, then said, "Take Boulevard de Magenta north and turn on

Boulevard de Rochechouart. Call me back when you find Place de Clichy."

Lyon ended the connection.

Caroline was still terrified. Ashby wondered if she might panic and try to flee. It would be foolish. A man like Lyon would shoot her dead in an instant—treasure or no treasure. The smart play, the only play, was to hope for a mistake. If none occurred, perhaps he could offer this monster something that could prove useful, like a bank through which to launder money where no one asked questions.

He'd deal with that when necessary.

Right now, he simply hoped Caroline knew the answers to Lyon's coming questions.

SIXTY-EIGHT

THORVALDSEN AND MEAGAN TRUDGED DOWN A graveled path adjacent to the basilica's north side, away from the plaza.

"There's a former abbey," Meagan told him, "located on the south side. Not as old as the basilica. Nineteenth century, though parts date way back. It's some kind of college now. The abbey is at the heart of the legend that surrounds this place. After being beheaded in Montmartre, the evangelist St. Denis, the first bishop of Paris, supposedly started to walk, carrying his head. He was buried where he fell by a saintly woman. An abbey developed at that spot, which eventually became"—she motioned at the church—"this monstrosity."

He was trying to determine how to get inside. The north façade contained three portals, all iron-barred on the outside. Ahead, he spotted what was surely the ambulatory, a half circle of stone pierced with colored-glass windows.

Rain continued to fall.

They needed to find shelter.

"Let's round the corner up ahead," he said, "and try the south side."

ASHBY ADMIRED THE BASILICA, CLEARLY A MARVEL of skill and craftsmanship. They were walking down a graveled path on the south side of the building, having gained entrance to the church grounds through an opening in a makeshift construction barrier.

His hair and face were soaking wet, his ears burning from the cold. Thank goodness he'd worn a heavy coat, thick leather gloves, and long underwear. Caroline, too, had dressed for the weather, but her blond hair was matted to her head. Piles of broken masonry, blocks of travertine, and marble fragments lay just off the path, which cut a route between the basilica and a stone wall that separated the church from some adjacent buildings. A construction trailer stood ahead on concrete blocks, scaffolding rising behind it up the articulated walls. On the trailer's far side, up a few dozen stone steps, rose a Gothic portal, narrowed from front to back through the thickness of the walls toward two double doors clamped tight with plates of blue-washed iron.

Lyon climbed the steps and tested the latch.

Locked.

"See that piece of iron pipe?" Lyon said, pointing to the rubble pile. "We need it."

He wanted to know, "Are you going to smash your way inside?"

Lyon nodded. "Why not?"

Malone watched as Stephanie dialed Ashby's mobile number one more time. They'd arrived at the Place de Clichy, an interchange busy with activity.

"South down Rue d'Amsterdam, past Gare St. Lazare," Lyon instructed through the speakerphone. "The church you seek is across from that train station. I'd hurry. It's going to happen within the next thirty minutes. And don't call again. I won't answer."

The driver heard the location and sped ahead. Gare St. Lazare appeared in less than three minutes.

Two churches lay across from the busy station, side by side.

"Which one?" Stephanie muttered.

Sam skirted the basilica's north side, following Henrik and Meagan through the rain. They'd already rounded the corner a hundred feet ahead.

This far side of the basilica was rounded, full of curves, different from the straight edges on the plaza side.

He carefully advanced, not wanting to alert Thorvaldsen to his presence.

He followed the church's half circle and swung around to the building's south side.

Immediately he spotted Thorvaldsen and Meagan, huddled beneath a covered section that jutted from the basilica and connected with an adjacent structure. He heard something clang from farther down, past where Thorvaldsen stood.

Then more clangs.

ASHBY CRASHED THE HEAVY METAL PIPE ONTO THE latch. On the fourth blow, the handle gave way.

Another swipe and the black iron lever tumbled down the stone steps.

Lyon eased the door open. "That was easy."

Ashby tossed the pipe away.

Lyon held his gun, incentive enough not to try anything stupid, and motioned with it toward Caroline.

"Time to find out if her suspicions prove correct."

MALONE MADE A DECISION. "YOU DIDN'T THINK Lyon would make it simple, did you? You take the church on the right, I'll go left."

The car stopped and they both leaped out into the rain.

ASHBY WAS GLAD TO BE INSIDE. THE BASILICA'S interior was both warm and dry. Only a handful of overhead light fixtures burned, but they were enough for him to appreciate the lofty nave's majesty. Soaring fluted columns, perhaps thirty meters high, graceful arches, and pointed vaulting conveyed an awe-inspiring sense. Stained-glass windows, too many to even count, dark to the dismal day, projected none of the sensuous power their luminous tones surely could convey. But the impression of seemingly weightless walls was heightened by the lack of any visible feature holding something so tall upright. He knew, of course, that the supports were outside in the form of flying buttresses. He was forcing himself to concentrate on details as a way to relieve his mind of stress. He needed to think. To be ready to act when the moment was right.

"Miss Dodd," Lyon said. "What now?"

"I can't think with that gun out," Caroline blurted. "There's no way. I don't like guns. I don't like you. I don't like being here."

Lyon's brutish eyes narrowed. "If it helps, then here." He stuffed the weapon beneath his coat and displayed two empty, gloved hands. "That better?"

Caroline fought to regain her composure. "You're just going to kill us anyway. Why should I tell you anything?"

All congeniality faded from Lyon's face. "Once we find whatever there is to find, I might have a change of heart. Besides, Lord Ashby there is watching my every move, waiting for me to err. Then we'll have a chance to see if he's really a man."

Ashby clung to his last tatters of courage. "Perhaps I might have such an opportunity."

Lyon's lips parted in an amused grin. "I do hope so. Now, Miss Dodd, where to?"

THORVALDSEN LISTENED FROM THE HALF-OPEN door that Ashby had battered. He and Meagan had crept forward after Ashby, Caroline Dodd, and the man in the green coat had slipped inside. He was reasonably sure that the third participant was the second man who'd leaped from the tour boat with Ashby.

"What do we do?" Meagan breathed into his ear.

He had to end this partnership. He motioned for them to retreat.

They fled the portal, back into the rain, retreating to their previous position beneath a covered walk. He noticed restrooms and an admission office and assumed this was where people bought tickets to visit the basilica.

He grabbed Meagan by the arm. "I want you out of here. Now."

"You're not so tough, old man, I can handle myself."

"You don't need to be involved."

"You going to kill the woman and the other man, too?"

"If need be."

She shook her head. "You've lost it."

"That's right. I have. So leave."

Rain continued to torrent down, spilling off the roofs, dashing the pavement just beyond their enclosure. Everything seemed to be happening in a hypnotic slow motion. A lifetime of rationality was about to be erased by immeasurable grief. How many substitutes for happiness he'd tried since Cai died. Work? Politics? Philanthropy? Lost souls? Like Cotton. And Sam. But none of those had satisfied the hysteria that seemed to constantly rage within him. This was his task. No others were to be involved.

"I don't want to get myself killed," Meagan finally said to him.

Scorn tinged her words.

"Then leave." He tossed her his cell phone. "I don't need it."

He turned away.

"Old man," she said.

He stopped but did not face her.

"You take care." Her voice, low and soft, hinted at genuine concern.

"You too," he said.

And he stepped out into the rain.

SIXTY-NINE

MALONE PUSHED HIS WAY THROUGH A HEAVY SET of oak doors into the Church of St. André. Typical of Paris, gabled apses, crowned by a gallery, a high wall encircling the ambulatory. Sturdy flying buttresses supported the walls from the outside. Pure Gothic splendor.

People filled the pews and congregated in the transepts on either side of a long, narrow nave. Though heated, the air bore enough of a chill that coats were worn in abundance. Many of the worshipers carried shopping bags, backpacks, and large purses. All of which meant that his task of finding a bomb, or any weapon, had just become a million times harder.

He casually strolled through the edge of the crowd. The interior was a cadre of niches and shadows. Towering columns not only held up the roof, they provided even more cover for an assailant.

He was armed and ready.

But for what?

His phone vibrated. He retreated behind one of

the columns, into an empty side chapel, and quietly answered.

"Services here are over," Stephanie said. "People are leaving."

He had a feeling, one that had overtaken him the moment he entered.

"Get over here," he whispered.

ASHBY WALKED TOWARD THE MAIN ALTAR. THEY'D entered the basilica through a side entrance, near one inside staircase that led up to the chancel and another that dropped to a crypt. Row after row of wooden chairs stretched from the altar toward the north transept and the main entrances, the north wall perforated by an immense rose window, dark to the disappearing day. Tombs lay everywhere among the chairs and in the transepts, most adorned with inlaid marbles. Monuments extended from one end of the nave to the other, perhaps a hundred meters of enclosed space.

"Napoleon wanted his son to have the cache," Caroline said, her words sputtering with fear. "He hid his wealth carefully. Where no one would find it. Except those he wanted to find it."

"As any person of power should," Lyon said.

Rain continued to fall, the constant patter off the copper roof echoing through the nave.

"After five years in exile, he realized that he

would never return to France. He also knew he was dying. So he tried to communicate the location to his son."

"The book that the American gave you in London," Lyon said to Ashby. "It's relevant?"

He nodded.

"I thought you told me Larocque gave you the book," Caroline said.

"He lied," Lyon made clear. "But that doesn't matter anymore. Why is the book important?"

"It has a message," Caroline said.

She was offering too much, too fast, but Ashby had no way of telling her to slow down.

"I think I may have deciphered Napoleon's final message," she said.

"Tell me," Lyon said.

SAM WATCHED AS THORVALDSEN ABANDONED MEAgan and she plunged back into the rain, running toward where he stood hidden by one of the many juts from the outer wall. He pressed his back against cold, wet stone and waited for her to round the corner. He should be freezing, but his nerves were supercharged, numbing all feeling, the weather the least of his concerns.

Meagan appeared.

"Where are you going?" he quietly asked.

She stopped short and whirled, clearly startled. "Damn, Sam. You scared me to death."

"What's going on?"

"Your friend is about to do something really stupid."

He assumed as much. "What was that clamor I heard?"

"Ashby and two others broke into the church."

He wanted to know who was with Ashby, so he asked. She described the woman, whom he did not know, but the second man matched the man from the tour boat. Peter Lyon. He needed to call Stephanie. He fumbled in his coat pocket and found his phone.

"They have trackers in them," Meagan said, pointing to the unit. "They probably already know where you are."

Not necessarily. Stephanie and Malone were busy dealing with whatever new threat Lyon had generated. But he'd been sent to babysit Thorvaldsen, not confront a wanted terrorist.

And another problem.

The trip here had taken twenty minutes—by subway. He was a long way from Paris central, in a nearly deserted suburb being drenched by a storm.

That meant this was his problem to deal with.

Never forget, Sam. Foolishness will get you killed. Norstrum was right—God bless him—but Henrik needed him.

He replaced the phone in his pocket.

"You're not going in there, are you?" Meagan asked, seemingly reading his mind.

Even before he said it, he realized how stupid it sounded. But it was the truth. "I have to."

"Like at the top of the Eiffel Tower? When you could have been killed with all the rest of them?"

"Something like that."

"Sam, that old man wants to kill Ashby. Nothing's going to stop him."

"I am."

She shook her head. "Sam. I like you. I really do. But you're all insane. This is too much."

She stood in the rain, her face twisting with emotion. He thought of their kiss, last night, underground. There was something between them. A connection. An attraction. Still, he saw it in her eyes.

"I can't," she said, her voice cracking.

And she turned and ran away.

THORVALDSEN CHOSE HIS MOMENT WITH CARE. Ashby and his two companions were nowhere in sight, vanished into the gloomy nave. Darkness outside nearly matched the dusky interior, so he was able to slip inside, unnoticed, using the wind and rain as cover.

The entryway opened in nearly the center of the church's long south side. He immediately angled left and crouched behind an elaborate funerary monument, complete with a triumphal arch, beneath which two figures, carved of time-stained marble, lay recumbent. Both were emaciated representations, as they would have appeared as corpses rather than living beings. A brass plate identified the effigies as those of 16th century François I and his queen.

He heard a clamor of thin voices, beyond the columns that sprouted upward in a soaring Gothic display. More tombs appeared in the weak light, along with empty chairs arranged in neat rows. Sound came in short gusts. His hearing was not as good as it once was, and the rain pounding the roof wasn't helping.

He needed to move closer.

He fled his hiding place and scampered to the next monument, a delicate feminine sculpture, smaller than the first one. Warm air rushed up from a nearby floor grate. Water dripped from his coat onto the limestone floor. Carefully, he unbuttoned and shed the damp garment, but first freed the gun from one of the pockets.

He crept to a column a few meters away that separated the south transept from the nave, careful not to disturb any of the chairs.

One sound and his advantage would vanish.

ASHBY LISTENED AS CAROLINE FOUGHT THROUGH her fear and told Peter Lyon what he wanted to know, fishing from her pocket a sheet of paper.

"These Roman numerals are a message," she said. "It's called a Moor's Knot. The Corsicans learned the technique from Arab pirates who ravaged their coast. It's a code."

Lyon grabbed the paper.

**CXXXV II CXLII LII LXIII XVII
II VIII IV VIII IX II**

"They usually refer to a page, line, and word of a particular manuscript," she explained. "The sender and receiver have the same text. Since only they know which manuscript is being used, deciphering the code by someone else was next to impossible."

"So how did you manage?"

"Napoleon sent these numbers to his son in 1821. The boy was only ten at the time. In his will, Napoleon left the boy 400 books and specifically named one in particular. But the son wasn't even to receive the books until his sixteenth birthday. This code is odd in that it's only two groups of numerals, so they have to be page and line only. To decipher them, the son, or more likely his mother, since that's who Napoleon actually wrote, would have to know what text he used. It can't be the one from the will, since they would not have known about the will when he sent this code. After all, Napoleon was still alive."

She was rambling with fear, but Ashby let her go.

"So I made a guess and assumed Napoleon chose a universal text. One that would always be available. Easy to find. Then I realized he left a clue where to look."

Lyon actually seemed impressed. "You're quite the detective."

The compliment did little to calm her anxiety.

Ashby had heard none of this and was as curious as Lyon seemed to be.

"The Bible," Caroline said. "Napoleon used the Bible."

SEVENTY

MALONE STUDIED THE CONGREGATION, FACE AFTER face. His gaze drifted toward the processional doors at the main entrance, where more people ambled inside. At a decorative font many stopped to wet a finger and cross themselves. He was about to turn away when a man brushed past, ignoring the font. Short, fair-skinned, with dark hair and a long, aquiline nose. He wore a knee-length black coat, leather gloves, his face frozen in a bothersome solemnity. A bulky backpack hung from his shoulders.

A priest and two acolytes appeared before the high altar.

A lecturer assumed the pulpit and asked for the worshipers' attention, the female voice resounding through a PA system.

The crowd quieted.

Malone advanced toward the altar, weaving around people who stood beyond the pews, in the transept, listening to the services. Luckily, neither of the transepts was jammed. He caught sight of

Long Nose edging his way forward, through the crowd, in the opposite transept, the image winking in and out among the columns.

Another target aroused his curiosity. Also in the opposite transept. Olive-skinned, short hair, he wore an oversized coat with no gloves. Malone cursed himself for allowing any of this to happen. No preparation, no thought, being played by a mass murderer. Chasing ghosts, which could well prove illusory. Not the way to run any operation.

He refocused his attention on Olive Skin.

The man's right hand remained in his coat pocket, left arm at his side. Malone did not like the look of the anxious eyes, but he wondered if he was leaping to irrational conclusions.

A loud voice disturbed the solemnity.

A woman. Midthirties, dark hair, rough face. She stood in one of the pews, spewing out something to the man beside her. He caught a little of the French.

A quarrel.

She screamed something else, then rushed from the pew.

SAM ENTERED SAINT-DENIS, STAYING LOW AND hoping no one spotted him. All quiet inside. No sign of Thorvaldsen, or Ashby, or Peter Lyon.

He was unarmed, but he could not allow his

friend to face this danger alone. It was time to return the favor the Dane had extended him.

He could distinguish little in the bleak light, the wind and rain outside making it difficult to hear. He glanced left and caught sight of the familiar shape of Thorvaldsen's bent form standing fifty feet away, near one of the massive columns.

He heard voices from the center of the church.

Words came in snatches.

Three forms moved in the light.

He could not risk heading toward Thorvaldsen, so he stayed low and advanced a few feet straight ahead.

ASHBY WAITED FOR CAROLINE TO EXPLAIN WHAT Napoleon had done.

"More specifically," she said. "He used Psalms." She pointed to the first set of Roman numerals.

CXXXV
II

"Psalm 135, verse 2," she said. "I wrote the line down."

She searched her coat pocket and located another sheet of paper.

" 'You who stand in the house of the Lord, in the courts of the house of our God.' "

Lyon smiled. "Clever. Go on."

"The next two numerals refer to Psalm 142, verse 4. 'Look to my right and see.' "

"How do you know—" Lyon started, but a noise, near the main altar and the door through which they'd entered, arrested their captor's attention.

Lyon's right hand found the gun and he whirled to face the challenge.

"Help us," Caroline cried out. "Help us. There's a man here with a gun."

Lyon aimed the weapon straight at Caroline.

Ashby had to act.

Caroline crept backward, as if she could avoid the threat by retreating, her eyes alight with uncommon fear.

"Shooting her would be stupid," Ashby tried. "She's the only one who knows the location."

"Tell her to stand still and shut up," Lyon ordered, the gun aimed at Caroline.

Ashby's gaze locked on his lover. He raised a hand to halt her. "Please, Caroline. Stop."

She seemed to sense the urgency of the request and froze.

"Treasure or no treasure," Lyon said. "If she makes one more sound, she's dead."

THORVALDSEN WATCHED AS CAROLINE DODD tempted fate. He'd heard the noise, too, from the portal where he'd entered. About fifteen meters away, past an obstacle course of tombs.

Somebody had come inside.

And announced their presence.

SAM TURNED AT THE NOISE BEHIND HIM, FROM THE doorway. He caught sight of a black form near the outer wall, approaching a set of stairs that led up to another level behind the main altar.

The size and shape of the shadow confirmed its identity.

Meagan.

ASHBY NOTICED THAT THE RUSH OF WIND AND rain from outside had increased, as if the doors they'd broken through had opened wider.

"There is a storm out there," he said to Lyon.

"You shut up, too."

Finally, Lyon was agitated. He wanted to smile, but he knew better.

Lyon's amber eyes were as alert as a Doberman's, scouring the cavern of faint light that enclosed them, his gun leading the way as he slowly pivoted.

Ashby saw it at the same time Lyon did.

Movement, thirty meters away, on the stairway right of the altar, leading up to the chancel and the ambulatory.

Somebody was there.

Lyon fired. Twice. A sound, like two balloons popping, thanks to the sound suppressor, echoed through the nave.

Then a chair flew through the air and crashed into Lyon.

Followed by another.

SEVENTY-ONE

MALONE KEPT HIS ATTENTION ON THE WOMAN, who elbowed her way out of the pew. The man she'd argued with fled the pew, too, and headed after her, both walking away from the altar, toward the main doors. He wore a thin, nylon coat, open in the front, and Malone spotted nothing suspicious.

His gaze again raked the crowd.

He spotted Long Nose, with the backpack, entering a half-full pew toward the front, crossing himself and kneeling to pray.

He spotted Olive Skin, emerging from the shadows, near the altar, still in the opposite transept. The man pushed through the last of the onlookers and stopped at velvet ropes that blocked any further forward access.

Malone did not like what he saw.

His hand slipped beneath his jacket and found the gun.

SAM SAW LYON FIRE TOWARD WHERE MEAGAN HAD headed. He heard bullets ping off stone and hoped to heaven that meant the rounds missed.

A new noise clattered through the church.

Followed by another.

ASHBY WATCHED AS THE TWO FOLDING CHAIRS pounded into Lyon, who was caught off guard by the assault, his balance affected as he staggered. Caroline had tossed both of them just as Lyon had been distracted by whoever had entered the church.

Then she had escaped into the gloom.

Lyon recovered and realized Caroline was gone.

The gun came level, pointed Ashby's way.

"As you mentioned," Lyon said. "**She's** the only one who knows the location. You I don't need."

A point Caroline had not seemed to consider.

"Get. Her. Back."

"Caroline," he called out. "You need to return." He'd never had a gun aimed at him before. A terrifying sensation, actually.

One he did not like.

"Now. Please."

THORVALDSEN SAW CAROLINE DODD TOSS THE chairs at Lyon, then disappear into the darkness of the west transept. She had to be working her way forward, using the tombs, the columns, and the darkness for cover, moving his way. There was no other route, since the far transept was too close to Peter Lyon and much more illuminated.

His eyes were accustomed to the dimness, so he stood his ground, keeping one eye on Lyon and Ashby, the other on the stillness to his left.

Then he saw her.

Inching stealthily his way. Most likely headed for the south portal's open doors, where the wind and rain continued to announce their presence.

Toward the only way out.

Trouble was, Lyon would know that, too.

MALONE'S FINGERS WRAPPED AROUND THE BERETTA. He didn't want to, but he'd shoot Olive Skin, right here, if he had to.

His target stood thirty feet away and he waited for the man to make a move. A woman approached Olive Skin and intertwined her arm with his. She gently kissed him on the cheek and there was clear surprise on his face, then recognition as the two started to chat.

They turned and walked back toward the main entrance.

Malone's grip on the gun relaxed.

False alarm.

His gaze returned to the nave as mass began. He

caught sight of Long Nose as he eased his way out of the pew toward the center aisle.

Malone continued to search for problems. He should order the whole place evacuated, but this could well be another nothing.

A woman stood in the pew Long Nose had abandoned, holding a backpack. She motioned to the man, signaling he'd left something. Long Nose waved her off and kept walking. The woman stepped out into the center aisle and hustled after him.

Malone remained in the transept.

Long Nose turned, saw the woman coming for him, backpack in hand. He rushed toward her, wrenched the black nylon bundle from her grip, and tossed it forward. It slid across the marble floor, stopping at the base of two short risers that led up to the altar.

Long Nose turned and ran for the exit.

Thoughts of Mexico City flooded Malone's brain.

This was it.

Do something.

SEVENTY-TWO

THORVALDSEN WAITED FOR CAROLINE DODD TO creep closer. She was skillfully using the wall's nooks, shielding her advance toward the basilica's south portal. He crouched and eased himself into position, waiting for her to pass. One hand clutched the gun, the other ready to snag his target. He could not allow her to leave. Over the past year he'd listened to tape after tape of her and Ashby conspiring. Though she may well be ignorant of all that Ashby did, she was no innocent.

He hugged the short side of a marble sarcophagus topped with an elaborate Renaissance carving. Dodd made her way down the tomb's long side, the monument itself, and one of the massive columns shielding them both from view. He waited until she tried to make a dash for the next monument, then wrapped an arm around her neck, his palm finding her mouth.

Yanking her down, he jammed the gun into her neck and whispered, "Quiet, or I'll let the man out there know where you are. I need you to nod your head if you understand."

She did, and he released his grip.

She pushed back.

"Who the hell are you?" she whispered.

He heard the hope in her question that he was perhaps a friend. He decided to use that to his advantage.

"The person who can save your life."

ASHBY KEPT A TIGHT GRIP ON HIS EXPRESSION AND stared at the gun, wondering if this would be the end of his life.

Lyon had no reason to keep him alive.

"Caroline," Ashby called out. "You must return. I implore you. This man will kill me if you don't."

THORVALDSEN COULD NOT ALLOW PETER LYON TO do what he'd come to do.

"Tell Lyon to come and get you," he whispered.

Caroline Dodd shook her head no.

She needed reassurance. "He won't come. But it will buy Ashby time."

"How do you know who we are?"

He had no time for explanations, so he aimed his gun at her. "Do it, or I'll shoot you."

SAM DECIDED TO MAKE A MOVE. HE HAD TO KNOW if Meagan was okay. He'd seen no movement from the top of the stairs, behind the altar. Lyon seemed more concerned with Caroline Dodd, forcing Ashby to have her return to where they stood, at the nave's far west end.

While Lyon was distracted, this might be the time to act.

"Hey, asshole," Meagan called out through the dark, "you missed."

What in the world?

"AND WHO ARE YOU?" LYON ASKED THE DARKNESS.

Ashby wanted to know the answer to that question, too.

"Wouldn't you like to know."

The echo off the stone walls made it impossible to pinpoint the woman's location, but Ashby assumed it was the same figure they'd spotted climbing the stairs into the ambulatory.

"I'm going to kill you," Lyon said.

"You have to find me first. And that means you have to shoot the good Lord Ashby there."

She knew his name. Who was this?

"Do you know who I am, too?"

"Peter Lyon. Terrorist extraordinaire."

"Are you with the Americans?" Lyon asked.

"I'm with me."

Ashby watched Lyon. The man was clearly rattled. The gun remained pointed directly at him, but Lyon's attention was on the voice.

"What do you want?" Lyon asked.

"Your hide."

Lyon chuckled. "Many covet that prize."

"That's what I hear. But I'm the one who's going to get it."

THORVALDSEN LISTENED TO THE EXCHANGE BEtween Meagan and Lyon. He realized what she was doing, creating confusion, forcing Lyon to possibly make a mistake. Reckless on her part. But perhaps Meagan had gauged the situation correctly. Lyon's attention was now divided among three possible threats. Ashby, Caroline, and the unknown voice. He'd have to make a choice.

Thorvaldsen's gun remained aimed on Caroline Dodd. He could not allow Meagan to take the chance she'd clearly assumed. He jutted the weapon forward and whispered, "Tell him you're going to reveal yourself."

She shook her head.

"You're not really going to do it. I just need him to come this way so I can shoot him."

She seemed to consider that proposal. After all, he did have a gun.

"All right, Lyon," Dodd finally called out. "I'm coming back."

MALONE PUSHED HIS WAY THROUGH THE NEAREST pew, filled with sitting worshipers. He figured he had at least a minute or two. Long Nose had apparently planned on surviving the attack, which meant he'd given himself time to leave the church. But the Good Samaritan woman, trying to return his left backpack, had eaten into some of that cushion.

He found the center aisle and turned for the altar.

His mouth opened to shout a warning, but no sound came out. Any alarm would be futile. His only chance was to get the bomb away.

As he'd studied the crowd, he'd also studied the geography. Adjacent to the main altar was a stairway that led down into what he assumed was a crypt. Every one of these old churches came with a crypt.

He saw the priest take notice of the commotion and stop the service.

He reached the backpack.

No time to know if he was right or wrong.

He snatched the bundle up from the floor—heavy—and darted left, tossing it down the steps where, ten feet below, an iron gate was open into a dimly lit space beyond.

He hoped to God no one was in there.

"Everybody," he yelled in French. "Get down. It's a bomb. Down to the floor, behind the pews."

Many dove out of sight, others stood stunned.

"Get down—"

The bomb exploded.

SEVENTY-THREE

Ashby breathed again as Lyon heard Caroline and lowered his weapon.

"Sit in the chair," Lyon ordered. "And don't get up."

Since there was only one way out of the basilica and he'd never come close to making an escape, he decided the safe play was to obey.

"Hey," the first female voice called out in the dark. "You don't really think she's going to show herself, do you?"

Lyon did not reply.

Instead he marched toward the altar.

Sam could not believe Meagan was actually drawing Lyon her way. What had happened to the **I can't** she'd uttered outside in the rain? He watched as Lyon walked down the center aisle, between rows of empty chairs, gun at his side.

"If all my friends jumped off a bridge," Norstrum said. "I wouldn't jump with them. I'd be at the bottom, hoping to catch them."

He tried to make sense of what he'd heard.

"True friends stand and fall together."

"Are we true friends?" he asked.

"Of course."

"But you always tell me that there will come a time when I have to leave."

"Yes. That may happen. But friends are only apart in distance, not in heart. Remember, Sam, every good friend was once a stranger."

Meagan Morrison had been a stranger two days ago. Now she was placing her ass on the line. For him? Thorvaldsen? It didn't matter.

They would stand or fall together.

He decided to use the only weapon available. The same one Caroline Dodd had chosen. So he shed his wet coat, grabbed one of the wooden chairs, and hurled it toward Peter Lyon.

THORVALDSEN SAW THE CHAIR ARCH ACROSS THE nave toward Lyon. Who else was here? Meagan was past the altar, in the upper ambulatory. Dodd was a meter away, terrified, and Ashby was near the west transept.

Lyon caught sight of the chair, whirled, and

managed to maneuver out of the way just before the chair struck the floor. He then aimed his gun and fired a round toward the choir and the episcopal throne.

SAM FLED HIS HIDING PLACE JUST AS LYON AVOIDED the chair. He darted left, between the columns and tombs, staying low, heading toward where Ashby sat.

Another shot rang out.

The bullet pinged off the stone a few inches from his right shoulder, which meant he'd been spotted.

Another pop.

The round ricocheted off more stone and he felt something sting his left shoulder. Intense pain shot through his arm and he lost his balance, careering to the floor. He rolled and assessed the damage. His left shirtsleeve was torn.

A blood rose blossomed. Sharp pain stabbed up from behind his eyes. He checked the wound and realized that he hadn't been hit, only grazed—enough, though, to hurt like hell.

He clamped his right hand over the bleeding and rose to his feet.

THORVALDSEN TRIED TO SEE WHAT LYON WAS shooting at. Someone had thrown another chair. Then he spotted a black form rushing past, on the other side of the monument that served as his hiding place.

Dodd saw it, too, panicked, and scampered off, putting a procession of tombs between her and the nave.

Thorvaldsen caught a fleeting glimpse of the face of the form as it hustled past.

Sam.

He heard two more shots, then the thud of flesh and bone meeting stone.

No. Please, God. Not again.

He aimed at Peter Lyon and fired.

ASHBY DOVE FOR COVER. THE NAVE HAD ERUPTED into a mélange of gunfire from all directions. He saw Lyon flatten himself on the floor and also use the chairs for cover.

Where was Caroline?

Why hadn't she returned?

THORVALDSEN COULD NOT ALLOW ANYTHING TO happen to Sam. Bad enough Meagan was involved.

Caroline Dodd had disappeared, surely toward the open portal where wind and rain continued to howl. It would only take a moment for Lyon to recover and react, so he scampered away, toward where Sam had headed.

MALONE SHIELDED HIS HEAD WITH HIS ARMS AS the explosion thundered through the nave, rattling the walls and windows. But his toss into the crypt had been true and the explosion's brunt force stayed below, only a smoke and dust cloud bubbling up from the stairway.

He glanced around.

Everyone seemed okay.

Then panic assumed control and people swarmed for the exit. The priest and the two altar boys left, disappearing into the choir.

He stood before the main altar and watched the chaos, mindful that the bomber had probably made his escape. As the crowd thinned, standing at the rear of the center aisle was Stephanie, holding her gun to the ribs of Long Nose.

Three Paris policemen appeared through the main doors. One saw the automatic in Stephanie's grasp and immediately found his weapon.

The other two followed suit.

"Baissez votre arme. Immédiatement," one of

the officers shouted at Stephanie. Drop the gun. Immediately.

Another non-uniformed officer appeared and called for the officers to stand down. They lowered their weapons, then rushed forward to handcuff Long Nose.

Stephanie marched down the center aisle.

"Nice catch," he told her.

"Even better throw."

"What do we do now?" he asked. "We've surely heard the last from Lyon."

"I agree."

He reached into his pocket and found his cell phone. "Maybe it's time I try to reason with Henrik. Sam should be with him."

He'd switched the unit to silent on the taxi ride to the church. Now he spied a missed call from about twenty minutes ago.

Thorvaldsen.

Placed after they'd talked.

He saw a voice-mail indicator and listened to the message.

"This is Meagan Morrison. I was with Sam today at the Eiffel Tower when you came. Henrik gave me his phone, so I'm calling at the same number where you called him. I hope this is Cotton Malone. That crazy old man has gone inside Saint-Denis after Ashby. There's another man and a woman in there. Sam told me the man is Peter Lyon. Sam went in there, too. They need help. I thought I could let Sam do this alone. But . . . I can't. He's going to get himself hurt. I'm going in. I thought you should know."

"We have to get there," he said.

"It's only eight miles, but the traffic is heavy. I've told the Paris police. They're dispatching men right now. A chopper is on the way for us. It should be outside. The street's been cleared so it can land."

She'd thought of everything.

"I can't send the police in there with sirens blasting," she said. "I want Lyon. This may be our only shot. They're headed there quietly."

He knew that was the smart play.

But not for the people inside.

"We should beat them there," she said.

"Let's make sure we do."

SEVENTY-FOUR

SAM CLUTCHED HIS ARM AND KEPT MOVING TOWARD the end of the church that, he assumed, faced the plaza outside. He'd succeeded in drawing Peter Lyon's attention away from Meagan, but he'd also managed to get injured. He only hoped that they could all occupy Lyon long enough for help to arrive.

Thorvaldsen had apparently come to his rescue, firing on Lyon and allowing him the opportunity for an escape.

But where was the Dane now?

He found the last column in the row that supported the vault. Open space loomed beyond. He pressed his spine close and risked a peek into the nave.

Lyon was running toward a staircase, left of the altar, that led up to where Meagan was hiding.

"No," Sam screamed.

ASHBY COULDN'T BELIEVE WHAT HE WAS HEARING. Lyon was finally moving away, toward the other end of the church, far enough that he could make an escape for the doors. He'd been patiently waiting, watching as the demon avoided whoever was shooting at him from the south transept. He didn't know who that was, but he was damn glad they were here.

Now someone from his immediate right had shouted out.

As if to say to Lyon, **Not there. Here.**

THORVALDSEN FIRED ANOTHER ROUND, DISTURBED that Sam was drawing attention to himself.

Lyon sought refuge behind one of the tombs near the main altar.

He could not allow Lyon to advance toward the ambulatory, to where Meagan was hiding. So he hustled forward, back through the south transept, away from Ashby and Sam, toward Lyon.

ASHBY FLED THE CHAIR AND SOUGHT PROTECTION in the shadows. Lyon was thirty meters away, enemies thickening around him. Caroline had never appeared, and he assumed she was gone. He should follow her lead. The treasure was no longer important, at least not at the moment.

Escaping was his only concern.

So he crouched low and crept forward, down the south transept, heading for the open doors.

MALONE BUCKLED THE HARNESS JUST AS THE HELIcopter lifted from the street. Daylight was sinking away, and only faint slants of light managed to pierce the rain clouds.

Stephanie sat beside him.

Both of them were deeply concerned.

A bitter, angry father bent on revenge and a young rookie agent were not the duo that should be facing a man like Peter Lyon. One wasn't thinking, the other had not learned how to think yet. With all that had happened, Malone hadn't had a second to consider the rift between him and Thorvaldsen. He'd done what he thought was right, but that decision had hurt a friend. Never had he and Thorvaldsen exchanged any cross words. Some irritation, occasional frustration, but never genuine anger.

He needed to speak with Henrik and work it out.

He glanced over at Stephanie and knew she was

silently berating herself for sending Sam. At the time, that had been the right move.

Now it might prove fatal.

SAM WAS PLEASED THAT LYON HAD HESITATED AND not, as yet, pressed his advantage and made a dash for the staircase that led up to the ambulatory. His left arm hurt like hell, his right hand still clamped on the bleeding wound.

Think.

He made another decision.

"Henrik," he called out. "That man with the gun is a wanted terrorist. Keep him pinned down until help arrives."

THORVALDSEN WAS GLAD TO HEAR THAT SAM WAS okay.

"His name is Peter Lyon," Meagan called out.

"So nice," Lyon said, "that everyone knows me."

"You can't kill us all," Sam said.

"But I can kill one or two of you."

Thorvaldsen knew that assessment was correct, particularly considering that he seemed to be the only one, besides Lyon, who was armed.

Movement grabbed his attention. Not from Lyon. But off to his right, near the doors leading out. A solitary form, moving straight for the exit. He first thought it was Caroline Dodd, but then he realized that the figure was male.

Ashby.

He'd apparently taken advantage of the confusion and carefully crept from the other end of the nave. Thorvaldsen turned away from Lyon and scampered toward the doors. Being closer than Ashby, he arrived first. He hugged François's monument again for cover and waited for the Brit to approach through the darkness.

The marble floor was soaked from blowing rain.

Without a coat, he was cold.

He heard Ashby, on the monument's opposite side, stop his advance.

Probably making sure that he could make the final ten meters without anyone noticing.

Thorvaldsen peered around the edge.

Ashby started forward.

Thorvaldsen swung around the tomb's short side and jammed his gun in Ashby's face.

"You won't be leaving."

Ashby, clearly startled, lost his balance on the wet floor and rolled to face the threat.

SEVENTY-FIVE

ASHBY WAS PUZZLED. "THORVALDSEN?"

"Stand up," the Dane ordered.

He rose to his feet. The gun remained pointed at him.

"You were the one shooting at Lyon?" he asked.

"I didn't want him to do what I came to do."

"What is that?"

"Kill you."

SAM COULD HEAR VOICES FROM A HUNDRED FEET away, near the exit. But the storm and the nave's echo made it difficult to distinguish what was being said. Thorvaldsen was there, that much he knew. Ashby had fled, so he assumed Henrik had stopped the Brit from leaving, finally confronting his nemesis.

But Lyon was still here.

Perhaps Lyon had already determined that only

one of the three was armed, since neither of the other two challengers had sent gunfire his way.

Sam saw Lyon flee his hiding place and advance across the nave, using the altar and its surrounding monuments for cover, heading straight for where the voices seemed to be.

He headed that way, too.

MALONE CHECKED HIS WATCH. ROUGH AIR BUF-feted the helicopter, and rain poured down the windows. His mind was in a tense communion with the whine of the rotors. Paris rolled past beneath them as they roared northward toward the suburb of Saint-Denis.

He hadn't felt this helpless in a long time.

Stephanie checked her watch and flashed four fingers.

Less than five minutes.

THORVALDSEN KNEW HE HAD TO ACT FAST, BUT HE wanted this son of a bitch to know why he was about to die.

"Two years ago," he said, "in Mexico City. My son was one of seven people who were butchered that day. A shooting you ordered. One that Amando

Cabral carried out. For you. I've already killed him. Now it's your turn."

"Herre Thorvaldsen, you are completely mistaken—"

"Don't even try," he said, his voice rising. "Don't insult me, or the memory of my only son, with lies. I know every detail of what happened. I've hunted you for two years. Now I have you."

"I was wholly unaware of what Cabral would do. You must believe that. I simply wanted those prosecutors discouraged."

He stepped back, closer to François' tomb, using its elaborate columns and arches as cover from Lyon, who had to be lurking behind him.

Finish this, he told himself.

Now.

SAM STILL GRIPPED HIS WOUNDED ARM AS HE MADE his way forward. He'd lost sight of Lyon, last seen crossing before the main altar, maybe fifty feet from Thorvaldsen and Ashby.

He must alert his friend, so he took a chance.

"Henrik. Lyon is headed your way."

ASHBY WAS IN A PANIC. HE NEEDED TO LEAVE THIS godforsaken place.

Two men with guns wanted to kill him, and somebody just yelled that Lyon was approaching.

"Thorvaldsen, listen to me. I didn't kill your son."

A shot banged through the church and rattled his ears. He jumped and realized that Thorvaldsen had fired at the floor, close to his left foot. The ping of metal to stone sent him staggering back toward the exit doorway. But he knew better than to try to make a run for it.

He'd be dead before he took one step.

SAM HEARD A SHOT.

"Stay where you are," Thorvaldsen yelled over the wind and rain. "You sorry excuse for a human being. Do you know what you did? He was the finest son a man could have and you gunned him down, like he was nothing."

Sam stopped and told himself to assess the situation. Act smart. Do what Norstrum would do. He was always smart.

He crept to one of the columns and stole a look into the nave.

Lyon was to the right of the altar, near another column, standing, watching, listening.

"I TOLD YOU NOT TO MOVE," THORVALDSEN SAID. "The next bullet will not hit the floor."

He'd thought of this moment for a long time, wondering what it would feel like to finally confront Cai's murderer. But he'd also heard Sam's warning, concerned that Lyon may be only a short distance away.

"Thorvaldsen," Ashby said. "You have to see reason here. Lyon is going to kill us both."

He could only hope Sam and Meagan were watching his back, though neither one of them should be here. Funny. He was a billionaire many times over, yet not a single one of those euros could help him now. He'd crossed into a place ruled only by revenge. Within the darkness, he saw images of Cai as a baby, then an adolescent. He'd owed it to Lisette to ensure the lad grew into a man. Over four centuries Thorvaldsens had lived in Denmark. The Nazis had done their best to eradicate them, but they'd survived the onslaught. When Cai was born he'd been ecstatic. A child. To carry on. Boy or girl. He hadn't cared.

Just healthy. That's what he'd prayed for.

Papa, take care. I'll see you in a few weeks.

The last words Cai had said to him during their last telephone conversation.

He did see Cai a few weeks later.

Lying in a casket.

And all because of the worthless creature standing a few meters away.

"Did you think for one moment," he asked Ashby, "that I'd allow his death to go unanswered? Did you think yourself so clever? So important? That you could murder people and there would never be consequences?"

Ashby said nothing.

"Answer me," he yelled.

ASHBY HAD REACHED HIS LIMIT.

This old man was deranged, consumed with hate. He decided that the best way to deal with the danger was to face it. Especially considering that he'd caught sight of Peter Lyon, on the far side of one of the columns, coolly watching the encounter. Thorvaldsen was obviously aware of Lyon's presence.

And the others inside, they seemed to be the Dane's allies.

"I did what I had to do," Ashby declared.

"That's exactly right. And my son died."

"You have to know that I never intended that to occur. The prosecutor was all that interested me. Cabral went too far. There was no need to kill all of those people."

"Do you have children?" Thorvaldsen asked.

He shook his head.

"Then you cannot possibly understand."

He had to buy more time. Lyon had yet to move. He just stayed behind the column. And where were the other two?

"I've spent two years watching you," Thorvaldsen said. "You're a failure in everything you do. Your business ventures all lost money. Your bank is in trouble. Your assets are nearly depleted. I've watched with amusement as you and your mistress have tried to find Napoleon's wealth. And now here you are, still searching."

This fool was offering far too much information to Peter Lyon.

Then again.

"You're mistaken. I have a wealth of assets. Just not where you can discover them. Only in the past few days I've acquired a hundred million euros in gold."

He wanted Lyon to know that there were a lot of reasons why he should not be shot.

"I don't want your money," Thorvaldsen spit out.

"But I do," Lyon said as he emerged from the shadows and shot Henrik Thorvaldsen.

SAM STOPPED AT THE REPORT OF WHAT HAD TO BE A sound-suppressed weapon. He hadn't been able to hear what was being said as he was some fifty feet away from the conversation.

He glanced into the nave.

Peter Lyon was gone.

THORVALDSEN DID NOT FEEL THE BULLET ENTER his chest, but its exit produced excruciating pain. Then all coordination among brain, nerves, and muscles failed. His legs gave way as a fresh rush of agony flooded his brain.

Was this what Cai had felt? Had his boy been consumed by such intensity? What a terrible thing.

His eyes rolled upward.

His body sagged.

His right hand released its grip on the gun and he crashed down in a palpitating mass, the side of his head slamming the pavement.

Each breath tore at his lungs.

He tried to master the stabs at his chest.

Sound muffled.

Location failed.

Then all color drained from the world.

SEVENTY-SIX

MALONE CAUGHT SIGHT OF THE SAINT-DENIS basilica through the rain, about a mile ahead. No police vehicles were outside, and the plaza before the church was deserted. Everything around the church was dark and still, as if the plague had struck.

He found his Beretta and two spare magazines.

He was ready.

Just get this damn helicopter on the ground.

ASHBY WAS RELIEVED. "ABOUT TIME YOU SAVED ME from that."

Thorvaldsen lay on the floor, blood gushing from a chest wound. Ashby could not care less about the idiot. Lyon was all that mattered.

"A hundred million euros of gold?" Lyon asked.

"Rommel's treasure. Lost since the war. I found it."

"And you think that will buy your life?"

"Why wouldn't it?"

A new sound intruded on the monotonous drone of the storm.

Thump, thump, thump.

Growing louder.

Lyon noticed it, too.

A helicopter.

SAM CREPT CLOSE TO WHERE ASHBY AND LYON stood and saw the gun in Lyon's hand. Then he spotted Thorvaldsen on the floor, blood pumping out in heavy gushes.

Oh, God.

No.

"WHERE IS THIS GOLD?" LYON asked ASHBY.

"In a vault. That only I can access."

That should buy him a reprieve.

"I never liked you," Lyon said. "You've been manipulating this entire situation from the beginning."

"What do you care? You were hired, I paid you. What does it matter what I intended?"

"I haven't survived by being a fool," Lyon declared. "You negotiated with the Americans. Brought them into our arrangement. They didn't like you, either, but would do anything to capture me."

Rotors grew louder, as if right overhead.

"We need to leave," Ashby said. "You know who that is."

An evil light gathered in the amber eyes. "You're right. I need to leave."

Lyon fired the gun.

THORVALDSEN OPENED HIS EYES.

Black spots faded, yet the world around him seemed in a haze. He heard voices and saw Ashby standing close to another man, who was holding a gun.

Peter Lyon.

He watched as the murdering SOB shot Ashby.

Damn him.

He tried to move, to find his gun, but not a muscle in his body would respond. Blood poured from his chest. His strength waned. He heard wind, rain, and the pump of a deep bass tone thumping through the air.

Then another pop.

He focused. Ashby winced, as if in pain.

Two more pops.

A red ooze seeped from two holes in the forehead of the man who'd butchered his son.

Peter Lyon had finished what Thorvaldsen had started.

As Ashby collapsed to the floor, Thorvaldsen allowed the surprising calm coursing through his nerves to take him over.

SAM CAUGHT HIS BREATH AND STOOD. HIS LEGS were frozen. Was he afraid? No, more than that. A mortal terror had seized his muscles, gripping his mind with panic.

Lyon had shot Ashby four times.

Just like that.

Bam, bam, bam, bam.

Ashby was certainly dead. But what about Thorvaldsen? Sam thought the Dane had moved, just before Ashby died. He needed to get to his friend. Blood flooded the marble flooring at an alarming rate.

But his legs would not move.

A scream rang through the church.

Meagan sprang from the darkness and tackled Peter Lyon.

"Papa, Papa."

Thorvaldsen heard Cai's voice, as it had been years ago in the final telephone call.

"I'm here, Papa."

"Where, son?"

"Everywhere. Come to me."

"I failed, son."

"Your vendetta is not necessary, Papa. Not anymore. He's dead. As certain as if you had killed him yourself."

"I've missed you, son."

"Henrik."

A female voice. One he hadn't heard in a long time.

Lisette.

"My darling," he said. "Is that you?"

"I'm here, too, Henrik. With Cai. We've been waiting."

"How do I find you?"

"You have to let go."

He considered what they were saying. What it meant. But the implications that their request carried frightened him. He wanted to know, "What's it like there?"

"Peaceful," Lisette said.

"It's wonderful," Cai added. "No more loneliness."

He could barely recall a time that loneliness had not consumed him. But there was Sam. And Meagan. They remained in the church. With Lyon.

A scream invaded his peace.

He struggled to see what was happening.

Meagan had attacked Lyon.

They were struggling on the floor.

Still, though, he could not move. His arms lay extended on either side of his bleeding chest. His legs were as if they did not exist. His hands and fingers were frozen. Nothing functioned. Hot pain gushed up behind his eyes.

"Henrik."

It was Lisette.

"You can't help."

"I have to help them."

SAM WATCHED AS MEAGAN AND LYON ROLLED across the floor, struggling.

"You son of a bitch," he heard Meagan yell.

He needed to join the fray. Help her. Do something. But fear kept him frozen. He felt puny, peevish, cowardly. He was afraid. Then he straightened up from his conflicting thoughts and forced his legs to move.

Lyon vaulted Meagan off him. She thudded into the thick base on one of the tombs.

Sam searched the darkness and spotted Thorvaldsen's gun. Ten feet away from his friend, who still had not moved.

He rushed forward and grabbed the weapon.

MALONE UNBUCKLED HIS HARNESS JUST AS THE chopper's wheels kissed the pavement. Stephanie did the same. He reached for the door handle and wrenched the panel open.

Beretta in hand, he leaped out.

Cold rain stung his cheeks.

SAM LIFTED THE WEAPON, HIS BLOODY FINGER FIND-ing the trigger. He was deep in the shadows, beyond where Henrik and Ashby lay. He turned just as Lyon jammed a fist into Meagan's face, knocking her head against the base of one of the tombs, her body set-tling at a contorted angle on the floor.

Lyon searched for his gun.

The thump of rotors outside had subsided, which meant the chopper had found the plaza. Lyon must have realized that fact, too, as he grabbed his gun, stood, and darted toward freedom.

Sam fought the pain in his left shoulder, stepped from the dimness and raised his weapon. "That's it."

Lyon halted but did not turn around. "The third voice."

"Don't move." He kept his gun trained on Lyon's head.

"I imagine you'll pull the trigger if I so much as twitch?" Lyon asked.

He was impressed at how Lyon clearly sensed the gun.

"You found the old man's weapon."

"That head of yours makes a wonderful target."

"You sound young. Are you an American agent?"

"Shut up," he made clear.

"How about I drop my weapon?"

The gun remained in the man's right hand, barrel pointed to the floor.

"Let it fall."

Lyon released his grip and the gun clanged away.

"That better?" Lyon asked, his back still to him.

Actually, it was.

"You've never shot a man before, have you?" Lyon asked.

"Shut the hell up," Sam said.

"That's what I thought. Let's see if I am right. I'm going to leave. You won't shoot an unarmed man, with his back to you."

He was tired of the banter. "Turn around."

Lyon ignored the command and took a step forward.

Sam fired into the floor just ahead of him. "The next bullet will be to your head."

"I don't think so. I saw you before I shot Ashby. You just watched. You stood there and did nothing."

Lyon stole another step.

Sam fired again.

MALONE HEARD TWO SHOTS FROM INSIDE THE church.

He and Stephanie darted for an opening in the plywood barrier that wrapped the church's exterior, this one facing south. They had to find the doors everyone else had used to enter.

The three sets in front were closed tight.

Cold rain continued to slash his brow.

THE SECOND BULLET RICOCHETED OFF THE FLOOR.

"I told you to stop," Sam yelled.

Lyon was right. He'd never shot anybody before. He'd been trained in the mechanics, but not in how to be mentally prepared for something so horrific. He yanked his thoughts into some semblance of disciplined ranks.

And readied himself.

Lyon moved again.

Sam advanced two steps and sighted his aim. "I swear to you. I'll shoot you." He kept his voice calm, though his heart raced.

Lyon crept ahead. "You can't shoot me."

"You don't know me."

"Maybe not. But I know fear."

"Who says I'm afraid?"

"I hear it."

Meagan stirred with a grunt of pain.

"There are those of us who can end a life with-out a thought and those, like yourself, who can't bring themselves to it, unless provoked. And I am not provoking you."

"You shot Henrik."

Lyon stopped. "Ah. That's his name. Henrik. Yes, I did. A friend?"

"Stay still." He hated the element of a plea that laced his words.

Ten feet separated Lyon from the open doors.

His adversary eased another step forward, his movements as controlled as his voice.

"Not to worry," Lyon said. "I won't tell anyone you didn't fire."

Five feet to the threshold.

"PAPA. COME TO US," CAI CALLED OUT through a tremulous blue radiance.

Strange and wonderful thoughts stole upon him. But Thorvaldsen couldn't be talking to his wife and son. The conversation had to be the rambles of a mind in shock.

"Sam needs me," he called out.

"You can't help him, my darling," Lisette made clear.

A white curtain descended in a muted fall. The last remnants of his strength ebbed away.

He fought to breathe.

"It's time, Papa. Time for us all to be together."

SAM WAS BEING ANTAGONIZED, HIS CONSCIENCE challenged.

Clever, actually, on Lyon's part. Goad a reaction, knowing that doing so could well prevent anything from happening. Lyon was apparently a student of character. But that didn't necessarily make him right. And besides, Sam had ruined his career by defying authority.

Lyon kept approaching the door.

Three feet.

Two.

Screw you, Lyon.

He pulled the trigger.

MALONE SAW A BODY CAREER FORWARD, OUT AN open set of double doors and thud to the wet pavement with a splash.

He and Stephanie rushed up slick stone steps, and she rolled the body over. The face was that of the man from the boat, the one who'd abducted Ashby. Peter Lyon.

With a hole through his head.

Malone glanced up.

Sam appeared in the doorway, holding a gun, one shoulder bleeding.

"You okay?" Malone asked.

The younger man nodded, but a dire expression crushed all hope from Malone's heart.

Sam stepped back. He and Stephanie rushed inside. Meagan was staggering to her feet and Stephanie came to her aid. Malone's eyes focused on a body—Ashby—then another.

Thorvaldsen.

"We need an ambulance," he called out.

"He's dead," Sam quietly said.

A chill ran across Malone's shoulders and up his neck. He urged his legs into tentative, stumbling movements. His eyes told him that Sam was right.

He approached and knelt beside his friend.

Stickly blood clung to flesh and clothes. He checked for a pulse and found none.

He shook his head in utter sadness.

"We need to at least try to get him to a hospital," he said again.

"It won't matter," Sam said.

Dread punctuated the statement, which Malone knew to be true. But he still couldn't accept it. Stephanie helped Meagan, as they stepped close.

Thorvaldsen's eyes stared out blindly.

"I tried to help," Meagan said. "The crazy old fool . . . he was determined to kill Ashby. I tried . . . to get there—"

Choking sobs pulsed from her throat. Tears flowed down her cheeks.

Thorvaldsen had interjected himself into Malone's life when he really needed a friend, appearing in Atlanta two years ago, offering a new beginning in Denmark, one he'd readily accepted and never regretted. Together they'd shared the past twenty-four months, but the past twenty-four hours had been so different.

We shall never speak again.

The last words spoken between them.

His right hand clutched at his throat, as if trying to reach through to his heart.

Despair flooded his gut.

"That's right, old friend," he whispered. "We will never speak again."

SEVENTY-SEVEN

PARIS
SUNDAY, DECEMBER 30
2:40 PM

MALONE ENTERED SAINT-DENIS BASILICA. THE
church had remained closed to both the public and
construction crews since Christmas Day, the entire
site treated as a crime scene.

Three men had died here.

Two he could not give a rat's ass about.

The third death had been more painful than he
could have ever imagined.

His father had passed thirty-eight years ago. He'd
been ten years old, the loss more loneliness than
pain. Thorvaldsen's death was different. Pain filled
his heart with an unrelenting, deep regret.

They'd buried Henrik beside his wife and son in
a private service at Christiangade. A handwritten
note attached to his last will had expressly stated
that he wanted no public funeral. His death,

though, made news throughout the world and expressions of sympathy poured in. Thousands of cards and letters arrived from employees of his various companies, a glowing testament of how they felt about their employer. Cassiopeia Vitt had come. Meagan Morrison, too. Her face still carried a bruise and as she, Malone, Cassiopeia, Stephanie, Sam, and Jesper filled the grave, each one shoveling dirt onto a plain pine box, not a word had been uttered.

For the last few days he'd hidden inside his loneliness, remembering the past two years. Feelings had leaped and writhed within him, flickering between dream and reality. Thorvaldsen's face was indelibly engraved in his mind, and he would forever recall every feature—the dark eyes under thick eyebrows, straight nose, flared nostrils, strong jaw, resolute chin. Forget the crooked spine. It meant nothing. That man had always stood straight and tall.

He glanced around at the lofty nave. Forms, figures, and designs produced an overwhelming effect of serenity, the church aglow with the radiant flood of light pouring in through stained-glass windows. He admired the various saintly figures, robed in dark sapphire, lighted with turquoise—heads and hands emerging from skillfully crafted sepia shadows through olive green, to pink, and finally to white. Hard not to have thoughts of God, nature's beauty, and lives gone, ended too soon.

Like Henrik's.

But he told himself to focus on the task.

He found the paper in his pocket and unfolded it.

**CXXXV II CXLII LII LXIII XVII
II VIII IV VIII IX II**

Professor Murad had told him exactly what to search for—the clues Napoleon concocted, then left for his son. He began with Psalm 135, verse 2. **You who stand in the house of the Lord, in the courts of the house of our God.**

Then Psalm 2, verse 8. **I will make the nations your inheritance.**

Typical Napoleonic grandeur.

Next came Psalm 142, verse 4. **Look to my right and see.**

The precise starting point—from where to look right and see—had been difficult to determine. Saint-Denis was massive, a football field long and nearly half that wide. But the next verse solved that dilemma. Psalm 52, verse 8. **But I am like an olive tree flourishing in the house of God.**

Murad's quick class on Psalms had made Malone think of one that more than aptly described the past week. Psalm 144, verse 4. **Man is like a breath, his days are like a fleeting shadow.** He hoped Henrik had found peace.

But I am like an olive tree flourishing in the house of God.

He glanced right and spotted a monument. Designed in a Gothic tradition, elements of an ancient-style temple sprang from its sculpture, the upper platform decorated with praying figures. Two stone effigies, portrayed in the last moments of their life, lay flat atop. Its base was figured with Italian-inspired reliefs.

He approached, his rubber-soled shoes both sure and silent. Immediately to the right of the monument, in the flooring, he spotted a marble slab with a solitary olive tree carved into the marker. A notation explained that the grave was from the 15th century. Murad had told him that its occupant was supposedly Guillaume du Chastel. Charles VII had so loved his servant that he'd bestown on him the honor of being buried in Saint-Denis.

Psalm 63, verse 9, was next. **They who seek my life will be destroyed, they will go down to the depths of the earth. They will be given over to the sword and become food for jackals.**

He'd already received permission from the French government to do whatever was necessary to solve the riddle. If that meant destroying something within the church, then so be it. Most of it was 19th and 20th century repairs and reproductions anyway. He'd asked for some tools and equipment to be left inside, anticipating what may be required, and saw them near the west wall.

He walked across the nave and retrieved a sledgehammer.

When Professor Murad related to him the clues, the possibility that what they sought lay below the church became all too real. Then, when he'd read the verses, he was sure.

He walked back to the olive tree carved in the floor.

The final clue, Napoleon's last message to his son. Psalm 17, verse 2. **May my vindication come from you; may your eyes see what is right.**

He swung the hammer.

The marble did not break, but his suspicions were confirmed. The hollow sound told him that solid stone did not lie beneath. Three more blows and the rock cracked. Another two and marble crashed away into a black rectangle that opened beneath the church.

A chilled draft rushed upward.

Murad had told him how Napoleon, in 1806, halted the desecration of Saint-Denis and proclaimed it, once again, an imperial burial place. He'd also restored the adjacent abbey, established a religious order to oversee the basilica's restoration, and commissioned architects to repair the damages. It would have been an easy matter for him to adjust the site to his personal specifications. How this hole in the floor had remained secret was fascinating, but perhaps the chaos of post-Napoleonic France was the best explanation, as nothing and nobody remained stable once the emperor had been ensconced on St. Helena.

He discarded the sledgehammer and retrieved a coil of rope and a flashlight. He shone the light into the void and noted that it was more a chute, about three feet by four, that extended straight down about twenty feet. Remnants of a wooden ladder lay scattered on the rock floor. He'd studied the basilica's geography and knew that a crypt once extended below the church—parts of it were still there, open to the public—but nothing had ever stretched this far toward the west façade. Perhaps long ago it had, and Napoleon had discovered the oddity.

At least that's what Murad thought.

He looped the rope around the base of one of the columns a few feet away and tested its strength. He tossed the remainder of the rope into the chute, followed by the sledgehammer, which might be needed. He clipped the lamp to his belt. Using his rubber soles and the rope, he eased down the chute, into the black earth.

At the bottom he aimed the light at rock the shade of driftwood. The chilly, dusty environs extended for as far as the beam would shine. He knew that Paris was littered with tunnels. Miles and miles of underground passages hewed from limestone that had been hauled, block by block, to the surface, the city literally built from the ground up.

He groped for the contours, the crevices, the protruding shards, and followed the twisting passage for maybe two hundred feet. A smell similar to warm peaches, which he recalled from his Georgia childhood, made his stomach queasy. Grit crunched beneath his feet. Only cold seemed to occupy this bareness, easy to become lost in the silence.

He assumed he was well clear of the basilica, east of the building itself, perhaps beneath the expanse of trees and grass that extended past the nearby abbey, toward the Seine.

Ahead he spotted a shallow recess in the right-hand wall. Rubble filled the passageway where somebody had pounded their way through the lime-stone.

He stopped and searched the scene with his light. Etched into the rough surface of one of the rocky chunks was a symbol, one he recognized from the writing Napoleon had left in the Merovingian book, part of the fourteen lines of scribble.

Someone had propped the stone atop the pile like a marker, one that had patiently waited underground for more than two hundred years. In the exposed recess he spied a metal door, swung half open. An electrical cable snaked a path out the doorway, turned ninety degrees, then disappeared into the tunnel ahead.

Glad to know he'd been right.

Napoleon's clues led the way down. Then the etched symbol showed exactly where things awaited.

He shone the light inside, found an electrical box, and flipped the switch.

Yellow, incandescent fixtures strewn across the floor revealed a chamber maybe fifty by forty feet, with a ten-foot ceiling. He counted at least three dozen wooden chests and saw that several were hinged open.

Inside, he spied a neat assortment of gold and silver bars. Each bore a stamped N topped by an imperial crown, the official mark of the Emperor Napoleon. Another held gold coins. Two more contained silver plate. Three were filled to the brim with what appeared to be precious stones. Apparently the emperor had chosen his hoard with great care, opting for hard metal and jewels.

He surveyed the room and allowed his eyes to examine the ancient and abandoned possessions of a crushed empire.

Napoleon's cache.

"You must be Cotton Malone," a female voice said.

He turned. "And you must be Eliza Larocque."

The woman who stood in the doorway was tall and stately, with an obvious leonine quality about her that she did little to conceal. She wore a knee-length wool coat, classy and elegant. Beside her stood a thin, gnarled man with a Spartan vigor. Both faces were wiped clean of expression.

"And your friend is Paolo Ambrosi," Malone said. "Interesting character. An ordained priest who served briefly as papal secretary to Peter II, but disappeared after that papacy abruptly ended.

Rumors abounded about his—" Malone paused. "—morality. Now here he is."

Larocque seemed impressed. "You don't seem surprised that we are here."

"I've been expecting you."

"Really? I've been told that you were quite an agent."

"I had my moments."

"And, yes, Paolo performs certain tasks that I require from time to time," Larocque said. "I thought it best he stay close to me, after all that happened last week."

"Henrik Thorvaldsen is dead because of you," Malone declared.

"How is that possible? I never knew the man until he interjected himself in my business. He left me at the Eiffel Tower and I never saw him again." She paused. "You never said. How did you know I'd be here today?"

"There are people smarter than you in this world."

He saw she did not appreciate the insult.

"I've been watching," he said. "You found Caroline Dodd faster than I thought. How long did it take to learn about this place?"

"Miss Dodd was quite forthcoming. She explained the clues, but I decided to find another way beneath the basilica. I assumed there were other paths in and out, and I was right. We found the correct tunnel a few days ago, unsealed the chamber, and tapped into an electrical line not far from here."

"And Dodd?"

Larocque shook her head. "She reminded me far too much of Lord Ashby's treachery, so Paolo dealt with her."

A gun appeared in Ambrosi's right hand.

"You still have not answered my question," Larocque said.

"When you left your residence earlier," Malone said. "I assumed you were coming here. Time to claim your prize, right? You've been working on some contract help to transport this fortune out of here."

"Which has been difficult," she said. "Luckily, there are people in this world who will do anything for money. We'll have to break all this down into smaller, sealed crates, then hand-carry it out of here."

"You're not afraid they'll talk?"

"The crates will be sealed before they arrive."

A slight nod of his head acknowledged the wisdom of her foresight.

"How did you get down here?" she asked.

He pointed above. "Through the front door."

"Are you still working for the Americans?" she asked. "Thorvaldsen did tell me about you."

"I'm working for me." He motioned around him. "I came for this."

"You don't strike me as a treasure hunter."

He sat atop one of the chests and rested nerves

dulled by insomnia and its unfortunate companion, despondency. "That's where you're wrong. I love treasure. Who wouldn't? I especially enjoy denying it to worthless pieces of crap like you."

She laughed off his touch of drama. "I'd say you're the one who's going to be denied."

He shook his head. "Your game is over. No more Paris Club. No more financial manipulation. No treasure."

"I can't imagine that is the case."

He ignored her. "Unfortunately, there are no witnesses left alive, and precious little other evidence, to actually try you for a crime. So take this talk as your one and only get-out-of-jail-free card."

Larocque smiled at his ridicule. "Are you always so gregarious in the face of your own death?"

He shrugged. "I'm a carefree kind of guy."

"Do you believe in fate, Mr. Malone?" she asked.

He shrugged. "Not really."

"I do. In fact, I govern my life by fate. My family has done the same for centuries. When I learned that Ashby was dead, I consulted an oracle I possess, and asked a simple question. **Will my name be immortalized and will posterity applaud it?** Would you like to hear the answer I was given?"

He humored her. "Sure."

"A good-humored mate will be a treasure, which thine eyes will delight to look upon." She paused. "The next day I found this."

And she motioned at the lighted cavern.

He'd had enough.

He raised his right arm, pointed his index finger downward, and twirled, signaling Larocque should turn around.

She caught his message and stole a glance over her right shoulder. Behind her stood Stephanie Nelle and Sam Collins.

Both held guns.

"Did I mention that I didn't come alone?" Malone said. "They waited until you arrived to come down."

Larocque faced him. Anger in her eyes confirmed what he already knew. So he said what she was surely thinking, "Delight to look upon it, madame, because that's all you get."

Sam relieved Ambrosi of his gun. No resistance was offered.

"And I'd keep it that way," Malone said to Ambrosi. "Sam there got dinged with a bullet. Hurt like hell, but he's okay. He's the one who shot Peter Lyon. His first kill. I told him the second would be a whole lot easier."

Ambrosi said nothing.

"He also watched Henrik Thorvaldsen die. He's still in a piss-poor mood. So am I, and Stephanie. We'd all three just as soon shoot you both dead. Lucky for you, we aren't murderers. Too bad neither of you can say the same."

"I've killed no one," Larocque said.

"No, you just encourage others to do it and profit from the acts." He stood. "Now get the hell out."

Larocque stood her ground. "What will happen to this?"

He cleared his throat of emotion. "That's not for me or you to decide."

"You realize this is my family's birthright. My ancestor was instrumental in destroying Napoleon. He searched for this treasure until the day he died."

"I told you to get out."

He'd like to think this was how Thorvaldsen would have handled the matter, and the thought provided a small measure of comfort.

Larocque seemed to accept his rebuke with the knowledge that she had little bargaining power. So she motioned for Ambrosi to lead the way. Stephanie and Sam stepped aside and allowed them both to leave.

At the doorway, Larocque hesitated, then turned toward Malone. "Perhaps our paths will cross again."

"Wouldn't that be fun."

"Know that that encounter will be quite different from today's."

And she left.

"She's trouble," Stephanie said.

"I assume you have people out there?"

Stephanie nodded. "The French police will escort them out of the tunnel and seal it off."

He realized it was over. Finally. The past three weeks had been some of the most horrific of his life.

He needed a rest.

"I understand you have a new career," he said to Sam.

The younger man nodded. "I'm now officially working for the Magellan Billet, as an agent. I hear I have you to thank for that."

"You have yourself to thank. Henrik would be proud."

"I hope so." Sam motioned at the chests. "What **is** going to happen with all this treasure?"

"The French get it," Stephanie said. "No way to know where it came from. Here it sits, in their soil, so it's theirs. Besides, they say it's compensation for all the property damage Cotton inflicted."

Malone wasn't really listening. Instead he kept his attention on the doorway. Eliza Larocque had sheathed her parting threat in a warm cloak of politeness—a calm declaration that if their paths ever crossed again, things would be different. But he'd been threatened before. Besides, Larocque was partly responsible both for Henrik's death and for the guilt that he feared would forever swirl inside him. He owed her, and he always paid his debts.

"You okay about Lyon?" he asked Sam.

The younger man nodded. "I still see his head exploding, but I can live with it."

"Don't ever let it get easy. Killing is serious business, even if they deserve it."

"You sound like somebody else I once knew."

"He a smart fellow, too?"

"More so than I ever realized, until lately."

"You were right, Sam," he said. "The Paris Club. Those conspiracies. At least a few of them were real."

"As I recall, you thought I was a nut."

He chuckled. "Half the people I meet think I'm one, too."

"Meagan Morrison made sure I knew she was right," Stephanie said. "She's a handful."

"You going to see her again?" Malone asked Sam.

"Who says I'm interested?"

"I heard it in her voice when she left the message on my phone. She went back in there for you. And I saw how you looked at her after Henrik's funeral. You're interested."

"I don't know. I might. You have any advice on that one?"

He held up his hands in mock surrender. "Women are not my strong point."

"You can say that again," Stephanie added. "You throw ex-wives out of planes."

He smiled.

"We need to go," Stephanie said. "The French want control of this."

They headed for the exit.

"Something's been bothering me," Malone said to Sam. "Stephanie told me that you were raised in New Zealand, but you don't talk like a Kiwi. Why's that?"

Sam smiled. "Long story."

Exactly what he'd said yesterday when Sam had asked about the name Cotton. The same two words he'd told Henrik the several times when his friend had inquired, always promising to explain later.

But, sadly, there'd be no more laters.

He liked Sam Collins. He was a lot like himself fifteen years ago, just about the time when he'd started with the Magellan Billet. Now Sam was a full-fledged agent—about to face all of the incalculable risks associated with that dangerous job.

Any day could easily be his last.

"How about this," Sam said. "I'll tell you, if you tell me."

"Deal."

WRITER'S NOTE

This novel took me first to France, then to London. For several days Elizabeth and I roamed Paris, scouting every location that appears in the novel. I wasn't particularly fond of being underground, and she disliked the height of the Eiffel Tower. Our various neuroses aside, we managed to discover all that we went there to find. As with those of my previous seven novels, this plot involved concocting, combining, correcting, and condensing a number of seemingly unrelated elements.

Now it's time to draw the line between fact and fiction.

General Napoleon Bonaparte did indeed conquer Egypt in 1799, and ruled that land while he awaited the right moment to return to France and claim absolute power. He certainly saw the pyramids, but there is no evidence that he ever ventured inside. A story exists that he entered the Great Pyramid at Giza and emerged shaken, but no reputable historian has ever verified that account. The notion, though, seemed intriguing, so I couldn't resist including my own version in the prologue. As to what happened inside with a mysterious seer (chapter 37), that was all my concoction. Napoleon's **savants,** though, did exist, and together they unearthed an ancient civilization heretofore unknown, creating the science of Egyptology.

Corsica seems a fascinating place, though I wasn't able to actually visit. Bastia (chapters 2 and 14) is described as correctly as photographs would allow. Cap Corse and its ancient watchtowers and convents are also faithfully rendered. Rommel's gold is an actual treasure lost from World War II, with a Corsican connection, as described in chapter 6. The only addition I made was the fifth participant and clues left inside a 19th century book about Napoleon. The actual treasure remains, to this day, unfound.

The Moor's Knot described in chapters 6, 12, and 39 is mine, though the coding technique came from **The Chalice of Magdalene,** by Graham Phillips, a book about the Holy Grail. I also was directed to Psalms, and the use of its many verses as clues (chapter 77) by that same book. The particular portions I chose are correctly quoted and proved uncanny in their applicability.

There is a Paris Club, as described in chapter 4. It is a well-intentioned organization, staffed by some of the world's wealthiest countries, designed to help emerging nations restructure their debt.

Eliza Larocque's Paris Club bears no relation. Likewise, her club's historical connection to Napoleon is purely fictitious.

The incident in Egypt, with Napoleon witnessing the murder of a mother and her infant (chapter 4), happened, but Napoleon found no papyri that day. Those are my invention.

All that's related about the Rothschilds (chapters 5 and 24) is a matter of historical record. They did indeed finance royalty, governments, and wars, profiting immensely from all sides.

Louis Etienne Saint-Denis (chapter 16) faithfully served Napoleon. He went into exile with his master on both Elba and St. Helena and penned all of Napoleon's writings (chapter 40). Napoleon bequeathed to Saint-Denis 400 books from his personal library (chapters 16, 17, and 25) and charged him with holding those books until Napoleon's son attained the age of sixteen. The addition of one particular volume on the Merovingians—supposedly named in the will—is mine, as is the manner in which Saint-Denis ultimately disposed of that collection (chapter 16).

Paris is accurately described throughout (starting with chapter 18), as is Shakespeare & Company, which stands on the Left Bank, facing Notre Dame.

The Creature from Jekyll Island: A Second Look at the Federal Reserve, by G. Edward Griffin, proved helpful in formulating Sam Collins' and

Meagan Morrison's views on conspiratorial economics. That book also pointed me toward Executive Order 11110 (chapter 24), issued by President Kennedy shortly before his assassination.

Westminster Abbey in London, along with its Poets' Corner (chapter 19), are fascinating. Jack the Ripper tours (chapter 43) occur on London's east side nightly (I enjoyed one myself).

France's Loire Valley is magnificent (chapter 20). Eliza Larocque's château is my creation, though I modeled it after the fabled Chenonceau, which also spans the river Cher. Paris' Latin Quarter (chapter 23) bristles with life twenty-four hours a day and is accurately captured, as is the Cluny Museum (first seen in chapter 26) with its vast array of medieval exhibits (chapter 28). The Invalides and its Church of the Dome (chapter 36) are both Paris landmarks. Napoleon's sarcophagus (chapter 36) is certainly grandiose. The part of the military museum at the Invalides devoted to Napoleon was undergoing renovation while I was there, so I incorporated that into the story (chapter 38). Only the addition of the book on the Merovingians (chapters 36 and 38) is fiction. The Ritz hotel, its Bar Hemingway (chapter 33), and Le Grand Véfour restaurant (chapter 37) are all there. Meagan Morrison's fascination with the Paris underground (chapter 44) mirrors my own with those subterranean passages.

Pozzo di Borgo (chapters 20, 23, and 35) lived.

He was, first, Napoleon's childhood friend, then his sworn enemy. Di Borgo's life and Corsican **vendetta** are accurately described. He was instrumental in convincing Tsar Alexander not to make a separate peace with France, which ultimately led Napoleon down his road to ruin. Di Borgo's interest in any lost treasure, and his family connection with Eliza Larocque, are purely my invention.

Abbé Buonavita (chapters 25 and 46) was on St. Helena with Napoleon and left shortly before the emperor died. He was permitted to take with him several personal letters for Napoleon's wife and child. The addition of secret messages within those letters is my creation. The visit to St. Helena in 1840 by Prince de Joinville, to retrieve Napoleon's remains and return them to France, happened as described (chapter 37). Those present, and their comments, are likewise accurately quoted.

The Eiffel Tower plays an integral role in this story. Like Sam, Stephanie, and Meagan, I climbed its several hundred metal stairs to the first and second platforms (chapter 39). The tower's sites and geography, including La Salle Gustav Eiffel (chapters 39, 48, and 49), all exist. And the surprising effect a kiss-like-you-mean-it has on human life expectancy (chapter 44) is real, as is the study Meagan Morrison refers to.

The 14 lines containing coded information in the form of raised letters (chapters 39 and 47) are from the legend associated with Rennes-le-Château, which I explored in my novel **The Templar Legacy.** While researching that story, I came across these two legendary parchments. Since no one has ever actually seen those documents, and since their secret message—**To King Dagobert II and to Sion belongs the treasure and he is there dead**—applied to this story, I appropriated them. The only modification made was the elimination of the designation **II.** Dagobert I was a great Merovingian king, and his 13th century funerary monument stands in the Basilica of Saint-Denis (chapter 61). Napoleon was indeed fascinated with Merovingians (chapter 33). With all of these seemingly unrelated facts suddenly bumping up against each other, a marriage seemed in order. Hopefully, Rennes-le-Château purists will forgive me.

The Basilica of Saint-Denis is a French national treasure. Given its location north of central Paris, few tourists venture there, which is a shame. They are missing something even more awe inspiring than Notre Dame. Chapters 67–77 accurately describe the church, including construction that was ongoing during my visit. Only the olive tree marker and tunnel beneath (chapter 77) are my additions.

The congressional legislation noted in chapters 51 and 52, known as The Financial Service Modernization (Gramm-Leach-Bliley) Act and the Commodity Futures Modernization Act, adopted in 1999 and 2000 respectively, are real and most experts now say that these disastrous attempts at deregulation contributed greatly to the economic meltdown of 2008. **60 Minutes** featured an entire segment on their effect.

The idea that Osama bin Laden may have profited from the 9/11 attacks through short selling stocks has, for years, been postulated by conspiratorialists. There was actually an American investigation, and the French article mentioned in chapter 52 was published, but no short selling was ever substantiated.

The idea that profit can be made through chaos (chapter 52) is not new. What's described in chapter 24 about Yugoslavia occurred. The political wisdom contained within the four papyri (chapters 27, 29, and 40) were adapted from **The Report from Iron Mountain.** According to that document, a 15-member panel, called the Special Study Group, was set up in 1963 to examine what problems would occur if the United States entered a state of lasting peace. They met at an underground nuclear bunker called Iron Mountain and worked in secret for two years. One member of the panel, an anonymous professor at a college in the Midwest, decided to release the report to the public and Dial Press published it in 1967.

Of course, only the part about Dial Press is true. The book was published and became a bestseller. The general consensus is that the entire report was a hoax. In fact, **The Guinness Book of World**

Records eventually labeled **The Report from Iron Mountain** as its Most Successful Literary Hoax. Still, the ideas presented within the "report" about war, peace, and maintaining political stability are, if nothing else, intriguing. The idea that society will allow in a time of threat that which it would never tolerate in peace is particularly relevant today.

The oracle relied on by Eliza Larocque is real. **The Book of Fate, Formerly in the Possession of and Used by Napoleon** is still in print. All of the questions and answers quoted in chapters 8, 10, 29, and 67 are taken from the actual oracle. The oracle's dubious history (chapter 8) is one of contradiction. Napoleon was highly superstitious and fate played a role in his decisions (chapter 10), but did he consult an oracle every day? No one knows. The idea, though, is captivating.

It is true, as Eliza Larocque noted, that save for Jesus Christ, more books have been written about Napoleon than any other historical figure, yet he remains enigmatic. He was, on the one hand, a capable and competent administrator, and on the other (as Eliza Larocque laments in chapter 35) a man with no loyalty, who consistently turned on his family, friends, and country. His hatred of financiers, and of incurring debt, is a historical fact (chapter 16). He also believed in plunder. In that regard, he was truly a modern Merovingian. Of course, he would say that his plundered loot was simply the spoils of war, and perhaps he's right. Whether he actually hoarded away some of those spoils for himself—Napoleon's cache, which plays such a central role in this story—remains a matter of debate.

No one knows. Nor will we ever.

Instead, Napoleon will continue to be studied and debated. Every volume that proclaims him a saint will be followed by another that decries him as a devil.

Perhaps, in the end, he said it best.

For all the attempts to restrict, suppress, and muffle me, it will be difficult to make me disappear from the public memory completely.

ABOUT THE AUTHOR

STEVE BERRY is the New York Times best-selling author of **The Charlemagne Pursuit, The Venetian Betrayal, The Alexandria Link, The Templar Legacy, The Third Secret, The Romanov Prophecy,** and **The Amber Room.** His books have been translated into thirty-seven languages and sold in fifty countries. He lives on the Georgia Coast and is now at work on his next novel. He and his wife, Elizabeth, have founded History Matters, a nonprofit organization dedicated to preserving our heritage. Visit www.steveberry.org to learn more about Berry and the foundation.

LIKE WHAT YOU'VE READ?

If you enjoyed this large print edition of
THE PARIS VENDETTA, here are a few of Steve Berry's
latest bestsellers also available in large print.

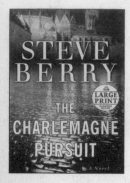

THE CHARLEMAGNE PURSUIT
(paperback)
978-0-7393-2699-2 • 0-7393-2699-6
$24.95/$27.95C

THE VENETIAN BETRAYAL
(paperback)
978-0-7393-2698-5 • 0-7393-2698-8
$25.95/$32.00C

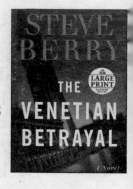

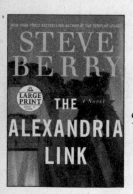

THE ALEXANDRIA LINK
(hardcover)
978-0-7393-2697-8 • 0-7393-2697-X
$27.95/$34.95C

Large print books are available wherever books
are sold and at many local libraries.

All prices are subject to change. Check with your
local retailer for current pricing and availability.
For more information on these and other large print titles,
visit www.randomhouse.com/largeprint.